"From Oxford's hallowed ha[...] don's seedy underbelly, Ami [...] for answers about a mysterious Egyptian artifact—and find far more than they bargained for. Don't miss all the romance, adventure, and danger in Michelle Griep's new page-turner, *Of Gold and Shadows*."

—Julie Klassen, bestselling author
of *Shadows of Swanford Abbey*

"Move over, Amelia Peabody, there's a new lady Egyptologist in town! Twisty, humorous, and with Griep's unique, dry wit, *Of Gold and Shadows* is a quick-paced adventure into curses, black markets, and irresistible romance that will have readers declaring it a 'bookshelf treasure!'"

—Erica Vetsch, author of the THORNDIKE & SWANN
REGENCY MYSTERIES

"Griep excels at the slightly madcap Victorian romp, and *Of Gold and Shadows* is no exception! With a style and voice reminiscent of her BLACKFRIARS LANE series, an independent-minded heroine, and a wealthy-but-tender hero, this Cinderella story is sure to please."

—Shannon McNear, 2014 RITA finalist, 2021 SELAH
winner, and author of DAUGHTERS OF THE LOST COLONY

"With intrigue, adventure, and toe-curling romance, *Of Gold and Shadows* is a masterpiece. This Victorian romance, complete with a quirky Egyptologist and a dashing would-be politician, kept me reading far into the night. Another dazzling story from Michelle Griep!"

—Tara Johnson, Christy and Carol Awards finalist,
author of *Engraved on the Heart*

"A sizzling romance, memorable characters, a hair-raising adventure, and a mystery to solve. Add in the curse of Amentuk, and I was lost for days in the pages of this great book. Michelle Griep never disappoints."

—MaryLu Tyndall, bestselling author of
LEGACY OF THE KING'S PIRATES

OF
GOLD
AND
SHADOWS

OF
GOLD
AND
SHADOWS

MICHELLE GRIEP

BETHANYHOUSE

a division of Baker Publishing Group
Minneapolis, Minnesota

Published by Bethany House Publishers
Minneapolis, Minnesota
BethanyHouse.com

Bethany House Publishers is a division of
Baker Publishing Group, Grand Rapids, Michigan

Printed in the United States of America

Library of Congress Cataloging-in-Publication Data
Names: Griep, Michelle, author.
Title: Of gold and shadows / Michelle Griep.
Description: Minneapolis, Minnesota : Bethany House, a division of Baker
    Publishing Group, 2024. | Series: Time's Lost Treasures; 1 | Includes
    bibliographical references.
Identifiers: LCCN 2024013523 | ISBN 9780764242564 (paper) | ISBN
    9780764244001 (casebound) | ISBN 9781493448104 (ebook)
Subjects: LCGFT: Christian fiction. | Romance fiction. | Novels.
Classification: LCC PS3607.R528 O3 2024 | DDC 813.6—dc23/
    eng/20240329
LC record available at https://lccn.loc.gov/2024013523

This is a work of historical reconstruction; the appearances of certain historical
figures are therefore inevitable. All other characters, however, are products of
the author's imagination, and any resemblance to actual persons, living or dead,
is coincidental.

Cover design by Dan Thornberg
Cover image of woman © Lee Avison / Trevillion Images

Published in association with Books & Such Literary Management, BooksAnd
Such.com.

Baker Publishing Group publications use paper produced from sustainable forestry
practices and postconsumer waste whenever possible.

24 25 26 27 28 29 30   7 6 5 4 3 2 1

To one of my dearest readers,
Susan Gibson Snodgrass,
who has since gone on to hear,
"Well done, good and faithful servant."

And as always,
to the One who I long to hear whisper
those very same words to me.

1

Cemeteries always smelled of earthworms and damp dog fur, especially after a rain, and Brudge rather liked it that way. It made death more tangible. Imminent. An irrefutable reminder that life balanced on a knife's edge. He patted the blade in his coat pocket, the hard lump of it a reassurance that the Shadow Broker wouldn't get the best of him. Not this night. Brudge would be the victor or die in the trying.

"Step smart, Scupper," he called over his shoulder, annoyed that the oaf he hired couldn't keep up with him. To be expected, though, if he really thought on it. A battleship aground wouldn't move with ease, and Scupper was a boatload of muscle and flesh.

Holding his lantern higher, Brudge studied the black shapes in the freshly fallen darkness. Not a particularly brilliant time for a rendezvous, what with the turn of wheels yet grinding along the cobblestones outside the hallowed ground of St. Sepulchre's. Midnight would have been better. Perhaps this Shadow Broker wasn't all he was cracked up to be.

Or it could be a well-calculated appointment to put him at ease before danger cuffed him in the head.

An involuntary shiver spidered down his spine as his gaze shifted left and right. Nothing moved save for the slight tremble of leaves on the trees, dripping leftover raindrops like so many drops of blood. Tombstones the colour of bleached bones popped up from the dirt, quiet sentries of the dead. Nothing out of the ordinary for a graveyard, but he didn't like it. Not a bit. In his line of work, it was the mundane that dulled the senses, and a trafficker of purloined goods ought never give in to passivity. Unless, of course, he didn't mind a gun to the back.

Which he did.

After rounding a bend in the path, Brudge crouched at the next gravestone on the left and squinted.

> *Beauty, wisdom, fame and wealth*
> *All are stolen by ill-health*
> *Bold or valiant, rugged or brave*
> *None escape the silent grave*

What a load of codswallop. Brudge turned aside and spit. If the Shadow Broker thought a few words carved in granite would put the fear of God into him, then the scoundrel clearly didn't know who he was dealing with.

He set the lantern on the ground as instructed in the note he'd received earlier that day. Scupper pulled alongside him, smelling of gardenias of all things. Either the man had a secret penchant, or he still lived with his mother.

"Now what?" Scupper's voice was a foghorn.

"Shsst!" Brudge kept his tone to just above a whisper as he scanned to the far stretches of the light. "No sense letting the whole world know we've arrived."

Scupper had opened his mouth to reply when hardened words hit them both in the back.

"I see you have brought company. That was not part of the deal."

Brudge wheeled about, brows shooting to the clouds as the

silhouette of a woman stepped from the shadows of a large tree trunk. She clutched a satchel in each hand, obviously prepared to do business. This slip of a woman was the Shadow Broker? No, it had to be a setup, and a nasty one at that.

"One can never be too cautious," he said, then murmured low to Scupper, "Be on alert." He eased his hand to his pocket, speaking loudly to draw attention to his words instead of the movement. "Had I known you were a skirt, I wouldn't have brought the extra muscle."

"Don't you know you ought not judge a book by its cover, Mr. Brudge?"

He chuckled, ending with a whisper to Scupper, "Check our flank, then circle round and get the goods." Upping his volume, he made a show of clouting the man on the back. "Off you go." Brudge smiled at the woman. "Is that better, miss?"

"There is no need to be condescending." A winter wind blew in her voice, stark against the July evening. "This is not my first purchase."

"So I hear tell." And he had, though he'd give Dandrae the sharp side of his tongue next time he saw him. The cully ought to have warned him the Shadow Broker liked to pull stunts. "How do you wish to play it, then?"

"I should like to inspect the artifact before I give you the money. Set the item down, then back off twenty paces. After I verify the authenticity, I shall put it in this empty satchel." She held up the bag in her left hand. "Then I will leave the money in its place, which is in this one." She lifted the other bag.

Brudge frowned. "Seems only fair I get to do some verifying as well. How do I know you've brought the full amount or even if there's anything in there?"

"In your own words, you have 'heard tell.' So no doubt you know I have never cheated anyone from the agreed-upon price."

A snort ripped out of him. "There's always a first in my line of business."

Though he couldn't see her face, he had no doubt her lips were pinched with irritation. Pulling out a stack of bills, she waved the wad in the air. "Would you like me to count them aloud?"

Sassy little sprite. A grin curved his mouth. "No need."

Shoving his hand into his pocket, he pulled out a cloth-wrapped bundle the length of his palm, hardly two fingers wide, then nestled it atop the gravel. He retreated no more than a step before the woman shot up her palm.

"Take the lantern with you."

He narrowed his eyes. "I thought you said you wanted to inspect the trinket."

Laughter bubbled out of her, more demeaning than humorous. He bristled. He'd never let a man insult him so, much less a woman.

"Just do as you are told, Mr. Brudge."

He snatched up the lantern, the flame casting a wild dance of light as it swung in his grip, then counted off twenty paces. How satisfying it would be when Scupper took this snippet down to the ground.

She approached the tiny parcel, skirts billowing like dark clouds. Setting aside the satchels, she retrieved the package and unwrapped it. Hard to say what she saw in the small figurine. He wouldn't give two coppers for the ugly chunk of clay. Not that it mattered, as long as she was willing to pay.

And since she was, that meant others would part with coins for it too.

Apparently satisfied, she opened the clasp on one bag and tipped it upside down. "As you see, Mr. Brudge, I shall be putting the item into the empty satchel and will leave behind the one with the payment." Like a grand entertainer, she flourished her hand in the air.

Brudge rolled his eyes. How this woman had earned such a shrewd reputation was beyond him. Then again, this could all simply be a charade while the real Shadow Broker hid behind some tombstone. If that was the case, hopefully Scupper could handle him. He'd certainly paid the brute enough.

"Let Mr. Dandrae know if you come across any other Egyptian artifacts. I am always in the market for such." She snapped the bag closed. "Good night, Mr. Brudge. A pleasure doing business with you."

Her skirts swirled as she shot down the gravel path. Brudge ate up the ground himself in a mad dash to grab the money. The clasp broke as he forced the satchel open. Sure enough, a bundle of banknotes sat inside. A slow smile eased across his lips, then broke into a grin as Scupper stepped out of the shadows and grabbed the woman. She'd have screamed were the man's big hand not over her mouth. He wrenched the satchel containing the artifact from her grip just as she elbowed him in the gut, followed by another sharp blow even lower. Scupper grunted.

Brudge winced. That had to hurt.

A curse bellowed out of the man, followed by a swipe of his meat-hook hand. The strike launched the woman sideways. She landed in a heap while Scupper lurched away, hunched over.

Brudge caught up to him and clapped the man on the back. "Good work. Now let's be off. Train leaves in twenty minutes . . . just about the time that chit will wake up with a real skull banger. Stupid woman. She has no business being in a man's world." He chuckled as he clutched both satchels. He could triple the money if he and Scupper pulled this little trick a few more times.

"But keep your eyes keen, eh?" His gaze swept the graveyard like the swing of a scythe. "For all we know, the Shadow Broker might yet be waiting to spring."

A twig in the mouth was as pleasant a sensation as gravel mashed into one's cheek—and a bruised one at that. Stifling a groan, Ami Dalton spit out the small stick, then pushed up to sit. Well. That hadn't gone exactly as planned.

Fingering the soreness in her jaw, she rose on stiff legs. Oh, but a hot soak in a rose-scented bath would be a welcome diversion this night. With quick sweeps of her hands, she dusted herself off, then glowered at a large tear in her hem. Must bullies always use force to get what they wanted? Then again, in order to bring history to life for the masses, one must be willing to face danger now and then—or so her father always said.

She huffed a disgusted puff of air as she picked her way through the maze of tombstones. The rear gate, while out of the way, was the safer route if Mr. Brudge and his hammer man came back. A beauty of a headache pounded in her temple as she upped her pace. Mr. Dandrae should have investigated this pair more thoroughly before suggesting she work with them. Such slipshod connections weren't like him . . . unless he'd taken a larger-than-usual cut of the profits. Possible. He was a consummate businessman even if his dealings were sometimes on the wrong side of the law. Perhaps Mr. Brudge had paid him too handsomely to refuse, or perhaps the man owned a little dirt on Mr. Dandrae. Regardless, Mr. Dandrae would hear of the heavy-handed horseplay that'd gone on tonight and make sure it didn't happen again, or she'd pull her business from him.

Hinges screeched like demons in the night as she opened the cemetery gate. Ahead sat a black cab with an even blacker horse hitched to it. The animal pawed the ground, a massive snort misting from his nostrils in the glow of the coach's lanterns.

"Ready to leave, miss?" the driver called from his seat.

"Yes, please." She boarded, taking care to tuck in her gown before shutting the door. No sense adding tear upon tear to the already battered fabric.

Sinking against the seat, she nearly closed her eyes. Yet no. This was a time not for rest but for celebration. With one quick movement, she pulled out the small bundle she'd jammed up her sleeve, then unwrapped the ancient shabti doll, the same shape and size of the rock she'd left inside the satchel Mr. Brudge stole. Mr. Clampstone would bounce on his toes when he got his hands on this gem. Another prize for the Ashmolean Museum's Egyptian collection and another step forward in her career to becoming a recognized Egyptologist. After six months of her identifying and acquiring unique pieces, Mr. Clampstone ought to be offering her that part-time Egyptologist position any day now. Which would be a boon. And yet even with such a title, she'd still be nowhere near gaining a smidgeon of the respect her father enjoyed. She'd never become a team member on an Egyptian dig without such respect. A sigh leaked out of her.

But even so, she smiled as she rewrapped the precious relic. If nothing else, the Shadow Broker had maintained her reputation, and for now, that would have to be enough.

2

Wut soft lite doth brake be-ond,
A donning, a yonning, a yell-oh

Hmm. A yellow what?
Frond?
Wand?
Vagabond?
Bah!

Tipping his head back against the velvet railcar seat, Edmund Price closed his eyes and gave in to the clickety-clack-clack of the train's wheels. It wasn't much more than half past nine in the evening, but even so he was weary of such a long journey. Usually poetry engaged his mind. Not tonight.

Outside the door to his private car, feminine giggles tittered like a gathering of hens. He opened one eye, and as he expected, a folded slip of paper slid beneath the door. A sigh deflated his lungs. He didn't need to retrieve the thing to know it dripped with some sort of floral eau de toilette. Loopy handwriting would entreat him to rendezvous in the dining car or invite him to call at such-and-such an address whenever he chanced to be in town. Such was the case ever since word got out that he'd left India. Women in gowns of all sizes, shapes, and colours had dogged his heels halfway across the world.

Knuckles rapped against the door. "Mr. Price?"

A male voice at least.

Setting aside his notepad, he opened the door. Behind the porter a few squeals rang out.

"There he is!"

"Ooh, he *is* a looker."

"Off you go now, ladies. Mr. Price has business to attend." The porter shooed them away with a flick of his fingers, then held out a white card to Edmund. "Here you are, sir. Oh, and we'll be arriving at the station shortly. I've made arrangements for a coach to be waiting for you."

"Thank you. I'll be sure to let your superiors know what a fine job you've done for me." Edmund swapped a few coins for the telegram before retreating to read the message—which took some time and effort. Why could letters and words never behave themselves? Were it not for his business partner, Gil, in London and his crack secretary, Anil, in India, he'd never be able to manage the correspondence portion of his business dealings. After several tries, though, he was finally able to decipher the thing.

CONCERNING OUR CONVERSATION, VIZ., YOUR FUTURE AS A PROSPECTIVE MEMBER OF THE HOUSE OF COMMONS. I SEE NO IMPEDIMENTS, PARTICULARLY NOT IF YOU'RE A MEMBER OF THE FAMILY, AND MY DAUGHTER, VIOLET, HAS NO OBJECTIONS TO THAT. WILL SPEAK SOON ON THE MATTER.

Well, well, well. Edmund set the message on the desk, then poured a glass of lemon water. Sipping the tart liquid, he mulled over Lord Bastion's proposal. Becoming a member of Parliament would be a stamp of success, but was the cost of a willful blond worth the price? Of course he didn't love her—would never love a woman again—but did such a concession have to rule out marriage? Weren't most unions marked by shallow conversations and cool looks across a dinner table? His parents certainly had perfected that art. He ran a hand over his face. My, how cynical he'd grown.

Still, there were other concerns to tackle first. He returned the glass to the drink cart, then doubled back to the desk and picked up a small piece of amber. Lamplight glowed through the specimen, highlighting the outline of a scarab—the only item he'd retained from the Egyptian shipment soon to arrive at his house. He frowned at the insect. Who knew what else was in that salvaged lot he and Gil had acquired from the failed venture with the Alexandria Merchant Fleet. He'd have preferred to be paid the debt owed him in pounds. If the cargo contained nothing but items such as this beetle caught forever in some hardened tree sap, resale would be a challenge.

And he needed that money.

He rubbed his thumb over the smooth surface of the resin. He was a man of business, savvy in buying low and selling high, but none of that experience would do any good with this load. He had no idea how to price such a bauble or—God willing— rare antiquities. He'd have to hire an expert to catalogue and value the relics, for there'd be crates upon crates of them . . . enough to put a huge grin on his business partner's face. And by the sounds of Gilbert Fletcher's recent correspondence, Gil had news that would make him smile as well—news he'd only tell face-to-face. Though Edmund was anxious to hear of it, Gil was tied up in a deal on the Continent. The soonest he could make it to Oxford was the end of next month.

Edmund closed his hand over the resin, the material now warmed to his body temperature. God had been good to him in many ways and yet sometimes not. A mystery, that. One he'd asked about in prayer many times and not once received a reply. How long would he sojourn in this land of uncertainty between gratitude for providence and the enigma of unanswered questions?

Brakes screeched, pulling him from his thoughts. The train juddered, and he grabbed hold of the table until the wheels stopped. The second they did, he pocketed the stone and dashed for the door. Thankfully the aisle was empty. Relieved, he grabbed his hat from a hook and darted to the exit, where a porter he'd not seen before dipped his head.

"Hope your journey suited you, Mr. Price."

"It did, thank you. But I'm afraid I'm in a terrible rush." He angled his head toward the door.

The porter swung the door wide. "Mind yer step."

Just as he'd feared, Edmund descended into a swirl of skirts and lace handkerchiefs. Bah! Such a gathering was completely beyond his control—which chafed, for he was accustomed to being in charge.

"Mr. Price! Remember me?" Eyelashes fluttered on the woman nearest him. Light from the station's gas lamps painted her very prettily, but he honestly didn't recall her face. "My cousin once removed said he'd mentioned me to you at a house party several years ago."

Behind her stood a stern-faced matron who'd been cajoled—or perhaps bribed—into allowing her charge out so late at night.

"I am sorry, miss. I do not recollect, but I am sure his words were kind." He edged past her, only to come nose to nose with a plump brunette.

"Welcome back to bonny England, Mr. Price. My father intends to hold a dinner in your honour. Naturally, I look forward to sitting next to you at the table."

"Yes, well . . . until then." He gave the woman a tight smile.

And so went the next eternity, all the way across the platform and through the station, until he finally—blessedly—reached his waiting carriage and sank against the leather seat. This mauling by the fairer sex was exactly why he preferred India to England. As the driver's tongue clucked and horse hooves clip-clomped, he couldn't help but wonder if coming home to Oxford had been the right thing to do.

Yet if he expected to land a seat in Parliament, he had no other choice.

A mad dash from the cemetery to the train station left Brudge with a throbbing bunion, a stitch in the side, and a very smelly Scupper. The big man sat across from him, filling the compartment with a most pungent body odour mixed with leftover gardenia. Brudge dabbed his brow with a handkerchief. They couldn't reach London soon enough.

But at least he was returning with a bag of money and the means to make more. The sooner he paid off Wormwell, the easier he'd breathe. Scupper was a mite of a man in comparison to that cully, and time was running out to give the most notorious smuggled-goods dealer in all of London his due.

The train lurched into motion, the jolt of it smacking Brudge's head against the seat. He tucked away his handkerchief as he peered out the window, not sorry in the least to see the lights of Oxford pass by the glass. A good foot soak was what he needed, that and several pints of ale.

He cracked open the window a few inches, letting in fresh air while hopefully sucking out Scupper's stink.

"Will ye be needin' me any more in London, then, guv'ner?"

He turned to the big man. "A time or two, I should think. We'll pull the same sell and snatch, draining what we can from this ugly little lump until I have enough money to pay my debts." He patted the bag at his side.

Scupper leaned forward, poking the small leather satchel with a thick finger. "Could I see it?"

"Ain't much to look at." Brudge shrugged. "It's just a clay doll hardly bigger than yer palm."

Eyes dark as boot blacking stared at him. "Why would anyone give a coin for it, then?"

"Pish. There's no accounting for some people's tastes. I once sold a stuffed patch-haired possum to a fellow with cages in his sitting room—and every cage held a different dead animal."

"Don't seem right, guv'ner, not for that stack o' bills ye collected." Scupper toyed with the curl of his moustache. "Maybe the value isn't in the item itself but what's inside."

Huh. Now there was a thought. "Good point. Could be more to it than I credited. Shame to break the thing open only to find it empty, though. We'd miss out on the resale."

"A risk, true enough."

But a risk he ought to take? If something costlier were hidden, he could pocket even more money. "I s'pose it wouldn't hurt to look the thing over."

He pulled the bag onto his lap and snapped open the clasp. Light seeped into the dark cavity, and rage leached into his soul. With a roar, he wrapped his fingers around a dirty chunk of rock.

"Guv'ner?"

"Conniving little vixen! No wonder she stayed in the shadows." He threw the rock across the compartment, nicking the paneling hardly an inch from Scupper's head. "We've been had!"

Scupper's long arm snagged the money bag from off the floor and pulled out a wad of bills. He fanned it in front of his face. "Appears to be all here."

"Let me see that!" Brudge seized the stack and counted each bill. "The full amount, what do you know?" He shoved the money inside the bag and slammed it to the floor. "Still, we're going back. I'll not be cheated. That little doll can and will bring me a coin or two more."

"Is it really a cheat, though, guv'ner?" Scupper's brow scrunched, making his thick forehead even more prominent. "Seems a fair deal. You got yer money. She got her goods."

"It's not a fair deal to my pride." He jammed his thumb into his chest. "Cyrus T. Brudge will *not* be bested by a woman."

"My mum used to say pride is a blind alley, the dead end bein' yerself. And she oughtta know. Kissed the grave 'cuz she were too stubborn to admit she were sick. Shoulda seen Doc Bones like I told 'er." Scupper sucked on his teeth. "But that's no nevermind when a coin's to be made, I s'pose."

Brudge scrubbed his face, irritated that Scupper always managed to lob truth nuggets at the most inconvenient times. It could be a death sentence to double back and swipe that blasted trinket from the girl, for it would eat up a day or two that might be better spent working a different angle to get Wormwell his money. Then again, if that smuggled relic did contain a hidden gem . . .

He blew out a long breath and folded his arms. "You're right, it is no nevermind. We will find out the identity of that woman, and when we do, I'll show that so-called Shadow Broker I'm not one to be trifled with."

3

Of all the hallowed halls and prestigious libraries dotting the many Oxford campuses, the stairwell down to the archives ranked highest on Ami's list of loves. Well, not so much the stairwell, perhaps, but the thought of retrieving a little piece of her father. Though he be a continent away, once she laid eyes on one of his old journals, she'd hear his voice loud and clear in every scrawled word.

Smiling at the thought, she had nearly cleared the last step when her ankle slipped sideways. She grabbed the railing just in time to avoid a nasty fall. *What in the world?* She bent to examine her left boot. A hairline crack fissured where the heel and sole met. Bother. These old balmorals would either have to be fixed or tossed in the dustbin. Yet neither option would do for the moment. She'd simply walk with more care until she could return home.

That settled, she shoved open the door to the University of Oxford record vault, where a ray of sunshine smiled at her from a massive desk. Clerk Polly Watkins never failed to dazzle everyone with her brilliant grin. Quite the contrast in this dimly lit crypt of files.

Ami approached the desk. "Good day, Polly."

"It's always a good day to see you, miss." She squinted, and a bouquet of little creases fanned out at the corners of her eyes. "Though I wonder if others will be of the same opinion."

"Whatever do you mean?"

Rising, Polly reached for Ami's hat. "For one, your boater is on all knurly. The bow goes on the side, goose, not the front. And then there's the whole matter of what some might consider an indecency."

Ami snapped a look downward. Sure enough, her bodice bulged out most unseemly where she'd missed putting a button into a hole, and her white shift showed through the gap. Bosh! With quick fingers, she righted the wrong, then tipped her head triumphantly. "There we are. All shipshape."

"True," Polly drawled, a flash of mischief lightening the deep blue in her eyes. "Yet I cannot help but wonder if you dressed in the dark."

Ami scrunched her nose. Either Polly was making a jest she couldn't understand, or there really was something wrong with her garments. "What could possibly make you say such a thing?"

"This." Polly circled her hand in the air, indicating Ami's figure from collar to hem. "Your bodice is embroidered with yellow and purple thread, that chemisette is red and green plaid, you've embellished it all with a striped chartreuse overskirt, and—" She narrowed her eyes on Ami's feet. "Ami Dalton, are you wearing one brown boot and the other black?"

Huh. How had she not detected such a faux pas when she'd taken note of her wobbly heel? "Unfortunately, yes." She smoothed her hands along her skirt. "But it's a matter soon to be righted. The black boot and its mate are going to the cobbler the moment I can manage it."

"Oh, my friend, what is the world to do with you?" Laughter, light as a summer rain, bubbled out of Polly while she doubled back to her desk chair. She plopped down, then planted her elbow on the tabletop and her chin on the heel of her hand. "Just imagine the man you could catch if you took a care with your looks."

What fiddle-faddle. If a man cared only about her outward appearance, then she most decidedly did not want him. And she had yet to meet a man who didn't. How her mother had managed to find her father had truly been a miracle, for as far as she knew, he was the only exception to the rule. It would have to be a very special man indeed to not only put up with her eccentricities but value them as well. She doubted such a fellow even existed, and as such, marriage seemed a distant prospect, overshadowed by the grandeur of someday leading a dig of her own.

But even so, she straightened her sleeve hems, now overly conscious about every aspect of her attire. "Actually, Polly, what I want is a particular journal of my father's to price a recent find."

The cluck of Polly's tongue echoed from stack to stack in the big room. "So you've been at it again, have you? It was an ill-fated day when you met Mr. Dandrae at that art auction, I tell you. He ought not be enticing you from your home while your father is out of the country. Speaking of which, what will your father say about you taking such risks in his absence?"

"He needn't know. Besides"—she shrugged—"I am always careful."

"Not careful enough with your face paint, though. That's quite the bruise you've got there." The slim little clerk aimed a finger at Ami's cheek.

Unbidden, her hand flew to her face, adding to the indictment. Evidently all the pains she'd taken with cosmetics before she'd left the house hadn't hidden last night's blow. And she still had a bit of a headache to contend with.

Polly shook her head. "Your fascination with ancient artifacts is turning into quite the star-crossed love affair. It's consuming you, goose, to your detriment. If Miss Grimbel sees that blemish, you'll be dismissed, and then what will you do?"

Ami dropped her hand, her lips twisting wryly. "Too late."

A snort riffled Polly's lips. "What did you do now?"

It was a fair question—if not a familiar one. Polly knew her long history of disappointing the headmistress of Grimbel's School of Conduct and Comportment. Ami tucked a loose strand of hair behind her ear. "I wanted my girls to understand there's more to life than knowing which fork to use or how to execute a perfect royal curtsey. History is so rich, you know?" She spread her hands. "I merely wished to impart a curiosity about it, that's all."

"I see." A prosecuting barrister couldn't have sounded more imposing—which was quite the feat for the petite clerk. "And how exactly did you do so?"

Ami smiled at the memory, a perfectly wicked thing to do, but oh how satisfying the girls' natural curiosity had been. "Easy enough. As a volunteer at the museum, I borrowed a mummified cat."

Polly's eyes rounded. "You didn't!"

"I did. Oh, Pol, you should have been there. The girls were wholly enthralled, asking loads of questions, but now that I think on it, perhaps I might have overdone fanning the flames of their curiosity. They simply couldn't stop talking about the experience. I still can't figure out if it was Lucy or Alice whom Miss Grimbel overheard." Ami tapped her lower lip for a moment. "But let us dwell on happier topics, hmm? I've brought you a little something." She shoved her hand into her pocket and retrieved a small white box, then pushed it across the desktop.

"Is it . . . ?" Polly's voice fairly squealed with anticipation.

"It is."

A green-sleeved arm shot out, and before Ami could say another word, Polly ripped off the cover and popped a piece of Turkish delight into her mouth. And a second. Followed by a third. "Mmm," she purred. A kitten with a dish of cream couldn't have showed more enthusiasm.

"Care to revise your opinion of my working with Mr. Dandrae? It does have its benefits, does it not?" Ami grinned. "Now then, while I hate to interrupt your obvious bliss, I should like to see an old journal of my father's. 1867 to '68, I believe. At least I hope that's the correct one. Can you give it a look, Pol?"

The clerk shoved one more candy into her mouth before dashing down an aisle to the right of her desk.

Minutes later, however, Polly returned empty-handed. "Sorry, Ami. That particular portfolio seems to be missing. The folders jump from '66 to '69."

Ami cocked her head. "Did someone else check it out?"

"Let's see." Polly ran her finger down several columns on the big ledger atop her desk, then glanced up. "Doesn't appear that happened."

"Well, bosh." Ami bit her lip. "That means I shall have to brave the abyss."

"Good thing you're not afraid of adventure, though I suggest you forgo any further opportunities provided by Mr. Dandrae. Your father won't be very happy about it, and you know it. He never has been."

"Then perhaps he ought to have finally taken me along on that dig of his to keep an eye on me. It's not like I haven't begged him to allow me to accompany him ever since I was a little girl." She sighed as bitter memories arose. Since her mother died when she was but seven years old, she'd longed to travel whenever her father pulled out his beat-up old trunk instead of being shuffled off to her grandmother's house. Not that it had been all bad, though. Grandmother had laid a strong foundation for Ami's current faith with all her Bible stories and insistence on attending services each Sunday. If she closed her eyes right now and inhaled, she might just catch a whiff of Grandmother's lilac perfume wafting across time. But even nineteen years later, she still wished Father would have relented to her request to allow her to go on a dig.

Well. Just wait until she was a recognized Egyptologist and managed to arrange her own dig. Perhaps he'd be the one asking her if he could go along!

Polly narrowed her eyes. "So you're walking headlong into danger out of spite, is that it?"

Ami snorted. "Now who's being the goose? It's not dangerous—usually—to purchase items from willing sellers. And if I don't rescue those stolen relics from careless criminals for the museum, who will? It is far better to see such artifacts purchased for all the public to enjoy than allowing them to get stuffed away in some private collection that benefits no one . . . though in a perfect world I'd rather them returned to the Egyptian people. But this isn't a perfect world now, is it?" She blew out a heavy sigh. "At any rate, I'm building quite a good reputation with Mr. Clampstone. Not only does he value my services, he's considering hiring me as an Egyptologist for the department. Well, part-time, that is. And not necessarily with an official title, mind. Not yet, anyway."

"That's wonderful, my friend. But truly, you needn't put yourself in risky situations to prove something that's already true." She aimed her finger at her. "Egyptologist or not, you are valuable. As God's creatures, we all are."

"God may think so—at least I hope He does—but men deem otherwise."

"Well, I suppose there's no accounting for those of lesser intelligence. I'm of a mind to scrap the whole lot of them after Charlie left me for that strumpet at the Eagle and Child. His loss, though." Polly wiggled her eyebrows before shoving the last piece of Turkish delight into her mouth.

"You are out of control, Pol. Until next time." Ami grinned all the way to the door.

Her mirth faded as she made her way up to ground level. Weaving past clusters of male students who paid her not the slightest bit of attention, she jammed her hat tighter on her head lest it blow away in the breeze. The truth was Polly had been wrong. Searching Father's office would be more of a nightmare than an adventure, for he was ever the disorganized pack rat. The notes she sought could be shoved in a box of chipped china that ought to be donated. Or for all she knew, the journal might be buried beneath a dish of sparrow feathers. For a man who appreciated fine Egyptian artifacts, one would think he could at least collect senet pieces or kohl pots.

Sighing, she trotted up the stairs to the humanities building, each step making her more cross. It could take her hours to find that journal. She ought to simply toss out all the worthless items and . . . wait a minute. What a brilliant idea. After she successfully priced the shabti doll—which she would, even if it killed her—she could thoroughly clean her father's office. Give him a real surprise when he returned to England, which wouldn't be for at least—

Crack.

The world tipped. She toppled sideways.

Ami flailed for the railing.

And missed.

Pulling his hat low on his brow, Edmund glanced right and left before stepping out of the carriage. In ten long strides, he made it inside the sanctuary of Oxford University's courtyard, where nothing but suits milled about. The tightness in his shoulders melted. Apparently he hadn't needed to borrow his steward's shabby hat and coat as a disguise. There wasn't a woman in sight.

Even so, he increased his pace toward the humanities building. There was no time to spare in securing the country's foremost Egyptologist for his shipment, which would arrive in two days. Hopefully the professor would not only be in his office but also able to devote the next month to Edmund's employ. He'd certainly make it worth the man's effort, far more than the fellow would pocket from teaching.

A gust of wind blew, nearly stealing his steward's old hat. He slapped his hand against the derby as he ducked around a marble column. The colonnade led to a staircase, where a shocking swirl of colour ascended. Edmund slowed his pace, giving the eccentric woman plenty of time for a lead. If she was this outlandish in her choice of garments, he could only imagine the trills and shrills that would squawk out of her were she to spy Oxford's most eligible bachelor.

Halfway up, though, her left heel gave, the black nub of it bouncing down the granite toward him.

Edmund took the stairs two at a time as she flailed. With a wide-armed lunge, he caught her before she cracked her head.

So much for avoiding women.

"My, my." Her words came out on a soft puff of air. Which was odd. Most women would've screamed at such an ordeal.

He guided her to the railing and was about to release her when she twisted in his arms, facing him head on. Eyes blinked at his, the colour of which was so mesmerizing it was impossible to look away. Were they blue? No, green. Hmm, not quite right either. Brown, then. But no. He leaned closer, staring hard. Great heavens. A master painter couldn't capture such a changeable hue. Depending on which way the light caught her face, one might say they were any of those shades.

"Thank you." She tipped her head, clearly dismissing him.

But when she did so, a shaft of sunshine landed on her cheek, where deep purple darkened the flesh beneath a layer of cosmetics. Either the woman was perpetually clumsy, or someone had struck her full-handed—and the thought of that clenched tight in his gut. "Are you all right?"

"I am fine." She smiled, surprisingly straight teeth flashing brightly.

"Of course you are," he murmured. She was a fascinating creature. Like a great portrait, the longer he studied her, the more details he saw, from the spray of freckles across the bridge of her nose to the darker dot of a mole at the edge of her jaw.

"You can let me go now."

"What? Oh. Yes." He released her, and she sank to the stairs, the top half of her body folding over her shoes. Alarm charged through his veins. Had he saved her from a fall only to have her swoon? He crouched by her side, arms at the ready to sweep her up should she need. "Are you certain you are all right, miss?"

"Yes, it's just . . . this . . ." She yanked off her shoe. "Blasted boot!" Her free hand flew to her mouth as a most becoming shade of dusty rose spread like the dawn on her face.

He laughed—really laughed—which was new. He couldn't remember the last time a woman made him feel anything other than the urge to run away.

"Please pardon my unconscionable outburst. It's just that, well"—she waved her shoe in the air—"it appears my heel has decided to completely run off without me."

"How inconsiderate of the thing." He retrieved the little fugitive, then returned and held out his hand. "Why don't you let me see what I can do?"

She offered him the broken shoe. He shook his head. "The other one, if you please."

Her lips lifted into a most adorable quirk, yet without an objection or even a question, she unlaced the other boot—a completely mismatched one—and gave it to him.

Eyeing the crisp marble edge of the wall just above the hand-rail, he swung back the shoe, then struck with all his might. Another heel flew high in an arc. He caught the nub before it hit the ground and handed all the broken bits and now-heelless shoe to the woman.

Glowering, she hugged the boot to her chest. "What did you do that for?"

"You had a problem. I solved it. Unless you wanted to hobble around like the hunchback of Notre Dame?"

"Hmph." She jammed her feet into her shoes. "I'm not quite sure if I ought to thank you or censure you."

"No need for either." He grinned. My, but she was spunky. "I am happy I came along when I did, or you may have been more seriously hurt. How about you try those out while I'm still around to be your safety net?"

"Thank you all the same, but I need no such thing." Rising, she smoothed the creases out of her skirt, totally ignoring him.

And he wasn't quite sure what to do with that.

"Don't let me keep you, Mr. Problem Solver. Good day." Clutching the railing, she mounted the rest of the stairs, leaving behind a smoky-cinnamon scent and a completely foreign emptiness in his chest.

He caught up to her three strides past the landing. "Actually, I am going the same direction."

"Is that so?" She slanted him a sideways glance, her step not hitching once.

Astounding. Any other woman would have needed smelling salts if he offered to escort her. "You really don't know who I am, do you?"

"Of course I do." She shrugged. "You are Mr. Problem Solver."

What an anomaly. Clearly the woman didn't read the social columns. Who was this peculiar lady? He matched his pace to hers. "It is rather unusual to find a woman gracing these halls of learning."

"Well, there you have it."

"Have what?"

"I *am* rather unusual." Her lips curved into a mischievous grin. "And this is where we part ways. Good day." Retrieving a key from her pocket, she opened an office door.

Edmund looked from the woman to the nameplate on the wall—then sucked in a breath. Professor Archer Dalton. The very man he was looking for. What were the odds?

He followed her inside to a small room filled with an assortment of empty ink bottles, spent candle nubs, rolls of rags, and broken crocks holding dried snakeskins. And was that a painted elephant tusk hanging by a frayed rope from the ceiling? Stars and thunder. This place was a curiosity shop, as varied and colourful as the woman's garments. . . . Ah, perhaps she was the supplier of the professor's odd collections.

"Do you work here?" he asked.

"In a sense. Now, if you don't mind, I am rather busy." She turned away.

A bold move, one he often employed when hoping to close a deal, but he hadn't even submitted his proposal yet. He planted his feet. "I should like to hire Professor Dalton to catalogue and price a shipment of Egyptian antiquities soon to arrive at the Price mansion, which is just outside of town. The work would require a fortnight or so of employment. Possibly more, but it will be very much worth his while."

She whirled back around. "Am I to understand you are in charge of hiring the professor for Mr. Price?"

"In a sense." Her pert little nostrils flared at his repetition of her own words, and he stifled a grin.

"That being the case . . ." She circled a cluttered desk and planted her hands atop two stacks of books. "I have both bad and good tidings for you."

"Intriguing. Start with the former—for things are often not as bad as they seem—and then I should like to hear the good."

"Very well." She tipped her chin. "Unfortunately, Professor Dalton is indisposed for another six weeks at a dig in the Biban el-Muluk valley. There is no possible way he could accept your offer."

"Hmm. That is a problem." He scrubbed his knuckles along his jaw, thinking aloud. "Those antiquities must be priced and moved within a month. It never pays to sit on a shipment over-long, and the funds are needed."

"Well, you can call me Miss Problem Solver, then." She grinned. "I have just the solution for you."

He narrowed his eyes. "You know of another Egyptologist for hire?"

"You really don't know who I am, do you?"

Instant admiration flared at her adept play of bandying his words against him. "I am afraid I am at a loss, Miss . . . ?"

"I am the professor's daughter." She threw back her shoulders, a soldier at attention. "Miss Ami Dalton at your service."

Well. That was a twist he hadn't seen coming. "Pleased to meet you, Miss Dalton." He dipped his head. "But how does that solve my problem?"

"I, sir, am a rescuer of forgotten fragments, a story guardian of the past, a fervent believer in bringing history to life for the masses. There is no one on this campus who knows as much about Egyptian relics as I do. I grew up living and breathing artifacts." She swept her hand around the room—though it didn't do much to prove her point. He wouldn't give two shillings for the lot of eclectic items filling the small space.

"If Mr. Price has a shipment that needs an accurate inventory and appraisal, I'm the woman for the job. I have a bachelor of art degree from Lady Margaret Hall, I currently work with the Ashmolean Museum's Egyptian department, and I have studied at my father's knee since a young girl. You won't find anyone in all of Oxfordshire who knows as much about Egyptology as I do. Well, except for my father, that is. And as I've already stated, he is not here."

He inhaled deeply. He'd been trying to avoid women, not hire one. "I am not so sure—"

"We'll just see about that." She rummaged through the books on the desk, then held out a thick one. "Here. Quiz me."

He cocked his head. "Pardon?"

"Clearly you have doubts. I mean to put them at an end. Ask me about anything." Leaning across the desk, she pushed the book into his hands.

She was a determined little firebrand, he'd give her that. He'd play her game, although with much trepidation. He paged to a random chapter and scanned the first paragraph, praying to find some words he could decipher. Sweat sprung out on his brow. He hated this weakness. It was a chink in his armor. Unmanly. Humiliating.

God, please, do not shame me in front of this woman. Help me to trust in Your strength, not my own—for in this particular instance, I have none.

He continued scanning and . . . perfect. A sketch with numbers beneath. Numbers were always easier than letters. He peered at her. "When was the Great Sphinx of Giza discovered?"

"Oh, bosh! Please don't go so easy on me. I am no novice, sir." Removing a ratty conquistador hat that looked as if it had died in the Spanish Inquisition, she sank onto the now-cleared-off chair and laced her fingers beneath her chin. "The Italian Giovanni Battista supervised an archaeological dig in 1817, at which point the Great Sphinx was first uncovered all the way up to its chest."

"And let's say by some miraculous movement of God that you were able to come into possession of that magnificent artifact. How much would you value it at for resale?"

She blew out a huff. "What a ridiculous question. It is beyond value, sir."

"Mmm. Fair enough." He flipped to another page, looking for something more obscure yet readable, leastwise to him. And . . . victory. Another sketch, this time with small words describing it. "What is the name of the dolls that are placed in tombs as servants in the afterlife?"

Her shoulders stiffened, and her voice dropped an octave. "Who sent you here?"

Odd. Hadn't he made clear his business? "As I said, I have a shipment that needs—"

"Yes, yes." She fluttered her fingers at him as she dashed to the door. Craning her neck, she swept a gaze along both sides of the corridor.

"Is there a problem, Miss Dalton?"

"Hopefully not." Tugging down her garish bodice, she resumed her seat.

"Say," he drawled. "You're not trying to stall on answering the question, are you? If you don't know the answer, there's no shame in admitting it."

Pah! What a hypocrite. As if he'd admit to the difficulty he had with reading. Granted, poetry had helped his affliction, but his lack when it came to the written word still haunted him.

She shook her head, loosening a strand of brown hair. "No shame involved. What you described is a shabti doll, sometimes referred to as a ushabti. It's a small figurine usually made of clay and frequently carries a hoe or a basket on its back. Along with scarabs, shabtis are the most numerous of all ancient antiquities to survive. In fact, I am about to sell one to the Ashmolean once I verify the price."

His brows rose. "Impressive. How much do you hope to gain?"

"Ten pounds." Folding her arms, she leaned back in the seat. "Go on, and be sure to make the next one a challenge, if you don't mind."

You better believe he would, for it was a downed gauntlet now to stump such an eccentric little beauty. This time he ignored the text and instead squinted at the footnotes in small print. A slow smile eased across his lips as he closed the book and thunked it onto the only clean corner of the desk. "What is a sister-um, Miss Dalton?"

Musical laughter bubbled out of her. "A—what did you say?"

Heat flared up his neck. She'd heard him all right, which could only mean one thing . . . he'd read it wrong. "Did I mispronounce it?"

She grinned, but she didn't poke fun. "A sistrum is a member of the percussion family, a U-shaped musical instrument made of bronze or brass, generally from the ancient Egyptian era. When shaken, small rings or loops—"

He held up his hand. "That's enough."

"Is it?" She rose from her seat and folded her hands primly in front of her as if ready for a recital. "I can do this all day if you like."

No doubt she could. He chuckled, for once savoring a battle he hadn't won. "I'll expect you at Price House two days hence. It's a large project, one that will take upward of two to four weeks' worth of work. Being that the manor is outside of Oxford's city limits, bring along a chaperone as you'll be expected to stay until you are finished."

She narrowed her eyes. "Are there no other women on the premises?"

"Of course there are. Price House prides itself on a full household staff."

"Then tell me, sir." Miss Dalton planted her hands on the desk and leaned forward. "If my father had been in this office today and you hired him, would you also have required him to bring along a chaperone?"

"That's a preposterous question."

"And yet it stands."

He blinked. What a headstrong young woman, and yet instead of being annoyed by her brash manner, oddly enough it amused him. "No, Miss Dalton, your father would not need an attendant."

"Then neither do I." She lifted her chin. "I expect complete professional courtesy, no matter my gender and with all the same benefits."

He eyed her, uncertain if he truly ought to take on such a firebrand.

"Very well," he said at length. "Nine o'clock Saturday morning. Don't be late."

"I shan't be." She grinned. "And thank you."

"I hope I am not making a mistake, so by all means, prove me wrong."

"I'd like nothing more."

He reset his hat as he headed toward the door. "Good day, then, Miss Dalton." Before he crossed the threshold, a new thought hit him, and he doubled back. Reaching into his pocket, he planted several bills on the desk.

Her brow wrinkled. "Is that some sort of retainer fee?"

He straightened, enjoying the confusion on her face far too much. "No, it's for a new pair of shoes—ones that match. I shall see you in two days."

He strolled out the door, wondering if he'd done the right thing by hiring a woman. When she discovered who he really was, would she turn into a lovelorn schoolgirl? He'd hate to terminate her, but he would in an instant if need be.

Strangely, though, deep down he hoped he wouldn't have to.

4

Ami stood in front of Price House with a bag in her hand and a scowl on her face. Father often scolded her for being too swift to form an opinion, but even without entering this house she knew exactly what she'd find inside. Arrogance. Strict protocol. And worse, a mawkish cloud of lemon beeswax permeating the air to a sickly degree.

Oh, but she could *not* abide lemons.

Tossing back her shoulders, she snubbed her nose at the carved granite lions on either side of the stairs and rang the bell. Off-putting smells or not, she was anxious to dig into Mr. Price's precious load of relics, though admittedly a bit apprehensive as well. She'd finished her business with the shabti doll, pleasing Mr. Clampstone just as she'd hoped to, but being tied up here could cut into her shadow brokering . . . a dilemma she'd been wrestling with the past two days. She'd instructed Mr. Dandrae only to contact her here if something extraordinary came up, but if that happened, how would she explain her absence to the indomitable Mr. Price? Wealthy men thought they owned everyone working for them, and the thought of being owned made her feet itch to run.

Moments later, a tall, thin butler cocked his head at her like a crow. His dark eyes assessed her in a hasty blink, and if the twitch of his upper lip was any indication, she fell somewhere between a traveling trinket seller and a gypsy waif.

"The servants' entrance is around back, miss." His voice was distinctly nasal.

Hmm. Perhaps Father ought to have his don't-judge-a-book-by-its-cover monologue with this fellow. She lifted her chin. "Thank you for the information, but I am no housemaid. I am here at the . . . em, steward's request. Well, actually, I didn't inquire after the man's position so that is an assumption, but nevertheless, it must have been Mr. Price's man of business who employed me to catalogue and value a soon-to-arrive collection of Egyptian artifacts."

He reared back his head. "*You* are the professor?"

A common response. Expected, actually. But all the same, she bit her tongue and curved her lips into a pleasant smile. "I am Miss Dalton, Egyptologist."

"I see." Humor glinted in his eyes. "Crawford put you up to this, did he? I should have expected some sort of retribution, I suppose. That imitation spider in the corner of his room was one of my better pranks. Shrieked like a little girl." A chuckle squawked out of him. "At any rate, you may tell Crawford you played your part well, and here is a penny for your trouble." He produced a coin from his pocket.

She fended off the payment with an upraised palm. "I don't know what sort of hijinks you and this Mr. Crawford have going on, but it sounds rather a jolly game. Even so, I assure you I truly am the Egyptologist employed by Mr. Price's steward, so if you wouldn't mind announcing me?"

Stooping somewhat, he narrowed his eyes. "This isn't a jest?"

"No, this is not a jest."

"Well, well. My mistake, then. Do come in, Miss Dalton." He flung the door wide and ushered her inside. "Jameson's office is this way."

She followed, purposely putting weight on the instep of her left foot. Though it was yet morning, a mighty fine blister would likely emerge on her pinky toe by nightfall. She'd bought a sturdy pair of new boots thanks to the steward's advance, but she had yet to break them in.

Bypassing the sitting room, the black-coated butler crossed a vast receiving hall. How many ball gowns and bespoke suits had graced this marble floor in years past? If she listened closely enough, would she hear the tinkle of flute glasses and strains of Haydn or Mendelssohn haunting the air? What a dreadful pastime. She'd attended a dance once and had been heartily glad when it was over. A good book and hot cup of drinking chocolate was much to be preferred.

As they skirted a collection of bronze pedestals at the center of the room, she slowed her pace, inhaling deeply. Each pillar varied in height and sported a crystal vase of multicoloured lilies. How delightful. If the housemaids had polished the baseboards today, the lemony scent was obliterated by this heavenly fragrance.

The butler turned into a corridor, and she scurried to catch up. He entered a door at the far end, announcing her the moment his foot crossed the threshold.

"Mr. Jameson? A Miss Dalton to see you."

"Is that so? Send her in, then."

Shoving her hat back atop her head, for the silly thing had slipped in her haste, she strode past the butler.

The man behind the desk glanced up at her. He was a ruddy-faced fellow, likely accustomed to the elements when not squirreled away with ink and ledgers. Side-whiskers drew to a point down his jawline, bristly as a Shetland's shorn mane. The coat he wore was familiar—dark green with a brown collar and oval patches on each elbow—but the fabric of it did not stretch as tightly across his shoulders. He didn't have dimples or a fine strong mouth or a manner that both chafed and intrigued simultaneously. And those eyes were certainly not the same dusky blue. She ought to know. Much to her chagrin, she'd revisited that face many times in her dreams over the past couple of nights.

Mr. Jameson set down his pen. "How may I help you, Miss Dalton?"

"Em . . ." Perhaps this really was a jest, but not one of the butler's design nor of the aforementioned Crawford. Had Polly set someone up to play a trick on her? Had Mr. Dandrae? Or maybe—

"Miss?"

She lifted her chin. If this was some sort of prank, she may as well go along with it for now. "I was hired two days ago to catalogue and price a shipment of Egyptian artifacts belonging to Mr. Price. This is Mr. Price's home, is it not? And he is expecting a cargo of valuable items?"

Mr. Jameson sucked in a breath. "*You* are the professor?"

She shoved down a sigh. Nefertiti probably hadn't been subject to such offense. Must she always prove to God and man that she was an intelligent creature? "For your clarification, sir, I am an Egyptologist, and I was under the impression the offer of employment had been made by Mr. Price's steward. Clearly that is not the case."

"Ah, I understand now." Mr. Jameson chuckled as he leaned back in his chair, lacing his hands behind his head. "Though I must say I am quite surprised he took on a woman."

She gripped the life out of her bag handles to keep from flailing her arms. "Who is *he*? Who took me on?"

"I did."

She turned at the deep voice—and there stood the man who'd refused to vacate a corner of her mind ever since he'd caught her up in his arms on a stuffy Oxford stairway. She popped her fist onto one hip, annoyed at the slight thrill fluttering in her chest. "And who, may I ask, in all the wide, wide world are you, sir?"

"I am Edmund Price, Miss Dalton." A crafty grin spread on those fine lips of his. "Welcome to my home."

Edmund grinned. Miss Ami Dalton was a sight, all right. One he'd been anxious to see again if only to confirm whether his memory of the anomalous woman was fact or fiction. And he was not disappointed in the least. There she stood in all her mismatched glory. A jaunty blue hat sat askew on hair that had slipped some of its pins. She wore a loose-fitting blouse with part of the collar folded in on her neck, a yellow cutaway jacket, and a striped burgundy skirt that would serve better as a pair of draperies. Shiny boot tips peeked out from the hem. New ones. So she had in fact used the money to get herself some shoes.

Even so, his grin faltered. Now that she knew his identity, would she transform into one of the many bubbleheaded women who swooned at his feet, hoping to become the new Mrs. Price, with all the wealth and prestige attached to that name?

Her eyes widened. Her fine little nostrils flared, the freckles on the bridge of her nose riding the wave.

Blast. Here it came. The fawning. The flattery. All the inane coy giggles and fluttering of eyelashes. Edmund stiffened.

"While I thank you for your greeting, Mr. Price, I cannot help but wonder if you are frequently given to deception? Because if I am to work here, that could be a troublesome problem, one I cannot abide."

Jameson snorted a laugh, yet to his credit, he quickly turned it into a cough by pounding his chest with his fist. The action did nothing, however, to hide the mirth in his eyes. Bah. The steward would have this little comeuppance spread from one end of the estate to the other, for the man was a bigger gossip than all the old tabbies in the Ladies Aid Society combined.

Edmund swept his hand toward the front hall. "How about we take our conversation to the sitting room, Miss Dalton? I am sure Jameson here has business to attend."

"As you wish." She strode past him.

He arched a warning brow at his steward. Not that it would do any good. Jameson could no more keep a good tale to himself than stop his heart from beating.

In several long-legged strides, Edmund caught up to the saucy Miss Dalton. "I trust your journey here went well?"

A playful grin lit her face. "I hardly traversed the Sahara to get here, Mr. Price, but yes. Aside from a squeaky spring, the coach ride was uneventful. Oh, could perhaps one of your staff collect my trunk from the drive? It was a bit too heavy for me to haul up the stairs."

"I take it that means you've decided to stay?"

She eyed him for several steps before answering. "For now."

Once inside the sitting room, he indicated the sofa. "Shall I ring for anything else? Tea, perhaps? Coffee?"

Surprise furrowed her brow. "I am not a guest, Mr. Price. I came here to work, and I am most eager to begin. But first, I'm afraid I must insist on an answer to my earlier question, for if a working relationship is not based on truth, then it isn't a relationship at all." She angled her head like a curious tot. "Why did you not tell me who you were when you offered me the job?"

"As I recall, Miss Dalton, I offered your father the job, not you. This employment is due more to your machinations than mine." If that made her prickle, she didn't show it. She merely stared up at him, a living Mona Lisa. "However"—he grinned—"if your career in Egyptology doesn't go well, I suspect you'd make a fine businessman."

"Ah, but I am a woman, sir, so that would go over about as well as my scholarly endeavors. But to the point, you purposely hid your identity from me, and I begin to think I can guess as to why."

A dog with a bone, eh? And an inventive one at that. He took the adjacent chair, intrigued beyond reason and not just a bit wary. "Go on."

"I was hoping you'd say as much." She settled on the sofa cushion, eyes gleaming. "Everyone knows you've been out of the country for years, and yet here you are now, showing up in Oxford incognito. It is my premise that you wish to keep your presence a secret because you're working undercover for the Crown. Maybe trying to crack some sort of smuggling ring that's moving relics from country to country or the like. No, no! I've got it."

She leaned forward, face alight with conspiracy. "You're not seeking to bring down smugglers but a counterfeiting gang that is flooding the market with fake artifacts. You've somehow managed to buy such a load of supposed relics and are eager to prove their fabrication. That's why you sought my father, for in the past he has worked with government agents. Am I correct, sir? If so, rest assured your answer will go no further than my ears."

He laughed. Really laughed. This was becoming a habit in her presence. An enchanting tale, but not nearly as endearing as the quirk of Miss Dalton's lips. Truly, it may have been a mistake to have invited her into his home, for this woman could leave an indelible mark if he wasn't careful. "Allow me to revise the career path I suggested. You have a very promising future in the publishing world penning novels of espionage and danger."

She frowned, which was just as appealing. Why, he'd not enjoyed a woman so much since . . . no. Dredging up that tragedy now would ruin the fun of bantering with Miss Dalton.

She shifted on the cushion. "I would prefer a career as an expedition director at an Egyptian dig."

Rising, he strode to the beverage cart and poured two glasses of lemon water. Miss Dalton shook her head at the offering, so he set hers on the tea table and drank a few swallows of his. "Well, at any rate, as much as I hate to dash your fine stories to bits, I am afraid my truth is not so clandestine. The sad fact is I merely wanted to avoid money-hungry mothers who wish to saddle me with their daughters."

She narrowed her eyes. "There wasn't a single mother or daughter in my father's office when we spoke."

"But there was you, and you are female."

"Surely you're not suggesting . . ." She gasped. "You *are* suggesting!"

Laughter pure as a summer morn rang out of her, so much that she dabbed the corners of her eyes with her knuckles. "Oh, Mr. Price, that is hilarious. Of course you cannot be expected to know my partialities for we have only just met, but you will soon find I am not the average female. My head is turned by a finely wrapped, mummified corpse, not a flesh-and-blood pile of muscles."

"Muscles, eh?" He set down his glass with a curve to his lips. "So you do find me attractive."

"What I find is a man who's been told he's attractive so many times that he's come to believe it." All her humor fled as she pressed her fingers to her mouth, a flush pinking her cheeks.

He blinked, unsure what to do with such candor from a woman. Though she clearly regretted what she said, was such a criticism true? Had he let all the feminine attention over the years get to him so he no longer recognized himself? Or was she being catty for the sake of retribution? Either way, such forthrightness was refreshing, if not a little stinging.

"Please pardon me, Mr. Price." She pressed her hands against her belly as if she were ill. "My tongue has been known to run away from me, and this time it has completely broken its leash."

A little girl caught with her hand in the biscuit tin couldn't look more contrite, which banished any remaining prickle from such rash words. "I would rather hear your unguarded thoughts, Miss Dalton, for as a wise woman once said, if a working relationship is not based on truth, then it isn't a relationship at all." He winked.

Relief flashed in a smile. "You are very gracious, sir."

They both looked up as his butler entered the room. "Sorry I'm late in answering your call, sir, but your shipment has arrived. I directed the lead driver where to go."

Edmund rose, rubbing his hands together. "And so it begins. Oh, Barnaby, will you have Miss Dalton's trunk brought up to her room?"

"Already taken care of, sir."

He might've known. The faithful retainer could set right an overturned applecart before one red fruit hit the ground.

"Very good." Edmund turned to Miss Dalton. "Would you like to see what you're up against?"

She hopped to her feet. "By all means."

He led her out the front door to view a line of wagons snaking around the side of the house. An impressive sight, if not a little daunting. Perhaps he ought to have rented a warehouse instead of expecting so many goods to fit inside Price House.

Miss Dalton craned her neck. "How many are there?"

"Ten drays in all. I wasn't jesting when I said it would take up to a month to sort through this lot."

"It could take much longer than that."

"Yet you will finish it in four weeks' time."

She peered up at him, a little scrunch to her nose that sent her freckles bobbing. "Why such a restraint?"

"Price House is not a museum. I wish to sell the lot as soon as possible. The money is needed elsewhere." Indeed, the woman could have no idea how much his old friend in India was counting on the proceeds from this sale. If he didn't get the funds to Sanjay before the new tariff was enacted at the end of September, the man's business would fail—and with it, the means to provide for his large family . . . and being destitute in India was a death sentence.

"But surely, Mr. Price, you do not need—"

An unearthly howl of pain violated the July morning. Shouts followed. So did more howls. Edmund set off at a run, calling over his shoulder, "Wait there, Miss Dalton."

He tore along the row of wagons, closing in on a huddle of men near the lead dray. By the time he reached the scene, several burly fellows were hefting an enormous crate off the leg of a man on the ground. His cries stilled as his eyes rolled back and his body went slack.

Lighter footsteps raced up behind him, a feminine "What's happened?" competing with the shout of a foreman to get a stretcher.

Edmund shot out his arm, holding back Miss Dalton. No woman—nor man, for that matter—ought to witness a leg broken to such a grotesque angle. Would that he could have done something to prevent such a tragedy, and yet this was beyond his control.

"I tol' ye this load were cursed! The whole lot of it." A sour-faced workman snatched his fallen hat from the ground and jammed it on his head as he stomped away. "I'll not have another thing to do with this unholy business, and if yer smart, none o' you men will either."

5

Miracles did still happen. Despite her frequent loose-lipped blunders around Mr. Price the past few days, Ami hadn't been dismissed yet, so there was that. And then there was this stunning alabaster vase. A marvel that stole her breath as she ran her gloved finger over the translucent curve of it. It was a valuable piece. A New Kingdom beauty, nearly four millennia having passed since its creation. Who had it belonged to? What sort of oil had been stored inside? Which crypt had it been stolen from? For indeed it was stolen. No self-respecting mummy would have authorized its removal.

She rubbed at a speck near the base, heart swelling with a deep love for this precious link to the forgotten past. A persistent internal whisper tugged at her ambition, urging her toward the sands of Egypt, where she might one day unearth a relic of her own. But was her true purpose to preserve finds such as this vase or to unravel the secrets of the untouched by exposing them?

Or was it something entirely else?

And what if—as Polly had said—her worth wasn't solely tied to what she achieved? Now, there was something to ponder.

"Will you take some tea, Miss Dalton?"

Ami startled, pulled from her thoughts by a now-familiar

nasal tone. In strode Barnaby, his steps echoing in the banquet-hall-turned-makeshift-valuation-room.

"Goodness." She smiled while peeling off her cotton gloves. "Is it that time already?"

"Afraid so. Where shall I . . . ?" He glanced at a sideboard she'd recently covered with a canvas tool roll, her various instruments peeking out from the pockets.

Good thing it was Barnaby serving the tea today instead of the housekeeper, Mrs. Buckner. She would have fussed about such an inconvenience. Nevertheless, Ami sprang into action, rolling her pouch into a bundle. "There you are."

He set down the tray, and as he poured the hot brew, she couldn't help but tease. "I heard from the maid that Mr. Crawford had his revenge on you this morning."

"He did indeed, the rotter." Barnaby's sharp cheekbones stood out as his lips curved upward. "Used the ol' salt-in-the-sugar-dish trick. I can still taste that first swig of coffee." His mouth puckered as he handed her a saucer with a rose-sprigged teacup balanced atop.

"Ah, so you are even, then." She eyed him over the rim as she took a sip.

"For now."

She blew on the hot Assam, hoping to cool it a bit. "I've never worked in such a grand house as this, so forgive my ignorance in asking you, Barnaby, but why do you play pranks on your underlings? I haven't heard of such a thing. Unless my preconceptions of upper staff are completely off-kilter."

"I suppose it is a rarity." He shrugged. "Most houses wouldn't allow such loose decorum. But that is exactly why I work here. You see, Miss Dalton, Mr. Price is rarely in residence, but when he is, he is an exacting employer who brooks no slack. That being said, he also understands that it takes faithful yet pliable people to work in a home where duties tend to be feast or famine. Thus, as long as the work hums along and everyone is happy, he's willing to allow good-natured jollity amongst the staff. For my part, I find it builds a sort of camaraderie, a sense of unity, if you will, in seeing that no matter the station or occupation, we are all brothers-in-arms."

A compelling premise. One she'd not thought of. She drank her tea, mulling on the enigma of Mr. Price and his home, the playful tomfoolery that established rapport amongst servants and—oh my. A rogue thought popped into her head. "Does Mr. Price partake of such antics as well?"

"Not at all, nor would I allow any of my staff to engage in such japery with him. The boundary between employer and employee ought never be crossed. I am strict on that rule." Barnaby covered the sugar bowl, then straightened. "Oh, I nearly forgot. Mr. Price insists you dine with him this evening, that he'll not take no as an answer as he has the past three nights."

Now, that was interesting. Where did she fall on the employee/employer line? Mr. Price had hired her, and yet he'd also asked her to dine with him every night since she'd started. If she did so, wouldn't that cross the boundary Barnaby spoke of?

She sipped her tea, conflicted by the thought. It would be nice to have a real meal instead of another bread-and-cheese plate left up in her room, eaten between yawns as the clock neared midnight. And Mr. Price had invited her. It wasn't as if she were trying to root her way into his good graces. Then again, that might not be a bad idea. Perhaps she could plant a seed for him to donate or sell the lot to an Egyptian museum instead of selling it to a private buyer who would hide it away in some mansion. This could be a fantastic opportunity to return to the Egyptian people what was rightfully theirs.

"Well then, Barnaby." She lifted her chin. "I suppose I ought not dally over a teacup if I'm to start on a new crate before changing out of my work apron." She drained her cup and set it down. "Thank you for the refreshment."

"Quite welcome, Miss Dalton." He gave her a sharp nod as he collected the tray, then pivoted with military perfection and strolled from the big room.

Passing by the alabaster vases and a large terra-cotta urn she'd already unpacked and valued, Ami reached for the crowbar. Her first crate felt like a victory, and she couldn't wait to see what the next container might hold. But as she approached it, her gaze landed on the damaged corner stained with . . . Was that blood? The tea in her stomach churned. This was the monster that had crushed the workman's leg so cruelly when it toppled from the wagon bed. The poor man had undergone an amputation to save his life. While she worked to pry off the lid, she lifted a prayer for the fellow. Only God knew if he had a wife and children to provide for, and if he did, they would surely need God's help.

A grunt and a heave later, she levered off the wooden cover, setting it—and the crowbar—on the floor. Backtracking to the table, she snatched up her gloves and snugged them on. She reached into the crate with care, fingers gently searching through the curly excelsior shavings for the next priceless piece to examine. When her touch met a cloth-wrapped bundle, she worked her hands beneath the shape and gently lifted it out with a grunt. My, but the thing was heavy! Cradling the package like a babe in arms, she carried it to the massive table and eased it down, then began the arduous process of untying the twine and removing the wraps, praying as she did so.

God, help me excel in my work here. Give me the intelligence to show Mr. Price he hasn't made a mistake in hiring me.

It wasn't a huge item. Two feet in length, half that as wide. A small statue, perhaps, or a figurine of some sort. Layer by layer she unwound the gauzy material, pulse racing faster as a golden glow appeared. Whatever it was would no doubt be spectacular.

But as she pulled off the last of the binding and studied the effigy from tip to base, her heart stuttered to a standstill. Could it be? Carefully, she stood the pure gold image on the table, then retreated a step, unable to look away from the legendary Golden Griffin of Amentuk—for surely it was. She'd studied the detailed sketches of this relic many times in her father's journal.

In a day of miracles, this was not one of them, leastwise not as far as legend was concerned. Despite her faith in a God who was good, a shiver snaked down her spine.

This artifact was said to be cursed.

Edmund snapped his pocket watch shut, a smirk lifting his lips. Most women would have been a quarter hour early instead of late for the chance to dine with him. Yet here he sat alone at a fully set table, waiting for Miss Dalton. She was truly singular, this woman, one he'd spent the past three days trying to figure out, and the only conclusion he'd come to was it would take a long time to decipher that quick mind. A lifetime, perhaps, yet a fine puzzle to keep a man occupied . . . *if* one were of the matrimonial inclination, that is. Which he certainly was not.

He tucked away his watch and leaned back in his chair. He'd known returning to Oxford wouldn't be easy. The lifestyle here was much more tightly wound than in India, and—bah! Who was he to complain? God forgive him! At least he was of sound mind and body to carry out his responsibilities, unlike the poor chap whose leg had been crushed. Oh, the fellow's life had been saved, and he'd learn to walk again, but Edmund felt inordinately responsible for the man's future. He'd have Gil set up a trust fund posthaste.

Footsteps rushed into the room, pulling him from his thoughts.

"I beg your pardon, Mr. Price. I lost track of time while cleaning a one-of-a-kind relic I wish to discuss with you." She dropped into the chair at his right hand, her plain blue gown rolled up at the sleeves, revealing porcelain-skinned forearms. Loose bits of hair tumbled down her neck. Clearly she'd put no effort into dressing for the evening. It was a wonder she'd taken off her work apron.

"You'll never believe it." She gripped the table edge as she leaned toward him, completely ignoring the bowl in front of her. "Though . . ." She bit her lip. "Come to think of it, you probably have no idea how rare the piece is. In fact, judging by what I've thus far unpacked, your whole collection is unique."

"I admire your exuberance, Miss Dalton, but your soup is cold enough as is."

"What?" Her nose scrunched, the faint spray of freckles all but disappearing.

Such a single-minded creature. He pointed at the consommé.

"Oh. Yes, of course." She gulped an obligatory mouthful, then set down the spoon. "Now, as I was saying, there is a history to this particular artifact I think you should know about and—"

"*And* I have no doubt you shall tell me, but in due time." With a wave of his finger, he signaled for the soup to be replaced with the fish. "I did not invite you to dinner to talk shop but rather to get to know you."

"Me?" A musical little laugh trilled past her lips. "I assure you I am far less interesting than what I've just discovered."

"Yet as your employer, I require it. Five minutes—just five— and then you can tell me all about your discoveries."

"You are a very insistent man, Mr. Price." Playfulness lit the golden flecks in her eyes. "If your career in business doesn't go well, you'd make a fine archaeologist."

How deftly she turned his words from days ago back on to him. He couldn't help but respect the complex thoughts behind that lovely face, storing away trivialities to be reclaimed at will—and to her own benefit. He grinned. "I shall take that to heart. Nevertheless, my request still stands."

Suddenly interested in her food, she took a bite of cod, chewing with a thoughtful tilt to her head. How curious. What sort of woman was not given to speak about herself for hours on end?

"Very well," she said at length. "What is it you wish to know about me?"

"All your deep, dark secrets, naturally."

Her lips parted slightly, her face paling to the colour of her fish, but only for an instant. Had he blinked, he'd have missed the slip. So . . . his instinct about her did prove true. The eccentric Miss Dalton was a woman of mystery.

"Do not fret." He arched a brow. "I merely jest. A lady ought to keep her secrets. While it is no great riddle you love all things Egyptian, I wonder if other interests ignite your passions. What else do you enjoy besides your work?"

"Well, you may think it silly, but there are two other things I adore. One is poetry—nonsense poetry, to be exact." She set aside her fork, cleared her throat, then flourished her hand in the air. "'Beware the Jabberwock, my son. The jaws that bite, the claws that catch.'" Her voice lowered to an ominous tone, her eyes narrowing. "'Beware the Jubjub bird and shun the frumious Bandersnatch!'"

So animated, so earnest was she, a great belly laugh ripped out of him. Sweet heaven. When was the last time a woman had so enthralled him? "Oh, Miss Dalton, I hardly think that a silly passion. After all, 'poetry is the record of the best and happiest moments of the happiest and best minds.'"

Her head reared back. "You are familiar with Percy Bysshe Shelley? I wouldn't think that standard fare for a man of your business savvy."

"Ah, but you see, Miss Dalton, I have my secrets too." He winked. "Besides poetry, what else do you love?" Once again he signaled for the next course.

Miss Dalton dabbed her lips with the serviette, leaning back slightly as her plate was replaced. Picking up her fork to tackle the beef and gravy, she paused before stabbing a piece. "Honeybees," she said simply.

Honeybees? He cocked his head. "Is that some sort of feminine delicacy like petit fours or bonbons?"

"Do you really think I'm the type to sit about and eat sweets, Mr. Price?"

"Surely you don't mean the sort that buzz and sting."

"The very same." She grinned, then chewed a mouthful. "Someday I hope to have my own apiary, though I suppose I shall have to learn the details as to how to go about that."

Of all the oddities. He set down his fork, more entranced by the enigma in a blue skirt than his beef and potatoes. "Why such an interest?"

"It's a bit of a story, but since you ask." She set down her fork as well. "I don't recall much about my mother, as she died when I was young, but I do remember her great love of gardening. I'd spend entire days with her outside, and it was the bee skep that most intrigued me. Flitting in and out, gathering pollen and nectar, those honeybees worked tirelessly, each doing their part to make the hive a success."

She leaned back in her chair, eyeing him. "There's a connection between teamwork and achievement, you know. Just like bees, people can accomplish so much more if they work together toward a common goal instead of insisting upon selfish ambitions."

"Lofty thoughts for a young woman. If I didn't know any better, Miss Dalton, I'd say you were trying to impress me."

"Bosh!" She snorted—quite unladylike but endearing all the same. "I didn't mean to imply I was a philosopher. Those are merely ideas that have come to me over the years."

"Well, whether you meant to or not, the fact is, I am impressed. And if you care to ruminate any further on the matter of bees or teamwork, Price House maintains a garden out back. You are welcome to visit it any time."

"Thank you. I may take you up on that offer." She tossed back her shoulders. "But now for you. Don't think for a moment you'll escape the same question. What does a businessman find captivating other than coins and ledgers?"

"I suppose it's only fair." He waved away their plates. She didn't seem any more interested in what was left of dinner than he was, not if the gleam in her eye was any indication. "I enjoy cricket, for one, though I am no champion of the game by any stretch of the imagination. Other than that, I adore traveling. I'll never turn down the chance to explore a new land."

She shook her head, lips twisting. "No good."

His brows shot up. "Do you presume to tell me what I do or do not care for?"

"Not at all. Your answers are simply too common. I daresay any man would spout travel and sport as a passion. You're going to have to be more creative than that. What do you, Edmund Price, find intriguing enough to spend time studying?"

You.

The thought hit him broadside. Where the deuce had that come from? Banishing the outlandish idea, he allowed a slow smile to curve his lips. "Point taken. All right, then. Besides the textile, tea, and spice markets, I know an excessive amount about drinking chocolate, as it is a particular favorite of mine." He wagged his finger at her. "And if word of that gets out to the social page, I shall have you boiled in the liquid."

She ran her pinched thumb and forefinger across her mouth, twisting it at the end and tossing away an imaginary key . . . the sprite.

He set his serviette on the table. "And my other interest is fingerprints."

Folding her arms, she tapped a bitten nail against her lower lip, adorably puzzled. "As in you'll scold a maid should some of the silver not get buffed clean of marks?"

"Clever, but no. I mean as in the mark of our Creator."

She shook her head. "I don't understand."

"Palmistry—unlike fortune-telling—is a way to admire the handiwork of God. We are each fearfully and wonderfully made, yet few take the time to appreciate the little details that are right in front of our eyes. God's character is displayed in creation as much as your character is revealed in visible ways." He held out his hand. "Will you let me show you?"

A bold request, one that flew out before he could snatch it back. What on earth had possessed him to suggest such a thing? But the moment she laid her bare palm gently in his, he knew. He *wanted* to hold her hand. Blessed stars above! He sucked in a breath, angry for having suggested this turn of conversation in the first place, and angrier still for entertaining such misguided thoughts about this woman.

"Mr. Price?"

He couldn't back out now. Not gracefully. Hang it all. He bent over her hand, trying not to notice her smoky-cinnamon scent for it was far too enticing. "These lines on your fingers are unique to you, each one formed in a pattern before you were born. I see a prominent whorl, indicating you have a strong sense of purpose and direction in life. The ridges are quite deep, suggesting you are a person with a sharp mind, one who pays close attention to detail. And here." He angled her index finger for a closer look. "These lines are long and curvy, suggesting you have a creative and imaginative streak."

"All that from a fingerprint? I never would have guessed," she murmured, then spoke louder as she pulled his hand toward her. "Let me try."

While she fixed her gaze on his finger, he studied the smooth arc of her cheek, the endearing little mole at the edge of her jaw, the pulse gently bobbing at the curve of her neck.

"Your lines are very symmetrical, Mr. Price. I suppose that could mean you're balanced." She glanced up at him. "In logic and intuition would be my guess, the necessary traits of a successful businessman."

He dipped his head. "Go on."

She lifted his hand closer, focusing on his thumb. "There are deep ridges here, same as you said mine were, so that's easy. Sharp mind, attention to detail. But this?" She squinted, her warm breath feathering against his skin. "Ah, a scar. From when you were young, no doubt. Good thing you didn't lose the finger. A tangible reminder for us both, hmm? That despite tribulation, God's goodness prevails."

The truth of her words, her soft voice, her softer touch, and the glass of wine he'd taken on an empty stomach while waiting for her . . . all made him feel suddenly light-headed. He pulled away, pushing back his chair to gain space from the bewitching woman. "Very good, Miss Dalton. Correct on all accounts. Now, about that discovery of yours?"

"Yes!" She grinned. "Would you like to see it? I'll tell you about the history along the way."

"Brilliant." Indeed. Better to walk side by side than entertain the idea of gazing into her eyes for the rest of the evening.

"I believe," she began as they strode from the dining room, "the item I uncovered today is a sacred artifact from the Old Kingdom, fourth century before Christ. According to legend, this statuette belonged to the Egyptian god Anubis. It is alleged to have the power to bring about great fortune and prosperity—until a rival kingdom stole it away for themselves. At that point, Anubis himself cast a curse upon his favorite relic."

"Allow me to hazard a guess." They entered the large front hall, steps muffled by Turkish carpets. "Anyone who now possesses that relic is doomed to ruin."

Peeking up at him, she furrowed her brow. "You know the story?"

He shrugged. "Don't all Egyptian tales end that way?"

"No. Some have happy endings. But you're right. This one doesn't. It is said that whoever owns this piece will face the wrath of Anubis."

"Good thing I don't believe in fairy tales."

"Nor do I."

Even so, it appeared a shiver ran across her shoulders. Was she merely chilled, or could it be the stalwart Miss Dalton hid an irrational fear based on myth?

But when she spoke, her voice didn't quiver in the least. "At first I was going to suggest that after cataloguing and pricing your collection, you sell it to the British Museum where others could enjoy viewing such finds. But now after unpacking such a rare piece?" She shook her head. "I think it better if you simply send the whole lot back to Egypt where it belongs."

"Don't tell me you believe such ancient poppycock, Miss Dalton." He snorted. "Some old chunk of pottery or figurine isn't going to do me in, I assure you."

"What I believe, Mr. Dalton, is that your collection isn't of commonplace items that could have been sold to anyone along the ancient trade routes. These are one-of-a-kind pieces that are an integral part of Egyptian history. They belong in Cairo, not in England."

They swung into the banquet hall, where the large wooden boxes lined the walls, only three of them with tops pried off thus far. She stopped in front of a two-foot-high statue of a creature with a lion's body and the head and wings of an eagle leering at him from the end of the long table. "Behold, the famed Golden Griffin of Amentuk."

He stooped over the relic, studying the familiar form from all angles. The hook-nosed beak, the slanted eyes, the powerful muscles and curved wings lifted to the heavens—he knew these things intimately, for he'd seen this creature time and time again. Clapping his hands together, he rubbed his palms back and forth. "What a find! I shall not sell this piece. It is too fortuitous."

"How so?"

Straightening, he faced her. "There is a golden griffin in the Price family crest, the very image of this one, and so I shall keep it as my own."

Her jaw tightened, her nostrils flaring slightly. "You cannot be serious."

"Don't worry, Miss Dalton." He flashed her a grin. "I am relatively certain that Egyptian curses do not work here in England."

6

Eyes were on her, boring down hard, staring into her soul. Usually, Ami preferred late evening as the best time to work, but not so much tonight, not in this cavern of a room where crates hulked like monsters in the shadows. The hair at the nape of her neck prickled as she swept a glance from corner to corner. Other than the slight flutter of curtains from the open window, nothing seemed amiss, so why the unease?

She smirked at the golden griffin on the table in front of her. "Probably because of you, eh?"

Her little story of the curse of Amentuk had been meant to prod Mr. Price into selling this lot of goods to the Cairo Museum where it belonged, not to frighten herself. What a goose—or so Polly would say.

With a half smile, Ami pondered the small statue. The griffin, a creature of myth, seemed almost sentient, its golden gaze challenging her skepticism. In her faith, she found strength, a conviction that transcended the bounds of mere reason. Still, no matter how strong her beliefs, there were moments like this when her scholarly pursuits seemed to clash with her faith and send a shiver down her spine.

She straightened her shoulders. Bosh! She would choose to trust God instead of pagan stories no matter how many shivers tried to attack her.

She reached for her gloves, and for a moment relived the feel of Mr. Price's touch sliding along her fingers. Even now her heart raced—*and* she still cringed inwardly at her bold move of taking his hand into hers. Not that she was never impetuous, but honestly, what must he think of her? An Egyptologist ought not act so unprofessionally. Besides, he was her employer, and she was no coy young miss in search of a man.

Disgusted with herself, she tugged on her cotton gloves and drew the golden statuette closer. Father always mocked her use of gloves, but to her it was an act of respect. These ancient pieces had been important to people—*real* people, who lived and laughed and loved just as anyone did today. It didn't seem right to handle such antiquities without extra care.

Picking up a small paintbrush, she dipped the tip into a vial of nitric acid, then gently eased the griffin back and placed a small dot on the bottom. Slowly, she counted to sixty and . . . nothing. Perfect! She smiled. Had the liquid turned a brackish green, it would prove the griffin wasn't gold. So far, so good.

She dabbed away the acid with a clean cloth, then examined the relic for a maker's mark or inscription that would verify her suspected date of origin. The base was dented, probably from some grave robber on the run, which made the symbol on the bottom corner hard to read. Only half a circle remained with the partial image of a knot at the bottom. A *shen* most likely, a hieroglyphic designating protection or divine power, another indicator this was part of the Amentuk hoard. Aside from that, though, there were no more engravings, making it difficult to irrefutably label this as the authentic golden griffin and not merely a copy.

Yawning, she leaned back in her chair and rubbed her eyes. Other than waiting around for curses to happen—which she doubted would occur—how could she verify this as the one and only griffin that'd supposedly been lost for centuries? Her father would know, of course, but it seemed a bit of a cheat to ask. Of course, it would take a while to hear back from him, and by then she might have figured something out. His letter would merely confirm it, so at that point it wouldn't actually be cheating . . . would it?

She shoved back her chair and strolled to the side table, when once again gooseflesh lifted on her arms. Someone was watching her! She was sure of it.

Squaring her shoulders, she marched to the open window and whipped back the curtains.

"Who's there? Show yourself."

Nothing moved out on the lawn. Nothing even made noise save for a few chirruping crickets and the bark of a dog from afar. Ami sighed as she slammed the window shut and locked the latch. Perhaps it was time to quit for the night, for clearly she was overtired.

But first the note to her father.

She settled back at the large table and penned her request for information about the Golden Griffin of Amentuk. Hopefully Father would send a timely response, but there were no guarantees when he was elbow deep in a dig.

She'd just finished addressing the missive when footsteps padded into the room.

"Oh, Miss Dalton. I hope I'm not interrupting. I expected you to be abed."

She rose at the butler's nasal voice and held out her letter. "Actually, Barnaby, I am on my way to retire. Would you see this gets into the post in the morning?"

"I'd be happy to, but speaking of the post—" He held up his index finger, then strode from the room.

What an odd fellow.

By the time she capped her ink and oxide bottles, he returned, a small envelope in his hand. "This came for you not long ago. I would have delivered it straightaway if I'd known you were still awake."

She arched a brow as she took the paper. "It seems you're a nighthawk yourself."

"I've never been one to sleep overmuch, which gives me time to pursue other interests."

"Such as devising pranks for your staff?"

He grinned. "You have a very clever mind, Miss Dalton."

"I suspect you do as well, Barnaby. Good night." She swept past him while unfolding the note. Familiar handwriting scrawled across the page.

> *Tomorrow evening. Half past eight.*
> *Physic Garden fountain.*
> *Five pounds for a collection of faience amulets.*
>
> *—Dandrae*

Hmm. She refolded the paper as she climbed the grand stairway. The museum was always happy to purchase amulets, and five pounds was a steal—literally.

She padded down the corridor, biting her lip. How could she reconcile taking time away to broker a deal with the fact that Mr. Price had made it abundantly clear she was to have all his artifacts catalogued and valued within the month?

Bother. She huffed a sigh as she reached her bedroom door. Should she take hours away from her job here? And if so, how would she explain her absence to Mr. Price?

She forced open her door harder than necessary. This was exactly the sort of dilemma she'd been hoping to avoid.

Of all the bloomin' greenery a wealthy Oxford estate could have planted beneath a window, it had to be rosemary? Brudge glowered as he duck-walked in the thin space between shrubbery and stone wall, the scent churning the beans he'd eaten for dinner. Bad memories barreled back of his mother forcing spoonfuls of vile rosemary oil down his throat, claiming it was good for a lad. Bogger! She may as well have whacked his head with a brick for all the good that had done him.

He edged closer to the only window with a lamp yet glowing in the big house. Blast that Scupper. They should've gotten here hours ago when there would have been more glass-peeping opportunities, but the oaf had insisted they stop by a barber for a quick yank of his sore tooth. What a blubbering baby. And he'd better not still be whimpering while he minded the horses. If the big dolt gave away their presence, he'd knock loose a few more of the man's teeth.

Anchoring himself beneath the windowsill, Brudge slowly rose, stopping when he barely cleared the wooden frame. What luck! There she was, the devious little Shadow Broker, sitting at the far side of a table that could seat at least fifty. A fortuitous find if expensive. Parting with that fiver to Dandrae to discover her whereabouts had considerably lightened his money purse.

Without warning, her gaze shot to him.

Brudge dropped. Then waited, ears straining for the woman's footfall, and . . . Ahhh, blessed silence from inside.

Once again he eased upward. This time his gaze locked on the ugly statue in her hands. Lamplight glinted on its golden surface. Now, there was a right royal piece! Quite an improvement from a hunk of carved rock.

His gaze drifted upward, mind whirring to calculate if he could stuff his body through the narrow gap of the open window. It had to be just shy of two handspans. He would wriggle through no problem, but she'd likely hear him. Not that a skirt could best a strapping man like himself, but one rip-snapping scream and who knew who'd come to her rescue. And at such a distance from the window to that golden gem, he'd never make it back outside before getting collared. No, snatching the thing now was out of the question . . . but besides a true-aim hand in a game of darts, patience was his strong suit. He'd simply wait her out. Slip in once she left the room.

And leave her to brunt the blame for a missing golden trinket.

He smiled at the thought. Served her right for crossing him. Thighs cramping, he shifted his position. He'd been hunkering down for who knew how long when footsteps clapped on the tiled flooring.

"Who's there? Show yourself." The woman's voice drowned out the crickets.

Brudge held his breath. If she spotted him now, would he be able to make it back to the horses before the gamekeeper released the dogs? Then again, with one quick swipe, he could simply jump up and yank the girl outside, knock her in the head, then—

Slam.

He winced lest shards of broken glass rain down from such a rude closing of the window. None did.

Well. That put an end to things.

For now.

Brudge waddled out of the bushes, rosemary branches scratching his face. Once cleared of the demon shrubbery, he paused while scanning the open lawn between the house and wood line. Satisfied no one was about, he sprinted. By the time he reached Scupper, his lungs heaved.

Scupper rose from where he'd leaned against a tree, one hand pressed to the sore side of his mouth. "Ye find 'er, guv'ner?"

"Aye." He huffed for air.

"So—" The big man turned aside and spit a mouthful of blood. "Where's the doll?"

"Don't want it no more. The woman's got something bigger. Better. It's a hideous-looking bauble, all right, but melt 'er down, and it'll bring in enough to set us up real fine, mebbe even for life."

"I dunno, guv'ner. Oof." Once again Scupper pressed his palm to his jaw, then tipped his head toward the big house. "Nipping a piece from a toff such as lives in that castle is a fair sight different than snatchin' it from a skirt. Ain't like we can jes' waltz in there and hold out our hands fer it."

"Din't say we would, ye daft slab o' meat."

"Then what's yer plan?"

Brudge rubbed the back of his neck, flicking away stray leaves. "Dunno yet, but I do know this. That gold statue will be mine, and somehow that woman will take the fall for it."

7

Edmund crouched next to Jameson, trying to focus on the steward's explanation of why and how the drainpipes needed replacing. It was conscientious of the man to include him on the mundane workings of the estate, but he didn't care a fig about gutters and water management. Of late he was much more interested in a certain Egyptologist.

Jameson tapped the rusty pipe. "Fifty pounds ought to do her nicely."

For a few pieces of metal? Edmund snorted. "What are you replacing it with? Gold?"

The steward shrugged. "It's a big house, and costs have gone up."

Edmund gave a noncommittal grunt as he rose. Sanjay could feed his entire family for a year on such an amount. Mayhap even two. And the fellow would need that and more if the tariff passed. So would many other men. The Indian Export Act the greedy members of Parliament wished to impose would harm countless natives by taxing the cost of certain goods coming from India into England, as well as by imposing new restrictions for attaining local business licenses. There were other ways of raising revenue besides hefting such a load onto the backs of those already struggling—and he'd do his best to present other options and stop this nonsense if he could land a seat in the House.

Stifling a scowl, he glanced at Jameson. "Get a few other estimates before you commit."

The steward's brows arched high. "Who are you, and what have you done with Edmund Price?"

Edmund chuckled. "I assure you I am one and the same, old friend."

"The man who left here eight years ago never would have suggested I shop around." A slow smile crept along Jameson's lips. "You've changed."

Pah! What an understatement. Absently, he rubbed the snakebite scar on the inside of his forearm. He'd have been a fool to face death and not be changed. "I suppose you could say I've learned a few things since then."

Jameson cuffed him on the shoulder. "Your father would have been proud."

"About my caution, yes, but motivation? Now, there's where we would have differed. He was a tightfisted old duff, and well you know it. All for the sake of greed." He huffed a long breath. His relationship with his father had been complicated at best. There had been many things to admire about his father—and even more to despise. But despite it all, he yet mourned the man's loss even after these past ten years.

Edmund shook his head. "God forbid I ever become such a miser, and if by chance I do, you have my permission to wallop me."

"Ho ho! We could sell tickets to that spectacle, earn a small fortune."

No doubt, for the loose-lipped steward would spread the news from one coast to the other. "Maybe so, but for now, just see what you can do about keeping down costs."

"Ought I and the staff be concerned about our jobs?"

Edmund chuckled. "No, nothing of the sort. I'm just a bit cash strapped at the moment, so I shall have to be more judicious when paying outright for goods and services. But don't fret, all my investments are secure. More than secure, actually. I hope to make a fortune off those relics in the banquet hall." He tipped his head toward the mansion's front door.

"Speaking of which . . ." The mirth faded from Jameson's tone.

Edmund suspected he knew why, for the man never could abide things out of place. These past eight years, he and Mrs. Buckner had had free rein to keep the house in perfect order. All that had changed now that their master had returned.

"Allow me to guess." Edmund eyed the man sideways. "The clutter is giving you a rash. But in less than four weeks the banquet hall will be returned to its former beauty."

"No, it's not that. I'm more concerned about thieves, and so I mean to increase security. I'm sure the word is already out about the priceless items inside, which is certain to attract every light finger in the area. I'll have some armed men on patrol, particularly at night." Carriage wheels ground on the drive, and Jameson craned his neck, peering over Edmund's shoulder. "Are you expecting someone?"

He turned. A dusty carriage pulled by a single horse rolled toward the house. Nothing fancy. Indeed, the transport was a bit on the rickety side with the way it leaned heavily to the right. At least no hopeful debutante could be expected to step from such a nondescript coach.

"I'll see to that while you see to a few more quotes on the gutter works." Edmund strode away as the driver halted the horse near the front stairs.

Out stepped a well-dressed gent, pressing creases from his trousers as he gazed up at the house. The garments were of quality, though ill-fitted and quite wrinkled, and as for the man? A strange unease prickled across Edmund's shoulders. If he didn't know any better, he'd be tempted to shoo the fellow away for the unnerving glint in his eyes as he studied the mansion . . . eyes that were familiar yet with a calculating gaze that was not. The broad forehead, wide nose, and cleft chin where whiskers didn't grow were all recognizable—but somehow different.

"Gil?" he wondered aloud. "Can it be?"

He hadn't seen his business partner, Gilbert Fletcher, since before he sailed to India. The silver threads in the man's dark hair were new, as were the sharp cheekbones and the pallor of his skin. My, how he'd aged, and not kindly.

Gil strode over and grabbed his hand for a hearty shake. "Good to see you."

"You as well." Edmund pulled back. "But I wasn't expecting you until the end of the month. You should have sent word."

Indeed. Fletcher was usually scrupulous about such minute details.

"Thought I'd surprise you." Gil slapped him on the back.

Edmund's eyes narrowed. "You hate surprises."

Gil laughed. "People change all the time, old man."

Edmund rubbed his jaw to hide a frown. First popping in unannounced and now such common language? The conservative businessman really had changed. "How have you been?"

"Never better. Quite invigorated, I should say. What man wouldn't be with the sun on his face and wind in his hair? I'm hoping we can strike up some new deals while I'm here."

He frowned. *New* deals? Did Gil think so little of the Egyptian antiquities? "I should think my recent acquisition would be deal enough."

"Oh? Already got a game on, have you? Capital!" Gil rubbed his hands together. "Say, you don't mind if I stay on here, do you? Save us both the trouble of commuting back and forth and, well, a hired coach isn't the way to go."

"Agreed. You shall stay here and have the use of one of my carriages. I cannot wait to hear about the good news you mentioned in your recent letter. But I suppose you'd like to see the cargo I've acquired first, eh?" Edmund swept his arm toward the house.

Gil cocked his head, a smile spreading, though it seemed

more a baring of teeth than anything. "Why, yes, I'd love to see it. Lead on, my good fellow!"

Edmund trotted up the stairs, conflicted about the changes in the other half of Price & Fletcher. It was to be expected, though, after so long an absence. Even Jameson had remarked on the changes in him.

They barely crossed the threshold when the butler strolled out of the sitting room, an empty decanter in hand. Edmund signaled him over.

"Yes, sir?" Barnaby asked.

"Mr. Fletcher will be staying with us a few days. See that he is taken care of, will you?"

"At once." He nodded, then faced Gil. "Price House always aims to make its guests feel comfortable. Let me know if there is anything I can do to be of service to you, Mr. Fletcher."

Gil grinned. "I have no doubt I shall be *very* comfortable."

A scream rang out, ruining the prospect of comfort for any of them. Footsteps pounded across the great hall in the corridor—the same passageway housing the room where Miss Dalton worked.

Edmund took off at a run.

Ami yawned as she entered the workroom. Spending the night scheming how to squeeze twenty-seven hours from twenty-four was never a good recipe for sleep. But a little sluggishness was worth it, for in all that tossing and turning, she had devised how to shave time off a run into town tonight to purchase those amulets . . . as long as Polly agreed to help her. Which shouldn't be difficult if Turkish delight was involved.

Her mouth stretched for another yawn when a scream from the far side of the room scared it away. Before she could even blink, a white-faced maid sprinted past her, apron strings flying in the air. What in the world had spooked her so?

Ami bypassed the golden griffin, giving it the evil eye as she strode to the dropped tote of brushes and rags the frightened girl had left behind. Something moved. Steadying her pulse, she peered into the thin space between two crates. A dark shadow twitched—one that stared right back at her. She stretched her arm into the abyss as footsteps pounded into the room.

"Great heavens! Miss Dalton, are you all right?" Worry pitched Mr. Price's voice to a husky tone. And no wonder. What a sight she must be contorted into such a strange position.

"I'm—ow!" Pain pierced her finger. She flinched. Bosh. She'd be hanged if she'd let this little demon get the best of her. Undaunted, she wedged her shoulder as far as it would go between the crates, stretching until her muscles ached. And . . .

Triumph!

She pulled out a cat as black as a moonless sky, one who was every bit as terrified as the young maid had been.

"Shh." She cradled the ball of fur while wiping the blood from her finger onto her apron. "All is well." She turned about to face three pairs of wide eyes all focused on her.

The butler's brows lifted clear to the rafters. "How did that get in here?"

"Odd place to keep a pet, old man." The stranger next to Mr. Price elbowed him in the arm.

Mr. Price was the only one to fix his gaze on her injured finger. In a trice, he whipped out a handkerchief from his pocket. "You're hurt. Barnaby, take that cat out to Phineas. No doubt he'll welcome a mole hunter in the rose bed."

"Take care, Barnaby," she told the butler as he reached for the feline. "She's a bit skittish, poor thing." Carefully, she nestled the cat into the crook of his arm.

Biting one corner of the cloth, Edmund tore a thin strip of fabric. He drew close, gathering her hand and winding the makeshift bandage around her finger. "This will do until you can see the cook for some salve, and the sooner the better."

She inhaled sharply, for his touch—while infinitely gentle—sent a strange wave of heat up her arm. Bosh, but she could get used to this man holding her hand, and she wasn't quite sure what to do with that craving, for she'd never experienced such a weakness before. Stranger still, the longer they stood this close, the more her knees threatened to give way. La! She didn't usually feel this giddy around anything but a mummy fresh from a sarcophagus. Perhaps that cat bite really was affecting her.

The man at Mr. Price's side snorted. "Such hubbub over a stray feline."

"I cannot say I am surprised." Mr. Price tied off the cloth and stepped back, taking his pleasant scent of curry along with him. "The village girls are given to superstition, and black cats are a bad omen."

"Ridiculous," Ami huffed. "The Egyptians believed just the opposite, thinking them to be a symbol of divine protection, not evil intent. It's all a matter of perspective."

"I didn't say I believed such poppycock." Mr. Price studied her. "But I must say your insight is quite astute."

Though she couldn't be sure, it looked as if admiration flickered in his eyes—which flared warmth into her chest.

"I will have my housekeeper speak with the maid. For now, allow me to introduce you to my business partner, Mr. Gilbert Fletcher." He swept his hand toward the stranger. "Gil, this is Miss Dalton."

"Charmed to meet you." Collecting her uninjured hand, the man bowed over the top of it and pressed his lips to her skin. An old-fashioned gesture, one that smacked of chivalry. And yet he was no knight of old. He looked more like one of the gin bibbers hanging about the Folly Bridge.

She pulled away, her stomach oddly queasy. "Mr. Fletcher."

Mr. Price tipped his head toward her. "Gil would like to see some of the artifacts."

"Well, I've not gotten any further than the griffin from last night, but over here are the vases and a mirror from the first crate I emptied." She led them to a long trestle table at the far end of the room. Soon that tabletop would be filled with treasures of the past, which carved a melancholy hole in her heart. She wouldn't have an infinite amount of time to persuade Mr. Price to sell—or better yet, donate—the lot to a museum in Cairo, and if she failed, all these historical pieces would be locked up in some wealthy man's curio cabinets. Someday—someday soon, God willing—she'd go on a dig of her own and bypass this whole ghastly process. Unearth her own treasures and put them where they belonged—on display in their homeland.

"Very nice." Mr. Fletcher moved from one item to the next. "How much are they worth?" He snapped a hawkish eye toward Mr. Price.

Ami clenched her jaw. Just because Mr. Price wore trousers did not make him more of an authority than her. "*I* have valued the vases at twenty pounds apiece, and this mirror"—she circled her hand in front of the ornate bronze looking glass—"is ceremonial instead of functional, which ought to fetch at least fifty."

Mr. Fletcher let out a low whistle, his head swiveling to take in the many crates filling the room. "And there's more where that came from, eh?"

Mr. Price nodded. "There's no telling what other riches may be uncovered. Just last evening Miss Dalton showed me this unique piece down here." He strode the length of the long table, stopping at the head, where the golden griffin sat.

"Do you mind?" Mr. Fletcher nudged him out of the way and reached out to run a finger over the griffin's wings.

Before he made contact, Ami batted away his hand. "Mr. Price may not mind, but I do. Your touch will mar the finish, and I have already buffed the gold."

"Gold." His teeth flashed in a wide grin. "How much is this beauty?"

Mr. Price shook his head. "It's not for sale."

Not yet, anyway. Not if she could impress upon him how important this particular relic was.

"Whyever not?" Mr. Fletcher jabbed his finger toward the griffin. "If that's solid gold, we could both retire here and now."

"I should like to keep it." Mr. Price arched a brow at her. "Curse or not."

"Curse? On this little gem?" Mr. Fletcher chuckled. "I suppose that explains the black cat, eh?"

Ami rolled her eyes. "Merely a coincidence. Now then, if

you gentlemen wouldn't mind, I really ought to be getting back to work."

Mr. Gilbert narrowed his eyes. "Should you not wait until the scholar in charge arrives?"

"I *am* the scholar in charge."

Mr. Gilbert's wide brow wrinkled. "But you're a woman."

"Nice of you to notice," she fumed.

Mr. Price laughed as his gaze bounced between them. "I own the situation is a bit unorthodox, Gil, but Miss Dalton has done a fine job thus far. Her knowledge is all-encompassing, and I find she takes great care with the relics, going so far as to handle each one with gloves."

Well. At least one man recognized her worth. She peered up at Mr. Price. "Thank you for your vote of confidence."

"Hmph." Mr. Fletcher grunted. "For your sake and mine, old man, I hope you are right."

"I have no doubt on the matter." Mr. Price smiled at her.

As did Mr. Fletcher. "I meant no offense, Miss Dalton. I am merely surprised to find such a beautiful woman tucked away in a room of dusty old artifacts."

"And on that note," Mr. Price cut in, "we shall leave you to your work. I look forward to hearing about what you uncover tonight at dinner."

"Oh, I'm afraid I won't be able to make it." She spread her hands. "If I'm to meet that deadline of yours, I really ought to keep at it."

"And yet you need to eat, Miss Dalton."

"A bowl of soup will serve just fine."

"Good. Then first course it is. Though I've asked the cook for Indian fare, which you might find more irresistible than cracking open another crate. Besides, with your zeal for the project, I have no doubt you'll finish your work before the end of the month." He tossed her a wink before pivoting away.

Ami grabbed the table for support. If she didn't know any better, she'd swear the man was flirting with her. And worse . . .

It was working.

8

It felt wrong to leave like this, which was frustrating. Ami pulled Price House's back door shut and stepped out into the late afternoon sunshine. It wasn't as if she was breaking the law—well, man's law, at any rate. But God's . . . ?

Her heels dug hard into the pea gravel pathway. Was it truly deceitful to have told Barnaby she needed to retrieve a book from her father's office in town? She would do so, of course, just to make good on her word, but she didn't really need one of her father's books. What she needed was to make haste in securing the amulets, then rush them back to the museum and hopefully return here in time for dessert. Mr. Price probably wouldn't even notice her absence. A man like him had more important matters on his mind than a hireling who missed a bowl of soup. Besides, he had Mr. Fletcher to dine with.

She followed the path around the garden wall toward the stables out back, hoping to talk the stableboy into saddling a horse for her. Honestly, in a sense it felt more wrong to stay here. Surely Mr. Price would understand the drive to transact a sale in a timely fashion. Why, she was just as much a person of business as he. Mr. Price simply happened to meet with his clients in a comfortable office instead of a deserted park at night.

With a seller who'd as soon cut a man's—or woman's—throat if crossed.

Shoving that thought aside, she upped her pace, absently rubbing where the bruise on her cheek had been. She'd be careful as always, so there was nothing to fear, especially since she'd made it clear to Mr. Dandrae that whoever he sent her way from now on must swear to conduct business without violence on pain of retribution—Mr. Dandrae's retribution. Since that would involve paid muscle of his own, he'd be sure to take extra screening precautions, or she'd quit doing business with him altogether. And more than anything, he did not wish to lose an income stream, so she had no doubt he'd comply.

As she rounded the backside of the garden wall, her steps slowed. Three wicker skeps sat in a row on a long bench, tempting her to pause for a moment. At this time of day, most of the bees were foraging for nectar, yet some buzzed around the dome-shaped hives. She really didn't have time to admire them. She could come back tomorrow. . . . Still, one little look wouldn't take but a minute.

Crouching slowly, she focused on one busy honeybee in particular. Its tiny wings flapped frantically, producing a soft hum as it closed in on the small entrance at the bottom. What a tireless worker, absorbed on the task at hand, not even noticing she was around. A frown creased her brow. Father often sang the merits of getting lost in one's work, a virtue she couldn't deny—except when it shut out someone you loved.

"Ye must have honey in yer veins, fer most women would admire from afar."

Startled by a deep voice, she shot to her feet, her hand flying to her chest. The man in front of her was a tall fellow, lean and sinewy, skin like a leather coin purse. He wore a straw hat with a broad brim and a blue work smock. Canvas leggings covered his trousers. In one gloved hand, he held a basket, and in the other, a tin smoke pot puffing out small clouds. The scent of beeswax clung to him, that and something more pungent. Manure.

Ah, the gardener.

"Forgive me." She smiled. "I didn't mean to intrude."

Despite his rugged appearance, a kind grin lifted his lips. "It ain't intrudin' if yer helpin,' missy. Care to give me a hand?"

She glanced at the sky, where the sun crept lower on the horizon. It would be a treat to work with the bees, but she didn't really have time for it.

"'Course if yer afeared," he continued, "then be on yer way. Agitates my pets somethin' fierce if they sense anythin' other than a calm spirit."

She lifted her chin. "I'm not afraid, it's just that I—"

"Good." He tipped his head toward a shed near the garden gate. "O'er there ye'll find a spare pair o' gloves and a netting fer yer face. Not that ye'll take a sting from these lovelies, but always pays to take a care."

"But I really can't—"

"Don't ye fret, now. Yer fine gown won't get mucked up a bit or my name isn't Phineas. I'll be right here a-waitin' for ye."

Biting back a ragged sigh, she strode past him. It would be faster to simply help the fellow than argue with him. She yanked the hood over her head and shoved her hands into the gloves, more annoyed with herself for having paused by the bees in the first place. It was a ridiculous obsession, one her father had never understood. Her mother, though . . . Ami's heart softened as she shut the shed door. When dabbling in nature, she always felt closer to her mother. And besides, there were only three skeps. How long could it take?

"All right," she said as she once again joined Phineas's side. "Now what?"

"Jes stand there and hold this." He handed her the empty basket. "I'll load 'er up, and tha's about all there is to it."

Humming an old folksong, he set to work, puffing out a great deal of smoke around the first hive. Carefully, he then removed the dome and began carving out pieces of honeycomb with a small knife. She held out the basket to collect each chunk.

He eyed her as he set a piece inside. "Ye must be that professor woman Jameson told me about."

Her brows raised. How novel. Finally, someone who didn't question her abilities. "My father is the professor, but I have studied at his feet since a young girl. I'm an Egyptologist, here in his stead, cataloguing Mr. Price's recent collection of artifacts."

"Not here for the man, eh?"

"No, just at his request."

"Well, well." His grey eyes twinkled as he replaced the dome and moved to the next hive. "I expect he finds that a mite refreshing."

Suddenly the disguise Mr. Price had worn when he'd hunted down her father's office made sense. "He is frequently beleaguered by women, then?"

Phineas clucked his tongue. "I expect that's what's kept 'im from home all these years. That and . . . well, other reasons, I suppose. He is the most eligible bachelor in all of Oxford, leastwise that's what I hear."

Ami cocked her head. Not that the man wasn't thoroughly charming and pleasing to the eye, but integrity and looks alone didn't make for such renown. "What makes him so sought after?"

"The name. Though they're not titled folk, surely ye've heard of the Prices."

"I, em, don't really keep up with the rumblings of society, unless that society has something to do with ancient Egypt."

"You are a singular woman, I'll give ye that." He chuckled. "The Prices made their money in the shipping industry, then expanded into other merchant investments. For all the talk of family lineage—of which there are some notable forefathers in the Price past—it is the wealth that attracts the women. His many estates, both here and abroad, lure 'em in like a fat leech on a hook."

Interesting information, though probably a good thing she hadn't known of it earlier, or she may have judged him more harshly. Wealthy men were notoriously arrogant, but Mr. Price had proved otherwise.

"You seem to know a lot about the Price family." A bee landed on the back of her hand, and she blew it away with a gentle huff of air. "How long have you worked here?"

"Long as I been breathin.' My family's served Price House for generations."

Two more bees tickled the skin near her wrist, and ever so lightly, she brushed them away.

Phineas paused before setting the next lump in the basket, his gaze holding hers. "Ye've a steady hand, miss, sign o' a steady heart as well."

Longing swelled in her chest. Would that her father had taken the time to notice such a thing. "It is kind of you to say so. Thank you."

The gardener went back to humming as he moved to the last skep. After a few more cuts of honeycomb, he finished his tune. "Did ye know bees are some o' the most consistent creatures around? They've a job to do, and they do it without fail. I reckon that's a lesson fer all o' us, keepin' our commitments no matter what distractions come our way. One could do worse than learn from these beauties."

Oh, the irony. Instant guilt churned in her belly. Of course old Phineas could have no way of knowing that his ruminations hit her like a hammer, for that's exactly what she was doing by sneaking away tonight. Taking time from her commitment to Mr. Price, being distracted from her work here. Then again, sitting at a linen-clothed table wasn't really working either.

Was it?

She frowned. If she missed this appointment, would Mr. Dandrae become wary of sending business her way?

Phineas replaced the dome, then pulled a soft-bristled brush from his smock pocket and handed it over. "Take a light touch, miss, and gently sweep away those what are still a-buzzin' about the comb, then I'll cover 'er up."

She barely kissed the bristles to the bees, and they took flight. One of them landed on her face netting, giving her a close-up view of the tiny hairs on its legs before it darted away. What a wonder. God's creation never failed to make her marvel.

Once she cleared the honeycomb, Phineas laid a white cloth over the top of her basket. Taking off his hat, he swiped his forehead with the back of his hand, looking pleased with their work. "Well done, lass. Let's wrap ye up a piece fer yer efforts. Come along."

She followed, heart full. Funny how such a small task could be so fulfilling, and it truly hadn't taken a great deal of time.

Inside the shed, she pulled off her netting and gloves. While Phineas packaged a small bundle of honeycomb, a quiet lap-lap-lap caught her ear. Curious, she ventured to the corner, only to spy the black cat enjoying a saucer of cream. She crouched and ran her finger along the silky fur of its back. The cat barely noticed, so tasty was its treat.

She grinned over at Phineas. "Spoiling him, are you?"

He approached, his grey eyes fixed on his new pet. "Jes' showin' him where his home is. One always returns to where they're cared for the most."

Ami blinked. This gardener was a regular philosopher. "You are full of wisdom, Mr. Phineas—"

"Jes Phineas, miss, and no, child." He chuckled as he handed her the cloth bundle. "I've no claim to wisdom other than what God teaches me here in the garden."

"Well, I should say you've learned a great deal." She tucked the package into her pocket. "And now I really should be going. Good day, Phineas."

He dipped his head. "Appreciate the help, miss. G'day to ye."

She'd barely reached the door before he called out, "Oh, and miss?"

"Yes?" She glanced over her shoulder.

"See that ye take a care with Mr. Price as well as ye did with my pets today. I'd not willingly see 'im hurt again, and ye remind me a great deal o' her."

Her brows knotted. "Her who?"

"I reckon tha's for him to tell ye, miss. Jes . . . tread as lightly with him as ye did with the bees, and all will be a'right."

"Of course," she murmured, confused as to why the old

gardener felt the need to tell her such a thing. It wasn't as if Mr. Price was interested in her when he could have any woman in society on his arm.

She strode outside, the sweet scent of roses thick on the air. The fact was that clearly some woman had hurt him in the past, which really wasn't any of her business. She was here to do a job, nothing more, nothing less—and the next stab of guilt hitched her step. Running off to broker a deal on a stolen artifact had absolutely nothing to do with the job she'd been hired for at Price House. Should she really be going?

But if she didn't, those faience amulets would more than likely end up stuffed away in some private home instead of being put on museum display for rich and poor alike to admire.

Edmund straightened his four-in-hand as he strode into the dining room, the blasted fabric nearly choking him, only to be intercepted by Barnaby the moment he crossed the threshold.

"A word from Miss Dalton, sir. She regrets to say she won't be at dinner tonight. Something about retrieving a book from her father's library."

A peculiar wave of disappointment washed over him. He'd been looking forward to the woman's lively conversation, but he hadn't realized how much until the opportunity was stolen. He did feel a bit guilty for flirting with her so frequently, but she made it far too easy with her witty banter and uncommon beauty. Too bad she wasn't Bastion's daughter, or he'd give that matrimony idea more of a consideration. It was so easy to be around Miss Dalton, to laugh, to banter . . . quite unlike the cool and distant relationship his parents had suffered—a marriage he would avoid at all costs. No, marrying Violet was out of the question, and he'd have to tell the man as much.

He gave a final tweak to his tie as he narrowed his eyes on the butler. "Why did you not offer to send a boy to fetch it for her?"

"I did, sir." Barnaby shrugged, his sharp bones lifting his

black suit coat at the shoulders. "Yet the lady claimed her father's office is such a fright that no one but her would be able to find it."

An image of the cluttered odds and ends he'd seen crammed into that small room came to mind. "True enough," he murmured. "Thank you, Barnaby." He made to sidestep the man.

The butler followed his movement, blocking his path. "There is one more thing I think you should know." He tipped his head slightly, indicating Gil on the far side of the room. "Mr. Fletcher did not bring any baggage."

Edmund wrinkled his brow. "What are you talking about?"

"There was no trunk on his carriage, sir, and as you'll note, he is not dressed for dinner. I daresay Mr. Fletcher will be wearing the same garments tomorrow . . . and the next day. All he came with was a small satchel he refused to let anyone handle but himself." Barnaby took a step closer, voice thinning to a whisper. "And he's been making rather free with the wine as well."

Edmund regarded his business partner. Sure enough, Gil tossed back a great guzzle as he peered up at the Price family portrait wall. How odd. He was a teetotaler.

Or at least he had been.

Edmund's gaze drifted back to Barnaby. "Thanks for the information."

Successfully sidestepping the butler this time, he strode the length of the dining table. He'd been hoping to ask Gil about his supposed good news tonight, but in his current state, that might be out of the question. "Good evening, Gil."

Gil faced him, the colour of his cheeks nearly matching the drink in his hand. How many glasses had he already downed?

"Good evening to you, Price." He toasted his glass in the air. "Nothing but the best, eh, old man?"

Edmund clenched his jaw, the new moniker beginning to grate. "Never let it be said Price House doesn't treat its guests well, and I would prefer you go back to calling me simply Edmund instead of old man."

"Oh? Ha-ha! Why, the term is all the rage in London. Though

with you having been gone for so long, I suppose you're not familiar with such things . . . which is good."

Edmund rubbed the back of his neck. True, he had been out of the country, but he wouldn't have expected such commonalities to become trendy in his absence. Even so, he willed a pleasant smile. "Say, Gil, you didn't happen to hire a second coach to bring your effects, did you?"

"Hmm?" His wide brow wrinkled.

"My butler informed me there was no trunk on your carriage."

"Oh yes. Ha-ha! About that." He slugged down the rest of his drink, then swiped his hand across his mouth. "Had a bit of a mishap on the way here. It appears my trunk was put on the wrong coach. I expect my suits are in Brighton by now, having a jolly holiday."

"I am sorry to hear it." He frowned as Gil snatched the decanter off the wine cart and refilled his glass. "I shall have Barnaby pull a few of my suits for your use until everything is sorted out."

"Good of you, old man." Gil slapped him on the back, sloshing wine onto the rug.

Edmund gritted his teeth. Barnaby hadn't been jesting about his partner's wine intake. "Some food is in order, I think." He swept his hand toward the table. "Shall we?"

"Should we not wait for the divine Mish—em, Miss Dalton?"

While it was true Miss Dalton was pleasing to the eye, it annoyed him that Gil had noticed. "She will not be joining us after all."

"Such a shame," Gil slurred as he sank sloppily into a chair. "I think she rather fancied me."

"I have it on reliable authority she only admires mummified corpses." He shook out his serviette with a sharp snap. Somehow the thought of Miss Dalton preferring Gil over him stuck like a fishbone in his throat. Which only irritated him further. He didn't have time to think about a woman. Lifting a finger, he signaled for the first course.

Gil motioned for more wine. "So how many buyers have you lined up for our 'Gyptian collection?"

"Only one thus far. I didn't wish to get too far ahead of myself. It's not even priced yet." The rich scent of curry filled the air as the footman removed the lid from the mulligatawny.

Gil picked up his glass instead of his spoon. "Say, do you really think that little filly is up to the task? Maybe you ought to get someone who knows—well, well, here she is now." The flatware on the table rattled as Gil grabbed hold of the tablecloth to steady himself while he rose.

Edmund glanced over his shoulder. In strolled Miss Dalton, hair loosely caught up at the nape of her neck as if she'd dashed across a field to get here.

And he wouldn't be astonished in the least if she had.

He stood with a grin and pulled out her chair. "Miss Dalton, what a surprise. I take it you found your book in record time."

"My—?" Her nose scrunched as she took her seat. "Oh. Yes. Well, you see, I didn't actually go to my father's office. I couldn't reconcile taking time away from working on your cargo."

"I hope you don't feel you're a prisoner here." He frowned as he reclaimed his chair.

"If I am"—she smiled—"then this is a lovely cage."

"Not half as lovely as you, my dear." Gil planted his elbow on the table, chin in hand, eyeing her like a cream puff on a silver platter.

Edmund was tempted to knock away the man's propped arm, not so much for the compliment but for the look in his eyes. What had gotten into his business partner to account for such a change? Clearly the spirits he imbibed played a role in his current mannerisms, but had something happened on the Continent that he was trying to drown out?

Miss Dalton lifted her chin, apparently ignoring Gil's blatant stare. "Thank you, Mr. Fletcher."

The footman leaned in, removing the tureen while Barnaby filled the empty spot with a large platter. He had barely lifted the cover when Gil tapped the rim of his empty glass. "A refill, if you please."

Barnaby nodded, the tightness of his jaw his only hint of displeasure. Clearly Fletcher's conduct was getting on the staff's nerves—and Edmund's.

Without waiting for approval, Edmund spooned out a healthy serving and plopped it onto Gil's plate. If the man didn't get some food into him soon, he'd pass out by the time pudding was served. "Try this chana masala, Gil. I think it will be to your liking."

"Miss Dalton is to my liking." He waggled his eyebrows.

Edmund's irritation flared. "Mind your manners," he grumbled for Gil's ears alone.

"Don't be such a prig, old man." Gil cut his hand through the air. "Just having a bit of fun. We are having fun, are we not, Miss Dalton?"

Miss Dalton merely picked up her fork—God bless her—and took a bite, overlooking his poor behaviour. "Mmm. This is delicious."

Pleasure warmed his chest. Granted, it was a small thing, but for the delicate senses of the usual Englishwoman, spicy food would've been tolerated at best, not praised. And it was spicy—exactly how he liked it. "You like Indian fare?"

"I adore all things exotic. Have you tried *koshari*?" At the shake of his head, she continued. "It's an Egyptian dish made of lentils, rice, and chickpeas in a rather fiery sauce. A little spicier than this, I should say. I love it, and it's one of my father's favorites."

"You're one of mine." Gil shoved away his plate, completely untouched.

The vein in Edmund's temple began to throb. Since when had his business partner become such a lecher? He reached for Gil's wine glass and moved it away.

"I say!" Gil objected. "What do you think you are—"

"So, Miss Dalton," Edmund interrupted. "What treasures did you uncover today?"

"Just one, but a rather large one at that, and its rarity only adds to the uniqueness of your collection." Her eyes sparkled in the lamplight. "A six-foot statue of Anubis carved from ebony and embellished with gold leaf. Your staff was helpful in unpacking the big fellow, as it is quite heavy. It took two men to move it."

"You should have called on me, my dear," Gil slurred. "I would help you with anything."

"And yet, Mr. Fletcher"—she skewered him with a sharp look, apparently tired of his innuendos—"after so much wine, I believe it is you who will be requiring help to make it to your room tonight."

"Oh?" he drawled as he leaned over the table toward her. "Are you offering for the task?"

That did it.

Edmund shot to his feet and hauled Gil up by the arm. "You're finished, Fletcher. Go sleep it off." He glanced over at Barnaby. "See Mr. Fletcher to his quarters, please."

"At once, sir." In four long strides, Barnaby shored up Gil with an arm around his shoulder.

Gil immediately pulled away. "I'll walk myshelf, thank you very mush," he slurred as he stumbled from the room.

Edmund sighed. There was a fine line between granting his partner the dignity to retreat alone and ensuring his safety . . . though in truth, after the way he'd just treated Miss Dalton, a wicked part of him wished the man would stagger right into a wall.

He met Barnaby's gaze. "Check on him after a few minutes, will you?"

"Of course, sir."

Edmund sank back to his chair, angling toward Miss Dalton. "I apologize for my partner's behaviour. It was unconscionable. He's not usually like that."

"Don't worry about me, Mr. Price. I am not a flower so easily crushed." She smiled as she took another bite.

His gaze lingered on her. He couldn't help but admire the

woman's unfazed resilience . . . the very trait he'd admired in Louisa as well. And look what that had done to him. Left him little better than a twisted wreck. He was tempted to slug back his own glass of wine at the thought, but he reached for his water instead. He'd do well to tread carefully around Miss Dalton.

She dabbed her lips with her serviette. "I met your gardener today. Phineas."

"He's a good man." Edmund chewed a bite thoughtfully. "Though given to roping in the unsuspecting. Let me guess. He asked you to deadhead the roses."

"Collect honeycomb, actually."

"A job you no doubt enjoyed, what with your passion for honeybees."

A lovely pink deepened her cheeks. "You remembered."

I remember everything about you.

Blast! So much for treading carefully.

He set down his fork, no longer hungry. "I realize it is far too early for you to estimate what my shipment is worth, but I do have an interested party stopping by my study tomorrow morning at ten o'clock. I wonder if you might be there to verify the value of what you've uncovered thus far?"

"I could, but . . ." She bit her lip.

"But what?"

She pushed away her plate, finished as well. "It might be better if I merely give you a tally for you to relate the information."

"If this is about your worry of taking time away from the cargo, think nothing of it. Meeting with sellers is part of the business as well. I find that bringing in an expert lends credence to a sale."

She met his gaze, fire in her eyes. "And I find that men have a hard time believing a woman can be an expert."

"Rubbish." He snorted. "You've proven to me you know what you're about."

Those same eyes suddenly glistened, and if he didn't know any better, he'd suspect the intrepid Miss Dalton was near tears.

"Thank you," she murmured.

For the life of him, he couldn't think as to why he'd evoked such a clear emotion. "While I appreciate the gratitude, I wonder what it is for?"

"In my line of work, Mr. Price, it is a rare compliment for a woman to be acknowledged as a historical authority."

He peered at her closely, saddened by whatever hurts she'd suffered for the sake of men's pride. "Some men are far too insecure in themselves."

"Yet you are not." She met his gaze—and held it.

"A trait I was forced to learn at a young age." As was every lad at boarding school, for it was either learn to stick up for yourself or take a beating.

"I suppose we have both learned, then, to stand our ground. It is an attribute I must hone if I ever hope to lead a dig in Egypt someday."

He angled his head. A commendable goal and quite bold for a woman. "So that is your great aspiration, is it? To lead an excavation in the Egyptian sands?"

"It is." She flashed a brilliant grin.

"Then I pray that one day your dream shall come true." He lifted his glass. "To dreams."

She lifted hers in response. "To—"

Footsteps pounded into the dining room, Barnaby's usual slicked-back hair hanging loose over his brow. "Pardon the interruption," he puffed, "but you must come at once, sir."

"Where?" He shoved back his chair. "What's happened?"

"It's Mr. Fletcher. I went to check on him as you asked and—" His gaze darted to Miss Dalton. Whatever he had to say couldn't be good.

Edmund dipped his head. "Lead on."

He followed Barnaby's long legs out the door, down the passageway, and across the great front hall to where Gil lay on the marble floor.

A pool of blood near his head.

9

Well. This day was off to a bad start. Ami shoved back a loose strand of hair, annoyed with the way it dangled in her eyes. Granted, her morning likely wasn't as awful as Mr. Fletcher's must be, for surely he suffered quite a skull banger today—from so much drink and a gash on his head. After such a nasty tumble down the stairs last evening, he was fortunate a few stitches had remedied the situation. It could have been much worse.

Her belly rumbled—loudly—and she pressed a hand to it. Thus far she'd missed breakfast, failed at yet another attempt to authenticate the griffin, and broken her thumbnail when prying open the next crate.

And now this.

She ran her finger through a pile of Roman coins, spreading them out on the tabletop. Were they tetradrachms? Denarii? Who knew? Certainly not her. Egyptians usually bartered small items or traded gold and copper rings—*deben*—as currency. Valuing this small cache of money would take someone familiar with numismatics.

Out in the great hall, the case clock bonged a low chime. Half past the hour—thirty minutes until Mr. Price's business meeting. It warmed her heart he wished her to be present. Too bad she'd have to disappoint. She reached for the valuation she'd penned for him and rose. As awful as this day was going, she had no desire to face the skepticism of some sour-faced buyer who'd undoubtedly question her credentials. Besides, she had plenty to do here, and that's what Mr. Price had hired her for in the first place.

On her way out, she paused in front of the jackal-headed statue she'd unwrapped yesterday. Bosh. Dusty already? Doubling back, she snatched a cloth off the table and swiped it over the figure's shoulders, the action not moving the heavy sculpture a whit. It seemed right having this guardian stand sentinel near the door as it would have been stationed in an ancient tomb. With a light toss, she landed the cloth over the back of her chair and strode from the room.

She didn't have far to go. The study was conveniently located close to the front entrance of Price House. The door stood open, but even so she gave a cursory rap on the frame. No one answered, which was perfect. She'd nip in and out before anyone noticed.

Once inside, though, she veered away from the big desk at center, drawn irresistibly to the massive bookshelves lining an entire wall. The scent of leather-bound books and polished wood—beeswax, not lemon, thank heaven—filled her lungs. Gently, she ran a finger along the spines, angling her head to read the titles. *Great Expectations. Middlemarch. Moby Dick.* Her brows rose. Mr. Price—man of commerce and business—had a soft spot for fiction? Even better, the shelf below bore a selection of Indian artifacts. Though she'd rather see these items in a museum, at least he had the good sense to keep them away from the sunlight and stationed at eye level to admire while seated behind his desk. There were many things she respected about the man. His love and care for antiquities added to the tally.

A tally that was rising day by day.

Across from the shelves, cozy armchairs sat in front of the hearth. She didn't need to close her eyes to imagine Edmund Price relaxing there, book in one hand, maybe a pipe filled with cherry tobacco in the other. His long legs would be stretched out, crossed at the ankle, his fine, broad shoulders nestled against the highbacked cushion. His dimple would crease as he concentrated. Ah, but he was a handsome fellow, one she didn't care to admit had visited her in her dreams of late. What would it feel like to wake up to those striking blue eyes of his every morning, focused on her, cherishing her?

She stiffened. Bosh! What in all of England was she thinking?

Pivoting, she slapped down her estimate on his desk a little too forcefully, the swift movement knocking a small notepad to the rug. She swiped it up, catching a glance of the masculine handwriting. Many lines were crossed off with angry X's. These were not the numbers a businessman ought to be calculating.

Curious, she peered closer, holding the paper up to the sunshine streaming through the mullioned window.

> *Wut soft lite doth brake be-ond,*
> *A donning, a yonning, a yell-oh . . .*

Oh my. *This* was Mr. Price's poetry? No wonder he'd labeled it abysmal. The sentiment was fine enough, but the spelling was atrocious. Almost as if a schoolboy first learning his letters had penned the words. How did he manage his business with such poor writing skills?

The low drone of men's voices traveled down the corridor. Whirling, she set the notepad back on the desk, but apparently not quite well enough. Once again it thwacked to the floor.

"You're here early, Miss Dalton." Mr. Price's rich tone entered the room.

Her heart banged against her ribs. If she bent to retrieve his poetry, he'd suspect she'd been poking about the papers on his desk. Which she hadn't been—mostly.

"I, em . . ." Stalling, she punted the notepad with a smooth kick, hiding the action with the hem of her skirt. Hopefully the incriminating evidence had sailed beneath his desk. Guilt tasted like ashes in her mouth, but she'd choke on even more shame if she admitted she'd read his verse without his permission.

Grabbing her estimate, she held it out. "Here is the valuation you requested. Now then, I am afraid I cannot stay. I really ought to be assessing more artifacts. You understand, I'm sure."

"Actually, I was about to suggest we convene this meeting in your work area." He tucked the paper into his pocket. "That way Mr. Harrison here can take a peek at some of the relics you've already uncovered and get a feel for how many more are in the load. And with that, may I introduce Mr. Harrison." He turned to the stout man next to him.

Ami stifled a sigh. As expected, the fellow was dour-faced and paunch-bellied, arrogance clinging to him as tightly as his suit coat. He needn't say anything for one to deduce he was a pound snatcher, breathing money, speaking it, rolling in it if he had the chance. Should she step closer, no doubt she'd inhale the metallic scent of old coins.

"Mr. Harrison," Mr. Price continued, "this is Miss Dalton, Egyptologist."

Both the title and the gleam in Mr. Price's eyes wrapped around her like a warm embrace. For the space of a breath, she relished the feeling.

Then steeled herself for the inevitable *You're a what?* from Mr. Harrison.

However, the portly fellow merely dipped his head, jowls blending in with his collar. "Miss Dalton, pleased to meet you."

Well, well, perhaps her bad day was turning a corner.

"Pleased to meet you as well, Mr. Harrison." She smiled at the fellow, then faced Mr. Price. "If you'll give me just a minute, I'll tidy up the display table. It's not in a fit viewing state at the moment."

"As you wish." Turning to his potential buyer, Mr. Price indicated the leather chairs. "How about we catch up on that recent hunting excursion of yours?"

Ami left behind the men's chatter of fox and hounds, conflicted at the suggestion she'd made. She ought not care about an appealing presentation of the goods, and in fact, should leave it a mess to dissuade a purchase. Who knew where Mr. Harrison would store the valuable items if he got his hands on them? It would be in her best interest—make that the relics' best interest—if the lot didn't sell to a private buyer . . . though that could be detrimental to Mr. Price.

And he'd been nothing but kind to her.

The debate raged in her mind all the way to the workroom—where it promptly flew from her head. Near the pile of Roman coins stood a man with a bandage wrapped around his head, back toward her, hand in his pocket.

"Mr. Fletcher?" Alarmed, she strode toward him. "Can I help you with something? You shouldn't be up and about so soon."

He faced her, half a smile lifting one side of his moustache. Other than the swath of white cloth on his brow, he appeared to be hale. "Don't fret about me, Miss Dalton. You'd be surprised at how fast I bounce back from an injury. I am no stranger to being knocked about. Ha-ha!" He shoved his other hand into his pocket, grin fading. A sheepish look tucked his chin. "Actually, I came to apologize. There is no excuse for speaking so crudely as I did last night. I hope you will forgive me."

He was right. He had been crude, but he'd also been intoxicated. And it wasn't as if she hadn't heard worse from the scoundrels with whom she brokered deals in dark alleys. "Yes, of course, Mr. Fletcher. We all make mistakes."

"You are a saint, dear lady. So then let us put the past behind us, eh?" He yanked out his pocket watch and, after a glance, snapped the lid shut and tucked it away. "While I'd love to stay and chat, I'm afraid I must cut this short, for I have a meeting with Mr. Price and Mr. Harrison. Until later, Miss Dalton."

He strode past her.

"But they will soon be . . ." She closed her mouth. There was no sense finishing the sentence. Mr. Fletcher was already out the door.

Reaching for the nearest pile of papers, she tapped them

against the tabletop, straightening them into a neat stack. She capped the ink bottle, relocated a pile of polishing rags to a nearby basket, and grabbed the pouch to stow the scattered Roman coins. After scooping them in, she pulled the drawstring and . . . wait a minute. She dumped them back onto the table and fingered through the gold tokens, mouth pinching. Either she'd miscounted the first time she'd unpacked them . . .

Or some were missing.

"Right this way, Mr. Harrison." Edmund led the man out to the corridor, thankful to leave behind the Pandora's box he'd unwittingly opened. Harrison had regaled him with detailed descriptions of his many hunts, right down to the various dogs he'd used over the years and what food he fed them. Not being overly fond of hunting, Edmund found the tales tedious at best.

"I'm sure you'll—" Edmund narrowed his eyes as they entered the great hall. "Gil?"

Striding toward them with a bandaged head and a smirk on his mouth, Fletcher closed the distance between them. "Sorry I skipped breakfast, old man. Bit of a sluggish morning for me, but I'm up to speed now. And you must be Mr. Harrison, I assume?" He shook the man's hand. "I'm Gilbert Fletcher, Mr. Price's business partner. I hope I haven't missed the entire deal, but if so, allow me to be the first to congratulate you on acquiring such a unique collection."

"You've missed nothing, Mr. Fletcher, for I've acquired nothing yet. We are just on our way to view the artifacts now." Mr. Harrison's gaze fixed on Gil's brow. "Looks like you were in quite a tussle."

"Just a quarrel with a staircase, but never fear, I came out the victor."

Edmund stifled a snort. Gil had gained such a victory by Providence alone, for had he climbed any more than the three steps he'd taken, that tumble could have very well broken his neck.

"The workroom is this way, Mr. Harrison." Edmund set off toward the refashioned banquet room, unaccountably perturbed by Gil's presence. The man really ought to be in bed.

"Fine home you've got, Price." Mr. Harrison puffed along beside him. For a fellow so given to hunting, he surely was unfit for physical activity. "I wonder you don't keep your recent purchase for yourself?"

"I am rarely in residence here and in fact soon hope to move to London once renovations are finished on my town house." If God showed him favor, that was . . . *and* if Lord Bastion did as well. He'd not heard from the viscount since that telegram on the train. But that was another matter for another time. For now, he smiled at Mr. Harrison. "Displaying such a treasure in this house would be wasteful as there would be none other than the servants to admire it."

"Treasure, yes!" Gil clapped his hands. "I daresay you'll want to jump on this lot, Harrison, before other buyers get wind of it. Will it be a problem for you to acquire the funds within the week?"

Edmund clenched his jaw. Gilbert Fletcher never used to be this high-pressured or ill-mannered. "That won't be necessary. As I've explained to Mr. Harrison, we are very early in the process, and not everything has yet been unpacked. Much as I'd love to sell the lot right now, it wouldn't be prudent to do so."

"Prudence is a nag to be goaded into motion. Ha-ha!" Gil's voice bounced from wall to wall as they entered the corridor.

Mr. Harrison didn't look amused. Neither was Edmund.

His irritation faded, though, as they entered the workroom, his gaze immediately drawn to Miss Dalton, who was handing a basket of rags to the housekeeper. Mrs. Buckner dipped her head at him as she passed by, but Edmund barely noticed. It was too hard to pull his eyes off Miss Dalton, for she was a veritable Cleopatra amongst these ancient relics. Sunlight illuminated her delicate features, her skin glowing as brilliantly as the alabaster vases. She was the true gem in the room, a timeless beauty even in an apron with her hair pinned haphazardly. The keen mind behind those sharp eyes only added to the allure.

He cleared his throat. "Are you ready for us to view the artifacts?"

"Yes. Why don't you gentlemen join me over here?" She turned toward the vases. "These urns"—she swept her hand over three slender pieces—"are from the New Kingdom, dating from the sixteenth century BC to—"

"Harrison doesn't care about such trivialities, Miss Dalton." Gil tapped the table. "Tell him what they are worth."

Her brow furrowed as she shot her gaze to Gil, clearly annoyed, and yet when she spoke, her voice hid any hint of agitation. "Twenty pounds apiece."

"And a bargain they are at that, eh, Harrison?" Gil nudged the man with his elbow. "I should think you'd want to buy the goods here and now."

"Perhaps. Perhaps not."

Miss Dalton moved on to the next item, circling her hand over a golden-framed looking glass. "Here we have a fine example of an article from the predynastic period, a ceremonial—"

"Yes, yes. We can all see it is a mirror, Miss Dalton." Gil chuckled. "What Harrison needs to know is the value."

Edmund's hands curled into fists, giving his fingers something to do other than throttle the man. He'd given Gil the benefit of the doubt yesterday, what with his travel and then overindulgence of wine, but there was no excuse for his poor behaviour today. A word or two was definitely in order after Harrison left.

Miss Dalton frowned. "The worth of an item goes far beyond a number, Mr. Fletcher. Take, for example, the golden griffin over there." She pointed across the room to the winged statuette. "If that piece truly bears the famed curse of Amentuk, then its value would—"

"Curse, you say?" Mr. Harrison's eyes widened. "How very interesting, Miss Dalton. I have an ardent curiosity in all things cryptically metaphysical, so do tell."

"If you like, though it is but a legend." She shrugged one shoulder. "Follow me."

Suddenly energized, Mr. Harrison tagged her heels like a playful pup.

Edmund grabbed hold of Gil's arm and lowered his voice. "Stop pressuring Mr. Harrison. I'm not ready to sell."

"That is why you need me, old man." Gil pulled away. "You cannot let a buyer like this slip through your fingers. The sooner the sale, the better."

"We don't even know what's in the rest of these crates!" he whisper-growled.

"That's why you name him a figure." Gil poked a finger into his chest. "Close the deal, then ship him only some of the items. He'll never know what he's missed out on, and the rest can be sold to another bidder."

Edmund stiffened. The idea was exactly the sort of underhanded scheme his father would have devised. "You know very well that I will have nothing to do with such a ruse. It's unethical."

"It's business!"

"Not my kind of business, and I'll hear no more about it. As planned, Miss Dalton will finish her valuations, and the cargo will be sold by month's end."

A vein stood out on Gil's neck. "No, it *must* be sooner."

Not that he'd mind getting the funds to Sanjay more quickly, but he wouldn't stoop to such a dishonorable sale. Interesting, though, that Gil was so insistent. "Why must the deal be made with such haste? What are you not telling me?"

"I—oh dear." Gil pressed his hand to his bandage and closed his eyes.

Instant guilt punched Edmund in the gut. Clearly the man wasn't one hundred percent yet, and he was being a bit harsh on him. "Pardon my severity, Gil. If you need a lie-down, why don't you—"

"No." His eyes shot open. "I am fine." He glanced over at Mr. Harrison and Miss Dalton, then swung his gaze back to

Edmund. "Look, the smart business move is to encourage Harrison to lay down his money. He's interested enough, especially about the folklore. Look at him over there. He's practically nose to nose with that ugly statue, eating up every word Miss Dalton is feeding him. He said himself he believes in that magic, so I say we play up that curse to entice him."

"But that's absurd. The griffin isn't cursed. It's just Egyptian folklore."

"Harrison doesn't need to know that. If a curse is what it takes to sell him, then a curse is what he shall get."

Edmund shook his head. "Like I said, Gil, stop pressuring the man. I mean it."

A disgusted sigh belted out of Gil as he turned toward Mr. Harrison, and though Edmund couldn't be sure, it sounded an awful lot like he grumbled, "You know nothing about making a situation better for yourself."

Edmund followed, hoping Gil took his admonition to heart.

Mr. Harrison looked up at his approach. "This is quite the find, Price—*if* all that Miss Dalton claims about this piece is true. The stories alone are worth a penny or two."

"Supposed curses aside, that item will not be sold with the rest for I intend to keep it."

"Hah!" Gil cuffed him on the back. "Such a jester. Likes to drive a hard bargain, you know. Why, Harrison, if a cursed artifact is what you're after, this little devil is just the thing for you. In fact, though I'd been hesitant to say so earlier, I believe my tumble down the stairs last night was because of the Egyptian spell hovering about that statuette. Something invisible pushed me. Something supernatural. What power that little gem holds! And were that power to be harnessed, why, who knows that it wouldn't turn into a good luck charm? A *golden* luck charm."

"Is that so?" Mr. Harrison scratched his jaw. "Now there's a thought."

Edmund rolled his eyes.

So did Miss Dalton.

Gil put his arm around Mr. Harrison's shoulder, propelling

him into motion. "How about we continue this conversation over a glass of sherry in Price's office?"

Blast! How could the man even think of drinking with a skull that surely had to be aching from his injury and overindulgence of the night before? Frowning, Edmund tipped his head at Miss Dalton. "Thank you. I shall leave you to your work."

"If you wouldn't mind, a word before you leave?"

He glanced at the door where Gil and Mr. Harrison had already disappeared. If he didn't keep that decanter out of Gil's reach, there was no telling what he might say to Mr. Harrison. "Yes, but it will have to be brief."

She plucked a small leather bag from farther down the table. With one hasty movement, she loosened the drawstring and small golden coins plinked onto the tabletop. "It's about this Roman currency."

"Roman?" He rubbed the back of his neck, thoroughly confused. "What are these doing tangled up with Egyptian artifacts?"

"Could be several reasons, actually." She held up one of the coins between them. "There was a Roman period in Egypt from 30 BC to AD 641, so it's not out of the realm of possibility for these to have been found in a tomb. Or perhaps they were stashed away elsewhere as Egypt was part of the ancient trading routes. Or—and this is what I'm leaning toward—it could be a collector or dealer of coins added a pouch to this mix of artifacts, someone hoping to sell a variety of relics together."

He plucked the coin from her fingers, studying it himself while she continued.

"Whatever the reason, here they are, and to be honest with you, I have no idea how to price them. You'll need a Roman antiquarian for that."

"Good thing I'm a problem solver, then."

She arched a brow. "What do you mean?"

He set the coin back with the others. "I happen to know just the fellow who can help us with this. An old friend of mine at Cambridge. I'll dash him off a note today. Thank you for bringing this to my attention, and for having the courage to admit the limits of your knowledge. Many a man wouldn't have been so bold."

For a few breaths she said nothing, but the pinking on her cheeks revealed his compliment had hit home. Most women would have tittered under his praise. She merely lifted her chin. "There is one more thing you should know."

"And that is . . . ?"

"There were twenty-five coins here this morning when I dumped them onto the table." With a few flicks of her fingers, she spread the golden circles so that none overlapped. "After I returned from your office, only eighteen remained."

The air whooshed from his lungs. Never once had his staff stolen anything. Why, Barnaby didn't feel he even needed to lock up the silver at night, such was his confidence in who he hired and the camaraderie he worked to instill in them. Though Edmund hated to doubt Miss Dalton, he couldn't help but ask, "Are you certain?"

"I wasn't at first, but I checked my tally sheet to confirm it." She pulled a slip of paper from her pocket, verifying her words.

Disappointment bowed his shoulders. Naturally, theft happened in other great houses, he'd just prided himself that it had never happened here. "I shall have Barnaby speak with the staff at once."

"You might first wish to ask Mr. Fletcher about it."

He wheeled about. "Why?"

"Because—though I cannot prove it—I saw Mr. Fletcher in here alone, standing near the coins, tucking his hand into his pocket."

10

There was a certain honesty in a game of billiards. Truth slid out easier with the clacking of balls, as if the sound of the game drowned out the fear of judgment. Closing one eye, Edmund sighted down his cue stick, then took his shot. The red ball banked off two sides, entirely missing the other two balls. A loss, but a respectable failure he could amend next turn . . . and that's what he loved about the game. Men could be vulnerable without feeling weak. And he especially hoped that sentiment proved true with the hornet's nest of a conversation he intended to open with Gil.

But better to ease into such a dialogue with a lighter topic. He faced Gil. "You have yet to tell me of your good news."

Across from him, Gil chalked the end of his stick. The man had indulged in a long lie-down earlier that afternoon and, while still sporting a pallid complexion and a bandage, appeared to be in good health. "What good news were you hoping to hear, old man?"

"Whatever it was you mentioned in your last letter."

"My—? Oh. Ha-ha! Nearly forgot. You should be happy to know I tidied up my office."

Gil was the most fastidious of men, so that didn't ring true in the least. Edmund fiddled with his stick, casting it back and forth between his hands, a twang in his gut. "While I am happy to hear all is in shipshape order, I am surprised to learn it was disheveled to begin with."

And even more surprised that such an event would count as good news—because it wouldn't. Clearly the man was hiding something.

Gil set down the chalk cube as if he hadn't a care in the world. "Just trying to keep the correspondence lighthearted, you know."

No, actually, he didn't. "Is there something you're not telling me? Because something is definitely off, and I demand to know what it is. What happened on the Continent? You were there at the behest of Mr. Durand, were you not? Did something go wrong with his investments?"

"Ha-ha! Nothing of the sort. I merely finished the Durand business in record-breaking time, hence my early arrival." He eyed the tip of his stick. "I wouldn't keep secrets from you, you know. We've been partners far too long for that."

He'd like to trust in their past history, and he would—*if* Miss Dalton's suspicion weren't roaming around the corridors of his mind. He cleared his throat. "Miss Dalton tells me there are some coins missing from the workroom."

"Is that so?" Gil drawled.

"Yes. You wouldn't happen to know anything about that, would you?"

"Perhaps you ought to ask her." He bent over his stick, lining up just the right angle. "She probably counted incorrectly."

Of all the blame shifting. How dare the man accuse the very one who'd caught him in the act! Edmund white-knuckled his stick so hard his fingers ached, yet he kept his tone casual. A cornered badger was never one to carelessly poke. "Miss Dalton saw you, Gil. She came upon you as you stood near the coins this morning, putting your hand into your pocket."

Gil jabbed at the cue ball and missed. Frowning, he straightened, the fresh bandage on his head stark white against his reddening face. "All right. If you must know, I took them."

"You—?" Edmund choked. "Why?"

"As a surprise for you." He shrugged. "I intended to get them restored and mounted as a gift when we make the sale with Harrison. It's your shot."

Edmund stood motionless. Why did everything about Gil seem so off? "And yet you took those coins before Harrison was even here."

"Well, I didn't mean him per se. The fact is, you'll sell the load to someone, and at that point, I planned to award you a congratulatory token of the deal. Blast it, Price! It wasn't like I stole them." He puffed a disgusted snort. "Besides, I didn't realize you were such a saint."

"And I didn't realize how much you'd changed while I'd been abroad." Seething, he smacked the cue ball with a satisfying clack. The white sphere slapped around from bumper to bumper, knocking his own ball into a pocket and following right behind it. He jammed his hand into the netting and yanked them both out, thwacking them on the table as he faced Gil. "What's happened to you?"

"Ha-ha! Don't be a fool." He took a shot and potted his own ball, then moved in for another shot. "Perhaps it is you who has changed. Ever think of that? I am the same as I always have been, old man."

Edmund gritted his teeth, the *old man* moniker proving his point. Gil had never called him anything other than Edmund, trendy terminology or not. "I beg to differ. The Gilbert Fletcher I know is a patient man, honest to a fault, doesn't imbibe, and wouldn't dream of lewd comments in the presence of a lady. You've hardly been here more than twenty-four hours and already blown those traits out of the water." He lowered his voice, the gravity of what he was about to say sitting like a brick in his gut. "I demand to know why, Gil. For though it pains me to say so, I am seriously considering cutting ties with you despite the fact that we've worked together for so many years. If I didn't owe the protection of my family wealth to you, I'd have already sent you packing."

A sigh sank his business partner's shoulders, and his next jab hit the ball sideways, sending it aimlessly spinning across the green felt. Gil straightened, his face ashen, the pool balls temporarily forgotten. "Very well. Though I hate to admit it, the truth is, you couldn't be more right. I haven't been myself lately, not for the past few years, actually. You see, I . . ."

Snapping his mouth shut, Gil snatched the chalk and rubbed the cube on the end of his cue stick as if his life depended upon it. "Loneliness has a way of carving the heart right out of a man."

Edmund shook his head as he strode to the end of the table. "With all your friends and associates in London? Surely you have far too many social engagements to fall victim to melancholy."

"It was like that . . . at least it used to be." Gil tucked his chin, eyes on his shoes.

Whatever was on his mind couldn't be good. Edmund set his stick to the table, focusing on the yellow ball.

"I met a woman," Gil began. "Charlotte and I were kindred spirits, or so I thought. I pursued her hard for a year, met her family, introduced her to mine. Things were going swimmingly." A low breath shuddered out of him. "But then she stopped seeing me. Not a word as to why. No excuses. Nothing. I have no idea what I did wrong, and it's been eating away at me ever since."

Edmund punched the stick against the ball, sending the thing over the edge of the table and cracking to the floor. He knew well how a woman could bring a man to his knees. "Women," he grumbled as he reset the ball on the table. "God's gift and torture."

"Would that it were only that." Gil spread his hands. "Business matters have been a struggle as well. You know the stock exchange. Of late it's been a battle to stretch my pennies—which weighs heavy on my mind. The failures. The loss. As you've noticed, I've turned to drink to cope with it all. I'm not proud of it, but I don't know how else to manage. Yet manage I must, and the only way to do that is to get more money." He tossed back his head, a desperate look in his eyes.

Edmund stared, stunned, and not just a little horrified. "Are you telling me our business is nearing bankruptcy?" His words were a growl.

"Ha-ha! Don't panic, old man. It is my affairs that are wanting, not yours."

He racked his pool cue, as done with the game as Gil appeared to be. "And yet many of our affairs are entwined, are they not?"

"True . . . and so perhaps you will now share the same urgency I feel in selling that lot of relics to Harrison."

Edmund exhaled long and low. "Why did you not tell me of this matter sooner?"

"Thought I could handle it on my own." Gil rolled his stick between his palms, back and forth, staring at the motion for a long while before snapping his gaze back to Edmund. "But no need to fret like a housewife. We'll simply sell the load to Harrison, and all will be well."

Edmund eyed his business partner, seeking truth. He'd trusted this man all the years he'd been in India, and never once had Gil let him down. Besides, he knew better than most the depths to which a heartless woman could drive a man. Save for the odd behaviour and the great amount of alcohol Gil had partaken of since yesterday, there were no other tangible reasons not to have confidence in him now—especially in light of his tale of womanly woe.

But that didn't mean he must continue putting up with such boorish manners.

"Very well, Gil. If you say so. But"—he leaned back against the table, pegging Gil with a resolute stare—"I will not tolerate any more drinking or dishonesty."

"Yes, yes! Of course." Gil racked his stick, then grabbed him by the shoulders. "I *am* trying to change, to become better, for my sake and for those around me. Please don't cut ties with me. I need your support now more than ever. I need that cargo sold at the earliest possible date."

The words hit home. Sanjay needed Edmund's half of the funds even more urgently than Gil did. Edmund rubbed the back of his neck, working out a tight knot. "Trust me, I share your sense of expediency. Your candor, however, is refreshing, though I wish you would have told me of these things as soon as you arrived."

Gil dropped his hands. "Lesson learned. Forgive me, old man?"

"Just see that you return the coins to Miss Dalton, and all will be forgotten."

The part about Gil pocketing the coins he could easily disregard. And it helped to know of Gil's woman trouble and subsequent money issues, for at least that accounted for much of the change in his partner's looks and demeanor.

And yet, despite the hope of selling the Egyptian cargo, none of this boded well for the future.

Candlelight flickered in the shadowy workroom, wind skritching branches against the windowpanes like the clawing of a beast set on breaking the glass. A night such as this was meant for letting the imagination run far and free. Ami sat on the parquet floor, back against a crate, her pencil flying across the page of her journal. The tale she'd been working on for so long was finally nearing a finish.

Pausing, she tapped the end of her pencil against her lip, rereading a few sentences. Strange. When she'd begun this saga of Egyptian adventure, she'd pictured the hero with almond-shaped eyes and a shaved head. Now, though she tried hard not to, all she could picture was the dusky blue gaze and dark wavy hair of Mr. Price.

Absently, she rolled the pencil between her fingers. The more time she spent with Mr. Price, the more she found herself navigating uncharted territory. It was now his warm laughter that echoed alongside her dream of leading a dig in Egypt, her personal and professional aspirations slowly tangling into a knot

. . . one she wasn't sure she'd be able to untie. Could one lead expeditions while also building a life with someone?

Her fingers froze at the sudden shift in her usual train of thinking. How could a blue-eyed man cause such a derailment from her formerly single-tracked ambition?

As if the mere thought of the man conjured him, Mr. Price stepped into the room, his presence warming her in ways she couldn't explain.

"Miss Dalton? I've brought you some—" His gaze shifted between her and the chair. "Why are you on the floor? Are you all right?"

With a soft chuckle, she rose, clutching the book to her chest. "Tell me, Mr. Price, do you like to write?"

He paused, his eyes searching hers. "Sometimes, particularly at the end of a grueling day. Ah, a rough one, was it? Don't tell me you're penning verse?"

She shook her head, a grin tugging her lips. "I am many things, Mr. Price, but I am not a poet. I couldn't make words rhyme for a king's ransom. What have you got there?" She tipped her head toward the mugs.

"Since you missed dinner, I thought you could tell me of today's discoveries over a cup of drinking chocolate. If you like, that is."

"How lovely!" Her heart fluttered at the kindness, yet she shoved away the feeling as she brushed aside the papers on the table. Laying her journal atop them, she then grabbed the candelabra from the floor.

As Mr. Price handed her a mug, their fingers brushed, sending a shiver down her spine. So much for shoving away random feelings!

"What were you writing?" he asked as he pulled up another chair.

"Nothing of consequence. Just a little story." But even as she spoke the words, an inconvenient truth rose up. It had been him she'd been writing of, not Amun. Her thoughts were beginning to be consumed with the man sitting across from her.

And as she gazed into his eyes, she couldn't help but wonder if he felt the same way.

Stars and lightning! What an absurd idea. What was happening to her?

She sipped her chocolate, delightedly distracted by the sweet, creamy flavor. If joy could be sold in a cup, this was surely it. "Mmm. Not only do I understand your obsession with this drink, I share it."

"I should like to hear it, you know." He took a sip of his own, his gaze lingering on her.

"Very well. Today I—"

"No." He eyed her over the mug's rim. "I mean, yes, I do want to know what made for such a rough day, but first I'd like to hear your story, if you're willing."

She toyed with the handle of her cup. She had no trouble whatsoever in submitting articles for archaeological journals, but this? This was far too personal. She shook her head. "I am certain you would not enjoy it."

He reached out, stilling her hand, and once again his touch jolted through her. "You'd be surprised. I have a fondness for fiction of all sorts."

An image of his massive bookshelves in the study flashed in her mind. She fingered her journal but didn't open it. Sharing her work was just so intimate.

She peered up at him. "I must have your word you'll not laugh at my storytelling attempts or have me committed to Littlemore."

He snorted. "It would be a crime to lock up your keen mind in an asylum, and I vow I shall not laugh." He slapped his hand to his heart.

She paused a beat more, then gave in to the sincerity in his eyes. "Very well." She flipped through the pages until she found the spot where she'd picked up the story earlier that evening.

"As the first blush of dawn kissed the sands of ancient Egypt, a solitary figure stood at the Nile's edge. Lotus

114

blossoms perfumed the air, but Amun took no notice, for his gaze fixed on the horizon where the ruins of a once-glorious temple rose from the earth like a phoenix reborn. Each weathered stone of Seti-Ama whispered to him from the past, like a lover long gone yet unwilling to let go."

Edmund arched a brow. "This *is* poetic! I had no idea you—"

She held up her hand, thoroughly embarrassed. "Either I read this all at once, or I don't read it at all, Mr. Price."

He pressed his lips tight, and for a moment, she reveled in her power.

Then she went back to reading.

"Amun splashed across the river with long strides, the water cool against his skin. If he didn't reach the ancient shrine before the sun fully embraced the sky, it would vanish—and wouldn't reappear for another hundred years. Or so it was said. He wouldn't live long enough to get another chance at snatching the healing balm from inside the temple.

And Safiyeh wouldn't live the week if he failed.

His heart quickened with each step. Lungs heaving. Thighs burning. Onward he pressed, taking the temple stairs by two. He tore past the entrance pillars, the acrid scent of sacrifices wafting across the centuries. Blinking in the sudden shadows, he pressed ahead to the altar and grabbed hold of the sacred urn. He had it! In his hands. The famed healing balm of Ko-tesh!

But then the earth trembled. The walls shook. Stones crumbled like the desert sands. Amun tore off like a whirl-wind, clutching the urn beneath his arm.

He had barely descended the last stair when a mighty force shoved him face first to the desert floor. Spitting out grit, panting for air, he pushed to his feet, clutching the urn to his chest. Slowly, he turned. Nothing but an end-less desert lay barren where once a mighty temple stood.

A triumphant grin stretched across his lips as he crushed the urn to his chest in a strong embrace.

'For you, my sister,' he whispered. 'Only for you.'"

Ami closed her journal, fearing to see what sort of reaction played on Mr. Price's face.

"I had no idea you were such a storyteller, Miss Dalton." Mr. Price's crooked finger lifted her chin, forcing her to look into his eyes. "That was beautiful."

Her heart raced. He'd always looked kindly upon her, but this time something more sparked in his eyes, almost as if he were seeing her in a completely different light—not just as a hireling but as a woman worth cherishing.

Her pulse galloped in her ears.

His gaze flicked to her lips, and her breath hitched. Could it be he wished to kiss her? The idea thrilled—and terrified—for she'd never been kissed before. Never had she time for such triflings. And yet now she leaned closer, drawn by his spicy curry scent.

But just as she was about to end the distance between them, a pang of self-doubt stabbed her chest. She was a bookish miss. He a sought-after bachelor of wealth and power. He couldn't possibly be interested in her—the person inside her, that is. He had likely pulled this same charismatic trick on countless other women. Used them and tossed them aside, for that was the way of businessmen, was it not?

Pulling away, she set her journal on the stack of papers. "Thank you, Mr. Price. I am happy you enjoyed the story."

"I did." He smiled warmly. "Very much."

Once again her pulse took off. Bosh! As much as she'd like to, she couldn't deny the attraction of his intelligence, his wit, his rugged charm. But it was more than unwise to pursue a romantic relationship with him. Quite frankly, it would be a train wreck. They were from vastly different worlds. She wouldn't know how to carry on inane conversation for hours on end at formal affairs, and he wouldn't have a clue how to read hieroglyphics if his life depended upon it. Besides, she wouldn't want to risk losing his friendship if the relationship didn't work out.

She cleared her throat, promptly changing the subject. "Now, about my day," she said, hoping to sound nonchalant.

"Indeed." He picked up his mug, finishing off his drink. "What was it that drove you to such distraction?"

"Several things." She sighed. "First there was the whole business of the missing coins with Mr. Fletcher, though to his credit, he did return them and explained the situation. Then there was this."

She beckoned him to the end of the long table to a broken mummy mask. "See here?" She pointed to a jagged edge on one kohl-blackened eye. "The cartonnage has been chipped, either from hasty grave robbers or during transport. Hard to say which. And down farther"—she slid her finger to the chin— "there is excessive discoloration, likely from light exposure, though it could be from moisture as well."

Mr. Price frowned. "Some missing coins and a damaged item are hardly worth ruining your day."

"That was just the beginning. When I opened a crate of papyrus scrolls, I found several of them badly torn and stained, one of them beyond repair or deciphering. But most troubling is this." She waggled her finger as she led him to the door, where a sobering jackal-headed Anubis stood watch.

Mr. Price's eyes flicked over the statue. "It appears to be whole."

"It is, but it's not in the same position as it was this morning."

"Somebody moved it." He shrugged.

Ami swept her hand toward the imposing figure. "Give it a go."

"Challenge accepted." He winked, then widening his stance, grabbed hold of the larger-than-life figure. His suit coat strained tightly across his broad shoulders as he put his weight into shifting the thing.

The statue didn't budge.

He tried again, the muscles on his neck bulging as he used all his might.

Anubis remained firmly in place.

Breathing hard, he retreated a step.

"As you see, Mr. Price, no man alone can move this piece."

He tugged down the cuffs of his sleeves. "True. So perhaps Barnaby had some of the staff shift the thing for cleaning."

Ami shook her head. "After the cat incident, I gave your butler strict instruction not to allow anyone in here."

"Well, clearly someone was . . . a few someones." He smirked.

"Impossible. I was in here all day."

"*All* day?" He cocked his head.

She bit her lip, reviewing how she'd spent her daylight hours and . . . Bother! "I guess I did go check on the cat, and when I did so, Phineas asked me to hold the ladder for him while he pruned some of the branches on the willow."

"There. You see? I shall speak with Barnaby and remind him no one is to be admitted to this room."

"Thank you."

Though the matter was settled, her gaze drifted back to the ebony snout and soulless black eyes of the god of embalming and mummification. It was kind of Mr. Price to reiterate her wishes to the butler, yet the fact remained it was highly unlikely Barnaby would have ordered two servants to shift this monstrosity a mere forty-five degrees. Doing so would serve no purpose whatsoever. But the worse alternative was that Barnaby hadn't asked his staff to move it at all, because then there was only one explanation.

The curse of Amentuk had shifted it, and she couldn't—she *wouldn't*—believe that.

11

In the past week since he'd heard Ami Dalton's Egyptian tale, Edmund had come close to kissing the woman at least three times. First, when she'd read her story, for he'd been both shocked and pleased that she'd share such a personal piece of writing with him. It had been a vulnerable move, one she'd entrusted to him simply because he'd asked, not because she expected anything from him for doing so. Days later, he'd come upon her in the workroom with wood shavings caught in her hair. Helping her pick them out had seemed the gallant thing to do at the time—until it turned into something more. Her bright laughter and smoky-cinnamon scent had nearly driven him to his knees. Then yesterday in the breakfast room, he'd almost pulled her into his arms for no reason whatsoever.

And now . . . well, he really ought to turn around and go back to his study instead of seeking her out, for the woman was becoming quite the preoccupation. He'd keep his distance this time, for her sake and his, and be thankful that Gil had been keeping his distance as well this past week.

He plowed his hand through his hair as he strode to the

workroom. He didn't have time for a relationship, not when he ought to be focused on pursuing a position in Parliament. And Miss Dalton had made it clear she aspired to be as renowned an Egyptologist as her father, so she didn't have the time for him either. No, at this point, anything more than enjoying quippy conversation with the woman was out of the question. He'd do well to keep that in mind.

Thus fortified, he stepped into the workroom, trying hard not to notice how the August sun streaming through the window highlighted the copper strands in Miss Dalton's perpetually ruffled hair. Most women couldn't pull off such a devil-may-care appearance, but on her, it looked heavenly.

He cleared his throat. "Miss Dalton, I have something to show you."

She peered over her shoulder at him. "Ah, Mr. Price. What a coincidence. I have something to show you as well."

She shoved back her chair and approached the looming figure of Anubis. "It's happened again. The statue moved overnight."

His gaze drifted past her to the ebony giant. Sure enough, the jackal's snout was now aimed straight at him. Despite his admonition to the butler, was Barnaby up to more antics?

"I shall have another word with Barnaby." Edmund heaved a sigh as he faced Miss Dalton. "But first come with me."

Her brow wrinkled far too adorably. "Where are we going?"

"You'll see."

"How cryptic," she murmured as she gained his side.

"You love a good puzzle."

She smiled up at him as they left behind the corridor for the great front hall. "You are beginning to know me far too well."

Not well enough.

Blast! There he went again. So much for mental determination . . . which actually might be something to explore in his next poem.

"I wonder if you know your business partner is seeking press for the collection I'm working on?" she asked.

The thought of Gil snapped him from any romantic notions

whatsoever. Though admittedly the man's behaviour had toned down, he was still becoming a bur in his side with his *ha-ha*'s and *old man*'s. "He mentioned it in passing last night, but I told him such publicity isn't the way to go about gaining serious buyers. I'd prefer it if Price House wasn't turned into a circus."

"Apparently Mr. Fletcher didn't take the hint. Not an hour ago he asked if I would write down the story of the curse. He believes the tale of the golden griffin will increase the price of the lot, particularly in Mr. Harrison's case."

"I hope you refused."

"Actually, I told him I could, but I'd make sure to include a disclaimer that any supposed curses are not included in the purchase price."

He laughed, the sound echoing in the large space of the front hall. What a quick-witted mind she owned!

She glanced up at him as they passed by the bronze vases, the sweet scent of lilies mixing with her cinnamon fragrance. "I hope you don't mind me asking, but I am curious about the exact nature of the business in which you've partnered with him?"

"I don't mind at all." In fact, he was pleased she took interest. "Shortly after my father died, so did his business manager. By God's grace and the recommendation of several trusted associates at the time, I approached Gilbert Fletcher for the job of managing my financial portfolio. Gil is a genius with numbers, even more so when it comes to investing. He has a broad reach and exposure to different business sectors and quite the flair for emerging markets. Currently, he manages my holdings here in England, and in return, earns a hefty percentage for himself. Part of our net worth is intertwined, but he does have other ventures, as have I in India. Overall, he is a good business partner."

"If not a rather erratic one."

He sighed. "I do admit he's been off-center."

"So why keep him on? It's not like you're married to the man."

"True." He chuckled. Leave it to her to drill to the center

of a matter. "But I owe him a great deal, enough to grant him some leeway."

Ami paused at his study door, the colour of her eyes hovering somewhere between blue and green as she stared at him. "What could a powerful man like yourself owe to such a feckless fellow?"

"My entire fortune. I know"—he held up a hand—"hard to believe, but true. In my earlier years, I wasn't quite as business savvy as I am now, and I entangled myself with some cutthroat capitalists. In the midst of a troubled business venture, Gil shielded me from impending legal disaster arising from a dubious investment that went sour. I was facing potential bankruptcy and accusations of fraud. But Gil—God love him—orchestrated a strategic defense, sparing no expense to protect my assets and reputation. His selfless sacrifice, shouldering legal consequences and fines on my behalf, forged a loyalty between us. So despite my suspicions of his recent behaviour, I find it hard to part ways with him. His actions during our darkest hour went beyond mere partnership. They represent a debt of gratitude I can never fully repay."

"Mmm," she murmured. "There are so many sides to you, Mr. Price, that I hardly know what next to expect."

"Well, I hope what I show you next will be a good surprise." He swept a hand toward the open doorway.

She grinned—but that smile vanished the moment they entered his study and her gaze landed on the mess near the bookshelves—the very same look the housekeeper had given him when she'd first seen the project. A large toolbox sat on the floor. A ladder leaned against the far side of the wall where sawdust mounded like fallen snow on the baseboards.

Miss Dalton slapped a hand against her chest. "Please do not tell me you are getting rid of the bookshelves."

"Just modifying them, and that's exactly what I wished you to see." Taking care to avoid the Ming Dynasty vase on a pedestal, he stepped past the toolbox, then held out his hand to help her cross over it as well. "I had the woodworker inset this shelf"—he ran his fingers over the freshly sanded wood—"to provide plenty of space, leaving no room whatsoever for the chance of the item falling and getting damaged."

"Very thoughtful," she murmured. "But what item?"

"The golden griffin. I thought it might ease your mind to see the care I shall take of such a valuable artifact. Furthermore, I assure you when I move to London, every bit as much precaution shall be taken there as well. I have instructed the renovators to build a secure shelf much like this one."

Her brow folded into deep creases. "I know that legally the griffin is your property to do with as you wish, Mr. Price, but I really think that artifact and the rest of the lot you purchased belong in the Cairo Museum. Those relics were created in Egypt and are an important part of the country's cultural heritage, the golden griffin in particular, as it is a religious piece."

When she was this fired up, he couldn't help but admire the flame on her cheeks and spark in her eyes. He grinned. "Then you should be pleased to learn I have already written the museum. If they agree to pay market value, I will be happy to sell the relics to them. I am a businessman, after all."

She pursed her lips, the mole at the edge of her jaw shifting in the most beguiling way. "Then why go to the effort of building this shelf?"

"I am open to selling the lot, not the griffin, but I will do everything in my power to keep it safe. Hence the fortification."

She shook her head. "Why is that one piece so important to you?"

"I told you, it's part of my family crest."

"No." She studied him as if he were a fresh find inside a sarcophagus. "It's more than that."

He huffed a long breath. The woman was far too perceptive. And as she'd already said, he knew her well enough by now to understand that she'd not retreat until she had the truth of the matter.

"In a sense, I suppose it is." He rubbed the back of his neck, working out the knot of tension that never failed to form when thinking of the past. "My father was an unyielding man, Miss

Dalton. Craving success more than anything. To be fair, he *was* successful . . . and I never measured up to his standards."

"But—" She spluttered. "How absurd. You are the most prosperous businessman I know, that all of Oxford knows for that matter."

"It is kind of you to say so. My father never did." He dropped his hand. He'd dealt with the bitterness of his father's coldness long ago, but the loss remained . . . and no doubt it would haunt him until his dying day. "That griffin, Miss Dalton, is a symbol of my family's heritage, one I will live up to or die in the trying. I don't expect you to grasp the sentiment, just to accept it."

The lines of her face softened, as did her voice. "Your father was wrong about you, but I know my saying so doesn't mean you'll believe it. That's the thing about fathers, they tend to have a way to make us feel like needy, negligible little children—save for our heavenly Father, that is." Her gaze drifted to the ceiling, a profound peace radiating from her. "We are never insignificant in His eyes. It's a promise I keep in my pocket and pull out when life takes a dreary turn."

He inhaled sharply. What a wonder this woman was. Stalwart in her faith. Intelligent. Innocent in a refreshing way, yet beneath that simple work apron was a spine of steel. If he didn't get away from her immediately, he really would pull her close and kiss those full lips of hers. "A good reminder, Miss Dalton. And now I shall let you get back to your work, as we should make way for the carpenter to finish up his labours in here."

Wheeling about, he hastily stepped over the big toolbox— almost, that is. The hem of his trouser caught on the handle. He flailed, hand smacking against the pedestal holding the vase. The movement helped him catch his balance—but not so for the vase. It toppled sideways.

Miss Dalton lunged, catching the valuable relic—*and* crashing headlong into him.

He went down hard, rolling at the last moment to bear the brunt of her tumble as he cradled her.

"Are you all right?" He shifted her in his arms, gaze sweeping over her face.

Frowning, she wrenched the vase from between them and gave it a good look then relaxed against him. "I am now."

Her eyes met his, her frown wavering. Good heavens. Was she near tears? He couldn't take it if she wept. A woman's tears were something he couldn't control.

But she burst into laughter, shoulders shaking.

And though for the life of him he didn't know why, he chuckled right along with her. Which only made her laugh all the harder. Eyes watering, heartfelt guffaws shook them both until at last they each lay flat on their backs, gasping for breath, the vase nestled safely between them. Why, he'd not enjoyed such a rollick since—

"Price?"

"Edmund?"

"Oh dear."

The words came in unison at the door from three different voices.

He pushed up.

Then wished he hadn't.

Barnaby, Lord Bastion, and his daughter, Violet, all gaped on the threshold.

"What is the meaning of this, Price?"

Ami eased into a sitting position as the question growled from wall to wall, an animal seeking prey. She revised that opinion the moment her gaze landed on the man who'd bellowed it. This was no beast but a fowl—a sharp-eyed falcon of a fellow with a beak nose. His pomaded hair was smoothed back like brownish-grey feathers, and she got the distinct impression she must move carefully around him, or he'd swoop against her.

And his talons would draw blood.

The woman next to him was just as dangerous, if the serrated stare she scraped over Ami and Mr. Price was any indication.

Ami clutched the vase in front of her like a shield. Behind the two, Barnaby tucked his tail and hastened away.

Mr. Price stabbed his finger at the overturned toolbox. "I'm afraid Miss Dalton and I took a tumble, my lord. As you can see, dangers abound."

Though it'd been but several breaths ago, already it felt like a lifetime since he'd broken her fall, caught her up in his arms, and shared laughter like a glass of sweet wine.

With a strong yet gentle grasp, he guided her to her feet, giving a steadying touch to the small of her back before facing the duo at the door. "While you are very welcome here, I am a little confused as to why you're at Price House, my lord. And why didn't my butler seat you in the drawing room?"

"There is no fault with your butler. I insisted he bring us to you while he arranged for refreshments." The man curled his fingers around his lapels, chest expanding. "I am afraid there is a matter of urgency that's come up that I wish to speak with you about. Of course, once Violet heard where I was going, she would not be put off."

Ami's gaze drifted to the perfectly coiffed blond as Mr. Price righted the pedestal—the last object between them and his guests. The woman—Violet, apparently—was too young to be Lord Bastion's wife. Then again, did age matter to a woman grasping for money? For no doubt she enjoyed a good shopping spree. Her emerald gown alone could finance an entire fieldwork project. The golden necklace and pearl earbobs would pay for travel costs to Egypt and back. There was an entitled air about her, as if the world owed her something, and though Ami really ought not judge so quickly, a seed of dislike took root deep in her gut.

Oh, how Father would scold her for not digging deeper before making assumptions.

Mr. Price tugged down the cuffs of his sleeves, rumpled from the fall. "Allow me to introduce you. Lord Bastion, Miss Woolsey, meet my resident scholar, Miss Dalton." He turned to her. "Miss Dalton, this is the Viscount Bastion and his daughter, Miss Violet Woolsey."

Still holding the vase, Ami bobbed a small curtsey. "Pleased to meet you, my lord, Miss Woolsey."

"What, may I ask, is a resident scholar?" Though the woman's tone was dulcet, there was a slight curl to her upper lip.

"I am an Egyptologist, Miss Woolsey." Ami lifted her chin. "Mr. Price has hired me to catalogue and value a recent shipment of artifacts he's acquired."

The viscount's falcon eyes narrowed on her. "But you are a woman."

Biting the inside of her cheek, she set the vase atop the pedestal.

"Miss Dalton is the daughter of the eminent Oxford professor Archer Dalton, hence she has a lifetime of learning from the very best." Mr. Price cut her a dashing smile. "I daresay her knowledge will one day surpass his."

"Egyptology. How quaint," Violet murmured.

Ami flattened her lips to keep from scowling. This sentiment was the exact reason she preferred dusty tomes and skeletons to the company of female society. Save for Polly, that is.

Lord Bastion sniffed. "If this professor is so proficient, then why did you not hire him?"

"He is in Egypt at the moment"—Mr. Price tipped the toolbox upright, tossing in the spilled gear as he spoke—"working at a dig."

"Speaking of working." Ami shoved a loose strand of hair behind her ear. "I should be getting back to mine. It was lovely to meet you, my lord, Miss Woolsey." She dipped her head respectfully, more than ready to be tucked away with a room full of silent relics that wouldn't judge her.

"Would you like to see what Miss Dalton is working on?" Mr. Price asked cheerfully. "It will take a moment for Barnaby to bring refreshments to the drawing room anyway."

Ami bit her lip.

Please say no. Please say no!

Violet snapped open a fan, giving her face a demure little puff of air. "I hope there aren't any mummies to view. Dreadful creatures. I don't see what the attraction is to such dirty old things."

Dirty old things! The woman could have no idea the treasures Mr. Price had beneath this roof. Ami flung back her shoulders. "There is a great deal more to Egyptology than mummies, Miss Woolsey. Mr. Price's acquisition is quite varied and extremely unique. There's not a mummy in the lot."

A relieved smile curved the woman's lips.

"Leastwise not that I've yet uncovered," Ami added, though she knew it was catty of her.

"It's settled, then. Off we go." Mr. Price strode to the door, and Lord Bastion fell into step beside him.

Leaving her to walk alongside Violet.

"So, Miss Dalton." The lady arched a brow at her. "How exactly did you and Mr. Price meet?"

And once again Ami felt his arms around her, protecting her against a nasty fall, taking the brunt of a spill . . . not that she'd breathe a word of that to this woman.

"At Oxford," she said nonchalantly.

"Ah yes, where your father is employed." Truthful words, but somehow Violet made it sound as if he were nothing more than a broom pusher. "I suppose if one must work, the halls of academia hold a certain dignity."

Ami focused on the broad shoulders of Mr. Price to keep from rolling her eyes. Definitely time to change the subject. "Did you travel a great distance to come here?"

"Oh no, we just popped up from London, though the train ride was tedious. First class was booked on the express, so we were forced on the intermediate and had to share the carriage with a matron and her young protégé. It was very tiring."

Hah! Rescuing that ushabti doll in the cemetery a couple of weeks ago had surely been more harrowing than a velvet-cushioned train ride. "Sounds grueling," she muttered.

"Just so." Violet eyed her as they entered the corridor to the workroom. "How long will you be staying here, Miss Dalton?"

"Until I've finished valuing the cargo, September at the latest." Just the voicing of it stirred a melancholy she'd been trying to ignore. Once she was finished, she'd likely never again see Mr. Price.

"I suppose your attendant is anxious to return to your home. I know my maid isn't fond of assisting me in a different house, even one as magnificent as this." She gestured toward the gilt-framed portraits lining the corridor. "Servants can be so territorial, you know."

Actually, no. She didn't have the slightest idea and was glad for it. How stifling it would be to have a maid hanging about all the time, not to mention what a damper it would be to her brokering activities.

She smiled at Violet. "I don't have an attendant, Miss Woolsey."

Musical laughter bubbled out of the woman. "Surely you're not staying unchaperoned beneath the roof of the most eligible bachelor in all of Oxford?"

"I am perfectly capable of taking care of myself, and I assure you Mr. Price is a perfect gentleman."

"Indeed." Violet's brow puckered, then just as quickly smoothed. "But you are correct. My Edmund is a man of integrity. You must think nothing of my silly meanderings, Miss Dalton, for we shall be boon companions, shall we not?"

My Edmund?

Best of friends?

"Em . . ." Words snarled into a ball in her throat. What was she to say to any of that?

Thankfully she needn't say anything, for they had finally arrived at the workroom. She immediately escorted Miss Woolsey to the display table, happy to stand on familiar ground. "Here is what has been uncovered thus far. As you can see, there are yet many more crates to go. It is quite an extensive collection."

Without so much as a by-your-leave, Violet swiped up an intricately carved amulet. Her lips pursed into a pretty pout as her gaze swept over the shine of the gold and inlaid gems. "What is this?"

Ever so carefully, Ami retrieved the valuable relic from the lady's hand, lamenting that neither of them wore gloves to handle such a precious item. "That is the only remaining scarab from the tomb of Seti."

"The gems are beautiful, but other than that, it is frightfully ugly."

"Every object has its own story, Miss Woolsey." She lightly set down the amulet. "That scarab is a symbol of rebirth, so I prefer to think of it as a hopeful promise. Beauty is in the eye and heart of the beholder, is it not? Take, for example, your necklace."

Frowning slightly, Violet patted her fingertips against the golden cross nestled against her bosom. "Surely you cannot argue its beauty?"

"I wouldn't dream of it, for it is lovely. I see the crucifix as a representation of a holy God who came down to rescue those who reviled Him. It's an icon of redemption, one I hold very dear. But other cultures wouldn't see that. To some, you are wearing an instrument of death around your neck, which they would consider 'frightfully ugly,' as you put it."

Violet dropped her hand, a soft intake of air hissing through her teeth. "You are very blunt, Miss Dalton."

Ami grinned. "I shall take that as a compliment, Miss Woolsey."

"While I am happy to see you ladies are getting on well," Mr. Price said as he and Lord Bastion joined them, "I suspect my guests should like some refreshment now, Miss Dalton. We shall take our leave and see you at dinner tonight."

Ami stiffened. Chatting with Violet for the past ten minutes had been taxing enough. "Oh, but Mr. Price, now that you have illustrious guests to dine with you, I hardly think you'll require my company at mealtimes."

"On the contrary, Miss Dalton." His gaze found hers—and

held. "Your knowledge of Egyptian artifacts makes for interesting table conversation."

Violet edged closer to him, her pert little nose lifting slightly. "Until later then, Miss Dalton."

As soon as they exited, Ami grumbled beneath her breath. She'd rather be buried in a tomb with live scarabs than sit through tonight's dinner with her new boon companion.

12

Old books. Worn leather. The last orange light of day seeping through the windowpanes. Edmund always loved this particular hour to visit Price House's library.

But not this evening.

He retrieved the humidor and held it out to the viscount. Truth be told, he'd been on edge ever since the Woolseys arrived. Could be because he had yet to find out what Bastion wished to discuss, but more likely the tightness in his neck was because of the possessiveness of a certain brown-eyed blond who assumed she already owned him. Not to mention her veiled rudeness toward Miss Dalton. In hindsight, his decision not to marry Violet had been spot-on. And then there was the matter of Gil. Would the man behave himself during their visit? It could prove to be very awkward indeed to try to manage the fellow. If Gil were any regular employee, he'd terminate him on the spot, but there was nothing regular about him. In addition to their friendship, his reputation in the business world was stellar, not to mention his knack for brokering lucrative deals.

The rich scent of tobacco filled the air as the viscount chose a cigar. "I suppose you'd like to know what my urgent business is, eh, Price?"

"The thought has crossed my mind." More like the thought was stuck in a deeply ground wagon rut. He closed the lid without taking one of Cuba's finest.

Bastion ran his fat cigar beneath his nose, sniffing it from end to end. "Your patience will serve you well in Parliament."

Pleasure warmed his gut as he took a seat across from the man, leather squeaking. "I like to think my background in business will also be a virtue."

"Mmm," Bastion rumbled.

Edmund sank back in his chair, waiting the man out as the viscount clipped the end of his cigar onto a small tray on the side table. Then he waited some more as the man lit the thing, cheeks sinking with each puff.

At length, the viscount finally quit fussing with his smoke and eyed him. "The thing is, Price . . ."

The unfinished sentence dangled in the air as he took a few more draws.

Sweet, blessed mercy! They'd be called in for dinner before anything was said. He wished now he had taken a cigar just to have something to do with his hands.

Bastion blew out a cloud of smoke. "I have it on good authority that William Mallory is going to resign next week. Apparently he's battling a dire health issue."

"I wish him well, of course, but what has that to do with . . . Ah, an unexpected opening for the Oxford seat, eh?"

"One that will move the election much sooner than you or I expected." Bastion rolled his cigar between his fingers. "It's an opportunity we must mount and ride hard."

His pulse took off at a run. If he could get elected and roll back that tariff due out by the end of next month, then Sanjay wouldn't need the money from the Egyptian cargo, nor would countless other men in the same situation be facing business failure. "When?"

"Mid-September."

"A little more than a month away," he murmured, calculating the odds. It would be a stretch—an all-out contortion, really—but with God's help it could be done.

"And that is exactly why I've come. We must move quickly." Bastion set his cigar on the ashtray and leaned forward. "While I am here, we must craft your campaign platform. I've taken the liberty to jot down a few ideas." He produced a paper from his pocket.

Edmund glanced over the list, struggling to make sense of the words. While it would take some time to comprehend the whole document, with some pointed concentration, a few items sank in. Investment in infrastructure to facilitate commerce he could get behind. He also agreed with funding institutional initiatives for education reform. But the third point instantly raised his hackles. Imperialism was a rabid dog as far as he was concerned, one an Englishman would do well to avoid.

He set the paper on the tea table between them. "Tell me more about this acquisition of territories. Surely the people of Oxfordshire don't have a keen interest in overseas conquest."

"Any good conservative does. It is our duty to expand our colonial landholdings in order to end lawlessness in other lands. Why, it's our duty as Christians, is it not?"

"I respectfully disagree, my lord." Edmund held up a finger, warding the man off. "I understand the importance of maintaining peace beyond our borders. Still, I believe acquiring territories through force is not the way to achieve that peace. It is better to respect the sovereignty of other nations, to work with them in cooperation and mutual benefit instead of wielding the mighty arm of the British military. Has history not shown such conquests come at great cost, both in human lives and resources? No, imperialism can lead to nothing but conflict and resentment."

The viscount picked up his cigar and took a long draw, blowing out a stream of smoke like a dragon. "I didn't realize you held such a liberal view, Price."

He stiffened. He'd played the wrong card—and this was too

important of a game to lose. He curved his lips into what he hoped was an easy smile. "I prefer to think of it as a personal view, but let us not dwell on our differences, my lord. Our common goal is to better the lives of the people of Oxfordshire, is it not? It is imperative we work together toward achieving such a purpose. And in light of that . . ." He swiped up his glass of lemon water and held it aloft. "Here's to a successful campaign."

Bastion hesitated a moment before grabbing his tumbler of brandy, not particularly enthusiastic, but neither did it seem he'd take any more issue with Edmund's stance on imperialism.

"Hear, hear." The viscount tossed back his drink, then set his glass on the table. "Now then, it will take some doing on such short notice, but I shall arrange a house party as soon as possible, inviting men who will be key in helping you get elected. Attendance could be sparse, considering it is summer recess. Nevertheless, it's important to get your face in front of England's powerhouses to gain their endorsements. While it's true you are the darling of Englishwomen, these men won't care about your handsome face. What they fancy is what you can do for them and the country, and your ties to mighty moguls—such as me. That's why it's crucial we pin down your message and a plan to execute it. Are you up for the challenge, Price?"

"Without doubt."

"Good." Bastion inhaled one last drag on his cigar, then ground it out. "The only other matter remaining is an engagement announcement for you and Violet."

Edmund's heart jumped to his throat. The mere thought of marrying Violet Woolsey made him choke. When the idea had first come up in the telegram, he hadn't seriously considered wedding the woman, but neither had he had such a visceral reaction as this. Miss Woolsey was a fine enough woman as women went, yet not one with whom he wished to share his life. But he couldn't very well tell that to the viscount, or his run for Parliament would be over before it began. He needed Bastion's title to get elected, and the viscount needed Price money for his land-rich, cash-poor coffers.

"Yes, about that . . ." Grabbing his water, he sipped it slowly, stalling for time, then set the glass carefully on the table. "Perhaps, my lord, it would be better to delay any thought of marriage until after the election. Wait to see how things develop." And in the meantime, hopefully Violet's head would be turned by a different man.

Bastion chuckled. "In this instance, your patience is a detriment. I'm afraid my Violet has her heart set upon a Christmas wedding. The sooner the engagement is announced, the sooner preparations can be made. It's not every day my only daughter weds, and I intend to make it a spectacular event."

Edmund sucked in a breath. He wouldn't allow himself to be forced into an engagement he didn't want, yet he couldn't risk offending the viscount either—and if he spoke what was on his mind, he'd never make it to the House of Commons.

He ran his hand along the arm of the chair. Now was as good a time as any to practice diplomacy. "Naturally I understand you love your daughter a great deal. But I would not wish my campaign to overshadow such an event. I think it is in Violet's best interest if we do not pursue the matter."

"Cold feet, eh?" Bastion arched a brow. "To be expected, I suppose. You've been a bachelor a long time."

Guilt punched him square in the gut. It felt wrong to lead the man on like this, pretending he'd consider Violet at some nebulous date in the future when in reality he wanted nothing more than to be left alone. Diplomacy be hanged! If he lost his chance for the viscount's sponsorship, then so be it. He still had the Egyptian cargo to sell, which would be enough to get Sanjay and his family by for a while until he could figure out a different way to stop that tariff.

He rose to refill his glass. Better to say what he must without making eye contact and enflame the man all the more. "Lord Bastion, I think you should know I cannot agree to mar—"

"Dinner is ready." Barnaby ducked his head through the doorway.

"Look at that! We're worse than two nattering hens." Slapping his thighs, the viscount stood. "Shall we?"

Edmund sighed. His butler's timing couldn't have been worse. Even so, he forced a pleasant tone to his voice. "Yes, let's."

As they strode to the dining room, his mind raced as to how to handle the situation. He couldn't keep avoiding the marriage issue forever. He'd have to say something . . . but did he really need to say it before the election? Or at least before Bastion's proposed dinner party? That event would be the perfect opportunity to rub shoulders with potential supporters and advance his campaign, enough that he wouldn't need Bastion's backing. If he could just bide his time until the Woolseys left tomorrow, perhaps he'd find a way to navigate through this mess. But for now, he had the gut-churning feeling this was going to be a long evening.

A very long one indeed.

It was to be a duel, then. That much was clear. The crustacean crouching on Ami's plate taunted her as ruthlessly as Violet's veiled comments had throughout the first and second courses.

"What a quaint gown, Miss Dalton."

"I don't believe I've ever seen such a unique hairstyle."

"My maid has a wonderful cream to hide blemishes. I'll have her drop some off at your room, and you can try it on your nose."

Condescension with a smile was the worst—and Violet was a master of the game. Ami dabbed her nose with her serviette, supremely self-aware of her freckles, her hair, her gown. And if that wasn't bad enough, now she must navigate how to eat a lobster while avoiding the horrid, sliced lemon guarding the thing.

While Violet was busy chatting with her father, Ami retrieved a silver pick at the side of her plate and poked at the shellfish.

Which got her absolutely nowhere. If only this were an ancient vase fragment with a bit of dried mud, she'd know exactly what to do.

Across the table, Mr. Price caught her eye, and her cheeks instantly heated. He'd noticed her ineptness. She could take Violet's barbs, but if he were to mock her—especially in front of the Woolseys—that would sting.

Yet there wasn't a hint of mockery in his regard. No pity. No scorn. Instead, there was something more, something . . . Her breath caught. The same spark lit his eyes that illuminated her father's when he wished to teach her about a new procedure in cleaning relics.

Mr. Price's gaze shifted pointedly to her hands, then back to her face. One brow lifted as, with an exaggerated movement, he picked up his lobster and twisted off a claw.

She mimicked.

He smiled—then twisted off the other claw and set the thing back down.

She did the same, her pulse quickening as he guided her through each step. Without a single word, he showed her how to extract the fine, white meat. Almost like a dance. His dusky blue eyes encouraging her every move, guiding her deftly, making her feel cared for in a way that went deep and took root.

And when his lips parted to take a slow bite, his gaze fixed on hers, she nearly swooned. What would it feel like to have that mouth pressed against hers?

Great heavens!

She set down her fork, stunned by the forbidden thought and even more so by a sudden realization. She was falling for this man. Hard. Fast. All because of a silly, wonderful lobster. Which of course was absurd. The most eligible bachelor in all of Oxford couldn't seriously be interested in her.

Could he?

"Don't you agree, Miss Dalton?"

Violet's voice pulled her from her musings, and she faced

the woman seated across the table. "I beg your pardon, Miss Woolsey. You were saying?"

Violet scanned from her to Mr. Price, then back again. A tight smile followed. "I asked if you think my Edmund will make a fine member of Parliament, assuming, of course, he wins the special election . . . which I have no doubt he will."

Again with *her Edmund*? Was there something between them?

"What's this?" Next to Ami, Mr. Fletcher cocked his head at Mr. Price. "Running for office, are you, old man?"

Mr. Price's brow creased. "Yes, I told you that in my last correspondence."

"Ah, well, you know, ha-ha!" He fluttered his fingers in the air. "So many plates to spin and all."

What an odd business relationship. Despite Mr. Price's assurance Mr. Fletcher was a good businessman, it was Mr. Price who seemed far more competent. Not that it was any of her concern, though. She smiled at Mr. Price. "Congratulations! I would vote for you."

Seated between Violet and Mr. Price, Lord Bastion snorted a disgusted puff of air. "Thank heaven you cannot, Miss Dalton. Women are far too emotional to make informed decisions at the ballot box. You would do well to take example from my daughter, who aspires to marriage, family, and minding her own home—which is where women belong. Isn't that right, Violet?"

"I am sure you know what is best, Father." Violet's pert little nose wrinkled, belying her words. Perhaps there was more to this pampered princess than Ami had credited.

Ami set down her fork, unwilling to drop the topic so easily. "I respectfully disagree, my lord. Some women can and do choose to keep a home, as is their choice. Others, however, feel called to a different vocation. Regardless, women are just as capable of making political decisions as men."

A smile twitched Mr. Price's lips. "Miss Dalton raises a good point, my lord. She and your daughter are fully capable of knowing their own minds. Furthermore, as citizens of the realm, they have a vested interest in the laws that govern their lives, and inasmuch, ought to have a say in who represents them."

Warmth flared in her chest at his thoughtful defense.

Lord Bastion went red in the face. "Do not tell me that if elected to office you will pursue the absurd notion of women's suffrage. It is a dangerous ideal that will lead to the instability of Britain's moral fiber."

Her warmth flared into hot fire. Sentiment such as this was the very reason she struggled so hard to be a recognized Egyptologist!

Even so, she smiled. If she could face brigands selling stolen goods in a dark alley, she could certainly take on this pompous politician. "And yet, my lord, is it not a moral obligation to allow those being governed a chance to participate in the democratic process? I fail to see how ensuring everyone's voice is heard will lead to instability."

"It is that exact failure to understand of which I speak." His sharp eyes homed in on her, a predator bent on shaking the life from his prey. "The fairer sex does not have the intellectual capacity to understand politics. Why, if women start voting, who knows what sort of chaos will ensue?"

"Nothing compared to the sort of chaos in a room full of cutthroat smugglers and opium eaters," Mr. Fletcher said under his breath.

Ami silently pushed away her plate, her stomach rebelling at the rich food and the viscount's snobbish remarks.

"I find no lack in Miss Dalton's intelligence." Mr. Price's gaze sought hers, and though he'd spoken for the room, his defense was somehow far more intimate.

Once again her pulse raced. Must he always have that effect upon her?

Violet cleared her throat, eyes narrowed on Mr. Price.

"Of course, Miss Woolsey"—he dipped his head toward the woman—"neither do I find lack in you."

"To the women, then!" Mr. Fletcher raised his glass.

Mr. Price lifted his as well. "Indeed. To the ladies."

Though he used the plural, Ami got the distinct impression his toast was for her.

Lord Bastion was slow to reach for his goblet, but to his credit, he did—though he purposely avoided eye contact with her.

Once they drank, Barnaby signaled for plate removal, easing some of the tension in her shoulders. Five minutes more. Just five. She could do this.

Several footmen appeared, placing silver dishes of raspberry sorbet in front of each diner. My, how things had changed in only a couple of weeks' time when Barnaby himself had waited upon her and Mr. Price. Had Mr. Price hired these servants only today with the arrival of the Woolseys, or did he have a secret cache of them on standby waiting for occasions such as this? The workings of a fine manor home were more mysterious than the hieroglyphics on a stone tablet.

Violet took a demure little nibble of her frozen dessert. "Will you play for us tonight, Miss Dalton?"

Ami blinked. Play what? The piano? She didn't know her right hand from her left. Cards? The only two games she knew how to play were senet and hounds and jackals. Or did this society lady wish to engage in a rousing round of charades? Whatever it might be, she'd had more than enough of Violet and her father's company for one evening.

Picking up her spoon, she forced a polite smile. "I am afraid I cannot join you after dinner. I have a few notes in the workroom I need to finish before I retire."

"Pity." A feline smile curved her lips. "Well, perhaps tomorrow evening, then."

"Tomorrow?" Mr. Price angled his head. "I thought you and your father would be taking the morning train."

"Heavens no. I packed enough gowns for at least a week."

Lord Bastion laid his wadded serviette on the table. "That's right, Price. Your platform must be nailed tight, remember?"

Whether he remembered or not was hard to say. Actually, it was hard to read any of Mr. Price's thoughts as he schooled his face.

Mr. Fletcher leaned close to Ami, the sour reek of wine on his breath. "Would you like some help with gathering those notes, Miss Dalton?"

"I am sure I can manage on my own, Mr. Fletcher." She dug into her sorbet, hoping he'd not press the issue.

"No doubt you can. I don't have a mind for such historical gibberish. What I meant was I wish to help you tidy up the room. Mr. Kane from the *Oxford Journal* is set to arrive in the morning. We must show him the collection in the best possible light in order to stir up interest, must we not?"

"We already have a potential buyer." Though Mr. Fletcher seemed oblivious, Ami didn't miss the tightness in Mr. Price's tone. "And I thought I made it clear I was not interested in press coverage at the moment."

"Indeed, you did."

"Then why invite the man?"

"Because as your partner, I *am* interested."

Lord Bastion tapped his finger on the table. "Journalist, you say? Now, that's something we can use to our advantage. Imagine the publicity for your campaign, Price, if you were seen as a man not only of wealth and stature but of culture, one who takes keen interest in preserving ancient artifacts. It could sway the hearts and minds of the voting public."

Leave it to the viscount to exploit cultural valuables for the sake of politics. Ami pushed back her chair before she dove headfirst into waters that were sure to be murky. "And on that note, gentlemen, Miss Woolsey, I bid you all a good evening."

The men rose, wishing her the same. Violet merely gave a nod as if she were the Queen herself bestowing her dismissal— and more than happy to have Mr. Price to herself for the rest of the night.

Ami strode away, conflicted thoughts crowding her mind. The dynamics between Mr. Price and Violet puzzled her. It surely seemed a strange tension tethered them together, making it difficult to decipher their true relationship. Clearly Violet believed Mr. Price belonged to her in some way. Yet Mr. Price's demeanor—while courteous—lacked the ardor one would expect from a devoted lover.

Bosh. What did she know? The realm of emotions and romantic entanglements had always baffled her, which in a sense, made it all the more desirable to escape into the tangible world of artifacts, where the age and value of an object could be precisely determined.

She swept into the workroom, then immediately wheeled about, facing the very statue she'd just passed. The enormous carving of Anubis now stood with its jackal snout to the wall. This was *not* to be borne! That figure was far too valuable to be used as a pawn for such antics.

Spinning about, she grabbed her notes off the table and shook the handful of papers in the air, shouting at whoever might be lurking in the shadows. "If you're trying to frighten me, it isn't working. Do you hear me? You're wasting your time, so stop it. The curse of Amentuk isn't real!"

She scanned the room from corner to corner, alert for movement of any sort . . . but there was none. Bah. What was she thinking? Whoever had moved the relic had clearly done the deed and departed. She'd have to hunt down Barnaby and question him once more, let him know this wasn't a laughing matter, especially if that statue were to topple and break. Heaving a sigh, she turned to leave, but as she did so, the hair at the nape of her neck prickled like sharp wires. No one was in the room. She was sure of it.

But that didn't account for the whisper of a sinister laugh at her back.

13

Ekonahmic. No, that couldn't be correct. Slashing a line through the word, Edmund redipped his pen and tried again. *Ecenamik*. He picked up the page and studied the letters—which looked as if a schoolboy had written them. Crushing the paper into a tight ball, he tossed it onto the ever-growing pile at the base of his desk, then glanced at the clock, thoroughly defeated. Nearly midnight and he had yet to compose a suitable outline to present to Lord Bastion tomorrow, one that promoted economic reform instead of imperialism.

Sighing, he planted his elbows on the desktop and scrubbed his face. Usually, he could count on Gil for drafting documents he required, but despite Gil's assurance he'd lay off the libations, the man had still managed to partake overmuch of the after-dinner sherry. He'd have to speak to Barnaby about locking up the spirits. No doubt Gil was even now gape-mouthed snoring in his bed from such excess. Despite his friend's tale of lovelorn woe, if he kept up his uncouth behaviour, Edmund would have no choice but to dissolve their business relationship for he couldn't socially afford such a connection. And yet . . . he toyed with the pen, uneasy about ending his long relationship with Gil. The man had been his right arm the entire time he'd been abroad, a more than astute businessman, and he did owe Gil for saving him from financial ruin all those years ago. Had the matter with that woman—Charlotte, was it?—so mangled the man's personality?

He dropped his hands. He knew too well the changes a duplicitous woman could wreak.

Shooting to his feet, he paced, frustrated with Gil, annoyed with his own limitations, and still a little bit irked at the way Violet had treated Miss Dalton during dinner. Catty woman. But irritated or not, he smiled as he recalled that dinner. The pert little Egyptologist had been far too proud to ask for help with eating her lobster, yet she'd followed his every lead, relied on him. Trusted him. A silent testament to the unspoken understanding that seemed to be growing between them—and there was no doubt in his mind there *was* something growing, a bond, one that filled him with an inordinate amount of pleasure. Throughout the entire meal his parents' distant exchanges had echoed in his mind. Were their cool looks truly the pinnacle of marital connection, or was there a depth that had been missing in their relationship he had yet to grasp?

He stole another glance at the mantel clock, feeling the pressure of getting the outline finished. Though he hated to admit it, he needed help. Jameson would be fast asleep by now. Barnaby couldn't write two words without speaking twenty between. Hmm. Would Miss Dalton be in the workroom at this hour? She'd said she had paperwork to finish tonight. Might she be willing to help him with his outline? A pretty big if, but better than coming up with another abysmal spelling of *economic* . . . though he would have to be crafty in how he worded his plea for assistance.

Doubling back to the desk, he grabbed the notepad and strode from the room. At this time of night, only dim light glowed from the wall sconces. Some might consider it romantic. Others ghostly. Either would work for a poem, but a political summary was far removed from rhymes and meters.

The thought caused his step to hitch. Was politics truly the path he ought to be following?

He crossed the great hall at a good clip, pushing away the question. This wasn't about him. It was about Sanjay and the others he could help by influencing economic policy.

As he swung into the corridor leading to the workroom, he spied a swath of golden light pouring out the door. Good. She was hard at work. Once this lot sold and Sanjay was taken care of, he'd see that she received extra payment for being so diligent.

"Miss Dalton, I—"

"Oh!" She slapped a hand to her chest, gasping.

"I beg your pardon. I didn't mean to startle you." He pulled a chair beside her, alarmed to note the paleness of her skin. Odd that this plucky woman would suffer such a fright from a mere casual entrance. He peered at her closely. "Are you all right?"

She pasted on a brave smile yet fidgeted with her pen. "Never better, now that I know it's only you in the room with me."

"Who else would be here?"

"Exactly what I'd like to know."

He narrowed his eyes. "A puzzling response. Care to expand?"

She nibbled her lower lip, scanning the room, yet she said nothing.

"Miss Dalton?"

She snapped her gaze back to him. "Oh, don't mind me. One too many hieroglyphics swimming about in here." She tapped the side of her forehead. "But what are you doing up at this late hour?"

"Looking for you. I was hoping you might help me with something."

"How can I be of service?"

He pushed the notepad across the tabletop toward her. "I realize you're busy with notating your own work, but I wondered if you'd like a break from detailing pottery shards and amulets to take dictation from me."

"You wish me to play secretary"—she shot a pointed look

at the wall clock, then arched a brow his way—"at this time of night?"

"If you wouldn't mind. I have a meeting with the viscount tomorrow and won't sleep a wink if I don't capture my thoughts on paper."

She studied him for a long moment. "Why not simply write them yourself?"

He shoved back his chair, uneasy with that all-seeing gaze of hers. He couldn't answer such a question. Not honestly, at any rate. Yet neither would he lie. So how to skate on the thin ice of grey without breaking through to black or white? She'd made it very clear she despised deception—as did he—but the last time he'd confessed his shortcoming to a woman, he'd been humiliated.

"I, em . . ." He strolled a few paces, thinking hard, then doubled back. "Well, to be frank, I find it easier to think aloud and allow someone else to capture my words, else I am prone to losing my train of thought."

"And you don't mind sharing those thoughts with me?"

Ah, but he'd share far more than that with her if he could.

He cleared his throat, banishing the rogue desire. "You've proven yourself a woman of integrity. I highly doubt you'll leak my political platform to the press tomorrow."

"I wouldn't, but even so, I ought not be privy to such confidential information. Are you sure you wouldn't rather write this yourself?"

"Completely certain."

She dipped her pen into the ink and held it poised above the paper. "Then let us begin."

Relief eased some of the tension in his shoulders but not all.

He still felt like a cad for not being completely honest with her.

Brudge whumped to the ground flat on his back, gasping for air like a landed halibut. Why must manor homes such as Price

House always be guarded by the requisite stone wall? Was it some sort of code amongst the wealthy? A status symbol? Or was it just a way to annoy honest thieves like himself?

After a few more breaths, he staggered to his feet. Oof. He was getting way too old for such rough-and-tumble jobs like this one. If Scupper were here, the tall oaf could've caught him, or at least broken his fall. But that whiner still moaned like a nursling in nappies about his sore teeth. Big baby. At this rate, they'd never get their hands on that statue.

Unless he was successful tonight.

Brudge gave his aching hip a good rubdown, then set off on a zigzag route from trunk to trunk. A crescent moon lent hardly any light, yet the clear sky and stars were bright enough. The closer he drew to the house, the more chance he could be seen if anyone happened to look out the window. Unlikely, though. Not at this late hour. It had to be well past midnight by now. He advanced.

Then paused. Ahead, a shadowy figure exited a side door of the house. Thunderation!

Like a startled squirrel, Brudge darted back to the safety of the previous oak tree, then carefully peered around the side of it. Sure enough, a man clutched a small parcel in one arm and . . . what was this? The fellow swiveled his head as he kept to the shadows—the very same move he employed when toeing about where he ought not be. Was one of the servants pinching the silver, then? Or—no! If that scoundrel was nipping off with his statue, he'd tackle the fiend and take what was rightfully his. After all, he'd spied that winged hunk of gold first!

Brudge squinted as the man followed the length of the house, picking his way toward the front drive. The canvas bundle in the crook of his arm didn't appear to be overlarge or too heavy. Brudge eased out a low breath. Not his piece.

With a last look over his shoulder, the man disappeared around the corner. Brudge gave him a moment or two out of professional courtesy before sidestepping the tree trunk. It never paid to shoehorn one's way too quickly into an active scene of another man's labour. No doubt Scupper had some sort of annoyingly pithy words about just such a thing.

He'd nearly made it to the next oak when he stopped and listened with his whole body. Something had snagged his attention. Something small but ominous. The swing of a gate? Sure did sound like the squeak of hinges. To be on the safe side, he doubled back to the previous tree, then the baying of hounds cut through the air.

Blast!

He sprinted, bunion screaming as he tore back to the stone wall. A straight shot this time. No need for stealth. He could practically feel the hot breath of the dogs at his back.

He lunged, scrambling for purchase, just as teeth sank into his ankle.

Double blast!

With a howl of his own, he kicked the beast in the head, barely freeing his leg before another set of snappers flashed in the night.

"You there!" a deep voice bellowed. "Stop!"

Brudge threw his arm over the top of the wall, hefting his body upward, leaving behind the bared teeth and vicious growls. With a great burst of strength, he flung his good leg over. One more breath and he'd be over the side and running for his horse.

A shot rang out.

Searing pain ripped across his thigh.

14

A good journalist could make a pile of manure into a bag of diamonds. A bad one, turn a saint into a sinner. Edmund hadn't decided which category he ought to file Mr. Kane under—good, bad, saint, or manure—but one thing he knew, he didn't like the fellow, mostly because he stood far too close to Miss Dalton. Or could be that the man smelled like a sardine tin. Probably both. And judging by the sour turn of Gil's lips, his business partner wasn't enamored with the journalist either, which was a bit ironic since he was the one who'd invited Kane here in the first place.

Pencil poised, Mr. Kane licked his lips, a habit he'd already engaged in countless times since he arrived. Judging by the chapped skin ringing his mouth, it was more a nervous tic than anything. "Miss Dalton, this love affair of yours with Egypt, how exactly did it begin? Remember, no detail is too small."

She offered him a tight smile as she set down the long-necked figurine she'd been showing him. "I appreciate your interest in my profession, Mr. Kane, but I hardly think Mr. Fletcher invited you here to take notes on me."

"Indeed, sir," Gil spoke before the man could respond. "While admittedly Miss Dalton is lovely to behold, just look at the great cache of beauties around you, in particular, this griffin." He swept his hand toward the golden statuette. "Did you know—"

"Yes, yes. We will get to that." Kane didn't so much as glance at the griffin, just sidled a step closer to Miss Dalton.

If he dared draw any nearer, Edmund would frog-march the man out to the drive.

"Tell me, Miss Dalton." Kane's tongue flicked out like a grass snake's. "As a woman in a man's world, what do you find most challenging?"

Edmund opened his mouth to redirect that line of questioning, then just as quickly pressed his lips tight. How would she answer such a query?

"That's easy." She tucked her ever-loosened hair behind one ear, not caring a whit that more oft than not, her appearance was that of an absent-minded professor. "My biggest trial is recognition. Even you questioned my title when Mr. Price first introduced us."

"Mr. Price, that's right. How could I have forgotten!" Kane's dark button eyes fixed on him. "Rumours abound as to why you left the country all those years ago. Most involve a woman. A Miss Louisa Allen, if I have my facts straight. Do I?"

The mere mention of her name made his jaw clench. "With all due respect, Mr. Kane, you are here to discuss Egyptian artifacts, not my personal history."

"Ha-ha! That's right." Gil guffawed. "Now, about this griffin here, have I got a tale for—"

"Personal insights are what make a story stand out in a reader's mind." The journalist flourished his pencil in the air. "Add in a dash of romance—such as an attractive female Egyptologist and one of the most sought-after bachelors in Oxford, housing together beneath the same roof—and voilà! A headline that'll drive sales to the sky."

If he clenched his jaw any tighter, his teeth would crack. This was exactly the sort of publicity he'd been hoping to avoid. "The only sale I am interested in is for this load of relics, which has nothing to do with either me or Miss Dalton."

"Now, there you are mistaken, sir. The more compelling the narrative, the more interest in your artifacts. The public will gobble up the story of how you left the country because of a lady and have now returned for a fresh start with a new woman, especially one so . . . novel. Do tell." This time he licked the tip of his pencil, then set it to paper, fingers poised to write. "How long have you two been in a relationship?"

The blush of a summer sunset lit fire on Miss Dalton's cheeks. "Mr. Price and I are not—"

Gil held up a finger. "About this griffin—"

"Stop right there, Mr. Kane." Edmund cut them both off. "Miss Dalton and I hold to a strictly professional relationship, nothing more."

"Perhaps." He hissed the *s* like the snake he was. "But once word of this arrangement leaks out, you can be sure another newspaper will sensationalize the situation. By giving me leave to write a wholesome yet intriguing account, not only will you endear the masses to you and Miss Dalton, you'll also be sure to attract potential buyers for your cargo in droves."

Edmund gripped the edge of the table to keep from throttling the man. Of all the oblique threats! Narrowing his eyes, he stared down the journalist, the sudden tension in the room thick enough to choke an elephant.

"Allow me to make myself abundantly clear, Kane." He used his deal-gone-bad tone, gunmetal hard and deadly low. Not only would a fake scandal damage his run for office, it would undoubtedly harm Ami. "Your purpose here is to present these artifacts in their historical and cultural context, not to gain blathering fodder to further your career or increase the *Journal*'s circulation. If you dare exploit Miss Dalton's reputation or tarnish the integrity of her work, I will not hesitate to take drastic measures."

Unease flickered across the journalist's face, his tongue darting in and out with a mind of its own.

"So"—Edmund leaned closer, driving home his point—"I suggest you tread carefully, sir. Mine is not a warning to take lightly. You may think you hold the power of the pen, but I assure you, I have means of my own. Stick to the story you were invited here to obtain, nothing more."

The words swung in the air like a noose in the wind. Miss Dalton stared wide-eyed. Gil smirked, his moustache twitching.

Red crawled up Mr. Kane's neck as he retreated a step. "I did not mean to offend, Mr. Price."

"Ha-ha!" Gil clapped his hands. "I'm sure you didn't. Now then, behold the golden griffin, Mr. Kane." He tugged the man to his side. "Trust me when I say you'll find nothing more sensational than the curse of Amentuk, and this is the very artifact that houses such a dark evil. Already this wicked little beast has broken a man's leg, sent a maid into hysterics, tripped me up on the stairs, and see that statue over there?" Clapping an arm around Kane's shoulder, he nudged the man to face the imposing Anubis standing guard at the door.

"Don't tell me that one is cursed too?"

"Not that I know of, and yet it mysteriously moves in increments each day. But here's the real kicker—it is far too heavy for a man to move alone."

Pulling away from Gil, the journalist turned back to examine the griffin. "Can you verify Mr. Fletcher's claims, Miss Dalton?"

"These things have happened, and there is a legend attached to the griffin." She frowned like a displeased school matron. "But I highly doubt they are related."

"Of course they are." Gil aimed his finger at her. "You're the one who told me the story in the first place."

"Of the curse, yes, but I don't recall speaking of the workman's broken leg or the movement of Anubis." Her brow arched at Edmund.

He gave a slight shake of his head. He'd not been the one to inform the man. Had Barnaby? "How did you know that information, Gil?"

"Servants talk." He shrugged. "But that's neither here nor there. The thing is, Kane, that whoever purchases this lot will no doubt have an exciting time in store for them."

"Or a dangerous one." Mr. Kane straightened, then flipped to a clean page in his notebook. "Tell me the details of this curse, then."

Gil rubbed his hands together. "It is quite the juicy tale. You see—"

A light touch to Edmund's sleeve pulled him away from Gil's story.

Miss Dalton peered up at him, whispering for his ears alone, "Might I have a word with you, Mr. Price?"

He glanced at the men, Gil animatedly serving up all the sordid morsels he knew—and no doubt sprinkling in even more imaginative tidbits—while Kane's pencil danced across his page with loud scratches. With both of them so engrossed, Edmund guided Ami aside. "My apologies for Mr. Kane's insinuation about us. When I hired you as a professional, I didn't think your reputation would be tarnished. Apparently I was wrong."

She clicked her tongue. "The only reputation I seek to protect is my Egyptologist status, which you very nicely defended." Her eyes narrowed. "In fact, I've never met anyone so keen for such validation on my account. Why is that?"

"Let's just say I understand how difficult it is to be recognized as proficient without acceptable credentials." Hah! What an understatement. Had it not been for the family name, he'd not be where he was now, though it was that very name he hoped to infuse with integrity instead of the often-unscrupulous dealings of his father.

Her nose scrunched, freckles bobbing. "What would a successful businessman know of that?"

"The answer may surprise you." He held up a finger, warding her off. "But now is not the time. What did you wish to tell me?"

Curiosity gleamed golden in those changeable eyes of hers, yet to her credit, she didn't pry—an urge Violet Woolsey would not have been able to conquer.

"I know you've got your hands full with houseguests and whatnot." She tipped her head discreetly toward Gil and Kane. "But I think you should know about something. When I came in this morning, I noticed a dusting of wood shavings on the floor near one of the unopened crates. Upon further examination, it appears as if the lid had been pried off, then reattached. Granted, that might've happened before shipping, but with the extra shavings on the ground, it is suspect."

"Is something missing from the crate?"

"I cannot say for certain as I hadn't had the chance yet to account for the contents inside it."

He scrubbed his jaw. Earlier this morning Jameson had told him of a breach in security. One of the hired guns had shot at a fellow last evening. Could that somehow be related to this? "May I see the crate?"

"Of course." She led him to one of the large boxes.

Sure enough, pry marks marred the wood on top. Had someone broken in and stolen a relic? His gaze drifted to the window and back. A possibility, but why would a thief go to the trouble of opening a crate when he could've picked up one of the antiquities ripe for the taking on the display table?

"I'll inform my steward of your concerns and have him increase the rounds of a night watch on the property."

"Perfect." She smiled. "Though again, I am not sure anything was taken. I do know with certainty, however, that something must be done about the moving statue. I'm afraid the thing will get knocked over and damaged if this continues."

He sighed. So help him if Barnaby thought this a lark. He'd have to give the man notice—which he was loath to do. For all his butler's eccentricities, it was Barnaby, Jameson, and Mrs. Buckner who held this great house together. "I'll have another word with my butler."

"I already did. Barnaby vows neither he nor the staff have had anything to do with it. He told me in light of recent events that he's sworn off any hijinks for the time being and not even Mr. Crawford has been pranking him of late."

"Well, clearly someone has been up to mischief. That thing"—he hitched his thumb over his shoulder—"isn't moving on its own."

"Exactly."

"Ah, you have suspicions." A slow smile traveled his lips. Leave it to this little pixie to unearth a real-life Egyptian mystery. "Who and how?"

"Obviously Mr. Fletcher is keen on playing up the curse aspect of this shipment. He thinks if word of it spreads, Mr. Harrison will be inclined to purchase the lot. Perhaps you might ask him."

"Gil?" His brows shot to the ceiling. "There's no way he could move that statue alone."

"Neither is there any way he should have known about the movement of it. I don't believe for a minute Barnaby breathed a word to him. He can't stand the fellow. Still, I've been thinking on the matter. The Egyptians were skilled in using all sorts of engineering techniques. It may be possible for someone to employ a combination of wooden levers and fulcrums strategically placed to create a rotational force. It's only being moved in small increments at a time. It wouldn't take that long to do."

Plausible . . . but not probable. He shook his head. "Even with such equipment, I highly doubt one man could do so unaided."

"Which is why Mr. Fletcher may have someone in this household helping him, though I don't believe it is Barnaby. He vows he keeps his tomfooleries to the understaff. He'd never try to dupe you or me."

It was endearing, this loyalty of hers—a trait Louisa hadn't owned. He rubbed the back of his neck, masking a wince from the memory of that duplicitous woman. "I shall question Mr. Fletcher about the matter, but don't get your hopes up. You've seen his physical state, not to mention how much he drinks. Plus, I doubt he'd risk damaging any of the items from which he hopes to gain a pretty penny."

Unbidden, he glanced over his shoulder to where the two men yet stood talking in front of the griffin. Gil grinned wide with one hand on the golden figurine. "I'm telling you this monstrous little thing is cursed."

Edmund frowned. Though he didn't believe in such dark

folly, at the moment, he could find no other explanation for all the odd happenings.

Some women loved the scent of jasmine or lilacs. Others preferred freshly baked bread or the peppery fragrance of the forest after a rain. An amused smile raised Ami's lips as she ran her brush over the snout of a mummified crocodile. While she didn't mind those aromas, she much preferred the tang of a good dammar resin mixed with a dash of turpentine . . . the scent of her father.

At the thought of him, she paused in her preservation work, brush hovered in the air. It was strange he'd not yet answered her telegram. Surely he'd received it. Luxor was only a few miles from the Valley of the Kings, where he was working, a modern city with the means to answer her query. His delay had given her time to continue examining the griffin, but still to no avail.

She ran her brush along the crocodile's back. What sort of tale belonged to this relic? For a long moment, she wondered about the hands before hers that had touched this item, the people behind the artifact, their tales of love and sorrow, prompting her to question if life held more than the preservation of the past. Her once unyielding career goals now shared space in her thoughts with the warmth of the unexpected companionship she'd found here with Mr. Price.

"Come, Miss Dalton. I find I am in need of—eew! What is that atrocious stink?" Violet flounced in with a lacy handkerchief to her nose, and when her gaze landed on the four-foot mummy on the table, her eyes widened. "By all that is holy, Miss Dalton, what is *that*?"

Ami smirked. Good thing the woman hadn't come in when she'd dusted off the glass case containing a preserved cobra in all its sharp-fanged glory. No doubt she would have swooned. "It's exactly as it appears, Miss Woolsey. A crocodile."

"How dreadful." With her free hand, Violet fanned herself,

noticeably keeping her distance. "Why wrap up such a horrid creature?"

"It's a religious object, leastwise for an ancient Egyptian." She set down her brush. Though the woman likely wouldn't care, Ami couldn't stop herself from giving further explanation—a trait she'd picked up from her father. He'd always been better at educating than showing affection. "Crocodiles were seen as a connection between the earthly and divine realms. One of their gods—Sobek—was believed to inhabit the waters of the Nile, and these reptiles were manifestations of his divine presence, which is why they took such care of it."

Violet gave a most unladylike snort, her handkerchief rippling from the force of it. "That is the most absurd thing I have ever heard. Let us speak of more pleasant topics as we take a turn about the garden."

Ami blinked, hardly believing her ears. Why would this uppity lady stoop to gracing her with her company? Intriguing to find out, yet even more distasteful to think of the woman's nattering on about her favorite topic—herself.

"While I thank you for the opportunity"—Ami picked up her brush and waved it—"I'm afraid I have work to do."

"Pooh. You are as bad as Edmund and my father. They have been closeted away since that journalist left this morning. They even had their lunch served in the study, leaving me alone with Mr. Fletcher. Odious man, if you ask me." Violet sighed, her eyes betraying a hint of weariness beneath her bravado. "I am bored, Miss Dalton. I crave a diversion. It seems the men in my life always find solace in their studies, leaving me on my own. Sometimes I wonder if there's more to life than waiting for a man to take notice of me."

A pang of empathy tightened Ami's stomach. The sentiment of being overlooked and confined within societal expectations resonated with her own struggles in the realm of academia.

Violet tucked away her bit of lace, revealing a pouty frown. "Besides, you need some fresh air. Your skin is as dull as one of your relics."

Ami clenched her jaw. Did this woman have any idea how abrasive she was? "Mr. Price hired me to catalogue these items, not frolic about in his garden."

"Don't be silly." She cut her hand through the air. "My Edmund wouldn't mind a whit."

And there it was again. *My Edmund*. Perhaps she ought to take a turn with the woman if only to find out the status of Violet's relationship with the enigmatic Mr. Price. Besides, a few minutes in the sun would be a welcome reprieve after a full day of bending over artifacts. Surely she could tolerate Violet's barbs for that long.

"Very well, Miss Woolsey. I suppose a brief stroll won't hurt."

She barely got to her feet before Violet linked arms with her and ushered her out the door. "Now, I simply must tell you about Lady Quilling's gown at the Evensons' ball. It was positively scandalous! I've never seen a neckline so low, practically to her waist, and if that weren't enough to draw attention, the overuse of sequins blinded one when the light hit just right. Such a Jezebel. Why, I hear she and Mr.—"

Violet droned on as they entered the garden, hardly drawing breath between sentences. My. She really had been in need of a diversion. Unbidden, a small amount of sympathy for the woman blossomed in Ami's heart. Did Violet have any friends, any *true* friends? Not that she had an entire stable of confidants herself, but she did have Polly.

Sidestepping an uneven cobble, Ami glanced around for Phineas. He really ought to replace that paving brick, though if he caught sight of them, he just might ask her and Violet to help him do so. An impish smile curved her lips at the thought of the dainty Miss Woolsey in her blush-pink day dress digging about in the dirt to reset a stone. It might do her some good, though, give her a sense of accomplishment other than having her hair curled to perfection.

"Don't you think, Miss Dalton?"

"Hmm?" She jerked her gaze to Violet, scrambling to answer a question for which she had no context. Violet gazed back, clearly waiting for a response. She couldn't very well admit she hadn't been listening, though, for the woman would take offense. She smiled and gave the best reply she could think of. "Yes, of course you must be right."

Violet gasped, a horrified pinch to her brows. "I should certainly hope not!"

Bosh.

Wrong answer.

Unwinding her arm from Violet's, she flung out her hand to the nearby rosebushes, quickly changing the subject. "Are these not divine, Miss Woolsey? There is no fairer flower than a Baroness Rothschild. I believe that's what these are, if my memory serves correctly. My mother was quite the horticulturalist."

Violet lifted her pert nose as she regathered Ami's arm and charged ahead. "Roses make me sneeze. I shall see them all ripped out once I am the lady of this grand house."

Ami schooled her face to keep her brows from lifting to the sky. "And when might that happy occasion be?"

"I am planning a Christmas wedding. White velvet for me to showcase my radiance and, hmm . . . I think a dove grey for Edmund would bring out the blue in his eyes. They're such a murky colour as is."

Murky was hardly the word she'd use to describe his eyes. More like the hue just before twilight, a deep azure, one that hinted of sweet dreams and kisses in the dark. Her face heated at the thought. If this woman really was to marry Mr. Price, Ami had no right to imagine such things. "I didn't realize congratulations were in order. How long have you and Mr. Price been engaged?"

"We're not. Officially, that is." Violet followed the curve of a low daisy hedge, clutching her hem up from a pile of forgotten trimmings. "But it shouldn't be long now. Why, I wouldn't be surprised at all if that's what Papa and Edmund are discussing this very minute."

Hmm. Were they? She hadn't seen any evidence that Mr. Price doted on the woman. Then again, what did she know of upper-class relationships? Maybe outward signs of affection were frowned upon as a societal faux pas . . . though Ami could've sworn she'd seen admiration flare in his gaze several times when he'd looked upon herself.

"At any rate," Violet continued, "it must be soon if Mother and I are to make my wedding the event of the season. Mother won't return from France until the first of October. But not to worry, she is a veritable Renoir of party planning. Society will speak of this event for years to come."

That sounded like a nightmare to her, and though she'd only known him a little while, she had a feeling Mr. Price would agree. "Don't you think Mr. Price ought to have a say in the matter? After all, it's his wedding too."

Violet trilled a laugh, startling a nearby robin to take flight. "Such naïvety, though I suppose you cannot be blamed for it. You see, my dear, a groom on a wedding day is an accoutrement to the bride, nothing more, nothing less. I have no doubt Edmund shall play his part with style, for he loves me dearly. Tell me, Miss Dalton." She paused, facing her with a tilt to her head. "Have you ever been in love?"

Ami chewed the inside of her cheek, thinking hard. There had been Peter, but they'd both been hardly more than children at the time. He'd held her hand once, and even picked a periwinkle to tuck behind her ear. It might have worked out with him had he not joined the navy. But that was years ago, and truthfully, she'd not thought of him since . . . unlike the dark-haired Mr. Price who'd set up camp in a corner of her mind.

A corner she visited far too often.

"Yes, actually. I happen to be in love right now." She gave Violet a tight smile. "I love my work, Miss Woolsey."

"Well, I suppose that explains it, then."

"Explains what?"

"Why you're a . . . well, you know." Her voice dropped to a whisper. "A spinster."

Air whooshed from her lungs. Though she'd heard such remarks before, she'd always been immune, having accepted the consequences of her choices. But for some reason, this one pompous woman's unfiltered opinion cut deep, exposing a longing for companionship she'd been trying to ignore—*unsuccessfully* trying to ignore—ever since she'd met Mr. Price. Was the path she'd chosen as an Egyptologist, all the social sacrifices she'd made, worth a life alone in a room full of dusty relics? For the first time, she questioned—really questioned—the life she'd made.

And she wasn't entirely sure she liked the answer.

Ami spun away. "I really should be getting back to work now, Miss Woolsey." Her feet pounded the cobbles, eating up as much ground as the width of her hem would allow. She was done with this walk and more than finished with any further scathing remarks from Violet.

"I hope you didn't take that the wrong way, Miss Dalton," Violet called behind her. "I merely meant that you—oh!"

A ragged scream ripped through the sanctity of the garden.

Ami wheeled about.

Violet sprawled on her belly, her slipper half-on and half-off her foot, having been snagged on the cattywampus cobble. Part of her body lay on the paving, the other part prone in a tangle of ivy.

Where Violet and a snake stared nose to nose.

15

Six hours. Enough time for a battalion to storm the walls of a fortified fortress and secure the perimeter, yet apparently not sufficient for the viscount to make up his mind on the finer points of the platform Edmund had drawn up last night—or rather that Ami had drawn up. Covering his mouth with his fist, he stifled a yawn. It was far too warm in here, making him even more drowsy. Though he'd had Barnaby open the windows, after being cooped up in the study for so long, the air was stale.

"Well?" he prodded.

"Mmm," Bastion mumbled noncommittally as he raised the last page of the document in the air, his sharp eyes fixed on the page.

Edmund leaned forward in his chair, his lower back aching from having sat in one position the better part of the afternoon.

"I think . . ." Bastion's lips pursed.

"Yes?"

Silence, save for the steady ticktock of the clock and a deep inhale from the viscount. For pity's sake! It was only a rough draft of a political strategy, not a plan to save humanity.

At last, the viscount slapped the page against his thigh and reached for his tumbler of brandy. After a sip, he cleared his throat, stared Edmund right in the face, and—

Once again folded over the infernal last page.

Edmund pinched the bridge of his nose. It was either that or shoot from the chair and bang his head against the wall.

"How am I to think with such agitation distracting me?" Bastion peered over the top of the paper, a slow smile lifting his lips. "Though it's to be understood, I suppose. I remember the days before I married the viscountess. All that hot blood running through one's veins. Hang in there, man." He winked.

Edmund's stomach roiled. It was wrong of him, this deceit simply to gain a seat in Parliament. Sanjay or not, he simply couldn't do it anymore. "About that, my lord . . . I think it best you know now I am not ready for marriage, not even to your daughter. It's nothing personal, I assure you."

For a long beat, the man said nothing, just stared at him, brow scrunching. Was this it, then? The death of his candidacy? An end of putting a stop to the tariff that would destroy men like Sanjay?

At length, the viscount once again disappeared behind the papers. "I understand, Price. I was young once too, you know."

That was it? It'd been that simple all along? For the first time in hours, he relaxed against the chair cushion, relieved beyond measure. "Thank you, my lord. If you'd rather I speak with—"

A rap pounded on the door, though the viscount gave no indication he'd heard the knock. Bypassing the man, Edmund swung the door open to Barnaby.

"You have a caller, sir. A Professor Bram Webb. In the sitting room."

"And you left him in there alone?" He shoved past the butler and dashed down the corridor.

"I didn't think you'd wish him to be brought in here, sir," Barnaby called after him.

Edmund swung into the sitting room just as Bram tucked a cigar into his pocket. Judging by the size of the bulge already there, his old friend had likely cleaned out the entire humidor. "I knew it! Always pilfering my cigars."

Bram wheeled about, flashing a grin. "It's your own fault, Price. You always did have the best, even as an undergrad."

"You can thank my father for that." With a chuckle, he clapped the man on the back. "How are you, my friend?"

"Walking a thin rope as always."

He did appear to be, if the shaggy hair in need of a trim and the threadbare fabric of Bram's suit coat were any indication. There were a few new lines on his face, mostly from having aged these past eight years, and a fresh scar on the topmost part of his right cheek. Bram Webb always had been—and apparently still was—a rogue.

Edmund's grin grew. "I'd expect nothing less from you, Webb. How long can you stay?"

"Just overnight." Lacing his fingers, Bram cracked his knuckles, the familiar habit unearthing memories of long hours of study with his college mate. "I told ol' Grimwinkle I was on college business, wooing a potential donor over an elaborate dinner."

"I suppose that means you must leave here with a full coin purse." Edmund smirked.

Bram mirrored it. "Is that a problem?"

It shouldn't be, not with his net worth, but the actual cash flow he had on hand worried him, what with half of his and Gil's capital tied up in that railroad venture. He kneaded a knot in his neck. He never should have agreed to bankroll the startup of the Bengal Express.

But Bram didn't need to hear of his woes. "I wouldn't call it a problem, my friend. More of an expectation. I'm always a few coins shy whenever I spend time with you."

"Speaking of coins"—Bram arched a brow—"I am anxious to see them."

"Then let's have at it, though we'll have to be quick about it. You're not the only guest I must attend to." He strolled from the sitting room, Bram at his side.

His friend cut him a sideways glance as they crossed the front hall. "I was surprised when I heard you returned to England. I didn't think you were ever coming back after . . . you know."

Honestly, he hadn't thought he'd return either. India had suited him, feeding his sense of adventure that his father had always tried to tame. Had it not been for the harsh tariffs funneling out of Parliament, he'd have been content to stay there.

"It's been eight years." He shrugged. "I should think the gossip has died down by now."

"There never really was that much, you know. You needn't have banished yourself for so long."

"It wasn't just that. It was . . ." A bitter taste filled his mouth. How to explain to Bram—to anyone, really—that he'd never conquered the shame he'd felt after Louisa's betrayal? He let out a long breath as they swung into the corridor leading to the workroom. "Let's just say it was for more personal reasons."

"Personal? Right." Bram eyed him. "Then you should be happy to know Louisa got what she deserved. I hear she turned into quite the sour pickle after marrying that walking corpse Lord Carlton. He whisked her away to Scotland, somewhere in the Highlands. Can't say I blame the change in her personality, though. Such a rugged climate is enough to drive the whimsy from the hardiest of souls."

Hah! *Whimsical* is hardly what he'd call Louisa's imprudent spirit, though he ought to feel sorry for her, he supposed. He should pity the fact that her vibrancy had been evicted to some obscure heathland. But all he felt was numb.

An improvement, that.

"Well, as my father always said, the past is not where we live."

"Thank heaven! Though in your case I imagine the present might be just as trying. You'll be beating off women with a stick now that you've returned home. You're nearly as handsome as I am, though admittedly your bank account is a monolith compared to mine. Toss in the allure of your travels to an exotic land and your mysterious return." Bram let out a low whistle.

"Indeed. I should think you're the most eligible bachelor in all of Oxfordshire, if not all of England."

"Which is why I'm holed up in my country estate for the moment. Once I get to London, I'll more easily blend in with the crowd. And here we are." He strode into the workroom, surprised at the eagerness in his step to see Miss Dalton. He glanced around for her bright smile.

Bram swiveled his head from wall to wall as well. "This is a treasure trove!"

"Yes, which will make it all the harder to find those coins for you to take a look at." He frowned. Miss Dalton was nowhere in sight.

Bram walked the length of the trestle tables, where those artifacts that'd been carefully unpacked and cleaned sat ready for sale. "Don't tell me you're organizing these items on your own. You couldn't even keep your books straight that first year at school, not to mention the disgrace your side of our bedchamber was."

Now there was a bittersweet memory, one that chased away his grimace. "No, I've hired someone."

Movement out the window snagged his attention, where Miss Dalton and Miss Woolsey stood face-to-face in the garden, and if the twist of Miss Dalton's lips was any indication, the discussion wasn't pleasant.

He turned back to Bram. "Come along. I'll introduce you to my resident scholar."

"Do you always keep your Egyptologist in the yard?" Bram asked as they worked their way to the rear of the house.

"Only when—"

A scream leached through the outside door. Edmund's heart plummeted. Had Miss Dalton been hurt? Violet was known to be verbally abusive, but surely she'd not taken to hair pulling.

He barreled outside, feet spraying up gravel. He and Bram had barely cleared the garden entrance when Miss Dalton flung a snake through the air.

Then she casually dusted off her hands as if she'd done nothing more than pick a few dahlias. "Calm yourself, Miss

Woolsey. It's not like it's an Egyptian saw-scaled viper. It's merely an adder, which isn't nearly as deadly."

Edmund's breath hitched as he charged ahead. What an extraordinary display of bravery and composure! He'd known she was an uncommon woman, one that intrigued him like none other, but this? Absolutely captivating, to the point that he barely registered Violet sprawled on the ground.

Phineas sped from the opposite direction, reaching the ladies before he and Bram. "Ho ho! That was quite a throw. Be ye all right, Miss Dalton?"

Violet pushed up, a scowl creasing her brow and dirt smudging her chin. "What about me?"

Miss Dalton hefted her from the ground with a pull to her arm. "It was just a small tumble, Miss Woolsey. You'll be right as a hen's feathers after a cup of tea."

"Who is that?" Bram huffed beside him.

"That is my Egyptologist."

His friend blew a low whistle. "You don't say."

"Oh, Edmund." Violet launched herself against his chest the second he and Bram reached the ladies. "I was so frightened."

Stiffly, he raised one arm and patted her back. How did one calm a woman without encouraging further attention? Thankfully, once her father talked with her about his refusal to marry, this sort of unwarranted attention would stop. "Yes, well, it looks as if Miss Dalton has squared things away."

"That she has." Phineas chuckled. "A right good toss o' that snake, lass, though if ye all will excuse me, I'll just be findin' where the little devil landed and send him on his way." Tugging his forelock, he wheeled about.

Miss Dalton swiped up a very dirty silk slipper and held it out. "Here is your shoe, Miss Woolsey."

The moment Violet released her grip to collect her shoe, Edmund stepped aside, putting distance between them. "Though this may be an inopportune time, I should nevertheless like to introduce you ladies to my old friend, Professor Bram Webb. Bram, meet Miss Dalton, Egyptologist, and—" He waited for Violet to straighten to full height after slipping her foot into her wayward slipper. "Miss Woolsey, daughter of Lord Bastion."

Bram dipped his head, a gleam in his grey eyes, particularly when his gaze landed on Miss Dalton. "Pleased to meet you, ladies."

"You as well, Professor Webb." Miss Dalton dipped her head.

"Professor." Violet sniffed, then turned to him. "Edmund, I should like a lie-down before dinner. Will you see me inside, please?" She wrapped her arm around his, tighter than any snake could coil.

"Of course." The words came out thinly, but at least they came out. "Miss Dalton, the professor has traveled from Cambridge and is here to value those Roman coins. I'll escort Miss Woolsey to her maid, then join you in the workroom."

Though it killed him to do so, he turned away with Violet, leading her off with a brisk pace. Leaving Bram alone with Miss Dalton was as dangerous as leaving him unattended in the sitting room, for his old friend didn't only have a reputation for pocketing cigars.

He was known to steal women's hearts as well.

The longer Ami assessed Professor Bram Webb, the more a slow smile curved her lips. Scruffy hair the colour of weak tea lay jagged against his worn collar. Whiskers that ought to be shaved shadowed the line of his jaw. The lower two buttons at the bottom of his waistcoat were missing, and the hem on his right trouser leg pulled from the seams at the outer edge. Was this what her father had looked like in his younger years? All harum-scarum and society be hanged?

Then again, she'd been accused of such on numerous occasions too.

With a jerk of his head, Professor Webb flicked back his unruly hair. "I must say, Miss Dalton, your snake-throwing skills rival those of the ancient gladiators."

"When you grow up with a father who has a fondness for ophiology, you learn at a young age how to handle them." She swung her hand toward the house. "Shall we go inside?"

A playful glint flashed in his grey eyes. "It seems you have a talent for not only taming serpents but the hearts of unsuspecting scholars as well. Lead on, m'lady, for I am eager to see what other surprises you have in store."

She turned away lest he see her smile. He was a playful pup, his tone nothing like the oily flirtations of Mr. Fletcher. How many women had fallen for that handsome face and rugged charm? He could turn a girl's head, all right. But not hers. Only one dark-haired man claimed that privilege. Perhaps she ought to introduce Professor Webb to Polly.

He fell into step beside her, matching her stride. "So you're the Egyptologist?"

"When I'm not occupied as a snake handler, yes."

"Apparently I've been stuck behind the walls of academia for too long. I wasn't aware there were any female Egyptologists in England. How did you come by your credentials?"

Bosh! Her degree in the classics had nothing to do with all the Egyptian knowledge she'd gleaned over the years. "Hard work and a father who heads the ancient studies department at Oxford."

"Mmm, interesting," he murmured, then snapped his fingers. "Dalton! You're Archer's daughter."

"I am." She waited as he shoved open the door and allowed her to pass. "And my position is not as novel as you may think, Professor. Flinders Petrie, one of our most renowned Egyptologists, didn't earn any degrees related to archaeology either. Technically, an Egyptologist is merely one who studies all things related to Egypt. Mr. Petrie's titles are honorary, yet his reputation as a scholar is undenied."

"Petrie." The name rolled slowly off his tongue. "Ah yes. I believe I know the fellow. Was he the one who discovered that large cache of Roman treasures at Hawara?"

"So you have heard of him—a man without a customary

formal education." Though she really hadn't meant to, a slight tone of vitriol slipped out with her words.

The professor held up his hands. "I meant no disrespect, Miss Dalton. In fact, it's refreshing to find a kindred spirit who defies the expectations of society. Though I admit I am surprised to find such a comely woman in a stuffy profession like this."

"Is that an oblique way of saying I've shattered your preconceived notions, sir?"

"Yes." He grinned. "And I can't say I like it. That's usually my job." His hand splayed over his chest. "But the world is full of wonder and contradictions, just like you, Miss Dalton."

"I shall take that as a compliment coming from a man of academia. Now, would you like to see those coins?"

"Lead on."

She strode into the workroom, and surprisingly, the professor passed right by the golden griffin without so much as a double take on the piece. Not that he'd have known about the curse, but its beauty usually drew one to it right away.

Pulling a small key from her pocket, she unlocked a safe box that Mr. Price had provided after the missing coin fiasco. She pulled out the leather pouch, then dumped the tiny cache onto the table.

He dragged over a chair and carefully scooped the coins closer to him. "That's it. Come to papa, little ones." He pinched a piece of the gold and held it in a ray of late afternoon sunshine streaming through the windows. His gaze was so intense, she doubted he knew she was still at his side.

"Can you value them, Professor?" She spoke low so as not to startle him.

"Can I?" He waggled his eyebrows as he set the coin down, then fingered through the rest. "Alexandrian, of course. Note the bust of the Egyptian god Serapis on some and the iconic Pharos lighthouse on others. Yet in addition to the Egyptian motifs . . ." He flipped over several of the gold pieces. "On a few you see the busts of Augustus and Tiberius—prominent emperors at the time—an eagle on this one and assorted Roman mythological deities on the rest. It was quite the fusion of cultures. I'd say they're worth forty to fifty pounds."

"That was fast. You certainly know your Roman antiquities."

"In my case"—he cracked his knuckles—"an education at Cambridge did serve its purpose."

Her gaze roamed the opulent room, albeit a bit cluttered with the remaining boxes to unpack. "It seems that education certainly paid off for Mr. Price as well."

The professor clucked his tongue. "Not so much as you think. Like Flinders Petrie, he never finished his formal education."

A frog in her soup bowl couldn't have surprised her more. "Whyever not?"

"Ahhh." His mouth quirked. "That's his tale to tell."

Unbidden, Phineas's words of weeks ago surfaced.

"Ye remind me a great deal o' her."

"Her who?"

"I reckon tha's for him to tell ye, miss."

Ami frowned. "Evidently there are several things Mr. Price has not told me."

"Well, you know the wealthy." The professor slid coin after coin back into the pouch. "They hold their secrets tighter than an old dame clutching her pearls."

Biting her lip, she turned away. First the gardener hinted at some sort of scandal involving a woman, and now Mr. Price had apparently also suffered some sort of disgrace at university. Was that what he'd meant when he'd told her he understood how difficult it was to be recognized as proficient without acceptable credentials? And then there was the supposed engagement Violet thought was in the making. What else was Mr. Price concealing? It seemed the man hid more intrigues than she did.

And she wasn't quite sure how to feel about that, for lately she wasn't sure she knew her own self anymore.

16

Stuck. Trapped. Cornered as securely as a fox hemmed in by a ring of hounds right there in the sitting room. Edmund stood wedged between Lord Bastion, his daughter, and a fat-backed sofa. What a night. While Violet nattered on and on about who'd become engaged to whom, he debated the credits and debits of hurtling his body over the ungainly piece of furniture.

And dinner had gone no better.

Bastion wanted to talk politics. Violet about her near-death experience with the snake. He'd given Gil several reminders to slow down on the wine, and worst of all, he never should have allowed Bram to sit next to Miss Dalton, for his friend had masterfully captured her attention.

As he was now.

Making her laugh.

Flashing his crooked grin.

His knee bumping against hers where they sat in adjacent chairs near the hearth.

Envy punched Edmund in the gut. He'd much rather be the one engaged in witty banter with the brown-haired beauty. Actually, he'd rather all his guests left, and he could return to having Ami Dalton to himself.

Across the sitting room, Gil turned off a gas wall sconce. Odd, that. Even more strange when he strolled to the next and turned that one off as well.

"Eh, Price?"

He jerked his attention to the viscount, scrambling to decipher what he'd missed—and came up woefully short. "I beg your pardon, my lord. Could you repeat that?"

Bastion's sharp eyes narrowed. "I said I should think one more day consulting about your platform ought to tie the thing up into a neat package."

Brilliant. Another stretch of endless hours watching the man squint and sigh. Still, if boredom was the price to gain that seat in the House, it was a small cost to pay. "Yes, my lord. I look forward to it."

Gil turned off another light. If the trend continued, they'd all be in the dark. He opened his mouth to rebuke the man, but Violet pawed at Edmund's sleeve before he got a word out.

"How do you feel about dove grey, Edmund? Miss Dalton seems to think I ought to get your opinion."

The question caught him off guard, diverting him from the dimming light in the room. "Why would she suggest such a thing? What were you two discussing?"

"Oh, you know. Female topics." She fluttered her fingers in the air. "Nothing to bother you about. I daresay it was only one of her provincial ideas at any rate. We will say no more about it."

Another light faded, this one close to Bram and Miss Dalton, leaving them in the shadows.

That did it.

"Pardon me." He shoved his way between Violet and her father. "That's enough with the lights, Gil. We're hardly ready to retire yet, and besides, I have staff for such tasks when the time comes."

Gil turned to them all, arms spread wide. "But the time is now, old man."

"Time for what, Mr. Fletcher?" the viscount grumbled.

"A ghost story."

"I've had enough scares for one day," Violet whined.

"Come now, Miss Woolsey." Gil swooped over to her and her father. "A good fright gets the blood flowing."

"So does a brisk walk through a dark cemetery in the dead of night," Ami cut in.

Bram leaned back in his chair, one long leg crossing over the other. "You speak as if you have experience, Miss Dalton."

Laughing, she caught Edmund's eye. "We all have our secrets."

Now, that was unexpected. What was the woman insinuating?

"Come, come." Gil herded the Woolseys around the sofa and practically pushed them down onto the cushions. "Let us have Miss Dalton regale us with a tale of Egyptian horror."

She shook her head, a curl of hair breaking free of the pins and cascading over her shoulder. "I'd rather not, Mr. Fletcher."

"Yes, let's play charades instead." Violet pursed her lips into a pout.

"What a perfectly stodgy idea." Gil snorted. "No, no. We must have a haunting tale to take to bed with us. Go on, Miss Dalton."

Her jaw stiffened, a distinct sign she was clearly irritated at Gil's insistence. Edmund tamped down the urge to intervene, curious as to how she'd respond.

"Reducing Egyptian culture to a trivial bit of entertainment seems rather disrespectful, Mr. Fletcher. And so I once again decline."

"Balderdash! Don't be such a killjoy. It's not disrespect at all, just a bit of thrilling diversion. Think of it as"—he twirled one hand in the air—"keeping their culture alive."

"I do not think of it in such terms." Steel sharpened her tone.

Edmund circled to the hearth, stationing himself next to Miss Dalton. "The lady has told you no, Gil. Leave her be."

"Very well." He spun in a circle, making eye contact with them all. "Then I shall have to tell a chilling tale of my own invention. Perhaps I'll even pen it down later tonight and have it sent to Mr. Kane. He may pay to publish such a story of intrigue."

Annoyance rippled on Miss Dalton's brow. Violet scooted closer to her father, patting the cushion next to her with an arched brow at Edmund.

Oh no. He'd not get tangled in her claws again. He set his glass on the mantel, the clink of it breaking the silence. "The hour is late. Perhaps we should call it a night."

"Oh, let the man regale us, Price." Lord Bastion draped his arm along the back of the sofa. "It shouldn't take that long."

"And so it begins!" Gil clapped his hands, the report as sharp as a gunshot. Unease permeated the air, as if the very house braced itself for the impending horror story. "Once, in the heart of ancient Egypt, stood a temple. Magnificent in beauty. Lethal by design. For inside, buried deep within an unholy labyrinth, lay a sacred artifact known as the Amulet of Death."

Miss Dalton rolled her eyes.

Edmund agreed.

Violet uttered a scared yip.

A wicked grin spread on Gil's face, teeth white in the shadows. "And there the amulet stayed for centuries, for you see, anyone who laid hands on this trinket would be forever bound to the realm of darkness. But that didn't stop the villainous Dr. Spencer from seeking its power. He crept through the treacherous passageways to reach the hidden chamber." Curling his hands like claws, Gil pranced about their circle.

Edmund angled his head, studying the man, unnerved. Something wasn't right about the twist of his partner's mouth or the wild gaze in his eyes. Was this a mere performance, or was Gil unraveling right here in the sitting room?

"It was dark!" Gil shouted, then whispered, "so dark. And cold. Bone-chilling. Enough to leach out your soul and leave it to die alone."

The Woolseys, Bram, even Miss Dalton seemed engrossed. Edmund shook his head slightly. He'd had no idea Gil was such a spinner of tales. The room vibrated with a macabre sort of energy, as if the taut string of reality were about to snap.

"At last Dr. Spencer came upon the golden charm and rubbed

his finger over the raised skull atop it. That's when the whispers began. Can you hear them? Listen," he hissed.

Miss Dalton swiveled her head to Edmund, pleading in her eyes—and it pleased him that she'd sought him out to end this charade instead of Bram.

He stepped from the mantel, grabbing Gil by the arm. "Your story is over."

Gil wrenched away, pointing a finger at each one of them in turn. "I may be finished, but remember, my friends, the moral of this story is that you must be cautious with relics that bear the weight of a troubled history, for there is a thin line between sanity and madness."

"What a horrid tale!" Violet flounced back against the sofa, arms clutched tightly about her. "I shan't sleep a wink tonight."

"Perfect!" Gil grinned. "Fear is a delightful companion in the night. Keeps you on your toes." He winked. "Nevertheless, allow me to make you a drink to calm your nerves, Miss Woolsey."

"I think turning up the lights would do so more quickly." Edmund strode to the nearest sconce, his frustration aimed squarely at his business partner.

No sooner had the words passed his lips than Gil's voice sliced through the air, stabbing him between the shoulder blades. "Gas lamps won't keep out the demons, old man. As you'll remember, Lucifer himself was an angel of light."

Edmund reached for the gas knob, eager to banish the eerie shadows.

Yet all the while he wondered if there was more to Gil's tale than mere fiction.

A scream blasphemed the night, yanking Ami from a deep sleep. She bolted from her bed, snatching her robe as she dashed across the room. Only she and Violet slept in this wing of the house. Was someone attacking her? Heart racing, Ami swiped up the letter opener on the desk. The silver blade was no dagger, but could anyone really tell in the dark?

She jerked open the door and ran pell-mell toward Violet's bedchamber, gaze snagging on a dark figure at the end of the corridor. Her step hitched as she squinted into the shadows. Was that someone running off, or were her eyes playing tricks?

"Who's there?" she called.

The only answer was another scream from Violet's room.

She sprinted to the woman's door and shoved it open. "Miss Woolsey? Are you all right?"

Violet's face was a stark white against the dark counterpane that she clutched in handfuls to her chest. She panted like a frightened deer, and even from steps away, the vibration of her shivering could be seen rippling the bedclothes in the dark.

Ami sank beside her. "What happened?"

Violet stared straight ahead, eyes fixed, the whites of which were huge, her pupils tiny dots. A medicinal stink tinged her breath.

"Miss Woolsey?" Ami tried again.

Even more colour drained from Violet's face. If she didn't bring the woman to her senses soon, the lady would swoon dead away.

"Violet!" Grabbing hold of her arms, Ami shook her like a mouse in a cat's maw.

With a great cry, Violet wrenched away. One of her arms snaked out from beneath the covers and raised an accusing finger, pointing across the room like the grim reaper come to call. "There. Right there!"

Hand covering the letter opener in her pocket, Ami tracked the imaginary line all the way to the closed white draperies. A dressing table graced the wall next to them. A chair. The hearth. Nothing seemed out of place.

But for good measure, she scanned the other shadowy corners before turning back to Violet. "You've had a bad dream, that's all."

"No!" She grimaced, skin taut against the bones of her face. "I saw the Amulet of Death, the black eye sockets, the grinning skull. It floated like a ghost in front of the draperies, and now

I'm going to die because no one can see it and live. No one!"
She yanked the covers over her head, wailing.

"Calm yourself. You and I are the only ones in here, I promise." Ami eased down the counterpane. "Chin up, now. There is nothing to fear. I shall prove it to you, all right?"

Rising, she padded barefoot across the carpet, praying her encouragement had been true. What if someone—or something—hid behind those draperies? She eased out the letter opener, taking care to hold it from view so Violet wouldn't go into hysterics. Moonlight crept beneath the curtains' hem. A thin line of promise . . . as long as she didn't see the tips of any shoes bumping out along that edge. Thankfully, none did.

But she'd seen stranger things happen during a midnight relic purchase.

Wrapping her fingers around the center seam of the drapery, she tugged. Curtain rings screeched. Silver light poured in, bathing the room in an ethereal glow. The windows were shut, but just to be certain, she gave them a tug as well. Locked.

She turned back to Violet with a smile. "See? Nothing whatsoever to fear."

But was that a lie? Had she seen a figure fleeing the scene?

Violet moaned as she buried herself deep against her pillows. "But I saw it. I know I did. I won't live until morning. I won't live to see my Christmas wedding!" Sobs broke, and the lady bowed her head into her hands, shoulders shaking.

Ami frowned. What was she to do about this? Her father had always comforted any stray bouts of her weeping with a mechanical pat on the head and a swift recitation of an ancient Egyptian text . . . which probably wouldn't work here.

She grabbed a nearby glass off a side table and filled it with water. "Have a drink, Miss Woolsey. It will help you feel better."

Violet shoved away the offering without even looking at it.

Well. That'd gone over as nicely as a rousing narration of *The Instructions of Amenemhat.*

Ami set the glass on the bedstand. "How about I retrieve your maid and have her sit with you? I won't be a minute."

A hand snagged out and grabbed her robe as she passed by the bed. "No! Don't leave me. Please. I . . . I'm afraid," she admitted, her voice barely above a whisper. "I don't like being alone. I'm always left alone."

A whimpering tot couldn't have sounded more pathetic. Pity welled, thickening a lump in Ami's throat. The lady really must be terrified to wish her to stay, and she could more than relate to having a father who was always preoccupied.

Sitting on the edge of the mattress, she gently pried Violet's grip from her robe. With the hem of the fabric, she dabbed away the woman's tears while humming "Nami, Nami," the same Egyptian lullaby her grandmother had used to quiet her after her mother's death.

"Mmm," Violet murmured, eyelashes fluttering. "Pretty."

With a light touch, she brushed back the locks of hair clinging to Violet's sticky face—and continued to do so until the woman's breaths evened and her eyes closed.

Rising ever so slowly, Ami tiptoed to the door. Out in the corridor, she debated a moment about turning back to her own bed, but it was probably better to alert Barnaby to summon Violet's maid in case the woman suffered any more nightmares.

At the end of the passage—right where she thought she'd seen the figure—her toe sent something skittering against the baseboard. Bending, she plucked up a small, thin piece of curved metal, like a broken part of a spectacles frame. Odd, that, for the maids kept the floor spotless. She pocketed the item. One more thing to ask Barnaby about.

The corridor opened onto a flat landing where the grand staircase descended. Overhead, a large domed glass window bathed the area in a ghostly glow. The perfect haunt for specters, if one believed in such things. Just past the stairway at the entrance to the east wing, where the men slept, another small lump sat on the carpet trapped in a ray of moonlight.

Pausing her butler-finding mission, Ami forged ahead and collected the trinket—the other half of the curved frame. She glanced down the passageway, scanning the floor, but it was too shadowy to see very far.

She tucked the piece away with the other. None of the guests she knew wore spectacles, nor any of the staff she'd had contact with. Unless she was wrong about the source and the metal had fallen from some other contraption. But why here?

Curiosity piqued, she set off down the men's corridor, sweeping an intent gaze from wall to wall as she went. A fruitless search. She made it all the way to the end, where a curtain billowed from an open window, flapping against a small table with a vase of red roses. If the breeze gusted any harder, that crystal container would crash and wake whoever slept behind the nearest door.

An easy fix, though. She grabbed the sash and pulled. The frame budged only an inch. Giving it a bit more muscle, she tried again, but the thing was wedged tight. Bosh! A quick coating of tallow would have made this a much easier task. This time she gave it a good valiant shove. The window plummeted.

And her elbow smacked into the vase.

Flowers flew.

Crystal shattered.

Glass glinted in the moonlight all around her feet.

Her *bare* feet.

Good heavens. That hadn't gone as planned. She crouched, carefully collecting as many large shards as possible when the nearest door brushed open.

"Miss Dalton? What are you doing here?"

She glanced up, and her jaw dropped. It couldn't be helped. Nor stopped.

For there stood Edmund Price in all his glorious manhood, bathed by moonlight. He'd donned a robe the colour of midnight, the silk accentuating the flesh—and darkly curled hair—on his chest where the material didn't close tightly. She ought to look away, for this was far too intimate a sight.

Yet all she could do was stare.

And he stared right back.

Instant heat flamed in her cheeks. In her shift and gauzy wrap, she was garbed no more decently than him.

"Miss Dalton?" He stepped closer. "Are you all right?"

She shot up a hand, forcing her gaze to fix on his face. "Stop right there. I am fine; however, the crystal vase that was on the table is not." Carefully rising, she held out her open palm, revealing the largest pieces she'd collected. "Step any closer and you'll be picking out glass slivers from your feet."

"Leave it. Mrs. Buckner can have a maid deal with the mess in the morning. I'll not have you risk getting cut."

"I appreciate that, truly, but I can't very well fly past this broken glass, and I'm afraid I've not got any shoes on my feet."

Humor pulled at his mouth. "It always comes down to shoes with you, eh? Wait there."

Wheeling about, he disappeared inside his bedchamber. Surely he didn't have a spare pair of women's slippers in there . . . did he? She set the glass pieces on the table, pondering what he might be doing.

A few moments later, he reappeared with shoes on his own feet, his heels grinding crystal into the carpet as he strode to her and slung her up in his arms. His chest was a fortress, his bare skin feverish. Or was that hers? Hard to tell, for fire licked along every nerve she owned. Such an embrace was wrong. Shameless. Forbidden. And yet as he carried her past the sharp bits littering the floor, she didn't care. She could live in this moment, relishing the shift of his body against hers. Forget about pyramids and mummies and think only of the life they might build together.

Three long-legged steps later, he set her down, yet by God's good grace, he did not move away. Nor did she. They stood toe to toe, breath mingling, his hands yet on her arms. His sleep-tousled hair for once as loose as hers. Promise, desire, need . . . all glimmered in his eyes.

And then his gaze flicked to her lips.

"Ami?" he whispered, a thousand questions in her name.

All she had to do was rise up. Murmur a yes. Claim his offering and feel what it was like to have that fine strong mouth pressed against hers.

A wave of yearning crashed over her, so strong it terrified her. Her! The Shadow Broker. The fearless buyer of stolen goods. Sucking in a breath, she pulled from his touch, thoroughly shaken by the effect this man had on her.

She lifted her chin defiantly. "Thank you, but I'm sure that after picking up a few more pieces of that glass, I could have safely made it through without a scratch."

One of his brows arched. "And yet you never answered me as to how you came to be here in the first place. Why are you roaming the halls of Price House instead of tucked safely in your own bed?"

"Violet had a night terror. I thought to wake Barnaby to summon her maid."

He cocked his head, suspicion flashing in his gaze. "Surely you know the butler's quarters would not be on this floor."

"Of course, but I got a little sidetracked." She pulled out the fragments of curved metal from her pocket. "I found these on the carpet, one part in the west wing, the other at the entrance to this one. And I thought I saw a figure leaving Violet's room shortly after her first scream."

He glanced from the pieces to her. "Who do you think it was?"

"I don't know. I was too preoccupied with Miss Woolsey."

"Hmm. Clearly something is afoot." He gathered the busted pieces of frame from her hand and slid them into a slit in his robe. "I'll see you back to your chamber."

Oh no, he wouldn't. Her heart couldn't take much more of this nighttime tryst. She shook her head. "I'm a big girl, Mr. Price, not given to flinching from shadows."

"And yet I insist." He tucked her hand into the crook of his arm and set off down the corridor.

For several steps neither of them spoke, which was to her liking. She couldn't string a sentence together without it unraveling.

"This terror of Miss Woolsey's, what did it involve?"

"She claims she saw the Amulet of Death hovering near her draperies, which I highly doubt for I examined the area thoroughly. I'm sure it was nothing more than her mind overworking Mr. Fletcher's story as she slept."

His lips twisted into a smirk. "His tale was a bit much."

"Indeed. He doesn't seem like quite the right business partner for you."

"Oh?" His gaze traveled her face as they walked. "And who would you choose for me?"

Anyone but that unstable fellow. She bit back the saucy retort. Still, it was a fair question, one she mulled over as they left the corridor for the expanse of the staircase landing. "I should think you'd need someone who is more unwavering. Someone discreet. A partner who is a truly hard worker."

"Add in beautiful and you've got the job, for you are all those things." He winked.

He was flirting, of course, but all the same she stowed the words away in her heart to revisit as she went to sleep. "I am already in your employ, Mr. Price."

"One of my best business decisions. I may purchase another load of Egyptian antiquities just to keep you on." He grinned, and in the soft moonlight drifting down from the dome window, she couldn't imagine any man more handsome.

Bosh! Better not to wander down that lane of thinking. She gave herself a mental shake. "I thought you were heading to London, Mr. Price."

"Please, I think we have moved beyond such formalities. Call me Edmund." He patted her hand in the crook of his arm, his touch warm against her skin. "And I have a big town house in the city. A simple word to the renovators and the entire third floor would fit you and some crates very nicely."

She stifled a snort. "I daresay Miss Woolsey would not approve of such an arrangement, nor would she appreciate me using your Christian name."

"Miss Woolsey's opinions matter naught to me."

Pulling away, she faced him before they strode down the corridor to her room. The need to finally sort out his relationship with Violet pounded stronger with each beat of her heart. "May I ask you a personal question, Mr. Price?"

"Hmm. That could be dangerous." He rubbed the back of his neck. "What would you like to know?"

She curled her toes into the carpet. It wasn't too late to back out. She could come up with a different query.

And yet she forged ahead. "Are you intending to pursue Miss Woolsey as your bride?"

He laughed, a merry sound in the dark, if not a little bitter. "Does she not seem like quite the right partner for me either?"

Ami shook her head. "Not at all."

"Who do you think I should marry, then?"

Me.

Egad! Where had that bold thought come from?

Banishing the impetuous musings, she tossed back her shoulders. "I think you must find someone who is kind yet not soft as pudding, for I don't think you'd admire a spineless woman. You need a lady able to keep your keen mind engaged. The future Mrs. Price should be a champion of your ambitions while also holding tightly to her own, for you wouldn't esteem a wife who is a mere shadow of yourself. And of course, you must marry someone full of surprises, for you have intrigues of your own."

"Again, add in beautiful, and you've once more described yourself." The words traveled on a husky breath, the gleam in his eyes suddenly primal.

Her hands flew to her cheeks. "I never meant to insinuate such a thing."

"What if I did?" He stepped closer, and once more they stood nose to nose in the night. "I know I don't compare to a cloth-wrapped corpse, but could you—*would* you—consider a man such as me to spend the rest of your life with?"

Was he jesting? In a heartbeat she would! But was he truly offering, or was this just a game to him? Her jaw stiffened.

"I would turn that question back to you, Mr. Price. I am no socialite."

"No, there is so much more to you than that."

The heat of his gaze. The subject they danced around. This was perilous ground, far more daunting than a back-alley deal gone bad.

Footsteps raced up the stairs. They turned in unison as Barnaby dashed toward them.

"Sir," the butler puffed. "A doctor must be sent for at once."

"Why?" Edmund stepped away from her, angling a bit, as if his body could block her from whatever ill tidings Barnaby carried. "What's happened?"

"Two of the staff members have fallen ill." Even in the dim light the distinct bob of the butler's Adam's apple could be seen. "*Deathly* ill."

17

"Quarantine. Preferably in a separate building. Trust me, it's the only way. You do not want to see this spread."

Dr. Greenwood's diagnosis was a brick to Edmund's head, driving away the final sweet memories of holding Ami in his arms last night. He pressed his fingers against his temple, where a throbbing pain started, the walls of the study closing in on him. "Are you certain it's influenza?"

"I'm afraid so. I've given your housekeeper instructions until I stop back later this evening. In the meantime, I suggest you go on holiday. Even with the quarantine, anyone staying beneath this roof runs the risk of contracting the illness." He collected the medical bag near his feet. "Good day, Mr. Price."

Edmund rounded the desk to shake the man's hand. "Thank you, Doctor. Oh, and let's keep this information out of the public eye. I don't wish to alarm the neighbours."

"Naturally." Greenwood sniffed. "Panic is never good for the community."

Edmund let out a long breath as the doctor departed, devising what to say so as not to cause a fright amongst his guests or staff. Barnaby would remain level-headed, as would his housekeeper, but there was no guaranteeing how everyone else might react. What an untimely disaster. He glanced at the ceiling, his heart looking far beyond the plaster.

Merciful God, spare the lives of my two maids and grant the illness be stopped. This is beyond my control—and You alone know how I loathe such a weakness. I have been here before . . . please do not let me fail this time.

Horrid memories of the '86 cholera outbreak crowded in, upping the pounding in his head. So many lives lost. So many that could have been saved if he'd stood up to Colonel McDonnough and forced him to isolate the sick.

He yanked the bell cord harder than necessary. Clearing his throat several times over from a scratchiness that had taken root, he paced the rug until Barnaby poked his head in the door.

"Yes, sir?"

"The sick maids must be moved at once. Have Jameson settle his belongings in the house, then set the women up in his cottage. After that, no one but Mrs. Buckner is to have contact with them. Is that understood?"

"Without question." Barnaby gave a sharp nod. "I shall see it carried out at once, sir."

Barnaby strode away.

As did Edmund. With clipped steps, he hurried toward the breakfast room—only to be stopped in the front hall by a whistling tune and the ever-present wily grin on Bram Webb's face. His friend held a travel case in one hand, his hat tilted at a jaunty angle.

Edmund's brow bunched. "Leaving without breakfast?"

"I've an early train to catch. As always, Price, it's been entertaining." He shot out his hand.

Edmund gave it a hearty shake. "As much as I hate to see you go, my friend, I was about to ask you to leave anyway. There is illness in the house, so take a care should you start to feel poorly."

"You know me." He clicked his tongue. "Slipping away just ahead of danger is one of my virtues."

"Always the cavalier, but beware. One day you just may get

caught in a dangerous net." He clapped Bram on the back. "Thanks for valuing those coins. I owe you."

"A promise I shall collect on in the future, Price. Until then, I leave you with your guests—or lack thereof, as the case may be. I'll spare a quick good-bye to Ami, then let myself out." With a mock salute, he wheeled about.

Ami?

The throbbing in his head banged all the harder. Her name on his friend's lips was a punch to the gut, a blow he'd not take without knowing why.

"Wait." The word came out more of a growl than a command.

Bram turned, one brow lifted.

In three great strides, Edmund closed the distance between them. "Is there something I should know about you and my employee, Miss Dalton?"

Bram chuckled, mischief flashing in his eyes. "Why? Are you jealous?" He waggled his eyebrows.

Oh, he was more than that. He'd lost many things to his friend—countless cigars, a prized antique snuffbox, too many card games to count—but old companion or not, on this he would stand his ground. "So help me, Webb, if you trifled with Miss Dalton, I swear I'll—"

"Calm down." Bram chuckled. "I know I'm devilishly handsome, but it's not like that. I assure you the lady and I connected on a purely academic level. Turns out we have a lot of the same contacts thanks to her father's position. But why such vitriol from you?" Bram's eyes narrowed as he studied Edmund's face, then widened. "Ah, I see."

Despite his friend's seemingly harmless explanation of his relationship with Ami, irritation still spread like a bruise beneath Edmund's skin. "What do you see?"

"Something you fear." An impish grin flashed across Bram's face as he reset his hat. "Good-bye, Price." Turning on his heel, he strode away, resuming his whistled tune right where he'd left off.

Blast that Webb! His friend ever had been too deuced cryptic, which had done him no good in his college days nor now. Scowling, Edmund set off at a brisk pace to the breakfast room, foul of mood.

And his ire only increased when Violet swooped over to him and linked arms before he had both feet inside the door.

"There you are, naughty fellow." She poked him in the chest. "I've already finished my crumpet and jam and was hoping for a short stroll with you before you closet yourself away with my father."

The viscount peered over the top of his newspaper. "Not now, daughter. Time enough for such diversions after he's won the election."

Across the table, Gil shoveled in a final bite of eggs, then dabbed his mouth with a serviette. "I'll accompany you, Miss Woolsey."

She cast him a dark look. "I must decline your offer, Mr. Fletcher. I wouldn't wish Edmund to get jealous."

Hah. No danger of that. He unwound his arm from hers. Clearly the viscount hadn't yet spoken to her about his denial to marry her. He'd do so himself right now were he not trying to get them out the door posthaste. "I'm afraid there will be no strolling or any further discussion about my electoral platform. In fact, I must ask you all to leave."

"But, Edmund!" Violet popped her fists onto her hips.

"See here, Price." Bastion slapped the newspaper onto the table, rattling the teacups. "If you have any hope of winning, we must square away not only what you stand for but what you stand against."

"Understood, my lord, but we will have to work out the finer details via correspondence." He poured a stout cup of coffee and downed a few swallows, hoping the dark brew would ease the slight ache in his throat. "There is sickness in the house, and I would not have any of you taking ill."

"Nonsense. Don't tell me you're the sort of man to let a few sniffles shut down your political ambitions."

"Influenza is more than a trivial cold. I have two maids fighting for their lives even as I speak."

A little shriek pipped out of Violet, and she edged away from his side as if he suffered the plague.

"Aha!" Gil rapped the table. "The curse of Amentuk strikes again, eh, old man?"

Shoving back his chair, the viscount rose. "You may be right, Price. The final wording can be accomplished via wire. You'll be hearing from me. Come along, Violet."

He strode out the door, Violet's steps in double time to match his long strides.

Draining his cup, Edmund set it on the sideboard, then faced Gil. "If you hurry, you can ride into town with the Woolseys."

Gil laced his fingers behind his head and leaned back in his chair. "I'm not going anywhere."

"To stay might very well mean risking your life."

He tipped his head, morning sunlight glinting an odd gleam in his eyes. "I will not leave until I have my portion of the profit from those relics."

"You'd risk your life in order to collect a few coins?"

"I don't see you dashing out of here."

He bit back a wince. That hit home, for more reasons than one. Naturally, as master of the estate, leaving during a crisis could be seen as a dereliction of duty at best, and at worst, show he thought his life above those in his employ. A noble reason to remain, but not the only one.

He needed those antiquities sold. Soon. But how to do that without Ami's expertise? For he must ask her to leave, yet she was only a little over halfway through valuing the artifacts. And when she did leave, there was no question she'd take his heart right along with her. He froze, a cold sweat breaking out on his brow.

Sweet, blessed mercy.

Bram had been right.

Edmund spun away from Gil, fists and jaw clenched. Gooseflesh prickled along his forearms. He *was* afraid. Terrified, actually. For eight long years, he'd steeled himself against ever going through this again, yet despite his carefully crafted barriers, somehow—some way—love had sneaked in like a killer in the night.

Only this time was different. During moments of solitude, he increasingly found himself contemplating the idea that perhaps his views on marriage were skewed. Maybe by witnessing the dismal relationship of his parents and experiencing his own shallow alliance with Louisa, he'd become soured on what ought to be a God-given gift. And, oh, how he yearned for something beyond the superficial, especially after holding Ami in his arms last evening. He knew for certain now he'd never loved Louisa as thoroughly as that mismatched pixie of an Egyptologist.

He swallowed hard, throat aching. If Ami betrayed him as Louisa had, he'd never survive it.

Pausing from yet again trying to authenticate the griffin, Ami flopped her arms on the worktable and buried her face, giving in to a few moments of rest. No doubt she looked a wreck, which was why she'd skipped breakfast. Violet would have engaged in several jolly pokes about the dark crescents beneath her eyes and her loose, unbrushed hair. It couldn't be helped, though, for she hadn't slept a stitch last night. Every time she closed her eyes, all she could see was Edmund's face, his eyes, those lips. Bosh! She'd never desired a man so strongly. Which was unfortunate. There was no way a relationship could work between them. She knew nothing about his world of fancy dinners and political intrigues. Besides, had he truly meant it when he'd asked if she'd consider spending her life with him? It wasn't actually a proposal, not a drop-to-one-knee-and-request-her-hand-in-marriage sort of thing. Surely his words were mere whispers in the shadows, a momentary lapse of formality caused by the late hour and romantic setting. And yet . . .

She pounded her forehead against the table. Why did she wish his proposal had been real?

Behind her, footsteps clapped on the parquet floor. She sat

upright, twisting her hair with one hand, then jamming the pencil through it to form a makeshift chignon.

Bram Webb entered with a grin. "Just popping in to say good-bye and extend a reminder that if you or your father are ever in Cambridge, I'm the man to show you a good time."

No doubt he was. This charming scoundrel was part pirate, part scholar, and altogether mischief. Half a smile quirked her lips. "Thanks for the offer, but I wouldn't hold my breath on that were I you. If I ever have the chance to travel, you can bet my best pair of cotton gloves it will be to Egypt. Still, it was a pleasure meeting you."

He cocked his head. "But even more pleasurable for you to meet Price, eh?"

Heat crawled up her neck. Schooling her expression, she lifted her chin. "Mr. Price is a good man to work for."

"He's a good man period, so mind you tread lightly. I'd hate to see him crushed again by a woman."

Interesting. First a warning from Phineas, and now him? She'd never once broken a heart, nor did she intend to do so. Shifting in her chair, she leaned her elbows on the table at her back. "You ought to be having this conversation with Miss Woolsey. She's the one who means to marry him."

"Maybe so, but Miss Woolsey isn't the one he loves."

Her breath caught in her throat. Was he seriously implying that Edmund was in love with her? Dare she believe such a thing? If she did, that could change everything. Her hopes. Her dreams. She bit her lower lip, worrying the skin between her teeth. Would she truly be able to set aside her aspirations of uncovering Egyptian relics, all for the sake of a man? No indeed. There was no way she could turn her back on her years of hard work for a mere man . . . and yet there was nothing "mere" about Edmund Price.

"A word of advice, my new friend." Bram clapped on his hat. "To protect the treasures of the past, one must understand the delicate dance between excavation, conservation, and the cultivation of present relationships . . . and I'm speaking as much to myself as to you." The case clock in the corridor bonged, and he gave a nonchalant glance over his shoulder at the sound. "That's my cue. Good-bye, Ami." He dipped his head before wheeling about.

"Good-bye, Bram," she called after him.

It felt a little strange calling the man by his Christian name after knowing him for only a day, but truly, Bram Webb seemed more of a brother than anything—unlike Edmund. After the way he'd spoken to her last night, and now with Bram's declaration that he didn't love Violet . . . had those words whispered in the dark been more than a fleeting flirtation? Could she— should she—develop a relationship with him? Suddenly she felt torn between her duty to protect history, the desire to make history, and the craving to make a life with a certain blue-eyed man. Little tingles ran down her arms. Absently, she rubbed them as she turned back to work.

"I was hoping to find you here."

Her heart skipped a beat at Edmund's low voice, the tingles turning electric—but this was not the time to give in to fanciful emotions.

Pull yourself together, girl!

Inhaling deeply, she turned, veiling her true feelings. "Did you hear from the doctor?"

"Yes." He pulled over a chair, lines creasing his brow. "It's influenza. You'll have to pack your things at once."

Her heart squeezed at the thought of leaving Edmund and abandoning her work. "There are at least a dozen crates left to unpack. What about your deadline?"

"Unfortunately, it remains." He rubbed the back of his neck, and judging by the slight tightening of his eyes, she guessed he had a headache. "I'll just have to sell what you've already priced to Mr. Harrison and add in the rest at a flat rate."

The thought of these priceless antiquities tucked away in some forgotten corner of England churned the milk and tea in her belly. "What about the Cairo Museum?"

He shook his head. "I haven't heard back from them yet, and

even if I did, I suspect they would want a verified tally of each item, not boxes of unknown relics."

She met Edmund's gaze unwaveringly. "Then I shall stay and continue working."

"No. I will not have you taking ill."

"I won't." She swept her hand toward the only somewhat-empty corner in the room. "I'll have Barnaby set up a cot in here so there will be no need for me to interact with anyone."

"Absolutely not. I won't risk it."

"But I will." She flashed him a smile, yet it did nothing to slacken his frown.

"Why?" The morning sun pouring through the windows highlighted the weariness in his eyes, and something more . . . what? Surprise? Suspicion? Irritation? He gave his neck one last knead, then dropped his hand. "Your loyalty is, well . . . I must say it astonishes me."

"That's an easy enough question to answer. For one"—she held the small clay seal she'd been cleaning in front of his face— "these items belong in the Cairo Museum, and if having them legitimately valued and priced is what is required, then I shall do it. It is imperative such rare antiquities be showcased and celebrated by their own people."

"You've made that abundantly clear already. What's the other reason?"

"Because *you* made it clear you need the money." She set the seal carefully down on the soft cloth, then angled her head at him. "Though for the life of me I cannot understand why the wealthiest man I've ever met should need more."

He splayed his hands. "I may be wealthy, but most of my money is tied up in investments at the moment."

"So what is your pressing need that makes you require cash in hand? Surely you have everything you could want for."

"By the grace of God, I do, but it's not for me."

She tapped her finger against the tabletop. Who would this man deem so important that he'd take on such a daunting task as this?

"Then who?" she asked point-blank.

A soft sigh escaped his lips—a mouth she'd been trying very hard not to stare at.

Thankfully, he rose and began pacing. "When I first arrived in India, I was quite green. I didn't understand the culture, and I most certainly did not understand the land. Like a fool, I tried to broker all contracts myself, not trusting anyone to do so in my stead. One such deal, however, needed to be transacted on the other side of a mountain. The one—and only—road had been washed out, so I set off with a machete and the swagger of a twenty-two-year-old. I didn't make it very far before I tripped and landed on a snake."

He stopped in front of her, and with a quick roll of his sleeve, exposed the inside of his forearm. Two jagged lines, slightly irregular in shape, marred his skin. Raised. Slightly rough. Deeply pink. Less than a quarter of an inch, but deadly all the same.

"Oh my," she breathed.

"And unlike Miss Woolsey's experience in the garden"—he straightened the cuff of his sleeve—"this one truly was a deadly viper."

A shiver ran the length of her spine. "A Russell's viper?"

Admiration deepened the blue in his eyes. "You do know your snakes, don't you?"

Unfortunately, she did. That particular venom was highly toxic. He'd have suffered internal bleeding in a matter of hours and died within a day. She pressed a hand to her roiling belly. "How did you survive?"

"God's providence." He sank into his chair, looking more tired than she'd ever witnessed. "A native found me shortly after the strike. He slung me over his shoulder and ran me to his village, straight up the side of that mountain. I still marvel at his strength. I outweighed the man by at least six stone. He knew exactly what to do, and though it took nearly a month of recuperation, he never left my side . . . which earned him the ostracism of his tribe. Sanjay lost all standing in the village for his care of me—a white man."

"And it is this Sanjay who is in need right now?"

He nodded. "Because of me, Sanjay was forced to move his family to Calcutta. I helped him start a small textile business, and he and his family had quite the knack for weaving the traditional fabric patterns they grew up with. He struggled to sell it, though, the Calcuttans preferring nothing so quaint, so I exported some samples to London. That's when his business really took off. Once his extended family heard of his success, they left the village and moved in with him as well. As you've likely deduced, he is a very conscientious fellow and would not turn any of them away, which has been fine up till the present."

"Why?" Her brows pinched. "What changed?"

"There's an exorbitant new export tariff set to go into action at the end of next month, one that will drain all of Sanjay's current English sales—which makes up the bulk of his income—dooming him and his family to poverty."

Ami tapped her lower lip with one finger. "So you mean to sell this cargo and send the money to Sanjay. I am surprised he would take such charity. Men are generally very proud creatures."

"Not when it comes to saving the lives of loved ones. But to ease any discomfort he might feel, I'll send the funds along with a contract, making us official business partners, so no charity involved." He lifted his chin, defiant. "That will get him through until I can figure out a way to reverse the pending tariff legislation."

Most rich patrons with whom her father dealt clutched their purses with a death grip. She found it sweet that Edmund had the opposite mindset. She laid a light touch to his sleeve. "I think it is very noble of you to help your friend."

His gaze flicked between her touch and her eyes. "Just as I think it is noble of you to wish to stay here." His eyes hardened to gunmetal grey. "But I still insist you leave, and I won't take no for an answer."

18

A killer bunion slowed a man down. Brudge knew that from experience. A dog bite and a gunshot, however, well . . . that had stopped him in his tracks for a week. Blast that Price for putting armed guards around his property! He'd barely made it to his horse before those men had scaled the wall behind him.

Turning aside, Brudge spit out a wad as he limped over the broken cobbles of Cranham Street. The past week had been insufferable, what with Scupper moaning about his tender jaw from yet another rotten tooth. The man really ought to have them all yanked out and be done with it. Brudge swiped his hand over his mouth, annoyed with his hired muscle, the ache in his leg, and most of all Wormwell. Time was nearly out for paying back that villain.

A frown weighted his brow. Hopefully his boy, Neddie, was still alive. Would to God he'd had some other form of collateral to leave with Wormwell than his only son.

Next to him, Scupper kicked a stray cat out of his way, the screech of the wiry creature an affront to the ears. "Don't quite remember it bein' this far, guv'ner."

"Quit yer whining." He shot the big oaf a dark look. "Heaven knows I've heard enough."

But apparently God didn't agree, for ahead a costermonger yowled behind his cart, attempting to sell onions that were more mold balls than anything edible. Their decomposing stink added with the other pungent stenches of the Jericho neighbourhood. A fitting name for the slum of run-down hovels. It wouldn't take an army of horn-blowing Israelites to cave in this rookery. A good wind could take it down any day.

Just past the end of the Black Raven, he veered down a narrow passage running the length of the nefarious pub. A door with a slot at eye level stood at the back, where he rapped once, thrice, paused, then twice. The metal covering the slot scratched open. A bloodshot eyeball appeared.

"Password?" The voice was as raspy as the slot casing.

Brudge sighed. What a tiresome game. Dandrae wasn't that big of a player to require such security. "Noose and needle."

The slot slammed closed. The door creaked open. He and Scupper passed by a man reeking of rum and unwashed stockings. Climbing the rickety steps took effort, wrenching a wince out of him with each lift of his sore leg. Though it was only afternoon, ribald singing from the public room haunted the narrow stairwell.

At the top of the landing, another man stood with a gun at the ready and a scowl on his face. Without a word, he eyed them, then banged his fist on yet another door. "Fresh fish for ya, Boss."

"Send 'em in." The words filtered out with a thick Jamaican accent.

The thug swung the door open. Brudge, with Scupper trailing behind, entered a thickly carpeted, multicoloured room. Fresh flowers perfumed the air. Bright textiles hung on the walls, woven with Caribbean motifs. Dandrae sat behind an enormous mahogany desk, the chair cushion at his back aswirl with reds and oranges.

"What are ye selling this time, Mr. Brudge?" There was a melodic lilt to his words.

Brudge shored himself up against a nearby bookcase, forsaking the chair in front of Dandrae's desk. He played by his own rules, and it was best to remind Dandrae of that. Besides, it was as hot as a blast furnace in here. Just the thought of parking his backside on the velvet-covered seat beaded sweat on his forehead. "I'm not selling. I'm buying."

"Is that so?" The big man laced his fingers behind his head as he leaned back in his seat. Not so much as a dot of perspiration glistened on his skin. "What ye in the market for?"

"A particular item about yea big." He held out his hands, roughly sketching out the size of the statue he had yet to claim. A waft of his own body odour curled his upper lip. "The piece is made of gold. Got an eagle head and wings on the body of a lion."

Dandrae narrowed his eyes, a knowing glint sparking. "Ye mean a griffin?"

He flung his hands wide. "I don't know what the thing is called!"

"Sounds like a griffin, man."

"Whatever it is, I want it, and I know who's got it." He hobbled over to the imposing desk and planted his palms on the top. "That snip of a Shadow Broker."

"Then you are out of luck, man." A wide smile split Dandrae's face. "The Shadow Broker never sells, only buys."

"Then we make the offer too tempting to refuse."

Dandrae shook his head. "The Broker is not interested in coins, no matter how many ye got jingling in yer pocket."

"Then what'll tempt her?"

"She cares only for restoring Egyptian artifacts to the museum for the fancy of all folk."

Straightening, Brudge swiped the sweat from his brow with a stained cloth. "I've got something she'll want, then. Something she'll be willing to hand over that hideous little statue for."

"And what is that, man?"

He shoved his cloth into his pocket. "A promise."

Though Edmund had asked her to leave, here she was, still at Price House three days later, and there was nothing he could do about it. There was nothing he could do about anything, actually, which grieved her. Despite sorrow and fatigue weighting her steps, she trudged up the stairs with a sense of gratitude. Though half the house was abed, stricken by illness, at least no one had died.

She set off from the kitchen with a tray of beef broth, oddly relishing the quietness of the house—the soft ticking of clocks, steady as heartbeats, and the occasional creak of a floorboard beneath her padding feet. Without guests or servants wandering the corridors, the great house was peaceful. In the midst of this tranquility, a question lingered like a shy child peeking round a curtain. . . . Was there a value in this quietude that she'd never before recognized? That of simply being? It was freeing indeed to not have to prove herself to anyone, to merely live in the quiet moments where the world spoke in whispers. Perhaps—just maybe—all her striving to prove her intelligence and credibility didn't matter a whit to God. If that was true, then perhaps her worth was in who she was, who God made her to be, instead of being measured by what she achieved. Dare she believe that?

Hmm. Now there was a thought she wouldn't mind dwelling on instead of wondering just how many breaths Edmund might have left in him.

She climbed the stairs, clutching the tray and humming "Blessed Assurance" for all she was worth. Focusing on things for which she was grateful was the only way she'd gotten through thus far. If she dwelled on Edmund's pale face and feverish skin . . .

Oh, Lord . . .

Once again tears welled, the song broken and bitter in her throat.

Please, Father, grant that Edmund will recover.

She sped past Mr. Fletcher's closed door, a garish rendition of "The Blue Danube" pulsing behind it. As short-staffed as they were, he'd still ordered someone to haul the Swiss music box to his chamber. Selfish man. But at least it kept him occupied.

Sighing, she traveled the rest of the passageway to Edmund's door. Visiting a single man's bedchamber was nothing out of the ordinary for a housemaid—the role she'd added to her repertoire. And besides, there wasn't the slightest chance of anything untoward happening, not with Edmund being so ill. Still, she hesitated before entering. Somehow, it just felt indecent. Not to mention pointless. He'd not been awake to eat since Saturday, shortly after he'd ordered her to leave.

Shoving aside the last of her reservations, she balanced the tray on one hand and fumbled with the doorknob. At the very least, she could swab his brow with a cool cloth, though reading from her story seemed to better calm him when he was restless. She'd nearly recited the whole tale.

She pushed open the door and, three steps later, froze. Bedsheets fell over the side of an empty mattress. A pillow lay on the floor.

And eyes the colour of faded twilight stared at her from an armchair near the hearth, where Edmund sat in a loose-fitting nightshirt, a lap rug drawn hastily over his bare legs.

"Ami?" His voice broke, and he cleared his throat several times. "Are you . . . are you really here? Or is this another dream?"

"I hope not," she whispered, hardly able to make her own words come out. He was awake! He was whole! Granted, he was paler than a New Kingdom mummy, but nevertheless, he would live.

The first real smile she'd owned in days stretched her lips. "Been dreaming of me, have you?" Closing the distance between them, she set the tray on the small table at his side. "But in answer to your question, yes, I truly am here, and it is good to finally see you stirring. You are feeling better, I take it?"

"Much." His brows gathered, a dark line against his ashen skin. "But why are you here?"

"Bringing your dinner, of course." She held out a spoon.

Ignoring the offering, he shook his head. "No, I mean you should be gone. I told you to leave."

"You did. I didn't. You took ill, as did Barnaby and much of the staff, and I couldn't very well leave you unattended. Now, take this spoon and get some nourishment in you." She shoved the utensil into his hand, then held up the bowl so he could scoop a few bites.

"You gave me quite a fright, you know," she murmured as he ate. "Three days of seeing you confined to your bed, weak and helpless—" A tremble shook through her. "It felt like an eternity."

His hand paused midair. "And you've cared for me all this time?"

"Well, that's not all I've been doing. I'm still working on the artifacts, inching closer to finishing every day."

"You are a wonder."

"And you have broth on your chin." Setting the half-empty bowl aside, she retrieved a cloth and dabbed away the liquid glistening on the stubble shadowing his jaw.

He grabbed her arm and planted a light kiss to her wrist, his gaze boring deep into hers. Oh, how she'd missed those eyes, that look . . . this man.

"Thank you," he rumbled, genuine appreciation warming his tone. "Not many women would do such a thing."

"Yes, well, I've been told I'm not like other women. But all the same, you are very welcome." She pulled her hand away before she gave in to running her fingers through his sleep-tousled hair.

He leaned back against the chair cushion, weariness sagging his shoulders. Clearly he was overdoing it.

Ami tossed the cloth onto the tray and took the spoon from his fingers. "Looks like you've had enough for now."

"Mmm. I think so," he muttered. "Tell me, how are the maids who first fell ill faring?"

She smiled. "On their way to recuperation. Barnaby, however . . ." That grin faded. "He yet concerns me and the doctor, not to mention Mrs. Buckner. I've never seen a housekeeper so aflutter on his and the rest of the staff's behalf. She's been the true heroine during this whole trial. A regular force to be reckoned with. You should give her a pay raise—once your friend Sanjay is on financially solid ground, that is."

"She's not taken sick?" His gaze drifted over her face. "Nor you?"

Ami shook her head. "Not a sniffle. Neither has Mr. Fletcher suffered anything more than a hangover, though I can't say I'm surprised. He's quarantined himself in his quarters with loud music and a crate of rum. Says alcohol keeps influenza at bay." She shrugged. "Keeps him out from underfoot. Oh, and surprisingly, the Anubis statue hasn't budged a whit this whole time. Apparently the curse is too busy keeping everyone under the weather."

"Sickness, curses, snakes . . . is there nothing that frightens you?" Though he no doubt intended humor, fatigue thinned his voice.

"You gave me a great scare when I thought you might never open your eyes again. Now, I suggest you don't overdo. Let me help you back to bed." Rising, she held out her arm the same way he'd offered his several times in the past.

He frowned. "I shall make it back to my bed by my own power once you leave. I am no invalid."

"I can see that. Still, if you wish to be up and about soon, the more rest you get, the quicker that will happen." She shoved her elbow closer.

"If you continue with such insistence, you may witness more than you anticipate, my dear, for I am not actually dressed for the occasion." Amusement flickered in his eyes.

Fire flamed in her cheeks as her gaze shot to his bare legs, the idea finally lodging that the man wore only his nightshirt. She toed the Persian rug, unwilling to look at anything other than the tip of her shoe. "I didn't think, I mean I didn't consider you weren't wearing any—" She slapped a hand to her mouth. What a dolt.

He chuckled, drowsy yet good-natured. "Did you know your freckles darken when you're embarrassed? It's quite endearing."

She shook her head vehemently. "Not according to my nursemaid. I spent the first five years of my life having my face scrubbed with lemons."

"So that explains your aversion to the fruit."

She angled her head, finally daring to peek at him. "You noticed?"

His gaze burned into hers. "I notice everything about you."

This time heat fired a line from head to toe. She turned her back to him, making a great show of gathering up the tray. "Yes, well, since you're finished, I'll be leaving." She hastened to the door lest he witness the effect of his words.

"Ami?"

She paused with her hand on the knob, still refusing to face him.

"Thank you again. I owe you much."

"You owe me nothing, Edmund. I am happy to have helped."

She fled the room. Short-staffed or not, this was the last meal she'd deliver to his bedchamber.

19

It felt good to be in his study, out of his bedroom, away from the stuffy air and wrinkled sheets. Edmund relished the feel of pencil lead against paper, the soft scratch of it, the satisfying lines of his campaign emblem taking shape—until his lungs spasmed. An ugly black mark ruined the drawing as he reached for his handkerchief. Whenever the blasted cough took over, there was nothing he could do but ride the wave.

Ami entered with a tea tray, a frown scrunching her brow. "That's exactly what I feared. You're overdoing it. You've only been awake since yesterday. Please go back to bed."

His body agreed. His very bones cried out for a lie-down, fatigue weighing as heavily as the pressure in his chest. But even so, he straightened as he tucked away his cloth. "You fret like a fishwife. I am perfectly fine."

Setting down the tray, she searched his face. Worry shone in her eyes like a beacon. "Liar. That sheen of perspiration on your brow says otherwise."

Blast. He swiped his forehead with his sleeve. Leave it to a restorer of antiquities to notice such a detail. "I will rest, but first I wish to sketch an emblem for my campaign. The election will be here before I know it."

She arched a brow at the page with the unruly black mark. "That's a bold statement, though I'm not sure it's a very good one."

He grinned. "I appreciate your—"

Another coughing fit hit. Once again he grabbed his handkerchief, this time a little too exuberantly. Papers flew off his desk, several fat folders loosing quite a flurry, and yet he was helpless to stop the mess or his cough.

Oh, how he hated such weakness!

Concern etched a deep furrow into Ami's brow as she swiped up paper after paper. "You really should go to bed," she singsonged.

Ah, but he could watch her lithe figure working like this for hours. Suddenly he felt feverish—and this time it had nothing to do with being sick. But as she gathered the last of the sheets and began tucking them into a familiar folio, his blood ran cold.

He knew what that folder held and—God help him—he knew exactly the sort of heartache those devilish documents could breathe to life.

"Leave it!" he barked.

Yet it was entirely too late.

Ami turned to him, papers in hand, a knowing light in her eyes.

His gut twisted. She'd seen the writing. She'd read it. And once again he'd been exposed for the half-wit he truly was.

Surprisingly, she dipped her chin sheepishly as if she were the one who was humiliated. "I suppose I should tell you that I . . . em, well, this isn't the first time I've seen your writing, Edmund."

He tensed, his guard immediately raised. "There is no way you could have possibly read any of my work."

"I'm afraid there is." A lump traveled the length of her neck. "That day Mr. Harrison came to view your cargo, I put a tally of the artifacts on your desk before either of you entered your study. A notepad fell to the floor as I did so. I picked it up, not intending to read it, but . . . it just sort of happened."

She'd known? All this time? Then again, she'd not really had an opportunity to shame him about the matter.

Yet.

Rising, he snatched his poetry from her hand. "I will thank you to keep this to yourself, Miss Dalton."

She scowled up at him, eyes flashing fury. "I can't imagine what you think of me. I would never share your private writings with anyone!"

"I've heard that before." The words ground out of him as foul memories surfaced. Things he'd run halfway around the world to forget stung as sharply now as they had eight years ago.

Wheeling about, he slapped the folio onto the desk just as another bout of coughing racked through his body. Shaken and weary, he sank into one of the leather chairs near the hearth, clutching his handkerchief in a tight fist.

"Edmund, I'm so sorry. I never meant to pry." She dropped to her knees at his side, skirts billowing around her. "There is nothing to be ashamed of, you know. Your imagery is vivid, your words sweet."

"And they're spelled all wrong." He shoved the cloth into his pocket. Annoyed. Exposed. Vulnerable once again to a woman, an event he'd sworn he'd never repeat. A sigh ripped out of him. "I suppose you may as well know I suffer from congenital word blindness."

If the slightest amount of pity welled in her eyes, he'd stomp upstairs, short of breath or not, and pack her bags for her.

She merely leaned back on her heels. "But these books." She swept her hand toward the towering shelves. "You are so well read. How do you manage that?"

"Time. Just because it's difficult for me to read doesn't mean it is impossible, though most who know of such a debilitation would label me an ignoramus."

"Then they are the real fools. You suffer a challenge, not an incapacity."

"Easy for you to say. You're not the one who got kicked out of school or fled the country because of it." A churlish response, and he knew it, but there was no way to explain the shame he'd been forced to swallow over the years. Especially from his father.

"What has any of that to do with putting letters in the wrong spot? Well, school I can understand, but leaving England?" Her eyes narrowed. "This is tied in with Louisa, isn't it?"

Despite his frustration, admiration for her quick mind sneaked up on him. "You are too smart for your own good."

"And you seem as if you've not dealt with the past." Rising, she brushed off her skirt and took the chair adjacent to him. She curled her legs beneath her, like a cat ready for a good long sit. "It might be good to speak of such things. Bottling up bad memories is a recipe for broken glass. So . . . what happened?"

The question loitered on the air, where he left it for several heartbeats. He didn't believe for one second that voicing what had happened would remove his scars . . . and yet he also knew Ami would not be put off.

Blowing out a ragged breath, he plowed his fingers through his hair. "A proposal gone bad is what happened. I thought she loved me, but it turns out the only one Louisa Allen ever really loved was herself."

He rubbed his hand along his thigh, antsy despite his exhaustion. "I poured my heart into a deeply personal poem for her, believing it would express the depths of my affection more than the spoken word. It wasn't meant for public consumption. Ever. It wasn't even ready to share with her when she found it. And instead of treasuring it as a token of my love, she saw it as an opportunity to elevate herself."

His voice crackled with bitterness as he continued. "Louisa claimed it was nothing but a lark, just a playful way to gain attention at the Witherspoons' ball when she read it aloud, making sure to point out my spelling blunders."

"How awful." Her words hissed in time with the sizzle of the coals in the hearth. "Why would she do such a thing?"

"At the risk of sounding conceited, I believe it was due to my looks and fortune. She came from blue bloods. I came from money. She wished to knock me down a few pegs, revel in the power she had by birth over me. Use my vulnerable expression of love as a means to diminish me in front of others." He looked away, reluctant to meet Ami's gaze. "You have no idea what it's like to be laughed at for baring your soul."

"Yes, I do."

He swiveled his head to face her, unsure if he'd heard correctly, so soft was her voice.

She toyed with the button on the cuff of her sleeve. "I'd written a paper once, a culmination of my research into Egyptian burial rituals. I thought it would spark an in-depth discussion amongst my father's colleagues, but all it earned me was derision. Most claimed it was my father's work. The rest scorned my findings, saying a woman couldn't possibly understand such a nuanced subject, that females are too simpleminded."

Ami Dalton was many things—unorthodox, outspoken, lovely—but before a court of law she could never be accused of being simpleminded. "You are the most intelligent woman I know. I am sure your insights were brilliant."

She faced him with a lift to her lips. "And I am certain Louisa was a fool."

He inhaled deeply, her words a balm. As her gentle voice faded along with the echoes of his own past struggles, right there in the middle of his study, weak and weary and worn, he felt the presence of God's love enveloping him. Enveloping them. Almost as if a divine hand reached out, assuring him his vulnerabilities were not signs of weakness but were in fact opportunities for God's love to be made perfect. Love, a sentiment he'd dismissed ever since Louisa, now lingered at the edges of his thoughts like an unexpected guest, challenging the cynicism he'd held on to for far too long—beckoning him to let go of it. Unbidden, he laid his hands in his lap, palms open, a silly symbol of release.

Yet one that resonated deep within.

Untucking her legs, Ami rose and once again knelt at his side. Her eyes were luminous, lit with the sort of ethereal glow that only a master painter could capture.

"You need never fear that I will shame you," she whispered.

His throat closed, and he reached out, gently laying his hand upon her cheek. "Nor I you," he whispered back.

How long they sat thus, he couldn't be sure, but he'd do so for all eternity would God allow it.

At length, she pulled away. "I suppose I should get back to work. After all, I'm not the recuperating patient, and those artifacts aren't going to tally themselves. Whoever ends up purchasing the lot will want a full accounting."

"Ah yes, about that." He rose and offered his hand, righting her before spilling the bad news. "I heard back from the Cairo Museum. They didn't offer anything close to what Harrison can pay."

"Enough for Sanjay?"

He shook his head. "I'm afraid not. Gil gets half of the profits, as per our business contract."

"But, Edmund, surely whatever the museum can manage would hold your friend over until you free up other funds."

"It's not that simple." Though it had seemed so at the time when he'd signed that contract for the Bengal Express railway. It would take at least nine more months before his railroad investment could be accessed—too late to help Sanjay.

Ami popped a fist on her hip, that one simple movement ending the closeness they'd shared. "Those relics are special. They belong—"

"In the Cairo Museum. Yes, I know, for so you've told me countless times." He pressed his fingers to his temple, the latent headache flaring to life.

A storm cloud darkened on her brow. "You make that sound like a bad thing."

"It's not, but neither is it a profitable thing."

"Money isn't the be-all and end-all!"

Hah! Said like a true working scholar. "It is when that's what is keeping your family from starvation."

"I understand that, truly, but . . ." She bit her lip, grief sagging her shoulders. "It's just that I cannot stand to think of those precious relics hidden away in a private collection, lost to obscurity. They should be accessible to the Egyptian people."

"I'm sorry, Ami, but my hands are tied in this matter. There are no alternatives." He didn't like voicing the words any more than she liked hearing them, yet they had to be said.

Uneasy silence descended, the occasionally pop of the coals jarring.

"Very well, then." She whirled so violently, the hem of her skirt slapped against his legs. "I shall get to work."

"Ami, please." He took a step toward her. "Don't be cross with me."

She did not turn back.

"I'm not cross. I'm just . . . frustrated." Flinging out her arms, she strode through the door.

For a long moment he stood there, listening to her steps clomp down the corridor, his chest tightening like a cloth wrung too tightly. Would to God he could please her and Sanjay, but how? Stuck between a rock and a hard place would be a holiday compared to this.

Like a rat with sharp teeth, the idea of those precious antiquities remaining in England gnawed at Ami as she stomped out the door, leaving Edmund to wonder at her childish behaviour. In truth, she barely understood it herself. On one hand, indignation practically choked her to see those relics anywhere except in Cairo. On the other, she couldn't help but admire Edmund's dedication to his friend.

Conflicted, she stomped up the stairs instead of heading straight for the workroom. She could use a good lie-down herself after the harrowing past few days, but she'd have to settle for draping her trusty old shawl about her shoulders. There was something comforting about her worn wrap. A shield from the outside world and from inner turmoil. Like an embrace across the years from her grandmother.

Once past her threshold, however, she bypassed the tasseled

green fabric hanging from a hook and strode straight to her nightstand. Perched atop a small silver salver was an envelope with her name penned on the front in familiar handwriting. Picking it up, she broke the red seal on the back.

I have a buyer for your golden griffin. Price is not a stumbling block.

She blinked. How did Mr. Dandrae know about that? Had that journalist, Mr. Kane, posted something? If so, this could be only the beginning of trouble—dire trouble.

It is the wish of Mr. Tariq Khafra to return the valuable piece to his homeland. Bring the item tomorrow night, Covered Market, outside the butcher stall, eight o'clock.

She sank onto her bed, envelope in hand, mind a mile away. An Egyptian wished to purchase the griffin? And bring it back to Cairo as she wished? Was this some sort of miraculous answer to prayer?

Aimlessly, she tapped the corner of the note against her thigh. She couldn't possibly take the man's offer . . . could she? The griffin wasn't hers to sell. But if price was no issue, she could meet with the buyer and negotiate a very pretty penny for it. Or better yet, tell him of the other riches and encourage the man to meet with Mr. Price about purchasing the entire lot. Wouldn't Edmund be pleased about that? Sanjay would have enough funds to survive, and the antiquities could be relocated to where they belonged.

A small smile curved her lips as she thought more on a plan. Perhaps beauty could be made of these ashes after all.

20

Night air wafted in as Edmund swung open the front door and stood aside so Mr. Harrison could pass. It was a mild evening. The sweet scent of roses a perfume. The moonlight soft and inviting. A perfect time for lovers to stroll hand in hand.

And yet he'd been holed up in his study with Gil and the man who wished to purchase the Egyptian antiquities. Harrison was eager. He'd give him that. The man hadn't been deterred one little bit by the lingering threat of influenza when he'd come to call earlier, though Edmund had made it clear there were several in the household yet abed. Apparently all the notes Gil had sent him about the cursed folklore behind the griffin had indeed lured him in. A tight grin stretched his lips. He had to hand it to Fletcher. The man knew how to reel in a buyer.

Edmund shook Harrison's hand. "As I said, once Miss Dalton has a completed list, I shall forward it to you at once."

"Very good." He clapped his hat on tightly. "Good night, Mr. Price."

"Good night, Mr. Harrison."

Edmund closed the door, drained beyond reason. His very bones ached with fatigue as he bypassed the study and went straight to the sitting room, hoping to spy Ami. It was hard to pull her from her work, harder still to have to tell her of Harrison's increased interest in the relics, and yet he must. Judging by the way she'd stomped out of his study that morning, she wouldn't like it.

Sure enough, she sat across the room, eyeing him from the sofa. "Mrs. Buckner said you wished to speak with me."

"I do." But first he detoured to the drink cart and poured them each a glass of water, omitting the lemon in hers. After handing her the refreshment, he sat next to her, thoroughly spent. "It's been a long day." He took a drink and side-eyed her. "How are you faring?"

"Better than you, I think." She set her glass on the tea table without so much as a sip. "You didn't sleep this afternoon, did you?"

Perceptive little sprite. He chugged the rest of his water and placed his glass next to hers. "I can neither confirm nor deny that."

"Just as I suspected." She reached for his hand, her touch gentle, her skin warm. "You've been through a lot."

His gaze fixed on her small hand holding his. There was nothing sensual about the act. Just one friend seeking to comfort another. And yet it did strange things to his heart.

She squeezed his fingers. "I'm sorry I walked out in such a huff this morning."

"Yes, well, you might do so again."

"Why?" She pulled her hand away.

"I just saw Mr. Harrison to the door. He's chomping at the bit for those antiquities. In fact, he's doubled his offer. I told you Gil was a good businessman. So after all this, I'm afraid once you've finished cataloguing the relics, I'll have no reason not to sell the lot to Mr. Harrison."

She deflated against the cushion. "I suppose that is good for Sanjay and his family."

He studied her. It wasn't like her to give up so easily. "Indeed."

218

"But what if"—she faced him, a mysterious glint in her eyes—"just imagine for a moment that there was a way to provide your friend the money he needs while at the same time get your cargo into the hands of the Egyptian people. Would you entertain such an offer if it could be arranged?"

"There is no other offer, though I suppose were one to present itself as you've described, we would both be satisfied, hmm?" Despite his exhaustion, he couldn't help but smile at her girlish enthusiasm. "Though I must say with you here, now, I cannot imagine feeling any more content."

A deep sigh expanded her chest. "Me too. And who knows? Perhaps just such an offer may come along. Miracles still happen, you know."

"Of course they do. You're here with me, after all." He snagged the curl she'd tucked away and freed it to run wild, relishing the silky feel of her hair against his skin. "As you'll note, Miss Woolsey fled at the slightest hint of danger, and yet here you are, despite accidents, illness, and all manner of unexplained phenomena."

"I couldn't very well leave you to fend for yourself." She smirked. "What do you know of amulets and scarabs?"

The arch of her brow, the pink in her cheeks . . . he could gaze at this woman forever and never tire of the sight. "What I know is that you are a very special lady."

Her lips parted, yet no words came out. None needed to. He didn't want flattery or platitudes. The genuine admiration in her eyes was enough. *She* was enough, eccentricities and all.

Somewhere in the distance a bell rang.

"Edmund?" Her name on his lips never ceased to thrill him.

"Hmm?" he murmured.

"Aren't you going to answer that?"

"Answer what?"

Half a smile quirked her lips. "The door. Barnaby isn't back on duty yet, and Mrs. Buckner is still short-staffed."

The bell rang again, breaking the enchantment that'd so thoroughly gripped him.

"Oh, em . . . yes." He pointed a finger at her. "But don't go anywhere. I'm hoping we can pick up where we've left off."

Still tired yet also surprisingly refreshed, he strode to the front door.

And opened it to a complete stranger.

The man on the stoop stared at him with eyes so intense, Edmund got the distinct feeling the sum of his character was being categorized and filed away to be used against him at some point in the future. The stranger was a gaunt-faced fellow, more lines carved into his cheeks and brow than those on a carriage-route map. He held a battered valise in one hand, a faded hat in the other—or it might be a dead hedgehog, so limp did the worn thing hang in his grasp. A shock of grey hair stood out on all ends of the man's head, as if the wiry bush wished to make a run from his scalp. Overall, the fellow would make a fantastic Dickens character.

Edmund angled his head. "Can I help you?"

"I should hope so." The man sniffed. "Are you Mr. Price?"

"I am." He nodded.

"Then it's the other way around." The man lifted his chin to an imperial tilt. "*I* am the one who can help *you*."

Leaning her head back against the sofa cushion, Ami closed her eyes, a smile on her lips. When Edmund looked at her, well . . . even now it stole her breath. No man had ever taken such notice of her before, looked past her haphazard appearance to the true woman inside.

Footsteps drew closer, and she sat up, taking care to tuck her hair into place. Whoever had come to call surely didn't need to witness her sprawled on the sofa like a loitering vagrant. Edmund strode in first, followed by her father.

Her—what?

She bolted to her feet. "Father?"

"Last time I checked I still was." He set down his suitcase, balancing his favorite hat atop it.

Ami dashed over and grabbed his hands. Rising to her toes, she planted a light kiss on his cheek. As always, he stood as stiffly as the statue of Anubis. Oh, he loved her, as a father must, though even now she yearned for more overt expressions of his affection. Over the years she'd learned to accept his lack, cherishing even more the rare times he graced her with a thumb to her cheek when she'd delighted him with a scholarly discovery.

She pulled away, taking his familiar scent of resin and turpentine along with her. "I expected a telegram, not you in person. Your dig's not over for three more weeks."

"Just like your mother." He clicked his tongue. "Always expecting me to keep a reliable schedule."

She frowned. "While I am happy to see you, you should know there has been influenza in the house. Several staff members are still abed."

"Pish!" He cut his hand through the air. "Just as I told your host over there"—he nodded toward Edmund—"I've recently come from a raging outbreak of malaria, and that didn't stop me. Can't imagine a silly little bout of coughing would slow me a whit."

Edmund chuckled as he strolled to the drink cart. "You are as strong-willed as your daughter, sir. And yet I admit I am every bit as curious as she as to why you are here."

"Great finds aren't all buried beneath pyramids. I hear there is a particularly valuable relic beneath your roof, Mr. Price."

She laid her fingers on his sleeve. "But, Father, I don't know that for certain. I hate to think of you cutting short your expedition for nothing."

"I didn't train those instincts of yours to be wrong, Amisi." He swept his hand toward the door. "Take me to the griffin in question."

She looked to Edmund. "I, em, I don't actually know where you've locked up the piece."

He set down the decanter, her father's request putting an end to his drink duty. "Follow me."

He led them across the vast receiving hall. Behind him, her

father frowned at her, his gait a bit off. "This is highly irregular, Amisi." The words were low, for her ears alone. "As the resident scholar, you should have control of the artifacts at all times."

The disappointment in his voice stung like a hornet. "I know, Father, but there's been extenuating circumstances."

"It had better be good."

"I wouldn't call it that."

He eyed her as they swung into the corridor opposite that of the workroom. "Then what would you call it?"

Exactly. What ought she call the ill-fated occurrences that'd been happening ever since she'd set foot in Price House? Her father might believe in curses, but she surely didn't. Even so, there was no solid explanation, so she pressed her lips flat.

And thankfully right at that moment, Edmund pushed open the door to his steward's office. "In here." He quickly lit the gas lamps as they entered.

She and her father took up a position at the corner of the big work desk while Edmund rounded it and fiddled with the brass lock on a black safe nearly the height of him. Moments later, he hefted out the golden griffin and set it atop the desk. Ami cringed that this precious piece must be locked away with gunpowder and birdshot, yet it was for the best to keep it safe.

"Well, well, well," her father mumbled as he elbowed past Edmund and took the steward's chair. Not sharing her qualms about fingering the object without gloves, he slowly turned the griffin in a full circle. "Light. I need better light."

Edmund retrieved a matchbox from one of the desk drawers, then brought a flame to life, touching it to the wick of a large oil lamp on the desk. Once lit, he shoved the globe closer to her father.

"What do you think?" Ami prodded.

"Mmm." He bent over the griffin, his ever-wild hair flopping onto his brow.

Edmund joined her side, whispering, "Is that a favorable sign?"

She shook her head. "Too early to tell."

After a few more incoherent mumbles, her father shot out his hand, palm up, never once pulling his gaze from the artifact. "A vernier caliper and some hydrochloric acid are needed, Amisi."

Ignoring Edmund's curious gaze, she raced to the workroom and snatched up her travel kit. On the way back to the steward's office, she rummaged for the requested items, so that by the time she returned to the desk, she could immediately set them both within her father's reach.

His arm snaked out, retrieving the caliper, and for the next endless minutes, he lightly set the points of the tool in different positions.

Edmund peered at her. "What is he looking for?"

"Measuring the dimensions." Wait a minute. Her father ought to have known she'd already have done so. She cocked her head at him. "I have taken stock of the measurements, Father. They match the griffin's description perfectly."

"Surely you should know I am not measuring the dimensions." Censure tightened his voice, and for the first time since beholding the statue, he glanced up at her. "I am tracing the contours of the wings, the curve of the beak, the ridges on the body. Slight nuances in design elements equate to different periods. Have I taught you nothing, Amisi?"

Shame burned in her belly. Suddenly she was eight years old again, receiving an ear-blistering lecture about wrongly assuming the false water cobra in the aquarium was a harmless rainbow boa—and she'd nearly been struck when she'd reached in her hand. Her father was right. Had he not taught her anything? Would to God the floor could just open up and swallow her here and now.

She dipped her head. "Of course, Father. My error entirely."

He went back to work.

Edmund stepped side to side with her, his tone thick with sympathy. "We are all wrong now and then."

His defense warmed her as the minutes ticked on.

"Aha," her father said at last. Setting down the caliper, he leaned back in his chair and untucked the hem of his shirt. Dust from his travels snowed off his shoulders as he ripped away a chunk of fabric, balled it up, then grabbed the acid bottle and dumped some of the liquid onto the wad.

"I have swabs, Father." She reached for her bag. "All you need do is ask."

He held up a finger. "It is unconventionality that yields the most extraordinary results."

Tipping the griffin back several inches, he gently wiped a spot on the belly, which was odd. The solution would do nothing. She'd already validated it was made of gold.

Tossing the cloth aside, he then reached inside his coat pocket and pulled out a brass-framed magnifying glass, the one and only tool he carried at all times. As he studied the small area he'd cleaned, a wide grin spread on his lips.

She and Edmund bent close.

"What is it?" she whispered.

Her father leaned back in his chair, pleasure radiating from his hazel eyes. "See for yourself." He offered over the magnifier.

She snatched it in a heartbeat and rounded the desk, cracking her hip on the way but so be it. What had he found? Squinting one eye, she studied the griffin's belly. Sure enough, in a patch hardly larger than her pinky fingernail, whatever had been painted to appear as gold in that tiny area had rubbed off—only to reveal more gold beneath.

And some very small hieroglyphics carved into the soft metal.

"Ka-ho-tep," she interpreted. "Kahotep?" She snapped her gaze to her father. "'The Ka is satisfied'?"

"Indeed." He folded his hands across his belly.

Edmund flapped his hands on the desktop. "What does that mean?"

"Yes, Father, what *does* it mean? I've never heard that name in association with the golden griffin."

Her father took the magnifier from her hands and cleaned the glass with his ripped shirttail. "Many years ago, I had the privilege of visiting a hidden temple dedicated to the sun god,

Ra, where I discovered an ancient inscription on the underside of an altar. This carving connected the name Kahotep to an animal with the body of a lion and the wings of an eagle."

"A griffin." She shook her head. "But that doesn't necessarily mean the Golden Griffin of Amentuk."

"True, yet remember, one should never jump to conclusions for or against a foregone conclusion." He tucked away his magnifier and once again leaned back in his chair. "Now then, according to the inscription, Kahotep was an esteemed priest of Ra, known for his deep devotion and unparalleled knowledge of solar magic. Some say he communed with the sun god himself. There is a story that during a sacred ritual, he transformed into a griffin to fly nearer to his god."

"I'm sorry"—Edmund shook his head—"but what has this to do with Amentuk?"

"Absolutely nothing." Her father chuckled.

Ami hefted a sigh. How could she have been so wrong? Edmund would never respect her work now. She could hardly respect herself.

"So," she drawled glumly, "this isn't the golden griffin after all."

Her father rapped the desk with his index finger, a habit he employed when annoyed. "Don't be ridiculous, Amisi. Of course it is."

She blinked. "How do you know?"

"Amentuk was not merely a geographical location or a forgotten kingdom. It was the sacred ground where Kahotep performed his ritual. The hidden chamber in which this little beauty was kept was where the divine energies of Anubis and Ra converged—where the golden griffin was believed to have been created. This artifact is powerful beyond any of our imaginations."

And there he went again, taking Egyptian religion much too far. She scowled. "Oh, Father, like Mother and Grandmother, you know I don't believe in Egyptian magic. God alone is the all-powerful One."

He wagged his finger. "Yet you cannot deny the very real powers of Pharoah's magicians during Israel's bondage."

"Smoke and mirrors, Father."

"Or demonically inspired acts," Edmund added.

"Yes, well, whatever your beliefs, this is the true Golden Griffin of Amentuk." He patted the little statue on the wings. "A cursed artifact if ever there was one."

21

"Ha-ha! So the curse is real. I knew it!"

Ami took a scalding sip of breakfast tea to keep from rolling her eyes at Mr. Fletcher's outburst. Across the table, her father fingered his chin—which was now freshly shaven. Despite his crooked bow tie and trademark explosion of hair shooting out in all directions atop his head, it appeared he'd slept well last night. She hadn't. Her mind had run circles trying to figure out how to talk Mr. Khafra into meeting with Mr. Price when she rendezvoused with him.

"Tell me, Mr. Fletcher." A twinkle danced in her father's eyes.

She pressed her serviette to her lips, hiding a smirk. She knew that look. Father was on a fact-finding mission.

"What indications led you to believe the curse is genuine? Have you any tangible evidence?"

Edmund strolled over from the sideboard, a plate of toast and jam in hand. Forsaking the head of the table, he sat next to her. "I assure you, Professor, Gil has nothing but conjecture on which to base his assumptions."

"Ha-ha! What does it matter, old man?" Mr. Fletcher slapped the table, rattling the flatware. "Harrison believes the curse is the cause for the workman breaking his leg, then the maid spooked by a black cat, the crack on my skull, and the continuing mystery of the moving statue."

Her father angled his head. "What moving statue?"

"The ugly mug in the workroom. Ask your daughter about it."

Her father arched a brow, silently indicting her as if she'd neglected to tell him about a lost manuscript detailing an ancient civilization. She set down her teacup with a sigh. "I'm sure there's a reasonable explanation for it, but for the past few weeks, the statue of Anubis has turned slightly whenever I return to the workroom. Hasn't happened for days now, though."

"I'm not surprised." Mr. Fletcher reached for the teapot, spilling dark liquid on the tablecloth as he sloppily poured a cup. "That curse was too busy frightening poor Miss Woolsey half out of her mind with a ghost, and let's not forget the influenza outbreak. Harrison ate up those additions like a dish of fine caviar."

Shoving away his plate, her father leaned back in his seat. "That seems like far too many coincidences to happen in such a short span of time."

"I rest my case." A smug smile curved Mr. Fletcher's lips, taking his moustache along for a ride. "Don't you think, Professor, that with such power tied to an artifact it ought to sell for quite a pretty penny?"

Her father shook his head. "Greed is the downfall of many a good man, Mr. Fletcher. Besides, that piece is valuable for its historical and social relevance, not for any supposed supernatural power."

Edmund set down his jam knife. "So you don't actually believe the griffin has caused any trouble?"

"What I believe or don't believe about it doesn't change the griffin's worth."

Mr. Fletcher lifted a finger. "But what others believe about it may."

La! The idea of tying power into an inanimate object for the sake of profit curdled the milk in her belly. Just like her father, she pushed her own plate away. "The truth is, Mr. Fletcher, that good and bad things occur every minute of every day, yet God is sovereign over all. Nothing happens that is not by His design. You cannot increase or decrease the price of a relic by attaching make-believe occurrences to it."

"The lady is correct." Edmund smiled at her, then leveled a steely gaze at Mr. Fletcher. "And yet the fact remains that no matter what, I am not selling the griffin."

Bosh. Could she and Mr. Khafra convince him to sell it? Would Mr. Khafra even be interested in the rest of the lot if the griffin wasn't included?

Edmund's gaze drifted to her father as he drained his cup. "Will you be going back to your dig now that you've confirmed the authenticity of the griffin?"

Her father shook his head. "By the time I got there, I'd have to turn right around and come back to Oxford. I thought, if you don't mind, that Amisi and I could work together to finish valuing your cargo. I'd dearly love to see what's in the rest of those crates."

Ami glanced sideways at Edmund, curious as to how he'd answer.

He hesitated a moment, crisply folding his serviette, then setting it beside his empty plate. "I suppose with two of you on the job, the valuation will go much faster."

Mr. Fletcher clapped his hands, the report of it sharp against the breakfast room's walls. "Capital! The sooner we can sell, the better."

"And the sooner you'll be gone," Edmund said under his breath.

She'd have missed it had he not been sitting so close. Interesting. Clearly he wasn't happy with his partner. He really ought to let the man go despite his repeated assurances that Mr. Fletcher was a good businessman.

Her father shoved back his chair. "Well then, let's have at it. Come along, Amisi."

She rose, giving Edmund's shoulder a light squeeze as she did so. "Try not to overdo it today. You're still recovering, after all."

"I shall take your words to heart." He winked.

Which never failed to zing a thrill straight to her belly. She scurried away lest Edmund see the pink that was surely flushing her cheeks.

By the time she caught up with her father, he was already halfway across the front receiving hall. "I am curious about something, Father."

"That's my girl!" He smiled. "Curiosity is the compass that leads to unexplored worlds."

"Yes, well, I haven't found any uncharted territories quite yet, but I did discover one of your journals is missing in the college archives. I was looking for the collection dated 1866 to 1869. Did you know it was gone?"

"Of course I did."

"Then where is it? Polly has no record of it being checked out."

He pulled a folded wad of paper from his coat pocket. "Here it is, well, part of it, anyway. And if Polly wishes items to be recorded, then she ought not take such long lunch breaks."

Ami crinkled her nose. "Why are you carrying part of your journal around?"

He tucked the papers back into his pocket as they swung into the workroom corridor. "Great-Grandmother Dalton's recipe is written on the back of one of the pages. I knew I'd never remember it while in Egypt, so I took it along with me. It's very helpful."

Hmm. Segmenting information instead of giving a full lecture was a favorite evasion tactic of his—and one of hers.

"What is the recipe for?" She studied him as they walked, spying for a nonchalant touch to his earlobe.

"A special herbal concoction, that's all." His hand raised.

And there it was. A jiggle to his ear—a sure sign he was hiding something.

In two quick steps, she blocked his path. "All right, Father, what are you not telling me?"

His lips pursed slightly, then parted as a sigh whooshed out of him. "Very well. I suppose you should know I've been battling chronic joint pain for some time now. The strain of expeditions is taking a toll on this old body. Nothing to fret about, though."

"Naturally I shall fret!" She popped her fists on her hips. "I am your daughter. I don't wish to see you in pain."

"For now, the recipe is doing its job." He patted her cheek as he sidestepped her. "But we have more pressing matters to attend."

Stubborn man. She followed behind him, this time intently studying his gait. Sure enough, his legs moved stiffer than she remembered. Either Great-Grandmother Dalton's recipe wasn't doing a nip of good, or that joint pain was too far advanced for it to help.

He entered the workroom ahead of her, and she nearly stumbled into him as he'd not gone more than two steps inside before stopping.

"Is this the position in which you last saw Anubis?" He swept his hand toward the long-snouted statue.

She glanced past his shoulders.

Oh dear.

Not again.

Meat hooks dangled overhead, the rank scent of blood so thick on the air Brudge could almost taste the metallic tang of it. He swiped his mouth with the back of his hand, more than pleased. Tucked away from the main thoroughfare, at the farthest end of the narrowest passage in the Covered Market, the butcher stall was the perfect setup. He'd be the one in the shadows this time.

Hunkering into the thin space between stalls, he took care not to bang his sore leg against the corner beam. He knew the woman's ways now. How she operated. Her movements. Then again, she also knew him—which was exactly why he'd ordered

Scupper to perch like an oversized duck atop the awning brace across the lane. She'd be expecting a grab from behind, not above.

A quick drop. A quicker capture. And that statue would be his.

Pulling out his pocket watch, he flipped open the dented cover and could just make out the minute hand slipping into position onto the twelve. Eight o'clock sharp. He ought to hear her footsteps any second now. Muffling the snap of the lid with the palm of his hand, he slid the watch into his pocket and flicked his gaze to look down the passage.

Then he startled to see the woman already there in front of the butcher stall. Ah, but she was a sly one. Were she not such a haughty wench, he'd consider making her his woman. Maybe even take her on as a partner. She'd certainly smell better than Scupper. Feel softer too. Maybe even be less whiny.

"Mr. Khafra?" Her voice echoed against the empty stalls.

Brudge's gaze drifted over her, from a collar half-upturned, to a—stone the crows! Was that a man's waistcoat over her blouse? Her skirt looked like she'd nipped it off a gypsy, and her shoes might be better suited to a dancer. Some sort of satin slippers. No wonder she'd glided in so quietly. But her hands were empty. She didn't clutch a bag nor was there one on the ground at her feet. And there was no way she could have tucked that heavy figure into her waistband.

Fury burned up his neck. Another one of her little tricks? Stashing the item elsewhere in the market until she saw the money for it?

"Mr. Khafra?" Slowly she spun in a circle. "I am ready to discuss the purchase of the griffin if you would but show yourself."

He licked his lips, coaxing out his best attempt at an Egyptian accent. "I prefer ze shadows, my friend. How much do you want for ze relic?"

She snapped her gaze toward where he hid, planting both fists on her hips. "You are no more Egyptian than my left stocking. I demand to know who I am working with, or there will be no exchange."

Blasted woman! Too smart for her own good. Ah well. She'd not outsmart him this time. He stepped from the shadows.

The whites of her eyes gleamed brightly, her surprise as pleasing as a frothy mug of ale. "Mr. Brudge! What are you doing here?"

"Where's the statue?" he growled.

"How do you know about—" She lifted her chin. "Mr. Khafra hired you to do his dirty work, did he?"

"Stupid woman. *I* am Khafra." He chuckled, triumphant in having outwitted her. "If you could see your face right now, love. Absolutely priceless. So where's that piece?"

"Pish." She snorted. "Surely you didn't think I'd bring such a valuable artifact to a deserted market?"

"You would have done so for an Egyptian buyer, which clearly you thought I was." He took a step closer, scanning the lane behind her in case she had brought company this time.

"You know nothing about me, Mr. Brudge, and I have nothing further to say to you. Good night." She pivoted.

He snapped his fingers.

Scupper plummeted, landing like a big cat at her back. In one swift movement, he slung his arm around her chest, pulling her against him, the flash of a blade at her throat.

A rabid filly couldn't have looked more feral than the woman's wide eyes and flaring nostrils. To her credit, though, she didn't cry out.

Brudge grinned. "And you know nothing about me, missy. I will have that flying lion, and I will have it now. Where is it?"

"I cannot speak," she ground out, voice raspy, "with a knife to my throat."

He glanced past her to Scupper. "Let her go, but don't let her get away."

"Ye sure, guv'ner?" The big oaf's curled moustache twitched. "Me mum used to say better a loaf o' bread on the table than a feast in the clouds."

Brudge spit out a curse. "I've had enough of your mother's blabberings. Do it!"

Scupper immediately loosened his hold, stepping back a pace, knife yet at the ready.

The woman gasped for air as she brushed herself off, ruffled as a peahen, then lifted her nose in the air. "The griffin is locked safely away, Mr. Brudge. Out of your hands and mine. I came here to tell the fictitious Mr. Khafra as much."

"Claptrap! I don't believe a word of it."

"Neither do I believe that even if I had the relic with me, you'd have enough money to purchase it. So it appears we are at a stalemate. I suggest we all walk away disappointed and call it an evening."

"Hah!" he barked. "You underestimate the lengths I am willing to go to get my hands on that moneymaker."

"Then you will have to deal with Mr. Price, not me. He's the only one with the combination to the safe." Her lips flattened into a smug line.

Blast it all! This was not going the way he'd so carefully planned. He rubbed at the ache in his hip, yet another part of his body gone wrong from all the limping over the past fortnight. What to do? How to salvage this?

Wait. Why take on the work of it himself?

"You're a crafty woman." He aimed his finger at her. "Find a way to wheedle that statue out of Price, then send word to Dandrae."

"It won't work. Mr. Price is a man accustomed to having his own way. No amount of cajoling from me will part him from the griffin, for his mind is set on owning it. I only came here tonight to encourage Mr. Khafra to come to Price House and make Mr. Price an offer. Too bad he wasn't a real man. Now then, if anything should happen to me as I walk out of here"—her gaze snapped to Scupper, then back to him—"Mr. Dandrae will hear about it. He doesn't take kindly to any sort of violence during transactions. Your hired gorilla may be able to overpower me, but neither of you can stand against the forces of Mr. Dandrae. He plays by Jamaican rules, not English. And so once again, I bid you good night, gentlemen."

She whirled, the slap of her hem hitting Scupper's shins.

Saucy wench. Brudge raised his fist, shaking with rage. "This isn't over, missy. You hear me? This is not over!"

22

Setting down his pen, Edmund leaned back in his chair. Late morning light filtered into the study, exposing dust motes hovering in the air. Most of the staff had recovered from the bout of influenza, but not all . . . and when they did, he'd request a thorough cleaning of Price House.

His gaze drifted back to the words he'd scrawled on the notepad.

> *What soft lite doth brake be-ond,*
> *At donning, a yonning, a yell-oh howr,*
> *In yor eyes, my wurld's reborn,*
> *New promis, new luv, for-ever sworn.*

He smiled. This was nearly as dramatic as the Egyptian story Ami had written. Had her tale influenced his thoughts? But no. He sucked in a breath. *She* had influenced him. She filled every crack and crevice of his mind, and this poem—God help him—was not only about her, it was for her.

He grabbed the pen and slashed a thick black line through the words. There wasn't a chance in all creation he'd ever go through that sort of humiliation again.

A knock rapped on the frame of his open door. Professor Dalton peeked in his head, his explosion of grey hair looking as if he'd just been struck by lightning. "I wonder if I might have a word, Mr. Price? Shouldn't take long."

"Absolutely. Come in." He rose slightly, gesturing to the chair in front of his desk. "I was going over the tally from yesterday. It's quite impressive."

"As is your collection." The professor chuckled while he sat. "I don't think you realize what an exceptional lot of antiquities you've purchased."

He stifled a snort. "So I've been told several times."

"Oh good. Then it should be no surprise when I advise you those relics must be returned to the Egyptian people."

This time he did snort. "I've been told that as well."

"Excellent." Shoving his hand into his coat pocket, the professor pulled out a calling card and shoved it across the desk. "Here you are."

Edmund collected the offering, skimming the sparse information.

Mahmoud Ali, 27 Al-Muizz Street, Cairo

He angled his head at the professor. "What's this?"

A distinct twinkle lit the man's hazel eyes. "The fellow to handle your donation."

He grinned. Ami's father was as presumptuous as his daughter. "I'm afraid I cannot simply give away the collection."

"Not to worry. Mahmoud will connect you with the Cairo Museum. I'm certain they will pay handsomely once they learn of the rarity of these findings."

Handsomely? That was a matter of opinion. Though to be expected from a scholar who spent more time buried in books than in ledgers.

Sensing this conversation could take a turn for the worse, Edmund picked up a pencil and twirled it around. "I've already

238

checked into that, Professor. The museum is not able to offer as much as the interested buyer I already have here in England."

"I see." He pursed his lips exactly as Ami might have. "Yet there are things in life that hold more value than money."

"Agreed." He flipped the pencil again. "But still, you must concede there is no getting around the fact that one needs money to survive in this world."

"Pardon my boldness, Mr. Price, but after enjoying your hospitality these past few days, it appears you are doing more than *surviving*."

So that's where Ami got her cheek. He grinned. "By God's grace, yes, I have had a measure of success."

Sinking back in his chair, leather squeaking, the professor steepled his fingers. "I wonder if you have considered the legal and ethical ramifications of selling looted artifacts to private parties. Engaging in such a practice not only undermines the integrity of archaeological sites but also fuels illicit activities and damages the nation's cultural heritage. Those items, sir, belong to Egypt and its peoples. Or at the very least, in a museum where the masses can and should appreciate them."

His grin grew. "You sound like your daughter."

The professor sighed. "Which brings me to my next point of topic."

The pencil stilled in his hand. "Your daughter?"

"Indeed. Tell me, Mr. Price." He tapped his fingertips together. "What are your intentions toward Amisi?"

Now there was a dangerous question. He set the pencil down lest it snap from the sudden wariness tightening his muscles. "What do you mean?"

"I may have only been here two days, but I've noticed the way you look at her, and more importantly, how she responds to you. She's never given a man a second glance before. I hope you do not take that lightly."

It wasn't anything he hadn't heard before. Fathers here and in India had often informed him of their daughters' affection for him. But this time, with this father, the words breached his wall of defense.

Rising, he strode to the window and looked out, unseeing. Too many thoughts vied for attention. Too many emotions thickened his throat. Better that the professor did not witness such a struggle.

At length, he murmured, "I regard your daughter in very high esteem, sir. She is bright, confident, able to stand her ground when challenged, and beneath that eccentric exterior of hers beats a rather soft heart. So, yes, Professor, I am honoured she considers me worth a second look."

"Honoured?" The word shot out like a cannonball. "Is that all?"

Hardly. Not if that poem he'd been working on was any indication. And yet could she be happy living the social life in London tied to an MP? Was it fair of him to ask her to give up her dream of digging about in the sands of Egypt? Sadly, he shook his head. "What more would you have me say?"

"I would have you say you love the woman, for clearly she is smitten by you."

He closed his eyes, and against his better judgment, savored the declaration.

"Well, Price?"

The professor was persistent, he'd give him that. Inhaling deeply, he donned his businessman mask. A cowardly retreat, perhaps, but the safest route for now. He'd do what he could to protect her—and himself—from heartache and disappointment, for well did he know those were the trappings of love.

He strolled back to his chair and met the man's gaze, choosing to handle the remainder of this discussion as if it were a deal to be negotiated. "I cannot deny I care deeply for your daughter."

The professor scooted to the edge of his chair, eyes narrowed, studying him so hard that Edmund wouldn't be surprised at all if he whipped out his magnifying glass. "No, Mr. Price, I sense there is more to your feelings than mere care. The question is, Are you man enough to admit it not only to yourself but to Amisi?"

By all that was right and good, was he ready for that step? To become vulnerable to a woman again? To open himself up to complete destruction? True, Ami was no Louisa, but loving anyone was risky.

He plowed his fingers through his hair, wishing now he'd kept his study door shut. "You give me much to think about, Professor Dalton."

"As is a professor's wont." The man stood, the many lines on his face softening. "I have made the mistake of putting my profession ahead of personal relationships, and I'm afraid I'm too old now to change my ways. You have many years ahead of you. Don't do the same. Woo Amisi. Pursue her. You will not find a finer woman, and she deserves to be cherished. God knows I've done a poor enough job in that department."

Wheeling about, he strode away, leaving the haunting words behind.

"Woo her."

"Pursue her."

Edmund pinched the bridge of his nose. He did love her, God help him, but even admitting that to himself drained the life out of his bones. As a young lad he'd loved his father, only to have it thrown back in his face in front of the family for being such a disappointment. He'd loved his mother as well, and she'd loved him right back, but a tragic fall down some stairs had ended that relationship when he'd been but eight years old. He'd also loved learning despite all the jumbled letters and strain to comprehend, and that had ended with a humiliating dismissal from school. And then there'd been Louisa. Opening himself up to that woman had stripped him of any shred of pride. Then again, Ami wasn't his father, his headmaster, nor a grasping, arrogant woman.

And she owned his heart as none of them ever had.

He scrubbed a hand over his face. Could he overcome the scars of the past to pursue her as her father suggested? *Should* he?

Another knock on the door was followed by Barnaby's rather pale visage entering with a paper in hand. "A message for you, sir."

Edmund rose to meet him. "Thank you."

The familiar header of a telegram from Lord Bastion scrolled across the top. He skipped to the content.

DINNER AND DANCE AT MY LONDON TOWN HOUSE NEXT SATURDAY. ARRIVE ON FRIDAY. TIME FOR THE BIG ANNOUNCEMENT.

Once again he strolled to the window, this time with a smile curving his lips. With the election happening in just shy of a month, it was more than time to publicly announce his run.

And more than anything, he wished Ami to be at his side when the declaration was made.

Ami put all her angst into rubbing the last bit of shine onto the hind leg of an ebony statue of Bastet, still shaken from last night's encounter with Mr. Brudge and his associate's knife. She'd never come so close to getting seriously hurt. And it was even more humiliating that it'd been such a ragtag operator who'd gotten the jump on her. Either she'd grossly underestimated him, or she was losing her touch.

Puffing out a breath, she surveyed the cache of relics she'd cleaned the past hour. Five clay figurines. An alabaster jar. A lovely ankh pendant, and ten pieces belonging to what must've been an extraordinary game of hounds and jackals. Amazing how much work one could get done when agitated—leastwise for her. Farther down the table, her father yet brushed at the same small Isis amulet.

An item he'd finished yesterday.

She set down her cleaning cloth. "All right, Father. Out with it."

"Out with what?" He spoke without sparing her a glance.

"Any more work on that amulet and there'll be nothing left.

You've been agitated ever since you returned from your morning constitutional. Whom did you cross paths with while on your walk?" Couldn't have been Phineas. Despite his penchant for asking any warm body to help him with a task, he was a delightful old soul who wouldn't put anyone in a foul mood. Actually, most of the staff were pleasant. She nibbled the nail on her pinky, thinking hard until an idea hit. "Let me guess, Mr. Fletcher?"

"Bah! I don't take anything that man says seriously." He glanced at her sideways, a mischievous twinkle in his eye. "Personally, I think he's got one too many bats in his belfry."

True. The man was a bit unhinged at times, but that didn't explain her father's sudden obsession with the amulet. "Well, if it's not Mr. Fletcher, then what has got you so preoccupied? And don't try to deny it." She aimed a finger at him. "I know your penchant for fixating on an object when you're deep in thought."

"Too smart for your own good," he muttered as he set down his brush. "The truth is, I didn't take my usual outside stroll. Instead, I stopped by Mr. Price's study. I thought to have a word with him about these antiquities."

Her lips twisted into a smirk. "So that's what did it."

His brow furrowed into lines deep enough to plant oats. "You know as well as I do where these relics belong."

"Of course I do, Father." She pulled out some fresh squares of cotton and began wrapping the game pieces. It was either that or flail her hands in the air. "But don't be too hard on Mr. Price. He has good reason to sell to the highest bidder."

"There can be no good reason."

"Normally I'd agree with you, but in this instance, I'm afraid I must side with Mr. Price."

Her father planted his fist on the tabletop, knocking his brush to the floor. "I taught you better than that."

True. He had. But after all Edmund's talk about Sanjay, she couldn't bear the thought of his family plummeting into poverty, starvation, and ultimately death. She shook her head.

"It's not my place to share Mr. Price's business, but trust me, there is a lot at stake if his cargo doesn't bring in a fair amount of money."

Her father snorted. "I never thought I'd see the day when you were more enamored with a man than with artifacts."

She'd never thought so either, and yet here it was. Heart sold to a businessman of all things.

But that wasn't the point.

She wrapped the last game piece, then shifted in her chair to meet her father's gaze squarely. "It's not a matter of being enamored. It's about understanding the complexities of life and the hard choices we sometimes have to make. As much as I love history and these relics, I do believe that current life and relationships must be given priority. There has to be a balance between preserving the past while existing in the present, else are we truly living? Somehow, Father—and don't ask me to explain this—but sometimes I feel my purpose is evolving and the relics are only a part of a much larger story. I just don't know what that story is yet."

Or if it involved a certain blue-eyed man.

His lips parted, several times, as if words would not come out.

Well. That was new. The great Professor Dalton at a loss for what to say? And was that, perhaps, a glimmer of admiration sparking in those hazel eyes of his?

He leaned back in his chair, a slight shake to his head. "Have you been studying philosophy in your spare time?"

"I hardly have time for such trifles." She grinned.

"Speaking of time, how did you manage to talk Miss Grimbel into letting you take off so many days?"

"Oh. That." She cleared her throat, stalling. She'd supposed the topic would come up sooner or later, but she'd dearly hoped for later . . . as in never. "I, em, I'm not currently employed by her anymore."

"Oh, Amisi." A sigh deflated him. "I am running out of schools to recommend you to. First there was the live scarab fiasco at St. Winifred's Academy."

"That's not fair," she shot back. "How was I to know there was a hole in the box?"

"Then there was your Cleopatra Day in which henna and kohl stained half the school's uniforms at Rosewood Hall."

"I never should have trusted those girls. Delinquents. Every last one of them."

"And Ivybrook Institute, that was just . . ." He shook his head, disgust pinching his lips.

"You have to admit that an archaeological dig in the school garden was a clever way to give the girls a hands-on experience."

"The gardener was not amused, as I recall. Nor was the gas company when you nicked a pipe."

"It was only a small explosion. No one got hurt."

He plowed his hands through his hair, fluffing the wild ends into complete chaos. "I suppose that is water under the bridge at this point. Tell me what happened at Miss Grimbel's."

"All I did was bring in a mummified cat. For all the hubbub, you'd have thought I'd brought in a fresh corpse from a body snatcher. She dismissed me shortly after you left for your dig, and I didn't want to ruin your trip with such news. I intended to tell you when you returned."

"So if you haven't been teaching, what have you been—no." His eyes suddenly narrowed. "You've been restocking the Ashmolean with new items, haven't you? I told you before I left there was to be no more shadow brokering!"

His voice bounced off the workroom walls.

Oh dear. This was going about as well as her meeting with Brudge last night. She stifled a cringe. "I know, Father, but I also know that had you been here, you would have wished for the relics Mr. Dandrae had come by to go to the museum."

"Hmm. Maybe so . . ." He blew out a long breath. "But one of these times, Amisi, you're going to cross the wrong man. It is a dangerous game you play, especially as a woman."

Unbidden, her fingertips fluttered to her throat—right where the cold metal of a blade had nearly taken her life. A shudder ran down her backbone. "You're right."

His jaw hardened to granite. "Then give me your word you're done with such risky business."

Truly she ought to be, especially after last night's threat. But next time Mr. Dandrae contacted her with a valuable find that deserved a home in a museum, would she truly have the gumption to turn him down?

"Amisi?" her father prodded. "I would have your word here and now on the matter."

She dipped her head. "I—"

"I hope I'm not interrupting anything." Edmund's deep voice turned both her and her father's heads. "But I have a rather urgent question."

"Sounds dire," her father rumbled.

"On the contrary." Edmund glanced at the artifacts spread on the table. "Though on seeing this progress, I suspect your answer will be more than satisfactory." His gaze flicked between her father and her. "I am wondering how much longer it will take the two of you to finish the artifacts."

"I'd say maybe a week more, if that." She arched a brow at her father.

He nodded. "We should be able to complete the valuations by next Friday."

"Excellent. That's when I must leave." Edmund gave her shoulder a light squeeze. "And I should very much like you to accompany me, both of you, that is."

She angled her head, noting the boyish gleam in his eyes. "Where to?"

"Lord Bastion is ready to announce my candidacy, so London it is."

Blast that woman! Blast her smug smile. Her snobby little nose. And especially blast that starchy look of hers tagging him as naught but a scabby bufflehead. Brudge tossed back his gin and slammed the glass onto the countertop, earning a cross look from the barkeep.

Scupper scratched behind his ear, wincing from the jostle to his jaw. "Seems to me we're but two foxes scamperin' after the moon. That prize is outta our reach. So what we gonna do, guv'ner?"

Exactly. What was he to do? He couldn't very well break into that fine manor home and crack a safe, not with armed men patrolling the place. A belch rose, and he pounded his chest, heartburn lighting a fire up to his throat. Only one week remained to pay off Wormwell. Seven days to raise more money than had dribbled through his fingers in the past year.

He never ever should have signed a contract with that devil. Never should have tried to deal with . . .

A deal?

Hmm.

Now there was a thought.

He shot to his feet, then grabbed the counter to keep from toppling. "Come on, Scupper. Time to move."

Scupper drained the rest of his drink, then swiped his hand across his thick lips. "Where we goin', guv'ner?"

"London. Time to negotiate a new pact with ol' Wormwell."

23

Bypassing the carafe of lemon water, Edmund poured three flutes of ginger beer, a tricky feat in the swaying train carriage. My, how different this ride was compared to last month's trek to Oxford, not only in his choice of drink but that he was no longer alone.

He delivered the first glass to the professor, seated near a window with a book in his lap, his eyes finally open. The man had napped nearly the entire journey, forcing Edmund to postpone his toast until now. Ignoring the man's arched brow at the offering, Edmund crossed over to Ami, opposite her father on the sofa. The thick tally ledger sat on the cushion next to her, the cover finally closed after she'd diligently gone over each and every item with him. Good thing the trek from Oxford to London hadn't been any shorter or she'd not have finished.

He handed her a glass, then sat beside her. He'd not fully taken her father's advice to woo her this past week, but he had gifted her a small golden brooch shaped as a honeybee, and it did his heart good to see it pinned to her collar—where she'd worn it every day since he'd given it to her.

"What's this for?" She nodded toward the bubbly liquid. "We're nearly to London."

"A toast is in order, I think."

A smile lit her face. "It is." She held up her glass. "To you, Edmund. May your run for election be a smashing success."

He shook his head, matching her grin. "Though I thank you for the sentiment, that's not at all what I intended to salute."

"Then allow me." Setting his book on the table, the professor extended his glass. "Here's to one of the finest collections of Egyptian artifacts I have seen in a long time. Though I can't say I approve of leaving behind Mr. Fletcher to close the deal with Mr. Harrison, I understand there is good reason for it, so cheers."

Edmund clutched his glass tighter. In light of Gil's recent erratic behaviour, he didn't necessarily approve of leaving him to conduct the transaction either, and yet in all the years he had worked with him, Gil had never once fouled up a sale. And Gil had just as much riding on the outcome as he did.

Edmund wagged his finger at the professor. "You are much closer to the mark, but not quite." He lifted his drink, indicating them both. "This toast is to the two of you for a job well done. Your expertise and work ethic has been invaluable. Truly, I couldn't have asked for a more knowledgeable pair. Professor Dalton, I am indebted to you for cutting short your dig, and to you, Ami, for sticking with the job despite the supposed curse of Amentuk. I owe you both my deepest gratitude. Cheers!"

They clinked their glasses together, but after hardly taking a sip, Ami scooched to the edge of the sofa and turned to him, lifting her drink even higher. "And to you, Edmund, cheers for taking a chance on me. If you'd not—oh!"

Brakes squealed.

The train jolted.

Ami clutched his arm, her drink splashing past the rim and dousing his waistcoat.

"Oh dear." She dashed to the drink cart and retrieved a cloth as the train came to a stop.

"Don't trouble yourself." He brushed away the excess liquid.

"Of course I will." She sank next to him, her cinnamon scent nearly overwhelming him as she dabbed the fabric. Were her father not here, he'd pull her into his arms and fill his lungs with her sweetness. But father or not, he couldn't stop himself from gazing deeply into her changeable eyes.

The professor cleared his throat. "If you don't mind telling me the address of where we're staying, Mr. Price, I should like to hail a cab and stop by the British Museum on my way. Shouldn't take long. Just wish to greet an old friend in the Egyptian department."

"No trouble at all. It's Seven Pembroke Terrace in Mayfair."

"Excellent." The professor retrieved his ratty old hat off the coat-tree. Clapping it atop his head, he tipped the brim at them. "I shall see you two later."

He disappeared out the door while Ami gathered her own hat and positioned herself in front of a mirror. By the time Edmund had donned his bowler, she was still fussing with it.

"Blast!" She slapped her hand to her mouth, whirling wide-eyed.

Though he ought to be shocked at such vulgar language from a lady, he couldn't help but grin. "Is there a problem?"

She waved her bonnet in the air—a single red ribbon dangling from one side—while her other fingers clutched the matching red trim. "I knew I should have restitched this ribbon before we left."

He held out his hand. "Why don't you let me see what I can do."

She scrunched her nose—an adorable trait he'd never get enough of. "There's hardly time to sew it now, but I am curious as to what you're about." She handed over her hat. "Here you are, Mr. Problem Solver."

He promptly ripped off the other ribbon and offered it back. "There. Problem solved."

She rolled her eyes as she jammed the thing on her head. "I should have known."

He grinned as he opened the train carriage door, where a porter stood at attention in the vestibule.

The fellow dipped his head respectfully. "There's a cab waiting just outside the station as you requested, Mr. Price. Your luggage will follow."

"Thank you." Edmund palmed him a few shillings.

"Thank you, sir." The porter opened the door and stepped aside.

Edmund strolled to the opening, where he abruptly stopped. Bah! He should've known word would get out that he'd be in town for Bastion's big soiree tomorrow evening, but this was more than the usual fawning females. This time there were journalists with pencils poised and even a camera or two.

Hands curling into fists, he glanced over his shoulder at Ami. "I probably should have warned you my arrival would cause a stir. Are you ready for London?"

She craned her neck to peer past him, then met his gaze with a spark in her eyes. "On the contrary, perhaps the question should be, Is London ready for me?"

Ami stared out at the multicoloured gowns and suits gathered around the train where Edmund descended, a mix of nerves and exhilaration fluttering in her chest. Pharoah himself couldn't have attracted more attention. And no wonder. His wealth. His renown. Not to mention the way his suit rode the strong lines of his body whenever he moved. The moment his feet touched ground, he turned his back to the throng and offered up his hand to assist her.

Her.

A female Egyptologist with no fashion sense whatsoever.

She couldn't have felt more chosen.

Warmth flared in her cheeks as she gripped his strong fingers. Some women sneered at her. Others looked as if they might swoon. And a select few gave her the distinct impression they'd drive a knife into her back to take her place without blinking an eyelash.

After only one step, a great gust of wind breezed in, pulling the hat from her head. Without thinking, she lunged for it. So did Edmund—but with a little too much gusto. He knocked into her.

She tipped sideways.

In one swift reach, he caught her and her bonnet. A collective "Oohh" hummed through the crowd as he set her on solid ground.

Pulling away, he handed her the hat. "Maybe you ought to just carry this for now."

"Good idea," she mumbled, far too preoccupied with the murmurs swirling about them.

"Did you see that gallant move? So chivalrous."

"He rescued her hat with such urgency. How I wish that would've been me."

"It was just like a romance novel."

"Who is that woman?"

"Yes, who is she?"

"Mr. Price. Mr. Price! Have you a few words for the *Times*?"

Edmund's jaw hardened, his voice lowering for her ears alone. "We'll have to make a dash for it. I'll lead, breaking a path through the crowd. You follow closely. Are you ready?"

She nodded. "Lead on."

"Pardon!" Edmund shouted above the swarm as he barreled ahead. "Coming through."

Ami dashed after him, alternately bumping against shoulders and sometimes the train. It took an eternity to plow their way along the platform, yet eventually they reached the station— where just as many travelers milled about.

Though she tried to stick close to Edmund's broad back, his long legs ate up way more ground than hers. The space between them widened—then widened some more when a man with a cane smacked against her as he passed by.

"Mind yer step, woman!" he grumbled.

She stiffened at the gravelly voice, a chill snaking down her spine when she realized who it belonged to.

And then her blood really did run cold when off to the side a tall monster of a man locked his gaze onto her. Unbidden, her fingers fluttered to her neck. If she swallowed now, she would no doubt still feel the cold metal of a blade pressed sharply against her skin.

"'Tis her, guv'ner! The filly with the statue."

She shoved ahead, feet hitting the tiles hard, unmindful of how many people she crashed into. The only thing that mattered now was catching up to Edmund. Mr. Brudge and his henchman wouldn't dare try anything with him at her side.

Would they?

"Hey now." Edmund caught hold of her arm as she nearly tore past him. "I'm right here."

She drew in a few deep breaths, desperate to pull herself together.

"So you are." She forced a smile. Hopefully it wasn't too wobbly.

"There he is," a woman's voice called loudly, growing in intensity. "Mr. Price is over there."

"Time to move again." Edmund pulled her out the station door. Not missing a beat, he lifted her into the carriage and hustled in behind her, slamming the door shut.

The moment he sat, he pounded his fist against the ceiling. "Walk on, driver."

The cab jolted into motion. Ami leaned back against the seat, supremely happy to be out of the press of humanity.

And especially glad to be away from Mr. Brudge.

Across from her, Edmund tugged at his sleeve hems, straightening his rumpled coat after the mad dash. As he did so, he peered at her. "Are you all right?"

"I am." Despite the chaotic experience, she grinned. "Is it always like this for you?"

"Unfortunately, yes." He chuckled. "Now you know why I wore Jameson's old set of clothes when I first met you."

"I didn't realize you were so popular. I mean, I did notice the looks you got when we boarded in Oxford, but I had no idea your good name would attract so much attention here."

He ran a hand over his face, inhaling deeply. "I suspect it will only get worse should I win the election."

"Of course you shall win, but even so"—she arched a brow—"that sounds perfectly awful."

"I can't say I like it much."

The carriage swayed around a corner, and she gripped the seat to keep from toppling sideways. At least it had good springs, or they'd both have been smashed against the side of the wall.

"So why don't you run away?" she wondered aloud.

"I did." He smiled. "To India."

"I thought that was because of Louisa."

"Mostly, but not the only reason." He grew pensive then, his gaze drifting out the window.

Which afforded her the best opportunity to study him un-watched. That jawline of his could intimidate the strongest of men should he choose to dig in his heels, and yet she'd seen it soften into compassion whenever he spoke of Sanjay. His blue eyes—ever dusky and intense—fixed on some point outside the glass, clearly not taking in the bustling street. He was miles away, lost in thoughts she couldn't begin to guess at, and yet she itched to know . . . just like so many other women, apparently. She hadn't realized he was so sought after, and yet somehow that just made him all the more vulnerable, sparking a sense of protectiveness toward him.

And not just a small amount of jealousy.

"I must say I feel very privileged to be here with you," she murmured, mostly to herself.

His blue gaze shot to hers. "No." He shook his head defiantly as he scooted to the edge of the bench. Leaning close, he gathered her hands in his, the heat of his touch drying her mouth to ashes.

"I am the privileged one to have met you." Without breaking eye contact, he lifted her hand to his lips and pressed a lingering kiss to her skin.

Oh my. It was stiflingly hot in here, yet she dared not pull away to fan herself. If her brow glistened, then so be it.

And it didn't get any cooler when his voice turned huskier. "I've grown very attached to your company, Ami. Actually, I've grown very attached to you."

There were promises in those words, hints of love, allusions to a happily ever after. Her heart, once solely devoted to her career, began to make space for the prospect of a shared journey with this man. She longed for him to choose her above all others, just as he had when he'd helped her off the train. But was that an absurd desire? The fact was, he could have any woman he wanted with naught but a crook of his finger.

She licked her lips, praying her voice would work. "I suppose I shouldn't have laboured quite so diligently on those antiquities of yours, for I must admit I am loath to part from your company as well."

A grin broke across his lips, so handsome her stomach flipped.

"Then it's settled." He squeezed her fingers. "I shall purchase another load of relics. Though you should know I value you more than your Egyptian savvy."

"Easy now!" the driver called out as the carriage wheels slowed. "'Ere we are."

Releasing his hold, Edmund stepped out, leaving a huge loss inside the cab without him. Of all the unfortunate timing. She'd much rather stay in this cocoon, soaking in his words of affirmation.

She grabbed her errant hat off the seat and followed, eager to once again grasp his hand as she descended.

Outside, however, that plan changed. She barely noticed his grasp. All she could do was gawk at the magnificent town house they'd parked in front of. The white stone walls shone fresh as if they'd been recently scrubbed of coal dust, as did the ornate cornices and mouldings up near the roofline. Lavish draperies peeked out at the edges of the many windows, and standing at attention on each side of the front door, tall columns reached to the heavens. It was a grand home, surprisingly more pretentious than Price House, as if it were a darling child who knew her ringlets and cherub cheeks inspired a second look. The renovators had done a brilliant job.

"What a beautiful house," Ami breathed.

"I am sure Miss Woolsey will love to hear you say so." Edmund guided her toward the front door with a touch to the small of her back.

Ami cocked her head. "Miss Woolsey?"

"Indeed." He rang the bell, then glanced at her. "The renovations on my town house are not yet finished, so we are staying at the viscount's."

Leaning heavily on his cane, Brudge wheeled about, a curse launching off his tongue. Just as Scupper had said, there she was. The wily little Shadow Broker. The swirl of her plaid skirt and flash of her flowery jacket disappeared into the crowd. Scowling, Brudge pressed light fingers to his swollen eye, where a headache now throbbed beneath. Blasted woman. He had her to thank for this aching blinker. Her and Wormwell. If he'd been able to wrest that little statue from her, he wouldn't have had to go to Wormwell begging for an extension of time.

And he wouldn't have had to bear the knuckles of Wormwell's henchman.

Scupper shoved his way closer to him. "Well now, guv'ner, we goin' after the woman or the statue?"

"Shut up! Let me think." Planting both hands on the cane's head, he anchored the thing front and center, a rock in the stream of station patrons. As people flowed around him, he debated what to do.

Yesterday's meeting with Wormwell had not gone as he'd hoped. The codger wouldn't budge a tittle on extending the deadline to pay back his debt—which only gave him until midnight tomorrow night. Worse, though he had yet to actually lay eyes on Wormwell's face, he had caught a glimpse of his own boy, Neddie. The young man was all knobs and sticks beneath his shirt and trousers, as if he'd not been fed a thing for days. A fresh hump disfigured his nose from a right hook. And when Brudge had complained to Wormwell about the treatment of his son, he'd taken a walloping himself.

No, it hadn't gone at all as he'd hoped. He never should have entangled himself with such an infamous antiquities runner. Though Wormwell was the most well-known buyer and seller of questionably acquired relics, he was also the most dangerous.

He glanced at the train ticket poking out of his coat pocket. Should he risk wasting time on a trip to Oxford knowing that the woman was here in London? She might very well have brought that golden trinket along with her, intending to sell the piece to a more lucrative market. But *he* needed that little statue!

And he needed it now.

"Come on, Scupper." Using his cane to knock travelers out of the way, he ignored the complaints and hastened to the door. And just in time too. The flash of a plaid skirt followed by a dark-suited man hiked into a cab.

He waved his arm, hailing a coach. "Cabbie! Over here."

The nearest black hackney rolled on by, the driver oblivious to his call.

"Hang it all!" He pounded his cane against the cobbles as the woman's coach lurched into motion.

An ear-breaking whistle ripped out behind him, Scupper's baritone voice tailing the obnoxious sound. "Oy! Cabbie!"

Sure enough, the next hack pulled over to the kerb. Irritation burned up Brudge's neck. Leave it to the long-limbed brute to get noticed.

"Follow that cab that's just turning the corner now," he shouted to the driver as he hoisted himself up. Pain shot through his leg as he landed on the bench seat, and even more so when Scupper banged into it as he folded his big body inside the coach.

The cab jerked into motion, and he bounced against the wall, adding further insult to his injury. "Blast it!" he howled. Would to God the festering gun wound would just heal already.

Across from him, Scupper ran his thumb and forefinger along his moustache, twirling it up at the ends. "So what we gonna do, guv'ner?"

"We'll find where that scrappy little Shadow Broker is staying and see if she's got that statue for us."

"And if she doesn't?"

He dropped his head against the wall, staring up at the stained fabric of the ceiling as he thought. If she didn't have that relic to steal, then he ought to just steal her out of vengeance.

Now, there was a thought!

Obviously she was a favorite of the rich fellow, and he just might pay a pretty penny to get her back, enough pennies, in fact, for him to get Wormwell off his neck.

He straightened. It would take some doing to get a forger to match Dandrae's handwriting, but in a town this size, he ought to be able to find someone to write her a note for a rendezvous she couldn't refuse.

24

Right there in the viscount's breakfast room, God smiled. So did Edmund. And why not? Last evening, Miss Woolsey had begged off early with a headache, which had given him time alone with Ami as he'd walked her to her room after dinner. Today, Gil was scheduled to sell the Egyptian collection to Mr. Harrison as per Edmund's instructions in the contract they'd finalized before he'd left town. Tonight, Lord Bastion would publicly announce his sponsorship for Edmund's political run. And here in this moment, Ami stood at his side, pouring him a cup of Darjeeling.

Indeed. Life couldn't be any better.

Setting down the teapot, Ami peered up at him while handing him his tea. "Are you ready for the big announcement this evening? It will be a life-changing event, I should imagine."

"Of course he is ready, aren't you?" Violet swept through the breakfast room door and entwined her arm with his—which jostled the tea in his cup.

He frowned at the liquid on his shoe. "I'd like to think I'm prepared."

Ami snatched a cloth from the sideboard, then bent and

swiped away the offense. Thoughtful on her part—endearing, actually—but far too humbling a stance . . . especially in front of Miss Woolsey.

He pulled away from Violet and guided Ami upright with a light touch to her elbow. "Please don't trouble yourself on my account."

"No trouble at all." She smiled as she set the soiled cloth onto the sideboard.

Violet merely scowled. "We have servants for that, you know."

Undaunted, Ami grinned at her as well. "I trust you are feeling better this morning, Violet?"

"Much, but even if I weren't, I wouldn't miss tonight's big event were I at death's door." Once again she coiled her arm through his.

And once again he pulled away. Had the viscount not yet spoken to his daughter about his refusal to marry her? The man had had plenty of time to do so . . . unless Edmund was wrong and this was some sort of way for Violet to intimidate Ami. Which of course wouldn't work. A mummy come to life wouldn't daunt Ami.

He faced Violet. "Did your father have a chance to speak with you about our agreement, or lack of one, I should say?"

"La." She flicked her fingers. "Father always drones on about everything, which can be very tedious at times."

He studied her a moment, trying to decipher such a cryptic answer.

"Well, I am famished. Shall we join my father?" Ami tipped her head toward the table.

Whatever Violet had meant, now was not the time for further discussion. He'd have to quiz her later—if there was time. He took the place setting at the foot of the table, Violet at his right and Ami sitting at his left, next to the professor.

Her father eyed him while slathering jam onto his toast. Though no doubt the fellow had every toiletry London could offer as a courtesy in his guest room, the man's hair had yet to meet with a comb. "As you know, Price, I stopped by the British Museum yesterday. A providence, that, for just this morning I received word my friend—the curator of the Egyptian collection—had dinner last night with the director. He's very interested in your artifacts and may be able to offer a higher sum than your Mr. Harrison."

Edmund reached for his own piece of toast from the rack on the table. "I appreciate the effort you went to on my account, Professor, but I am sure Mr. Fletcher will close the deal today—if he hasn't already."

"That would be a shame." Ami's father took a bite, chewing thoughtfully. "Perhaps you could send a telegram to confirm the sale? And if the deal hasn't been finalized, then send another one to delay it?"

He shook his head. "I'm afraid the time for negotiations is finished."

"Such dull conversation!" Violet rapped her knuckles on the table, then smiled at Ami—a little too felinely for his liking. Clearly she was up to something.

"Your gown, Ami?" she purred.

"Oh dear." Ami dipped her chin, glancing at her bodice. "Have I spilled something?"

"No, darling. I meant I should like to hear about what you are wearing to the dance tonight."

Aha. So Violet was trying to bully Ami, and it pleased him far too much when Ami merely dished a large spoonful of scrambled eggs onto her plate, completely impervious to the wiles of the viscount's daughter.

Ami enjoyed a bite before facing Violet. "Oh, my mistake. I brought my best gown. It's green, mostly. Though I suppose the trim isn't. Nor is the sash. Neither are the sleeves, come to think of it." She scooped another forkful yet allowed it to hover over her plate. "At any rate, it really is a dazzler. I got rid of the traditional bustle and added a peacock feather arrangement at the back, cascading from waist to hem."

Edmund's gaze immediately shot to Violet's face, and he wasn't disappointed. She looked positively nauseous. Just wait until she saw Ami in the fabric creation with her own eyes. He stifled a grin with his serviette.

Violet cleared her throat. "I thought as much, which is why I have a little gift for you." Raising her hand, she wiggled her index finger.

The footman stationed near the door stepped briskly to her side, giving her a little bow. "How may I be of service, miss?"

"Please see that my maid delivers my lemon-yellow gown to Miss Dalton's room."

Lemon yellow? Edmund's gaze drifted to Ami. She hated anything to do with lemons.

To her credit, she didn't fuss. She merely shook her head. "Thank you, but there is no need."

"I insist. A memento of our friendship, if you will. Besides, you do want to look your best tonight, don't you?"

So that was her game. Knock Ami emotionally off-center. A ruthless business move he'd witnessed by more than one unscrupulous capitalist. He set down his half-eaten toast, appetite fleeing at Violet's underhandedness. "I am sure whatever Miss Dalton has brought along will suit her very nicely, and I for one am eager to see it."

Violet grabbed her teacup, lips folded into a sneer.

Like daughter, like father, for in swept the viscount, a thundercloud darkening his brow. He slapped a folded newspaper onto the white linen tablecloth in front of Violet, rattling the dishes.

"Father! Such atrocious behaviour."

"You may not think so when you see the front page." He stabbed the paper with his index finger.

Interesting. What had Miss Woolsey done to earn such censure? She was her father's little princess. As she picked up the *Times*, Edmund was tempted to lean aside and glance at the headline along with her. Judging by the widening of her eyes and sudden pallor on her face, though, he kept his distance. It never paid to step between two fighting dogs, and this promised to be a sharp-toothed tangle. The very walls of the room seemed to hold their breath.

Violet's chest rose and fell in increasing succession, each huff gaining in intensity, until she whacked the paper every bit as violently against the table as her father had.

She turned a gangrenous eye not at the viscount, but at him.

"What is the meaning of this?" Her voice rang shrill, inducing winces from Ami and her father. She shoved the newspaper toward Edmund, faceup, where a photograph of Ami wrapped in his arms stared back at them all, followed by a banner that punched him in the gut.

Love at Last for Oxford's Most Eligible Bachelor?

Ami's fork clattered to her plate as her gaze locked onto the image of her caught up in Edmund's embrace. Her hair was half-loose, caressing his face like a wanton hussy. Her cheek practically pressed against his. Of course the photographer had chosen to crop out her runaway hat they'd both been reaching for and omitted the way her foot had slipped from the step in the process. The angle made the innocent and rather gallant save on Edmund's part look like a torrid love affair right there in front of the train. Heat burned a trail up her neck. If she didn't know any better, she'd swear she and Edmund were lovers of the most shameful variety.

And worse, deep down, she wished it were so. Oh, not the shameful part, but she longed to hear words of love whispered from his lips.

Her father looked at her askance—and she couldn't blame him.

"Amisi?" It was more of an indictment than a query.

Her throat closed at the disappointment weighting his brow. All her life she'd tried to please this man only to have let him down yet again. Would that she could just slide off her chair and hide beneath the table, but that would only endorse the incriminating photo.

Inhaling for courage, she faced her father head-on. "That

picture is not as it seems. The truth of the moment is far from what the photograph depicts."

"Then what is the truth?" Lord Bastion boomed, his voice rattling the breakfast room's windowpanes. "What are my daughter and I to believe, Miss Dalton?"

She sank in her chair, all her hard-won bravery fleeing. No wonder this man was one of the most powerful in Parliament. He could intimidate the Queen herself.

Edmund leaned closer to the table. "All that happened, my lord, was an ill-timed gust of wind that caught Miss Dalton's hat. She lunged for it, as did I. In my haste, I knocked her off-balance. I merely righted her and saved her bonnet, nothing more. You know the press. Always printing the most sensational front pages to drive up sales."

"It is sensational!" Violet wailed. All eyes turned toward her as she expertly flourished a white handkerchief, her tears sprouting faster than she could dab them away. "Edmund, how could you?"

Violet's dramatic sobbing seemed to flow like a well-practiced performance. It was as if she relished the opportunity to be the center of attention, basking in all the tragedy and drama of the moment.

But even so, Ami softened her tone. "Mr. Price is a gentleman, Violet. You've said so yourself. Do you really think he'd behave in such a lurid fashion right there in front of God and country?"

"I-I should hope not!" She sniffled like a tot.

Lord Bastion shook his head. "Good intentions or not, that photograph is scandalous and blasted poor timing."

Ami swallowed the lump in her throat. He was right. It was an indecent display that was likely even now making the rounds on breakfast tables across the city. This would most definitely not look good for Edmund's candidacy announcement tonight, and all because she'd not taken the time to stitch that horrid little red ribbon. Hopefully her lack of domesticity wouldn't ruin his chances to get elected.

Though it took every ounce of pluck she could muster, she faced Lord Bastion. "I would be happy, my lord, to go to the *Times* and explain the situation. Surely they can run a retraction."

His sharp eyes narrowed on her. "You have done quite enough already, Miss Dalton."

"Now see here, Lord Bastion, I understand your frustration for I am every bit as incensed." Tossing down his serviette, Edmund rose and rested his hand protectively at the back of her chair. "But taking it out on Miss Dalton is unacceptable. I claim full responsibility for the situation and will do whatever it takes to mitigate the damage that photograph may have caused."

"It's already out there, Price. Your status has taken a hit. There is nothing to be done for it."

"But, Father!" Violet sobbed. "What about *my* reputation?"

And there it was. The real reason for her tears, just as Ami suspected. The woman cared more for herself than she did about Edmund.

Shoving down her irritation, Ami attempted to paste on an encouraging smile. "All will be well, Violet. Things like this blow over."

"That's easy for you to say, stuffed away with your relics like a hermit." She slumped in her chair. "I'm the one who shall have to bear the gossip."

"I don't see why," Edmund cut in. "You're not the one in the picture."

"You don't understand," Violet wailed.

Ami tried hard not to roll her eyes. "You're stirring a tempest in a teapot. Every onlooker who witnessed that mishap when I stepped off the train can attest to the fact that Mr. Price was reaching for my hat, not for me."

"The point is, Miss Dalton"—the viscount swept up the newspaper and waved it in the air—"my daughter should not have to listen to any vicious rumours."

"Nor should mine have to bear your censure, my lord." Next to Ami, her father calmly reached for another piece of toast. "I agree it was an unfortunate event, but surely a few well-placed words from you to your guests tonight can right the whole situation. You hold more sway than the *Times*, do you not?"

"Hmm," Edmund rumbled behind her. "The professor raises a valid point. Your reputation and influential position can greatly impact public opinion, especially since you've invited the most esteemed of society for tonight's announcement. If we both address this article openly and honestly, it will show I run a campaign of the highest integrity."

"It could do . . ." Lord Bastion murmured as he stroked his chin. "Perhaps we can use this to our advantage." He wheeled about, calling over his shoulder as he strode away, "Come, Price. We have much to discuss."

Edmund gave her shoulder a little squeeze an instant before following the man. "Excuse me, ladies, Professor."

The moment the two men disappeared out the door, Violet tucked away her handkerchief and stood as if she hadn't a care in the world. "I shall take my leave also. One must look one's best for tonight's festivities. You would do well to take a care with your appearance, Miss Dalton, for the highest of society will be in attendance tonight." She flounced away.

Ami watched her go. Apparently they were no longer on a first-name basis.

"It's been an eventful morning," her father commented as he reached for the jam jar. "I cannot help but wonder what tonight will bring."

"Indeed." Pushing back her chair, she stood. Her father may yet have an appetite, but hers was ruined. "I suppose I shall do as Violet asks and prepare my gown, which, come to think of it, I should have hung up last night."

Her father chuckled, toast crumbs flying from his lips. "You always were better at deciphering hieroglyphics than managing your wardrobe."

Of course she was. Without a mother to teach her, what did she know of pretty garments and such niceties? Oh, Grandmother had tried during the summers she'd stayed with her while Father was on a dig, but she'd never truly been interested. She'd much rather don her work apron and lose herself in returning an ancient artifact to its former glory.

She ascended the staircase to her room, and the instant she opened the door, she pressed a hand to her stomach. There, lounging on the bed in front of her, was a gown of the most horrid lemon hue. She didn't know much about fashion, but that monstrosity surely couldn't be considered comely in any sense of the word.

"Pardon me, miss."

She turned to the maid's voice. "Yes?"

A slim lady in a spotless black gown and starched white apron stood in the doorway, a silver tray extended with a single envelope on it. "For you, miss."

"Thank you." Ami collected the missive, her brow bunching as she recognized Mr. Dandrae's penmanship on the front. A bit smudgy, but his nonetheless. Odd that he'd send her a message here in London. How had he even known where she'd be?

A chill traveled across her shoulders. Had Mr. Dandrae had her followed? Did he keep such close surveillance on all of his sellers and purchasers?

Despite her sudden doubts of the man, she hurried over to the writing desk and slit the seal with a silver letter opener, then held the card inside up to the light.

> *Rare canopic jars holding the remains of Akhenaten.*
> *Five hundred pounds. Tonight. Nine o'clock.*
> *Angel Alley. Whitechapel.*

She sucked in a breath. No wonder he'd taken the time and effort to track her down. This was more than important! Akhenaten was one of the most mysterious and enigmatic of all the pharaohs. If she could acquire those jars, what a gem that would be for the Ashmolean. As impressive as the golden griffin. But tonight of all nights?

She deflated into the chair. Of course she couldn't go. Not

with Edmund's big announcement, one he'd specifically asked her to attend. He valued her. He'd said as much. Leaning aside, she dropped the envelope and the card into the small waste-basket.

Being there for him in the present was more important than chasing a relic of the past.

25

A blend of too many perfumes hung on the air, thick as a November fog and about as pleasant. Edmund tugged at his cravat, struggling to breathe in the crowded ballroom. His election announcement and following dinner couldn't happen soon enough for his liking. Anything to escape this press of humanity, particularly the clinging vine in an emerald gown who had attached herself to his sleeve the moment he'd stepped foot past the threshold. To be fair, though, at least Violet had calmed down since this morning.

As had her father. Stationed next to Edmund, Lord Bastion stood like a monarch, fingers curled around his lapels, his hawkish eyes surveying the room with aristocratic authority.

Edmund preferred to scrutinize the scene behind them, which he did frequently, hoping to spy a glimpse of some outlandish peacock feathers. Where was Ami? She'd missed the grand reception nigh on an hour ago. Even her father had appeared—albeit late as well—and was now engaged in what appeared to be a lively conversation with two matrons and a retired brigadier off in a corner. Had something happened to keep her up in her room? Or was she too mortified to appear in public after this morning's fuss at breakfast? He'd tried all day—unsuccessfully—to speak with her, to let her know that despite the humiliation of such a public declaration of love, it was entirely true. He *was* in love with her. So much so that he'd reworked the first stanza of his poem and would—if given the chance tonight—share it with her. Once again he tugged at his cravat, the very thought of being so vulnerable cutting off his air supply.

And yet somehow he knew to the marrow of his bones that Ami would never treat him as Louisa had.

A rap on his arm pulled his attention back to Violet's frowning face.

"You are very preoccupied, Edmund."

"To be expected, daughter." The viscount looked down his nose at her. "The man's life is about to change tonight, eh, Price?" Chuckling, Bastion cuffed him on the shoulder.

And that's when he saw her. Not entering from the front foyer, as expected, but sweeping in from a side door, Ami created quite a stir from those around her. Or rather the peacock feathers draping down her marvelous backside did. Edmund couldn't help but grin as she ignored the stares with a defiant—and adorable—tilt to her chin.

"You are right, my lord," he murmured. "This is an auspicious evening, and as such, I must beg your pardon and part ways for a few minutes."

"Oh, Edmund, now?" Violet pursed her lips into a grand sulk. "Of all times!"

"Let him go, Violet." The viscount freed her grip from Edmund's sleeve and tucked her hand into his crooked elbow, then speared him with a sharp look. "But see that you return shortly, Price. Remember, I shall make the announcement at eight o'clock sharp. Don't be late."

He dipped his head as he pivoted away. While shouldering through the crowd, he met Ami's gaze across the room, pleasure surging in his chest that she'd known he would seek her out. With a quick jerk of his head, he signaled for her to follow, then turned toward the front foyer. It wouldn't do to attract attention. Not with her. Not now.

He handed out empty greetings and tight smiles as he worked his way to the master staircase, mind filled with a certain eccentric Egyptologist. He'd not had a word with her since the breakfast debacle. Which grieved him. Hopefully she'd not fretted about the situation overmuch.

He trotted up the stairs to fresher air and a quieter background—only a dull drone instead of the raging buzz of merrymakers. Crossing the landing, he paused at the entrance to a side-shooting corridor just long enough to make eye contact with Ami as she hiked her skirts up the stairway.

The din grew even quieter in this passage. He strode to the very end, where a cushioned window seat graced a curtained alcove. A perfect spot for reading—or an impromptu meeting without prying eyes and gossiping tongues.

Arriving ahead of Ami gave him time to appreciate her figure as she floated toward him. The closer she drew, the more his pulse raced. Her hair was done up, for once flawlessly pinned and curled into the latest fashion. Not a smudge of resin or dust marred her face. And though her colourful gown was unorthodox, it hugged her curves in all the right places. Her free spirit sparkled in eyes more green than blue or brown in this dim light, and her lips curved into a playful smile—one that hinted of shared secrets.

"Are you sure this is a good idea?" Stopping in front of him, she glanced over her shoulder, then back at him. "After this morning's newspaper article, if anyone should see us alone, I would think that would only add kindling to the rumour fire."

Grabbing her arm, he pulled her close, then yanked one of the draperies halfway, hiding them both. "There." He smirked. "Problem solved."

"Just like old times." She grinned. "Mr. Problem Solver."

Her nickname for him warmed his heart, but she was entirely wrong. This was nothing like the first time he'd met her on those college stairs. He'd been oblivious to her charms that day, and now . . . well, now he could see—he could *want*—no other woman but her.

Slowly, he traced his fingers along the gauzy fabric of her sleeve. "I'm sorry to have left you to navigate the day on your own. Bastion sequestered me in that fusty study of his, and there was just no getting away."

"I wasn't weeping into my pillow all day if that's what you're worried about. Oh bother!" Reaching, she pulled out a hairpin and gave her head a little shake, freeing a length of hair to cascade down the side of her neck. "I am no frail flower except when it comes to puncture wounds on my skull." She waved the hairpin in the air. "Nasty little torture devices."

He grinned. "I could accuse you of many things, but never of being a frail flower."

"Oh?" Her eyes twinkled. "Then what charges would you hold against me, sir?"

"For one, you have an impossibly keen mind that keeps me on my toes. For another, you are irrefutably true to yourself and to others, not caring a mite for popular opinion, which speaks highly of your character. And lastly . . ." He stepped toe to toe and breathed in her ever-present cinnamon scent. Surely that's what heaven would smell like. Unbidden, his voice dropped to a husky whisper. "I would indict you with filling a man's mind so that he can think of none other."

Her smile faded, a vulnerability he'd never seen before glistening in her eyes. "I assume you came up with a plan to refute that incriminating photograph of us?"

His gaze never once left hers. It couldn't. The pull of her was too strong. Meeting with her here had been a poor choice, yet he was powerless to step away now. And for once he didn't mind such a weakness. "The *Times* will retract their insinuations of you and me in tomorrow's edition."

You and me. What blessed words.

Would that it might always be so.

Her nose scrunched ever so slightly. "How did you manage that?"

"By giving their lead reporter a press invitation to tonight's gala."

"Ah." Her lips curved. "Bribery."

"I prefer to think of it as incentive."

"Ever the businessman *and* soon to be member of Parliament. I'm very happy for you, you know." Her smile vanished, replaced by a sadness in the press of her mouth, a sorrow he couldn't begin to understand.

At length, she murmured, "Oxford won't be the same with you here in London."

"About that . . ." Once again he ran his hand along her arm, more than pleased when she leaned into his touch. A good sign for a favorable answer to what he was about to propose. "I was wondering if, perhaps, you could be persuaded to take a position at the British Museum. Your father is friends with the Egyptian curator there. I'm sure he could get you in. It's a purely selfish suggestion, mind you, but the thing is, I cannot bear the thought of such a distance between us."

"Nor I." Tentatively, she reached up and rested her palm against his jaw. "I've grown rather accustomed to seeing this face every day, and I should sorely miss it."

"And I've grown rather accustomed to the lift of your brow when you're curious." He brushed his finger across her forehead. "Furthermore, I have adapted to the way you blush when I catch you looking at me." His touch trailed to her cheek, then over her nose. "I am completely attached to your delightful freckles and . . ."

Boldly—quite irresistibly—he glided his hand beneath her chin, tipping her face toward his. "I find I can no longer live without tasting those lips of yours."

Her chest rose and fell visibly. Several times.

"Then by all means," she breathed, "do so."

He didn't require any further invitation.

His mouth came down hard on hers—or was that deep hunger of her lips against his? He'd kissed Louisa before—and kissed her well—but never had it been anything like this. The connection he shared with this woman went far beyond the physical . . . and yet there was no denying just how pleasurable the physical aspect was.

He pulled away, heart racing, wanting more than he had a right to. "Ami, I . . . I know this is too soon for convention, but . . . well, what I mean to say is . . . I wonder if—" Hang it all! He couldn't put two words together if half the Queen's army aimed guns at his chest.

Drawing in a huge breath for courage, he shoved his hand into his pocket and pulled out a slip of paper.

Then held it up.

Ami struggled to breathe, her heartbeat so erratic she gripped Edmund's sleeve to remain standing. Polly had once tried to explain how a kiss felt, but this was nothing at all like the gushy warm feeling her friend had described. This was fire. Dangerous. Eternal. And altogether intoxicating. Either the small alcove she shared with this man was spinning or she was.

With her other hand, she plucked a torn piece of paper from Edmund's fingers. A curious offering, given the circumstances, and yet when she gazed at the misspelled words, her heart melted.

> *Wut soft lite doth brake be-ond,*
> *At donning, in this golden morn,*
> *In yor eyes, my wurld's reborn*
> *New promis, new luv, for-ever sworn.*

He'd written this for her? More than that, he'd risked showing it to her even after having his heart crushed when he'd done so with Louisa?

Overcome, she wrapped her fingers around the slip of paper, wrinkling it but not caring, owning it, possessing it, more than willing to become one with this man's sentiment.

"Ami?" Edmund's brow knit into worried lines.

"Oh, Edmund." She cupped his cheek, relishing the feel of his freshly shaven skin. "I cannot imagine my world without you in it, for I love you as none other."

He closed his eyes, nuzzling against her touch.

She stood stunned, hardly believing she'd voiced such intimate words to a man—and not just any man. To the most eligible bachelor in all of Oxford. How many times had he heard that same sentiment before? And yet here he stood with her.

Her!

Belowstairs, the deep reverberation of a gong sounded. Once. Twice. Thrice.

Edmund's dusky blue eyes opened as he pressed his brow to hers, their breath mingling. "So how do we manage from here on out, with your heart set on Egypt and mine on Parliament? For I will not take away your dream."

"And yet it seems you won't have *your* dream if we linger here any longer. You heard the gong. Your election announcement is at hand. Time for you to pursue the path meant for you."

Ever so slightly he shook his head. "You are my path now."

A thrill charged through her, settling low in her belly. "I am happy to hear it, but I will not be a hindrance to your career. You need to run for office to change those tariffs that harm innocent men like Sanjay. If we are meant to be"—she pulled back and collected his hand, pressing a kiss to his knuckles—"then God's will shall not be thwarted. He always makes a way."

"You, my love"—mimicking her, Edmund pressed his lips to the back of her hand—"are an inspiration."

"And you are going to be late." Wrapping her fingers around his, she tugged him from the alcove and down the corridor, stopping before it opened out onto the landing of the grand staircase. Despite his declaration of love, it wouldn't do to be seen together now. This was his night to shine, not to be shrouded in a cloak of romantic scandal.

Keeping to the shadows of a doorway, she turned to him. "You go first. You're the man of the hour. I'll slip in the side door of the ballroom like I did earlier."

"Very well, but only if you promise me the first dance after dinner."

"That won't sit well with Violet." She smirked. "This is her territory, after all."

"True, but I am not." He bopped her on the nose with a playful touch. "And I wish to dance first with the woman I love."

Once again warmth surged in her chest. The words. The sultry look in his eyes. She swallowed hard. It was so much to take in, more than she'd ever imagined. He loved her. *He* loved *her*. She held the knowledge close inside, protecting it like a freshly picked rosebud to be admired as it bloomed.

Then she lifted her chin. "I suppose you are used to getting your own way. So, yes, I will dance with you, sir. Now off with you before the viscount sends out a search party."

A grin spread on his lips—lips he pressed against hers in a mischievous kiss before he dashed away.

For a few more breaths, she lingered in the passageway, fingering her mouth in wonder. She relived every part of those stolen minutes alone with him in the alcove, branding his taste on her memory that she might never forget. Sweet mercy. If she'd have answered that call tonight to meet with Mr. Dandrae's seller, she'd never have known Edmund's kisses.

And if she loitered here any longer, she'd miss the big announcement for his candidacy.

Hastily, she tucked Edmund's cherished poem up her sleeve, then scurried down a different corridor, taking the back stairway to ground level. And just in time too. The viscount's voice was already booming as she entered the ballroom and lifted to her toes, scouting for her father. She caught his eye, thankfully, and he motioned her to the front of the circle, where he'd gotten a good position for the event.

"My esteemed guests," Lord Bastion began. Edmund stood at his right hand, Violet next to him, all in the center of the crowd's rapt attention. "It is my honour to have invited you here tonight, but as you may have guessed, this evening's gathering is more than merely an opportunity to socialize. I have an important announcement to make, one I am supremely pleased to share in public."

Murmurs bubbled all around. Edmund's gaze found hers and held.

"I am sure everyone here knows the illustrious Mr. Edmund Price." The viscount swept a hand toward him. "He is a man of remarkable achievements, a visionary leader in the realm of business, and a staunch advocate for the betterment of society. Edmund Price embodies the values and principles the heart of every Englishman holds dear."

Ami smiled. She couldn't be any prouder of Edmund. He would make such a fine MP. A stalwart one, championing causes for those who were powerless.

"And so"—Lord Bastion rubbed his hands together—"it is with great delight that I proclaim to you, my friends and colleagues, what can only be described as a monumental moment for me and for society at large."

A collective breath whooshed around the room, ladies leaning closer, gentlemen tilting their heads.

The viscount grinned broadly, clearly reveling in the response. "It is my joy to announce the engagement of my daughter, Miss Violet Woolsey, to Mr. Edmund Price."

Ami clenched every muscle from head to toe, waiting for Edmund to refute the absurd proclamation. Any second now he'd take command and tell the world this was a mistake. That he couldn't possibly marry Violet because he loved her. He *did* love her! He'd told her so only minutes ago.

But he merely stood there, jaw tight, saying nothing. Absolutely nothing. She grabbed her father's arm, craving support until Edmund laughed and said what a grand jest this had all been.

And still he said nothing.

Her stomach roiled, threatening to rebel right there on the ballroom floor. Thoughts from the very pit of hell swirled in her head like so many bats. Had Edmund known all along this would be the announcement tonight? Had he purposely led her to believe otherwise? Spoken so intimately—*acted* so intimately—only to secure her as his mistress before taking a wife? It wouldn't be a stretch to believe a man of material conquest would carry that trait over to his personal affairs. That's what the powerful and wealthy did, didn't they? Yet he'd seemed so different from men like the viscount and other rich patrons she'd met over the years. Had she been so captured by his practiced charisma that she'd fallen victim to it?

But no. No! She wouldn't—couldn't—believe such lies. For that's what such thoughts were. Vile, cancerous lies. Edmund couldn't refute the viscount's proclamation because to do so would be a stake in the heart of his candidacy. If he didn't comply with Lord Bastion's wishes, his chance at becoming a member of Parliament would be over before it began.

And she was the one standing in his way.

Hot tears burned in her eyes as she turned and fled, not caring who she shoved out of her way.

26

Edmund stood gut punched. Fists clenched. Jaw rock-hard. He hadn't been this stunned since the day he'd been dismissed from college for allegedly cheating on a test he couldn't even read. And yet this was worse. The confusion on Ami's face. The horrified parting of her lips. Surely she didn't believe—

She turned and dashed through the crowd.

"Ami," he whispered, stepping toward her retreating figure.

And getting yanked back just as quickly.

Violet wrapped her arms around his waist, smiling up at him. A snake swallowing a rat couldn't look more victorious. "Oh, darling, isn't it wonderful?"

Wonderful! Bile rose up his throat.

He peeled her off and wheeled about to face the viscount, his whole body shaking. "I must speak with you, my lord. Alone."

"Not now, man." Lord Bastion grinned. "Enjoy the moment with your betrothed."

"She is not my betrothed!"

Silence fell like shattered glass, so sharp it cut the ears and made them bleed. Everyone gawked, save for Violet. She slapped her hand to her chest as if she'd been shot.

"Of course she's not." The viscount chuckled and pinched her cheek. "You are so much more than that, aren't you, my dear?" Without missing a beat, he whacked Edmund on the back—too hard to be considered friendly. "Ever the jester, eh, Price?"

Before Edmund could get in a word, the man flung his arms wide and circled the gathered crowd. "And now, friends, if you would be so kind as to make your way to the dining room, you shall find a sumptuous feast where we will toast the happy couple momentarily." Under his breath, he said, "My study, Price," before he stalked away.

Edmund followed. Or tried to. Once again Violet grabbed his arm and tugged him back.

"Surely you know the dining room is this way, darling."

"I am not your darling," he ground out as he wrenched from her grip.

Ignoring the well wishes and raised brows of skirts and suits alike, he shouldered his way through the horde and, once he reached the stairs, took them two at a time. What a nightmare! He couldn't wait a minute more to set straight this whole debacle.

The second he set foot inside the viscount's lair, the man turned on him. "What the blazes was that all about?" Venom laced his tone.

"You tell me." Edmund slammed the door, giving vent to his fury. "You were supposed to announce my candidacy tonight."

"And I will as the pièce de résistance at the end of the evening." Spitting out a curse, Bastion paced in front of his desk, a tiger on the prowl. "What has gotten in to you?"

Edmund planted his feet, arms folded. How dare the man turn this back on him! "I never agreed to wed your daughter, my lord. In fact, I told you the very opposite when I clearly stated I wasn't ready for marriage—and *you* said you understood."

The viscount spun toward him, nostrils flaring. "No man is *ever* ready for marriage. That is what I understood, not that you were slapping away Violet's hand. My sponsorship was based solely on you taking my daughter as your wife." His lips thinned into a sharp-edged sneer.

"Do you think this is some sort of game?" Edmund flailed his arms. "Marriage is not a bargaining chip to be played so casually. It's a lifetime commitment. A vow before God. I will not be manipulated into such a union, nor do I think your daughter would thank you for a loveless marriage."

"Love has nothing to do with it."

"Love has everything to do with it!" Edmund sucked in a breath. Looking back, he marveled at the transformation within. After witnessing his parents' dismal marriage and suffering through the whole Louisa debacle, he'd perceived love as a weakness. Not anymore. He understood now just how wrong he'd been. Love was the strength of marriage. Faith played a huge part, as did hope, but the greatest of these *was* love.

Scowling, Bastion crossed to the drink cart and poured a large glass of brandy. He tossed it back, then tossed back another before facing Edmund once again. "Don't play the innocent with me, Price. This alliance benefits us both, securing your political position and adding prosperity to me. Violet understands that, and I should think you would as well."

Edmund ground his teeth. So that was it. No wonder she'd always claimed him as hers though he had never once given her any indication of his regard. The vixen had been in on Bastion's scheme the entire time.

"Now that you've had your little tantrum, Price, it's time to march downstairs and play the part of doting bridegroom. Then—and only then—will I announce your run for the House." The viscount strode to the door. In that moment Edmund knew, without a shadow of doubt, the man had manipulated this entire affair for his own benefit. And Edmund had blindly walked right into his trap.

Edmund dropped his hand, gut sinking as well. He'd had his back against a wall before, but this one had spikes in it. Bastion had been his only hope of getting into the House of Commons on such short notice. What did he know of campaigns? Without Bastion's sponsorship, his candidacy would be a farce. He'd never win.

"God's will shall not be thwarted. He always makes a way."

Ami's words rose to the surface. Wise words. Heartfelt.

But what if God's way didn't include stopping the tariff that would ruin men like Sanjay? Was the sacrifice of an empty marriage for the greater good what God was calling him to do?

He needed time. Alone. To think. To pray. To sort through how to navigate this tangled mess.

And yet, as wealthy as he was, that was a luxury he'd not be afforded.

"Well, Price?" Bastion stood with his hand on the doorknob, a single burning question afire in his gaze. "What's it to be?"

Ami braced herself against the wall inside the dark cab. It was either that or smash her face up against it. Cursed broken-springed hack! What a wretched excuse for a public conveyance. She should have waited to hail a properly functioning carriage, and she would have if the need to flee Lord Bastion's town house hadn't been so brutally fierce.

"Oof!" She grunted as the cab hit a bump, juddering her very bones. And yet she was glad for it. The harrowing ride made it all the easier to hold on to her fury, each jolt a physical reminder of the throat-hold the viscount had on Edmund. And Edmund hadn't refuted the man—which still rubbed her heart raw. Did he really love her as he'd claimed? Did he even know what true love was?

Oh my. Now there was a troubling thought. What if she was right on that account? What if Edmund honestly didn't know what love was? She propped her elbow against the wall to keep from tumbling sideways. Perhaps Edmund's definition of *love* was not the same as hers. After all, they were from entirely different stations in life. Likely worlds apart in thought and expectation. And what sort of love had he ever known other than that of a disapproving father and a woman who'd claimed she cared for him yet embarrassed him in front of his peers?

She blew out a long breath. Perhaps instead of running off like a petulant tot she ought to have pulled him aside and at least tried to understand his version of the situation. Be the bigger person and hear him out instead of flouncing away as Violet would have done. She owed him that much, she supposed.

The cab bounced to a stop. The door handle stuck, and she ended up kneeing the thing while cranking the lever at the same time. She tumbled out, the angle of the listing carriage much too sloped to do anything other. Arms flailing, she barely caught her footing before planting her face on the broken cobbles.

"Oi!" the driver called from up on his perch. "Mind yer step, sparrow, though ye might wanna turn yerself aback to that fancy 'ouse ye came from. Whitechapel ain't for the likes o' a dainty bird like yerself."

He was right. She should have taken the time to change out of her evening gown. Those peacock feathers on her backside would attract undue attention in this neighbourhood. But she was already running late, *if* the seller of those jars was even still here. Not that she had the money to make a purchase—yet— but she could reschedule a meeting for tomorrow and have her father secure funds from his friend at the British Museum.

She fished out a coin from her reticule and held it up to the driver. "Thank you for your advice, but I can manage. Please wait until I return."

He snatched the money with a frown. "Foolish nip, ain't ya? I'm not staying here like a fat duck to be plucked. Yer on yer own, sparrow, may God 'ave mercy on ye." He snapped the reins. "Walk on!"

The old horse clip-clopped away, dragging the sorry excuse of a carriage behind. Feeling suddenly vulnerable, Ami tucked her reticule up her sleeve, or tried to. Bosh! She fidgeted with the fabric, annoyed. It was a tight fit, leaving a bulge, but better that than allow it to swing and attract a cutpurse. Even so, just let someone try. In the foul mood she was in, she'd welcome such a fight.

Turning, she entered the narrow throat of Angel Alley,

scrunching her nose at the stench of urine. It wasn't soon enough before the short corridor spit her into a small courtyard.

The relief didn't last long. She stopped but six paces inside the shadowy area. Off to one side a brazier licked flames into the night, painting hellish light onto the leering faces of three monstrous men. One of them held a knife in the air, the blade gleaming silver. Over in the corner, a drunkard bent double, retching loudly, and in another corner, the whites of two eyeballs violated her in ways that clenched her stomach.

Gooseflesh lifted on her arms. The worst parts of Oxford were nothing like this. Brokering a deal in London was apparently quite a different animal—one she didn't think she could tame even with her years of bartering with thugs. A set of canopic jars, as rare as they were, was not worth the price of her virtue.

Or her life.

She spun about, only to see the opening blocked by a caveman. Next to him stood his shorter counterpart, leaning on a cane. A cleft in his jaw. One eye blackened. Wearing a tatty plaid suit coat the same as the last time she'd seen him. Of course! She should have known. She folded her arms, disgusted with herself for falling for such a trick. "I see you're up to your usual hijinks, Mr. Brudge. No wonder Mr. Dandrae didn't add a seller's name for those jars, though I doubt very much you have them."

"And yet here you are, missy," he said with a feral grin. "I knew you couldn't resist a fat worm."

"If this is another attempt to coerce me into getting you that griffin, you've wasted your time. I don't have access to it anymore. I am finished with Mr. Price." She grimaced at those words, more final than the bang of a coffin nail.

"Ah, but I'm not finished with you, love." Mr. Brudge snapped his fingers in the air.

The big oaf at his side advanced, pulling a length of rope from his pocket.

Swallowing back fear, Ami retreated—then stopped when she remembered the horrors behind her. What a beastly situation!

She never should have let that cab driver roll off. Even a broken carriage was better than no getaway.

She yanked out her reticule, careful not to dislodge Edmund's—hold on. Panicked, she fingered her sleeve. Her *empty* sleeve. Had the slip of paper with his poem fallen out when she'd jammed her purse beneath the fabric? Still, that was the least of her worries at the moment. She'd have to search for it when she left this putrid place.

If she left it.

Channeling all her frustration, she threw her reticule at the big man's feet. "That's all I have. Take the money and go."

Mr. Brudge spit out a crude laugh. "I don't want your coin, girl. I don't even want your ugly statue anymore."

"But I have nothing else." Great heavens. Had that frightened little girl's voice really come from her? She fisted her hands on her hips, praying the stance would infuse some sort of courage. "What more could you possibly want, Mr. Brudge?"

His lips twisted into a smug line.

"You."

27

"Get out!"

The words were thunder. The viscount's face black with rage. Edmund widened his stance in the storm, knowing full well it was a tempest of his own making. He never should have let Lord Bastion so much as entertain the thought he might marry the man's daughter.

But it was too late for that now.

He held up a hand, more of an appeasement than a surrender. Showing any hint of weakness would be a death knell. "Allow me to make amends, my lord, to your daughter, to your guests. Explain that this was all a misunderstanding and—"

"You heard me, Price." Bastion shot out his arm like an arrow to the kill, indicating the study door. "Pack your bag and leave at once while I mop up this mess. I will have nothing more to do with you and neither will Violet."

"But, my lord, if we could just discuss—"

"Now!"

Inhaling deeply, Edmund hesitated a heartbeat longer, debating if there was anything more he could do to keep from jumping off this cliff. Hah! Not likely. It'd been a downward spiral ever since he told the viscount in no uncertain terms he would not wed Violet, even if his candidacy depended on it. Which it did. Or it had. There was no chance at Parliament anymore.

"Very well." Sighing, Edmund strode from the room and signaled one of Bastion's staff members standing by. "Please see that my valet is summoned and have him make arrangements for three rooms at the Langham Hotel. Then he is to accompany my luggage and the Daltons' belongings over there. Is that clear?"

The man nodded. "Yes, sir."

"Very good. Thank you." The low drone of the party followed him like a moaning ghost as he bypassed the gentlemen's wing of the town house and trotted over to where the ladies' quarters smelled of perfume—rose, lilac, jasmine. Sniffing, he stopped at the door with a faint scent of smoky cinnamon lingering on the air.

"Ami?" He rapped on the wood.

No answer.

"Ami, please." He knocked again. "I saw you run off. I know you're in there. Let me explain."

And . . . nothing.

He dropped his forehead against the hard door, completely deflated. He could bear Lord Bastion's fury. Could take all the humiliation the society page would dish out in tomorrow's edition. But this was not to be borne. It cut too deeply, burned too hot to think of the hurt he'd caused this precious woman. Could she even hear him, or was she weeping into her pillow?

Swiveling his head, he pressed his ear to the wood. No sobbing whimpered from within. No anything, actually. Which in a way was worse. Was he already dead to her?

"Please, Ami, open the door." His voice shook. His whole body did. "I understand how it must seem to you, but it's not true. I am not engaged to Miss Woolsey. I do not love her. I love you. Do you hear me? I will have no one but you!"

Spent, he sagged against the wood. If she opened the door now, he'd fall against her. A dream, that. Heaven. And yet each second that ticked by was more hellish than the last.

At length, he straightened, giving it one last try. "We must leave here. Tonight. I'm booking rooms at the Langham, and we'll return to Oxford tomorrow. I'll be in my room packing, waiting . . . hoping."

It was a funeral march to his room, every step away from her a fresh grief. If Ami wouldn't speak to him through the door, there was no way she'd seek him out in his room.

He yanked his suitcase off the top of the wardrobe and flung it on the bed, angry with himself. He'd let her down. And not just her. He'd let down all the struggling men who were in Sanjay's same situation. Oh, he could still help his friend with the funds from the sale of the Egyptian cargo, but now he could do nothing to stop the new tariff from destroying other men's lives. Just like his father always told him . . .

"You are a disappointment of the highest degree."

He ripped off his cravat, relishing the burn of fabric at the back of his neck. Like Icarus, he'd aspired too highly, reached for things that were never meant for him. His once-optimistic aspirations were nothing but dung.

Wrenching out of his dress coat, he threw it at the suitcase, then lifted his face to the ceiling.

Why, God? Why did You let this happen? Ami doesn't deserve a broken heart any more than those men in India merit certain death by poverty. It's all my fault, and yet You could have stopped it. Why not? Why!

His head dropped, the last of his fury strangled by shame because he was right. This whole debacle had been his fault, not God's. Flirting with power and fame was his own undoing. A deep sense of remorse draped over his shoulders, the weight of responsibility squeezing the breath from his lungs.

"Forgive me, God," he murmured. "I ran ahead of You and made a mess of things. Heal the hurts I've caused. Protect the men I cannot. I don't know how, Lord, but somehow would You make beauty out of this ash heap I've created?"

A sharp rap on the door abruptly ended his prayer. He sprinted toward it, hardly believing God would answer so quickly.

And yet that spark of hope was doused when he opened the door to a wild-haired man in a crooked bow tie.

"I thought I might find you here." The professor swept a glance over him from head to toe. "Though I must say you don't appear to be as ill as Lord Bastion claims."

So that's what the viscount had told everyone. A stalling tactic, one that didn't bode well for it would give the man ample time to figure out how to crucify him. Edmund rubbed his hand over his face, weary of intrigue. "I am neither ill, Professor, nor engaged to Miss Woolsey."

"I thought as much." The man shoved past him without invitation and plopped into the overstuffed chair near the hearth. "Though I daresay Amisi could believe otherwise. Might I have a word?"

Edmund closed the door, dreading what this man might say. Better to make the first move himself. "I tried to explain, sir, to tell her she owns my heart, not Miss Woolsey, yet Ami would have none of it. She wouldn't even open her door to me."

"Nor to me." The professor peered up at him, stroking his chin. "That's why I tried the handle. She's not there. She's not in the ballroom, the dining room, the ladies' lounge, and for good measure I even checked the conservatory out back. Dark as a pharoah's tomb in there at this time of night."

Alarm prickled up his backbone. If Ami wasn't inside the town house, she must be wandering the dangerous streets of London at night. His gut clenched, and he grabbed his coat off the bed. "Have you any idea of where she might have gone?"

The professor produced a crumpled paper from his pocket. "I found this in her wastepaper bin."

Edmund palmed the offering, arching a brow at the man. "Why would you be digging in her wastebin?"

"I know my daughter better than she thinks."

He glanced at the short missive, though he may as well have been reading Sanskrit. "I don't understand." He glanced from the paper to the professor, looking for answers.

The man rose and, lacing his fingers behind his back, struck a lecturing stance. "Though you've likely already noticed, Amisi is not like other women. She doesn't spend hours in needlepoint or at the piano. Her favored pastime has a decidedly more dangerous flair to it. In certain circles, she is known as the Shadow Broker, and she is no doubt going after the canopic jars mentioned in that note."

"Shadow Broker?" he muttered, though even voicing it didn't help to comprehend the words. He'd worked with brokers before. Most were determined, some ruthless, all intelligent. Edmund kneaded the back of his neck, thinking on what he knew of the fearless little Egyptologist. "What sort of negotiations would she . . ."

His words died. So did part of his soul. She was brokering a dangerous deal for the canopic jars. He'd bet everything he owned on it. His hand dropped lifelessly at his side.

"I see you've figured it out." The professor looked down his nose at him.

"But this is foolishness!" He flailed his arms. "What sort of father allows his daughter to deal in such a treacherous fashion?"

The professor shot up his palm, staving off the accusation. "Amisi has a mind of her own, one that is not keen to bend to my will when she thinks there is a greater good at stake."

"Thunderation!" he roared. "She's gone to Whitechapel, hasn't she? The most crime-infested rookery in all of London. We've got to get to her."

"I was hoping you'd say that. I'm not nearly as intimidating as you. Shall we?" The professor angled his head toward the door.

Where yet another knock rapped.

Edmund's pulse soared as he dashed to the knob.

Please let it be Ami. Please let it be!

But it was a fresh-faced footman in midnight-blue livery holding out a tray with a telegram perched on top. "For you, sir."

Bitterly disappointed, feet itching to race out of there to find Ami, Edmund snatched the message a little too forcefully. The tray clattered to the floor, and he couldn't work up one bit of sympathy for it. He wheeled back to the professor and offered the paper. "What do you make of this?"

The professor looked at him askance for a moment, as well he should. In times like these Edmund scorned his affliction more than any other, but it would take too long to sound out each and every word—time he didn't have. Time Ami didn't have!

Thankfully, the professor merely squinted at Barnaby's telegram and mumbled aloud as he read.

"'The curse has struck again—or rather Mr. Fletcher has. He moved the artifacts yesterday, leading Jameson and I to believe Mr. Harrison had purchased them. Not so. Mr. Harrison arrived tonight for a final viewing and is not happy to see the relics gone. Please advise.'"

His leg ached. So did his bunion. And Brudge's fingers were working up a fairly strong cramp as well, especially in his pinky. Blast the struggling little Shadow Broker. She was more of a scrapper than he'd counted on.

Gritting his teeth, he limp-hustled along with Wormwell's cribbage-faced escorts, one of them so pockmarked it looked as if he'd been hit in the face with a meat hammer. Brudge would have made it to the smuggling kingpin's warehouse at least twenty minutes ago if it hadn't been for lack of cabs from a sudden rain that'd broken and for Scupper. The traitorous wretch. Of all the places in all of London, what were the chances one of the big goon's old mates would show up in Angel Alley for some late-night skullduggery? And worse, offered Scupper a fatter purse than he could supply the man. Well, good riddance! Him and his guv'ner this and guv'ner that. Scupper was a brainless wad of twaddle, and he'd told him as much.

Which hadn't really helped the situation.

But that was neither here nor there. The fact was, he had about ten minutes until midnight to get Neddie and himself out of Wormwell's clutches. With a little luck and a quick tongue, he just might be able to pull it off.

Inside the warehouse—which was really just a huge cavern of damp and darkness better suited to bats than men—the pile of muscles in front of him turned down a well-lit passage and stopped at a closed door. After a cursory knock and a requisite "Enter," the big man slid the wide door aside, top wheels screeching on their track like a shaken cage of mice.

The guard behind him grunted. "Move it."

Brudge lugged the woman inside the large room, her mumbled complaints worthless against the rag he'd tied around her mouth. A single chandelier dangled overhead, spreading a circle of light that he and the woman were prodded into. Ahead, in the darkness where the light didn't reach, a single spot of burning red flared, the scent of cigar smoke acrid on the musty air.

"I was wondering if you'd make the deadline or if I'd have to send out a retrieval squad." Wormwell's bass voice was surprisingly dull thanks to the thick layers of Persian rugs covering the area. It was a little disconcerting, though, not to be able to see him as he spoke. "Five minutes to spare. Impressive. Your son has been waiting ever so patiently to see if you'd show. Bring the man in, Flick."

Brudge tensed as the colossus who'd led them to the room disappeared out a side door. Neddie was still alive, but how much had his boy suffered over the past month and a half? At seventeen, his son was resilient, but not even a young brawler could last long drudging for Wormwell.

Moments later, the guard reappeared, this time with Neddie, one thick arm wrapped around his son's neck. The other pressing a gun to his temple.

Sweat collected on Brudge's brow, moist and cold. He shivered as he clutched the woman's arm tighter, telling himself it was more for balance than for comfort in the face of such a threat. The Shadow Broker whimpered, and he almost did too.

But to show fear would get him and his boy killed.

"Let Neddie go!" he rumbled. "I've brought the payment before the deadline, just as we agreed."

A bushel basket rolled out from the darkness, landing on its side in the circle of light.

"Put the money in there, and your son will be released."

With his free arm, Brudge swiped his brow, mopping the sweat with his sleeve. He couldn't very well wad up the woman and pack her in that basket.

"I didn't bring money," he admitted, then propelled the woman forward. "I brought something better."

Outside rain dripped against the tin roof, hardly more than a thick mist yet almost deafening in the sudden silence. If he listened hard enough, he might even hear the steady sizzle of Wormwell's cigar.

"A tasty morsel," the dismembered voice said at length. "But if I wanted a doxy, I'd have picked one up on Flower and Dean. The money, Brudge, or your son pays your debt, the one that's due in four minutes."

The woman's backbone straightened to a ramrod. She was on edge.

So was he, and without the woman to prop him upright, he leaned heavily on his good leg to keep the pain at bay in the other. "She's not a moll," he clarified. "She's your ticket to wealth. The woman belongs to Mr. Price, *the* Price, wealthiest gent in all of Oxford. He'll fork over a pretty sixpence or two to get her back. More than I could ever pay you. You'll pocket a tidy profit because of me."

Again silence. The red dot dulling somewhat, then flaring back to life after an ash had been flipped away.

"Do you think I'm stupid enough to extort such a prominent man?" Wormwell's tone was a bucket of ice water. "I'd have bluecoats swarming all over my prosperous business here. I don't need her. I need my money. And you've got three minutes to toss it in that basket, or your Neddie is done."

Panic tasted sour at the back of Brudge's throat. "Then don't ransom her! Use her. She's a historian who knows her trinkets. She can jack up your trade, give you credence, tell which pieces are fake and which are real."

"Is that so?"

The dot disappeared, as if Wormwell had turned the thing around and was studying it while deep in thought. Could be. And if so, now was his chance to drive home his point.

"God's truth! She's an expert, she is, a renowned Egyptologist up in Oxford. Ask Dandrae. With her knowledge, you can mark your collection as authentic, not mere forgeries. It'll fetch you more coin in the long run, earn you money that will overflow that little basket of yours." He nodded at the bushel container lying like a dead soldier on the rug.

"One minute, Brudge."

No! This couldn't be happening. His gaze shot to Neddie, all gangly limbed and as grey as yesterday's porridge. His son's pleading eyes bored holes into his soul.

"Fine, then don't take her!" he shouted into the darkness. "Take me. My life for Neddie's. I'm the one what owes you!"

Genuine laughter rumbled in the shadows. The burning dot of red reappeared, waving in the black void. "Your life's not worth a pot to spit in."

"I'm the one who failed you, not Neddie. Take me and let him go. I'll do whatever you ask, work off my debt. Serve you till my final breath if need be. Just spare my son!"

"You make me sound like a heartless devil. Is that what I am, boys?"

Eerie laughter crept out from every dark crevice. Dash it! How many men were in this room? Too many for him and Neddie to take on, that's for sure.

And that's when he knew.

There would be no escaping this situation.

Neddie would die here. He would die here. Even the woman wouldn't get away with her life.

As if in agreement, the red dot blinked out, snuffed into oblivion.

Brudge pulled at his collar, unable to breathe.

"Release him," Wormwell murmured.

In a flash, the muzzle of the gun tipped impotently to the

ceiling. The guard's beam of an arm dropped. Neddie fell to his knees, chest heaving, a string of spittle hanging from his lips.

"Off with you now, boy," the disembodied voice ordered.

Neddie shot to his feet, his gaze seeking his father's as he sped past Brudge.

Brudge teared up. What luck. What unmitigated, unadulterated luck! "Thank you, Wormwell. Oh, thank you! May this deed be spread far and wide. May your great name be hailed amongst men."

"You see?" The voice floated placatingly out of the darkness, benevolent in tone, like a grandfather to a beloved heir. "I am not the unreasonable monster you make me out to be, but . . ."

The unfinished sentence hung on the air like an off-key chord.

The Shadow Broker edged back, leaving Brudge front and center.

Wormwell cleared his throat. "I find that neither can I allow the word you so dearly hope to spread on the street. It wouldn't be seemly to appear soft. I have a certain reputation to maintain. So, yes, I will take your offer of service until the debt is paid, but as an astute businessman, that value will be better serviced by someone of keener intelligence than yourself. In that respect, the woman will work out just fine, I think. Better than you could ever hope to do."

Brudge blinked, unsure of Wormwell's meaning. Somewhere a clock struck. The low bongs throbbing inside the warehouse like the beat of a heart. One. Two. Three.

Could he leave the woman here and tag out on Neddie's heels, then?

. . . Seven. Eight. Nine.

Oh, the relief. The blessed, soothing relief!

. . . Eleven. Twelve.

"So I am free to—"

A shot cracked out of the darkness.

And that was the last thing Brudge ever knew.

28

Ami whirled from the sight of Mr. Brudge's body toppling backward. She wouldn't allow the image of blood spreading like gangrene over his chest to be imprinted on her mind. The sound, though. Well, that was quite another thing. With her wrists bound behind her back, there was nothing she could do to shut out the whump of his corpse on the rug.

"Tully, get that meat out of here before it leaks onto the carpet. Flick, see to the woman."

The man's words were a death sentence—hers. Pain was coming. Sharp and unstoppable. Her heart banged against her ribs, pulse staccato, breathing wild . . . the very things that would soon quit functioning forever. She'd always known she would die, just like every other human on the face of this blue ball, and yet, probably like Mr. Brudge and anyone else who'd ever lived and breathed and loved, she wasn't ready. Not yet. A whimper struggled in her throat, blocked by the rag jammed in her mouth.

Oh, God, I've been such a fool thinking I'm invincible. I am not, but You are. Please, Mighty One, grant mercy. Spare my life.

Footsteps drew near at her back, muffled on the carpet, making the sound all the more menacing. Fingers bit into her upper arm. She scrunched her eyes shut. This was it, and not at all how she'd imagined. She should be older, greyer, lying in a bed surrounded by her husband and children. Ushered into the next realm with hymns and prayers, not with rank breath snorting hot against the back of her neck. How much would this hurt? How long would it last? Would it take a while for her soul to float to heaven, or would she see Jesus right away?

Cold metal bit against the base of her skull. Every muscle she owned tensed. How she wished her father were here. That Edmund were holding her hand, making things less frightening. *Oh, Edmund.* Tears escaped past her clenched eyelids.

A quick jerk.

Her head snapped, and the putrid gag fell away.

Her eyes popped open. Sure enough, the stained rag lay atop the toe of her shoe.

Another jolt to her arms. A strong slice. Her wrists broke apart.

Freed.

She wheeled about, rubbing the chafed skin at the base of her hands, hardly daring to believe her lungs still worked, her heart yet beat.

"May I—" She cleared her rusty throat. "May I leave?"

"Not so fast, love." Mr. Wormwell's voice sailed out of the blackness. "You have a debt to pay off first. Your friend Brudge's there."

She kept her gaze fixed on the wall of darkness past her circle of light, refusing to look at the body being dragged past her. "He was not my friend."

Coarse laughter rumbled in the shadows. "It doesn't matter to me if he was your blasted hairdresser. The fact is he brought you here, and you will service what he owed me . . . that is *if* you're all he said you were. Are you well-versed in Egyptian artifacts and their value, or are you not?"

Bosh! Of all the times she longed to be recognized as a renowned Egyptologist, this was not one of them. Yet it was that very fact that might save her life.

Summoning any shred of courage she had left, she straightened her shoulders and spoke into the inky void. "I am."

"Good. Otherwise, I'd have two bodies to dispose of."

A shiver spasmed across her shoulders. She had no doubt he'd get rid of her as easily as he had Mr. Brudge. The question was if she could please him long enough to figure out how to get away.

A match struck in the darkness, its small flame sizzling into life. For the briefest of moments, she glimpsed the man behind the voice—then wished she hadn't. No wonder he preferred the shadows. Half his face was melted, the skin all puckery and purple. The eye socket on that side black and empty. The flame crawled into the end of a cigar, and after several puffs, expanded to a glowing red orb, too dull to illuminate any more of Mr. Wormwell's frightening visage.

After a few more draws, he said, "I have a shipment of Egyptian artifacts that's even now being unloaded. Before I pay the seller the exorbitant amount he's asking, I should like to get your opinion of what it's worth. Can you manage that?"

"Yes." She swallowed, knowing her voice sounded impossibly small.

"If you're lying," he drawled, "you're dead. If you try to escape, you're dead. If you cat-scratch my men, you're—"

"Dead," she finished for him, perspiration popping out on her brow. "Yes, I get the picture."

"Clever woman. Perhaps ol' Brudge really did pay his debt by bringing you in. Imagine that." The cigar bobbed in the darkness. "Take the woman to the loading dock, Flick. And if she doesn't play nice, you know what to do."

The pockmarked man next to her grabbed her arm. "Come along, darlin'."

She didn't object. In fact, she'd have to go along with anything and everything this Mr. Wormwell and his cohorts threw at her until she could devise a way to escape.

Mr. Flick led her down a labyrinth of passages, most lined by towering shelves of unmarked crates. The light from his lantern bobbed about, breathing life into ghoulish shadows, none of which were as menacing as him, though. Coming to a side door, he produced a key from his pocket and unlocked it. Air dampened by what was now a light rain smelled of musk and brackish river water. Mr. Wormwell's warehouse sat on a Thames wharf. Which one, she didn't know, so even if she did somehow get loose, she had no idea which way to go.

The brute tugged her across the thin space between buildings, steering her into the next warehouse. Inside this one, a hive of activity buzzed about. Lanterns hung on hooks, illuminating a huge unloading area. Big doors at the opposite end gaped open, allowing wagons to pass in and out. Burly men hefted crates off the drays, stacking them in rows, some of them with pry bars popping off the wooden lids. The closer she and Mr. Flick drew, the more her heart stalled. She didn't need to look inside to see what treasure she was to evaluate. She'd already done so.

These were the same crates she'd worked on at Price House.

Missing relics were bad enough, but if Edmund couldn't find Ami before anything awful happened to her, he'd never forgive himself—and neither would whoever dared to harm her, for he'd more than throttle the man. Or men. With all the fear and fury pumping through his veins, he'd mow down anyone and everyone in Angel Alley if she was hurt.

The cab jerked to a stop, his head and the professor's snapping forward from the abrupt halt. Edmund jumped out into the light rain, then immediately wheeled about and held up his hand, barring the professor from doing the same.

"Wait here," he said.

The professor's eyes widened, the whites stark against the night shadows. "You can't go in there alone!"

"Ami did." And the thought still scraped his heart raw. Why did she care so much for ancient remains and so little for her own life? He handed a bill up to the driver. "Stay put until I return or until the gentleman inside orders you to leave. Is that understood?"

The cabbie's jaw dropped as he stared at the exorbitant payment. "Aye, sir! Ye can count on me, sir."

"Very good." Edmund once again faced Ami's father. "I need you to summon the police if I'm not back in a few minutes."

The professor shook his head, a scowl digging a deep furrow in his brow. "You're as foolhardy as Amisi. We should have the police here with us now."

"We don't know if she's in there, nor do we know if a crime has been committed. We don't know anything—which is what I plan on finding out. And the longer I stand here chatting with you, the more it delays discovering where Ami is."

"Very well." The professor huffed as he pulled out his pocket watch and flipped open the lid. "You've got two minutes, Mr. Price."

"Make it three. There's no telling how large the courtyard inside is. Here, I won't be needing this." He handed his coat up to the professor, ignoring the questions in the man's eyes and pivoting away before he could voice any.

Four strides later, he paused before entering the narrow throat of Angel Alley. Stooping, he swiped his fingers along the sludge of the broken cobbles, then wiped the grime on his brow, cheeks, and jaw. Not as good of a disguise as Jameson's old coat and hat, but it would have to do. Wouldn't hurt to dirty his arms as well, so he shoved up his sleeves and once again smeared his fingers on the ground and— What was this?

He pinched a scrap of paper, and when he glanced at the penned words, his heart stopped. His poem. No, Ami's poem. He sucked in a breath.

She was here! Ami was here, or at least she had been.

He jammed the paper into his pocket and scrubbed the rest of the dirt furiously on his arms. Buoyed by hope, he ripped open the front of his waistcoat, buttons pinging against the brick opening, and set off.

He strode through the dark passage, gut revolting at the

putrid stench permeating the moist walls. Nor did it get any better when the channel opened into a dank courtyard of filth. Sweeping a glance around the area, he prayed to see the flash of some bodacious peacock feathers on a multihued gown. But no. Only black and grey met his eyes. Colour didn't live in this place, save for the hellish flames of a small brazier spitting against the rain. Four men stood about it, eyeing him. In a nearby alcove, a couple was all arms and legs, doing what ought not be seen in public. And off in the corner lay a body, drunk to the world.

Edmund swaggered over to the four men, dipping his head as he approached. A strange waft of gardenia hovered around the tallest fellow.

The man closest to him turned aside and spit, then swiped the back of his hand across his mouth. "Do I know ye?"

Edmund met his gaze. "Doubtful."

The man next to that fellow nudged his friend with his elbow. "Don't be daft, Muggs. That toff ain't from round 'ere. Them threads is too fine fer the likes o' the Angel."

"He's right," the third fellow said as he pulled a knife. "So move along, toff."

The tallest man said nothing, but the set of his jaw wasn't any less threatening than the blade in his comrade's grip.

Though everything in him screamed to fleet-foot it out of there, Edmund forced a grin. He didn't know a thing about knife fighting, but he did know how to negotiate—and thug or suit, every man was a businessman at heart. "Easy there, gents." He held up his hands. "Just looking for a bit of excitement in this dreary place. Heard this is where a man can find some action."

Muggs narrowed his eyes. "It'll cost ye, dependin' on what sort o' fluff up yer wantin'?"

"I'm looking for a woman. Colourful gown, feathers down the backside. Dark hair. Slight of frame."

The men exchanged glances, though all seemed to single out the tallest fellow. He toyed with the tip of his curled moustache, saying nothing. Ah. He did know something about Ami.

"I'm willing to pay for the information," Edmund prodded.

The tall one cocked his head. "What ye want her for, guv'ner?"

To love. To cherish. To make her my own and never allow a single harm to come to her.

He shoved down the passionate thoughts. These men wouldn't respect such soft sentiment—and that blade yet gleamed in the firelight. He forced a slow curve to his lips. "What does a man ever want a woman for?"

Coarse laughter guffawed out of them, curling Edmund's hands into fists.

The tall one's tongue poked about his cheek. He winced, sucking air through his missing front tooth. "What's it worth to ye, guv'ner?"

"I can make it very worth your while if you tell me where she is."

The man with the knife aimed the tip at him. "Or we could jes' take it from ye. A toff like you is child's play."

Sweat mingled with the rain dripping off the ends of his hair, trickling down his neck. Showing weakness now would be waving red in front of that bull.

"You could," Edmund admitted, "but I doubt you could dispose of my body before the police show up. If I'm not back on the street in one minute, my associate will alert the bluecoats. So either we conduct this business in a profitable fashion or in one that involves shackles and very poor meals." He pulled a wad of bills out of his pocket—which was either a baited hook or a death warrant. Hopefully the former.

The tall man's eyes locked onto the money. "I know where she is, guv'ner. The Shadow Broker's in Wormwell's warehouse over in Rotherhithe. Leastwise that's where ol' Brudge were takin' 'er an hour or so ago, an' tha's God's truth." He held out his hand, palm skyward.

It always paid to examine a man's chin when cutting a deal. If it twitched to the left, he was lying. To the right, no malintent, but it was a bluff all the same. The big man's jaw didn't move a hair. Edmund handed him the money. "Good doing business with you."

The big fellow tucked it inside his shirt. "'Tweren't a fair hand Brudge dealt the little woman, but as me mum always said, shadows may bend, yet they ne'er break. Keep that in mind with whate'er you intend concerning the woman."

Huh. He might almost think the man had a care for Ami. Even so, Edmund backed away, keeping an eye on the lot of them while listening for any movement behind him. He didn't know a thing about the Wormwell warehouse, but he did know a fair amount about the Rotherhithe wharves.

And they weren't any less dangerous than here.

29

How could it possibly be? Ami bit her lip to keep from gaping at the priceless artifacts being unloaded by men who wouldn't know an amulet from an ax-head. These items should have been in Mr. Harrison's possession, not here in a dirty warehouse smelling of dead fish and sweaty men. Besides an engagement to Violet, had Edmund kept this sale a secret as well?

She rolled the thought around in her head as the brute beside her led her closer to the treasures. But, no, the idea of Edmund negotiating a deal with Mr. Wormwell was even less plausible than him wedding a pampered princess he couldn't possibly love. Surely he'd have gotten more money from that private collector than a criminal like Mr. Wormwell . . . wouldn't he?

Then again, Mr. Dandrae had been known to outbid the Ashmolean when there was a piece he wanted for himself, and he operated on a much smaller scale than it appeared Mr. Wormwell did.

The brutish man hustling her along stopped in front of what appeared to be a side office and pulled a slate off a nearby hook. A broken piece of chalk was tethered to it by an unraveling piece of string, and he shoved it in her hands. "Get to work."

She clutched the board lest she anger the fellow. "I must know who brought in this shipment. Who is the seller?"

"Yer to price the lot, not ask questions." He rammed her shoulder with a thick finger, prodding her toward the unloaded crates.

She stumbled, then planted her feet. "It is imperative I know where these relics came from in order to give Mr. Wormwell the value he desires." A lie. Sort of. It was helpful to know where items came from to provide context for historical and cultural significance, which tied into price . . . not that this thug needed to know she already knew the answer, however.

And the more she stalled, the more time she'd have to figure out a way to escape.

God, please, help me think of a way!

"Ask the man yerself, and be quick about it," he grumbled. "Ye've a load o' work to do by sunup. And if ye don't get it done, Wormwell will have you fer breakfast. Ye'll find the hawker waitin' fer his due in here." He hitched his thumb toward the office door, then shoved his face into hers. "But mind ye don't run off. This wharf belongs to Wormwell, and he don't take kindly to runners. Neither do I."

She clutched the slate all the tighter to keep from whapping him over the head with it, for such an action wouldn't do any good. Even if she managed to crack his skull, the other men would see and come to his aid.

She strode the few steps to the closed office door, fighting to keep her composure despite the fear weakening her legs. She never should have fled the Bastions' town house. What an impetuous move! Her father and Polly had warned her that shadow brokering would catch up to her someday.

And this was the day.

Angry with herself, she yanked open the door—flinching as a gunshot split the night outside. Apparently there was just as much danger on the other side of these walls. She strode inside the office.

Then gaped.

"Mr. Fletcher?" The name on her lips made about as much sense as seeing Edmund's business partner pacing in front of a scarred hulk of a desk. His trousers were muddied. His hair stood on end, wilder than her father's. A grey pallor shadowed his face as if he might swoon dead away.

Concerned, she set the slate on a nearby chair and approached him. "Mr. Fletcher? You look unwell. Perhaps you ought to sit down."

Stopping in his tracks, he turned frenzied eyes upon her, and a shiver snaked down her spine. She'd witnessed a rabid horse put down for just such a look.

"Miss Dalton? What the devil are you doing here?"

"I would ask the same of you. What happened to the sale with Mr. Harrison? How did you get involved with Mr. Wormwell?"

His eyes narrowed. "How did you?"

"I have nothing to do with the man! I just wish to leave. Can you help me?"

"Ha-ha! I can't even help myself." He sagged against the desk. "I've dealt with Wormwell's associates before but never him—and now I realize I shouldn't have. He didn't pay me up front as he said he would, and I need that money. I need it now! You would think the most notorious smuggled goods dealer in all of London would know the value of a load right off. But no! I'm shut in here, left to sweat and wonder if he'll pay me or pop me off. Blast it all!"

He pulled at his hair, sweat raining from his face, so caught up in his own misery she wondered if he even knew she was there.

She stood stock-still, unsure if she ought to advance and comfort the pitiful man or retreat from the horror of him. "Why would you need money? Mr. Price says you're a good businessman."

He threw back his head, rough laughter pouring from his mouth.

Ami frowned. What sort of mess was this? "Mr. Fletcher, I demand to know what is going on right now."

"Demands are naught but smoke in the wind." Stepping

away from the desk, he puffed a stream of air at her, the stink of rum on his breath. "See? Gone."

Alarm prickled the nape of her neck. Something was definitely not right about him. Suddenly she preferred the pockmarked Mr. Flick to this unpredictable man. She edged toward the door.

Mr. Fletcher rocked forward to his toes. "Would you like to know how I did it?"

"Did what?" She humored him as she took another step backward.

"The curse, of course. After all, you were the one who gave me the idea." He tapped his temple. "Oh, the look on your face, my dear! As priceless as Miss Bastion's screams when I set up the makeshift magic lantern I created in her bedroom. Didn't even hear me doing it, so effective was the laudanum I slipped in her drink. I'm surprised you didn't find the broken spectacle pieces that I crafted the lens from when I made my hasty escape."

She paused, stunned as the puzzle pieces he threw out started to form a picture. "And the whispers I heard?"

"Easy enough." He shrugged. "I paid off a servant. Handsomely, too, thanks to the set of scarabs I pinched when you weren't looking. Brought in a pretty penny, bought me enough opium to get me by for quite a while."

Her stomach sank. So. That's what this was about. The man was an addict. What sort of Egyptologist had relics stolen from right under her nose for the purchase of such a devilish substance? "And the Anubis statue? There's no way you could have moved that."

"A magnificent feat, was it not?"

"So it was you!" Her mind whirled. Even with ropes and levers, he couldn't have pulled that off single-handedly. "But how did you manage it all alone?"

"Ah yes. Same servant. Loves a good prank, he does, and an added bottle of gin. Not so difficult after years of practice."

She shook her head. "But you didn't have years. You didn't have any time at all. You arrived at Price House after I did."

He spit out a curse. "Try moving chests of opium bricks and you'll gain the skills quick enough."

"I don't understand."

"Don't you?" He advanced, his head twitching one way, then the other, as if he were losing control of his own body. "You know, you're very pretty with your rabbity nose."

She backed up another step, almost to the door. If she kept him talking, she could make it out of here, not that a warehouse of Mr. Wormwell's men was much better, but at least they were more predictable.

"The workman with the broken leg." She flourished her hand in the air, hopefully distracting him as she slid her foot back another step. "The frightened maid. You couldn't have had anything to do with them."

"I didn't. Ha-ha! Good fortune, though, eh?"

"As was the influenza?"

"So intelligent." His voice dropped an octave. "So attractive." He licked his lips, a predator on the prowl.

So much for keeping him talking.

She spun, bolting for the door.

He beat her to it, blocking the exit. "Come with me. Yes, yes! That's it! Once I sell this load to Wormwell, I'll have enough to sail to China. Right to the source. Do you have any idea how much opium can be found in a Shanghai warehouse?"

Ami sucked in a breath. So that was his game. Steal Edmund's artifacts, sell them, then run with the money. What a cad! "How can you do this to your business partner? Mr. Price would never cheat you in such a foul manner."

"Then he shouldn't be so easy to dupe. Stupid man." He took another step toward her.

Heart pounding, she backed up, a quick glance over her shoulder revealing a window. No good, though. Beyond the glass were iron bars, protecting the office from break-ins. But she could swing around the desk and Mr. Fletcher behind it, then she'd have a clear shot at making another pass to the door.

"So China, hmm?" She forced a pleasant tone to her voice, the rest of her shaking like a leaf in a gale.

Maniacal laughter ripped out of him, spittle spraying from his mouth. "You do fancy me after all, eh?"

He lunged.

She bolted around the desk, straight toward the slate on the chair.

Fingers dug mercilessly into her arm, jerking her away from the only weapon in the room. Though she wrenched and wriggled, Mr. Fletcher's hold was superhuman. "You're hurting me!"

He yanked her to him, the reek of spirits so strong she gagged. "Ha-ha! I know all about hurt. And I will be the one to teach you."

Edmund paced in front of Sergeant Newell's desk. He shouldn't have taken time to come to the police station. Should have just gone straight to Wormwell's warehouse and demanded Ami's release. And yet . . .

He closed his eyes as a ragged sigh leached out of him. The professor had been right in that neither of them was trained in anything other than clawing at dirt with pointy tools or wielding a sharp business deal.

"Sit down, Mr. Price!" The sergeant bellowed behind his desk. "I don't appreciate the rut you're wearing into my floorboards. I've sent my two best men, so trust the process."

"That's just it," he grumbled under his breath. "I don't trust the process." He whumped so hard into the chair the thing wobbled back on two legs.

Leaning aside, the professor laid a hand on his forearm. "Amisi is a resilient girl. This isn't the first time she's gotten in over her head, and she always lives to talk about it. I am certain the fine officers the sergeant sent to retrieve her shall return with her any minute now."

Edmund pulled away from the man's touch, antsy, angry, agitated beyond measure. Despite it being the wee hours of the morning, it was abominably hot in this stuffy little office, which only added to his irritation.

"Are you not the slightest bit worried about your only daughter?" he snapped—and instantly regretted his tone of voice. Ami's father didn't deserve his contempt. The brigands who held Ami did.

The professor tugged at his bow tie, magnanimously ignoring the tetchy words. "In my line of work, Mr. Price, one becomes accustomed to uncertainty. I have learned over the years that worrying doesn't accomplish anything other than a headache. Besides, Amisi is like her mother, able to read people, understand their motivations, and rearrange bad situations to her advantage. I have no doubt she can and will survive the harshest of circumstances."

Edmund narrowed his eyes. "And yet you've never once taken her on a dig with you. Why is that, I wonder?"

"The world of archaeology is a cutthroat sort of existence, filled with rivalries, academic politics, personal agendas. I've always tried to protect her from the ugly side of the profession."

He couldn't help but snort. "It seems to me she's currently facing a threat far more dangerous than an academic rivalry."

"Indeed." He stroked his chin. "A fact that makes me reconsider."

Shouts boomed in from the main hall, followed by a few choice curses. Edmund shot to his feet as quickly as Sergeant Newell. He tagged the man's heels out the door only to see one of the two "finest" officers helping the other one sink onto a bench. Blood soaked that man's trouser leg, his face as pale as the waning moon outside. Edmund shot a glance beyond him to the door.

No sight of a perky brown-haired woman.

His gut clenched rock-hard. "Where is Miss Dalton?"

"What the blazes happened?" the sergeant thundered.

The officer yet standing faced the sergeant. "We din't make it through the door a'fore Hobson here got popped. Whatever

Wormwell's sittin' on, he ain't gonna part with it so handily. We'll need more men to get into that warehouse, Sarge."

For such a large man, Newell nipped into action faster than expected. Orders rose to the rafters. Blue-coated figures appeared from all corners of the station. Granted, not as many as Edmund would've liked to see going after the woman he loved, but for this unearthly time of day, it was a surprising number.

In all the hubbub, Edmund grabbed hold of the professor's arm and tugged him to the door. "Come on."

"Where are we going?" The professor huffed beside him as he tore down the street.

"I'm not leaving Ami in that thug's clutches for another minute."

The professor stopped cold. "What can we possibly do? You saw that officer back there." He flung his arm toward the station. "If this Wormwell had no qualms about shooting a man of law, what do you think he'll do to us?"

Edmund gaped. "What do you think he'll do to Ami?"

"Look, Price." He squeezed Edmund's arm. "I know you find this hard to believe, but I care about my daughter as much as you appear to. Even so, we will do her no good if we're dead. There has to be another way that doesn't end in our demise."

Edmund's mind raced with a torrent of thoughts. The professor was right, but he had to do something. He didn't have time to plan, to scheme. The urgency of the situation pressed down hard on his shoulders, compacting his frustration. Honestly, there was nothing for him to do but pray—and actually, somehow, this time that option didn't seem like a failure but more like a beginning.

God, please. I am helpless here. Give me an idea. A way to rescue Ami. Use me for Your purposes, not the other way around, and may You grant that Your purpose is to spare all of our lives.

Inhaling deeply, he collected what faith he could find and faced the professor. "I understand the risks, Professor. But every moment we waste puts her in greater danger. I would willingly give my life for her, a sacrifice I am prepared to make, and yet I hope it doesn't come to that. If I can reach the warehouse ahead of the officers, perhaps I can spy a safer way for them to enter and avoid needless violence. Clearly knocking on the front door didn't work. So"—he pulled away, trusting that God would allow for some sort of provision in this fiery furnace—"are you coming or not?"

"You're as bullheaded as she is."

"Then we make a good pairing." Wheeling about, Edmund dashed down the cobbled lane, surprised and gratified to hear the professor's footsteps echoing behind him. He veered into a smaller, dimly lit lane leading to the ominous Rotherhithe wharves, keeping to the shadows as he approached the row of hulking warehouses. It had stopped raining, but everything smelled like a freshly dug grave. His heart raced, keeping time with his pace. Even with the professor at his back, he felt an overwhelming sense of solitude as he plunged into the unknown. He was a businessman, after all, not a hurly-burly brawler. Hopefully it wouldn't come to that.

God, go with me. Provide a way in that doesn't begin and end with bloodshed. This is something I cannot do on my own—and I freely admit it. Please, keep Ami safe until I reach her.

Tall structures loomed ahead, windows like dark eye sockets peering into the night—save for the two buildings closest to the end of the stretch. Faint light flickered inside those, small fires in the belly of the beast. Had to be Wormwell's. He clung to the far side of the narrow lane, eyes darting nervously as he scanned for signs of trouble.

"I don't think we should go any further," the professor whispered, caution roughening his voice. "Let's wait here for the police."

He glanced from Ami's father to the foreboding warehouse, where dark shadows moved inside. The professor's words resonated in his gut. There was no telling how many men were in that place. Monstrous odds! And yet that's where Ami was. His fists clenched involuntarily, fingernails digging into his palms.

He had to get to her. Find where she was being held. Ensure she was unharmed and usher her to safety.

Determination and desperation warred within, the words slipping past his lips as taut as a bowstring. "No, you wait here."

He took off before the professor could argue against him. Giving the black monolith a wide berth, he crept from shadow to shadow, his heart pounding against his ribs. Each step was a calculated gamble, each movement a possible giveaway of his presence. He reached the edge of the building and paused, senses on high alert. Swiveling a look from side to side, he detected none of Wormwell's men, so he darted across the road and flattened against the side of the building. Just in time too. Coarse laughter barked out of a man exiting the front door, the sound slicing the night air like a blade. If he'd crossed that lane a moment later, he'd have been spotted.

Thank you, God!

He duck-walked to the nearest window, then rose ever so slowly. Inside was nothing but black upon black, so he skulked to the next. Faint light dribbled into the area, backlighting large boxes on rows of shelves. But that was all. No men. No woman either.

At the next window, his breath hitched. The warehouse opened into a cavernous expanse, where men hefted crates from the back of a wagon with practiced efficiency. He pressed his face to the glass, taking it all in. At the far end, doors stood open, allowing another wagon passage out the back. No brown-haired figure in a peacock gown met his sweeping gaze. This could be the perfect spot for the police to swarm through. He could turn back now. Clue in the bluecoats the moment they arrived. And yet . . . his jaw hardened.

Oh, Ami.

Sweat popped out on his brow, his unease growing. The possibility that Wormwell might be hiding her somewhere else gnawed at him. And then a worse thought . . . What if the thug back at Angel Alley had given him false information, and she wasn't here at all?

No.

No!

Better not to think such dire thoughts. Better to focus on the task at hand.

Two more windows remained on this side. It wouldn't hurt to finish what he had started, especially if he could catch a glimpse of her. Despite what he'd told the professor, he moved on.

The next window gave him a better view of the ham-fisted men unloading only God knew what. On the other side of the wagon, another team of Wormwell's workers pried off lids with crowbars. He squinted, but it was too hard to make out what they unpacked through the grimy window. Which was neither here nor there. Ami took priority over whatever illegal shenanigans Wormwell might be up to.

He crouch-walked to the final window on this wall and eased his head just past the sill—and his blood turned to ice.

Inside, Gil clutched Ami to his side, her face turned from his, her eyes squinched shut.

White-hot fury burned along every vein. This was no longer a mere rescue mission. This was a battle against time to save Ami from the grasp of a man he never should have trusted.

And there was no way he could wait around while she was in such danger.

30

Ami's heart hammered inside her chest, a captive fighting to be free. Just like her. She arched away from Mr. Fletcher's defiling touch. If she could make it out of the office, she'd have a much better chance at negotiating with the criminals in the warehouse than the traitor in this room.

But that was a pretty big if.

There was nothing for it, then.

She jerked backward, drove her knee upward, and connected sharply with his groin.

Pain grunted out of him—strained, guttural—his mouth contorting into a big O.

Breaking free, Ami dove for the slate on the chair. Mr. Fletcher roared behind her. Her fingers closed around the slate's cool surface, her grip desperate but her determination rock-solid.

She swung with all her might.

The slate cracked into Mr. Fletcher's jaw, just below his ear. His head snapped to the side, his eyes wide with shock. Almost in slow motion, his legs buckled. A macabre sight. One that would surely haunt her in nightmares to come.

He collapsed to the floor with a heavy thud.

Sickened by her own violence, she leapt over his fallen body.

And bolted into bedlam.

Curses fouled the air. Men ran everywhere. Crates tipped. One brute rammed against her shoulder as he sped past. She stumbled to a halt, mind barely grasping the cause of the mayhem. There weren't just drab-coated workmen here anymore. Bluecoats wielding clubs scurried about as well, rounding up those within reach. Could it be? Could help truly be here?

Once again she clutched the slate to her chest, this time filled with hope instead of despair. Peace poured over her like an anointing oil. God had seen fit to rescue her despite her failures and shortcomings. Despite her striving and reaching and trying to be an Egyptologist and a shadow broker saving relics of earth and dust.

Thank You, God. Oh, thank You for saving me—in more ways than one.

She took a step toward the large receiving doors ahead of her.

And was instantly yanked backward.

Hard metal poked against the side of her belly. Hot breath huffed against the back of her neck. The arm wrapped around her neck was an iron band.

"I walk free, ye cuffin' coves, or this woman bleeds out here and now!" Mr. Flick's gravelly voice rumbled at her back.

The three policemen nearest her exchanged glances. One nodded.

And they all retreated.

No! This couldn't be happening. Not now. Not when she should be walking out that open door!

A sinking ship full of rats scurrying for safety couldn't writhe more than the thugs pouring out of Wormwell's warehouse. When the police wagon had first passed Edmund, he'd been worried the bluecoats would hold him at bay while they rounded up Wormwell and his men. A vain concern, that. The moment the lawmen were spotted, shabby-coated ruffians fled from every possible exit, fully occupying the attention of the officers. Every curse, each panicked bootstep reverberated through the night air. The frenzied lawlessness mocked the very concept of law and order.

Which was perfect. The frantic scuttle unwittingly shielded him from the gaze of the law. Not that the bark of a policeman would have stopped him anyway. Edmund stormed through the open front door, shouldering past two thugs as if they were nothing but gnats. They were too intent on bolting out of there. In this half of the building, darkness reigned. Large rows of shelving blocked most of the light from the far end of the warehouse. He ran pell-mell down the main aisle toward that glow, two thoughts powering every stride.

Save Ami.

Stop Gil.

Yet before he left the cover of shadows, he stopped. So did his heart. Ahead, a broad-shouldered brute wrapped one of his thick arms around the neck of a woman in a green gown, peacock feathers drooping from waist to floor. His other hand pressed a knife to her side.

And the police—the defenders of the weak, the protectors of the frail—were backing off.

Edmund's gut twisted. This would be quite a different tussle than wrestling Ami away from Gil. One that could be deadly.

God, please. Give me strength. Give me wisdom.

"Tha's it! Scuttle off to the corners like the cockroaches ye are." The monstrous man advanced as the line of three officers retreated.

"You won't make it far, cully!" the largest bluecoat sneered, a veneer of false confidence belied by his next backward step.

Thunderation! If those lawmen didn't hold their ground, the villain would have free passage out the loading doors in a matter of seconds.

And who knew what would become of Ami at that point.

Edmund's mind raced, desperate to devise the next move in this dangerous game. He cast a wild look about, searching for something—anything—to combat the blade at Ami's belly.

A length of chain coiled on the floor. No good, though. Too far ahead. The thug would spot him before he could reach it. A broken board leaned against the wall to his left. That could work but . . . hold on. He squinted. There in the shadow of a large crate lay a gift from God.

A forgotten crowbar.

Edmund snatched it up.

Dashed ahead.

And swung.

The iron bar hit off-center on the back of the man's head, but it hit! Thank God, it hit! For a fraction of a second, nothing happened other than a slight stiffening of the brute's shoulders. Then in a surreal cascade, the villain's colossal frame plummeted, taking Ami down with him. The dirty floorboards rushed up to meet them with a sickening thwack, the impact jarring the ground under Edmund's feet.

Ami scrambled from beneath the weight of the unconscious man's arm, and Edmund pulled her into his embrace, holding her close, his grip a mix of protectiveness, urgency, and heavenly relief. She was here. In his arms. Safe. Whole. Breathing. The realization nearly buckled his knees.

"Edmund?" She tipped back slightly, her nose scrunching in adorable confusion. "What are you doing here?"

"Solving a problem, of course. Namely that you were missing. Are you hurt?" His voice rasped, a blend of concern and longing, exposing a vulnerability he hadn't intended to let her hear. He searched her brow, her cheeks, her chin, mapping every contour, seeking the slightest sign of injury. Then his gaze drifted lower to her side, where the cruel knife had torn the fabric of her gown. No blood, though. Just a ruined bodice. He shuddered. Oh, how close he'd come to losing her!

Thank You, God. Thank You!

"I am well," she whispered. "But how did you know where to find me?"

"Your father." He brushed back a loose lock of hair, relishing the moment despite the hellish howls and shouts around them, ignoring even the body at their feet. "Apparently there's more to you than I realized, hmm, Shadow Broker?"

The name curved her lips into a sad smile. "I made the same mistake about you. Shouldn't you be at your engagement party right now?"

The question was a bittersweet reminder of the tangled obligations that had driven them to this precipice.

He shook his head, his eyes never once leaving hers. "There is only one woman for me. And she's right here in my arms."

She sucked in a breath, her face turning ashen. Not the response he was hoping for but—

"Oh no." Her gaze fixed just past his shoulder.

A yowling screech shattered the air like a stone against glass. Edmund wheeled about, his body instinctively shielding her from whatever new threat plummeted toward them.

Gil staggered out a nearby door, his face twisted by malice. Blood oozed from the corner of his mouth, a walking, breathing nightmare.

"You!" Gil advanced, swinging a jagged-edged slate like a scythe. "Don't think you're taking my prize now! I went to too much trouble bringing those blasted relics here. Wormwell owes me!"

Edmund swiped for the crowbar. He had no idea what the man was talking about, but he did understand the murderous gleam in his eyes. "Gil, listen. Just—"

A bluecoat charged, hitting Gil sideways. They both flew. The officer landed on top. In a trice, the lawman snapped on a pair of darbies and hoisted Edmund's former business partner to his feet, then dragged him toward the dock door. Gil wriggled like a speared fish, shrieks spewing from his lips.

"Mr. Price!" A steamroller in sergeant stripes barreled toward them. "I thought I told you and the professor to remain at the station." Newell pulled up in front of him and Ami.

"You did, Sergeant. But see?" In a single motion, he pulled Ami to his side. "I found the lady I was looking for."

"And a good thing Mr. Price is here, sir." Though she spoke

to the sergeant, she grinned up at Edmund. "You'll need him for verification of the stolen goods."

Edmund tilted his head. "What stolen goods?"

Ami swept her hands toward the crates strewn about, some overturned and spilling out their contents. "Your Egyptian artifacts."

31

It was mesmerizing, this clickety-clack. The gentle swaying of the train. The enchanting land between sleep and awareness. Slowly, Ami fluttered open her eyelids, scorning the loss of the delicious nap she'd been enjoying on the velvet sofa in Edmund's private car. Truly, she ought not have given in to such a decadent rest, but after a full two days of police interviews and helping to haul Edmund's antiquities to a workroom at the British Museum, she'd been exhausted.

Without moving a muscle, she narrowed her gaze on Edmund. He sat across from her at a table with pen in hand, afternoon sunlight a halo on his bowed head. My, but he was handsome . . . and yet so much more. What a warrior he'd been on her behalf, both inside Wormwell's warehouse and in the aftermath. So attentive to her needs. So protective of her safety. She couldn't help but admire the scratches on his hand, the bruise near his wrist—all a tangible reminder he'd risked his very life to rescue her. How fiercely she loved this man!

As if feeling her perusal, he swiveled his head toward her. Affection glimmered silver in his blue eyes, twinkling all the more as a disarming smile lit his face. "Good timing. I was just about to rouse you. We're nearly home."

Home. What a slap in the face. What did she have to go home to but the empty rooms of a small cottage? A lonely life of . . . what? She didn't have a job anymore. And even if she did, it wouldn't matter. Nothing would be the same after living the past month at Edmund's side. Just the thought of leaving behind his daily companionship felt like death.

She pushed up to sit. Continuing that morbid line of thinking would only burst the dam of hot tears gathering in her eyes.

Edmund padded over to her, the cushion sinking next to her as he sat. "What's this?" His knuckle crooked beneath her chin, and ever so gently, he tipped her face to his. Concern marred his brow. "Are you not glad to forget everything that happened in London and return to Oxford?"

She forced a smile, though in truth it probably looked like a pathetic sort of grimace. "I am glad."

"But?"

She squared her shoulders, eager to end such a close scrutiny of emotions that not even she wanted to deal with right now. "You don't believe me?"

"Not at all." He traced his finger along the side of her eye. "Your left brow droops ever so slightly right here when you're sad."

Bosh. He knew her far too well. Not even Polly had ever recognized such a telling gesture.

She angled her head, retreating from his touch. "I should think you'd be the gloomy one. You've lost your chance at Parliament. And after such rough handling of your artifacts, even with my father staying behind to salvage what he can, I daresay Mr. Harrison will renegotiate for a much lower price. It may not be the sum your friend Sanjay needs."

"Those are my worries, not yours." He bopped her on the nose, a playful move, one that only increased her melancholy.

"Come now," he murmured. "What is it that troubles you?"

A great question. One she wasn't sure how to answer. After the exhilarating—albeit deadly—adventure they'd shared, she was loath to go back to normal life . . . but how did a lady gracefully say such a thing? She inhaled deeply, scorning such an aberrant notion. She was tired, that's all. Weary. Which was to be expected after such a harrowing experience.

Steeling herself to live in the moment instead of borrowing sorrow from the future or past, she faced him. "Right now, I haven't a care in the world."

Brakes screeched, and the train juddered to a halt.

Edmund steadied her with a touch to her arm. "And yet time moves on. I would know what it is that worries you so I can vanquish it."

She grinned, genuinely this time. "You cannot fix everything, Mr. Problem Solver."

"If it concerns you, I will die in the trying."

The scratches on the back of his hand backed up his words, doing all sorts of strange things to her heart. "I believe you would."

"Then tell me."

She sighed. The man was a hound with a mutton bone. A perfect trait for a successful businessman, but she wasn't so sure she liked such an attribute when turned on her.

And that set of his jaw would not be denied.

"It's just that . . ." She huffed against the sofa cushion. "Well, now that we're back to our former lives, you'll go your way and I'll go mine. As it should be, naturally." She flung her hand into the air, thoroughly frustrated. "You'd think after all these years of parting with my father when he goes on a dig, I'd have mastered saying good-bye. Apparently, I haven't, so there you are."

"Then don't say good-bye." He grabbed her hand, entwining his big fingers with hers.

A bittersweet smile trembled across her lips. "Saying 'until later' isn't much better."

"That's not what I meant." Bringing her hand to his lips, he studied her fingers as he kissed them one by one.

Her breath caught, far too many tingles running up her arm. "Then what did you mean?"

"After spending so much time with Lord Bastion, I have

come to realize there are different measures of success. The viscount's measure is money and fame—the very things he hoped I would bring to his family. The same ideals my father valued."

His gaze shot to hers. "But it is in your company, in the richness of our discussions, that I have discovered a world of depth that goes well beyond material pursuits. The way your mind works, the passion you hold for your interests, the bond we've formed, these things are truly valuable. People matter more than a hard-fought business deal. *You* matter more. So what I propose is that you don't say good-bye at all, but rather that you say yes."

"To what?"

He doubled back to the desk, then returned to her side with a paper in hand. Slowly, meeting her gaze with an unyielding stare of his own, he slid to one knee, pressing that paper into her fingers. "Say yes to this."

But what was this? A sketched-out new business venture? Some sort of contract? An invoice or . . . The words began to soak in, and the more they did so, the more her heart fluttered.

> *Wut soft lite doth brake be-ond,*
> *At donning, in this golden morn,*
> *In yor eyes, my wurld's reborn*
> *New promis, new luv, for-ever sworn.*
>
> *Eturnal plej, owr harts in-twined*
> *For-ever yors, for-ever myn,*
> *Lite or shadow, blis or strife,*
> *Wil yu, my darling, be my wife?*

The paper trembled beneath her touch. Could this be?

"Ami." Edmund's voice dropped to a husky tone. "Say yes to the possibility of building a life together—you and I. Say yes to facing as one whatever comes our way. Say yes to being my wife."

The words hung on the air like a promise, a joy, a dream she'd never quite dared allow herself to embrace. This sort of proposal was for other women, the genteel type, not a scarab cleaning, mummy scavenger like her. And from the most eligible bachelor in all of Oxford?

"Is this real?" she whispered.

"It is." He grinned, the feel of his thumb rubbing along the inside curve of her palm, a maddening distraction. "So what say you?"

"On one condition." Truly, it was wicked of her to string him along like this, but she didn't get proposed to every day, and she didn't want it to end. Not yet.

His eyes widened, but his voice didn't falter. "Name your condition, and it shall be done."

"Promise me another poem on our wedding day and every anniversary thereafter."

"You must be jesting." He snorted. "As you've just witnessed, I write abysmal poetry."

"And that, sir, is a mere fraction of your charm." She pulled his hand to her lips and kissed the back of it.

His grin grew cheeky. "And the rest?"

"You are brave. Witty. You make me smile like none other, and your loyalty and compassion for others is quite frankly astounding."

His smile faded, a serious glint replacing the playfulness in his gaze. "You didn't mention my wealth or status."

"That's because I would marry you, sir, were you the ragged-iest pauper in all of England."

He sucked in air. "So your answer is yes?"

"My answer is . . ." Bending close, she kissed him full on the mouth and didn't stop until his chest heaved. Only then did she pull away. "Yes."

In one smooth movement, he yanked her from the sofa, both of them tumbling to the train car's plush carpet, where he gathered her into his lap. "Then, my dear"—he looked down his nose with an imperial yet impish gaze—"allow me to state my one condition before I agree to be your husband."

"Intriguing. What is it?"

"No more shadow brokering. As my wife, I would not have you in harm's way ever again."

She bit her lip, the delicious waft of his ever-present scent of curry making it hard to concentrate on the many reasons why his simple request bothered her so much. Of course he was right, but still . . . she'd been rescuing relics for years now, placing them where they rightfully belonged, and yes, were she honest, perversely relishing the thrill of the deal—except in London. She could easily agree to never broker another deal there ever again.

"Ami?" Questions darkened the blue in his eyes.

"I . . ." She rested her palm against his cheek, seeking an anchor in her swirl of thoughts. "I'm not sure I know how to be me without rescuing the forgotten fragments of history."

He covered her hand with his own. "I'm not requiring you to give up who you are or to forsake your God-given desires. I'm merely asking you to find a method of salvaging those forgotten fragments without putting yourself in danger. There is always more than one way to fulfill your calling in life. The Red Sea didn't stop Moses from leading his people to safety. We shall both pray—and trust—that God will make a clear route for you to preserve artifacts without the threat of having your throat slit. Is that not reasonable?"

Sighing, she rested her head against his shoulder, peace washing over her despite the racket of departing train passengers. "There you go again," she murmured.

"What?" The question rumbled against her ear.

"Solving all my problems."

"Not me, love." He chuckled. "Only God can do that."

All was right in the world. Edmund had smiled for the entire carriage ride to Price House. She'd said yes! He still could scarcely grasp the idea that soon Amisi Dalton would be his wife. *His* wife! What a wonder. What a God-given wonder. Not only that she loved him but that he was able to fully love her in return . . . a miracle he never expected to experience after Louisa.

Yet now as he trotted up the few stairs to the front door, his step hitched. Though he'd soon be wedding his best friend, it was time to let go of an old one—and the thought of it punched him in the gut. He may as well be cutting off his right arm.

But it must be done.

He doffed his hat and set it on the foyer table, running his fingers through his hair. Like yanking off a soiled bandage, it would be painful to confront his butler, and yet sooner would be better.

Hardly a few steps into the great hall, he spied Barnaby crossing the expanse, hefting a tea tray. The moment the butler's gaze landed on him, the man smiled.

"Welcome back, sir! Happy to see you home."

"Thank you." Edmund advanced. "But I don't think you'll be so happy once I say what I must. Why don't you set down that tray?"

"As you wish, sir." Barnaby's brows furrowed as he complied. Once relieved of his burden, he faced Edmund, chin dipping. "How can I be of service?"

"Allow me to come straight to the point. I cannot abide lying, Barnaby, especially not under my roof and by my most senior staff member at that. If what I have heard is true, then I am afraid I must ask you to pack up your belongings and leave posthaste."

"But, sir!" Barnaby's head snapped back as if he'd taken a hard slap. "I assure you I have never once deceived you about anything."

Oh, if only that were true. But Ami had gotten it straight from Gil's mouth that a certain prank-loving servant had been his right hand in pulling off the supposed golden griffin curse. Edmund rubbed his jaw, hating to ask a horrible question for which he already knew the answer. "Did you or did you not aid Mr. Fletcher in turning the Anubis statue as part of a prank to further the rumours of the curse of Amentuk?"

Barnaby straightened to full height. "I most certainly did not, sir! And as a matter of fact, I had intended to discuss this very matter with you tonight."

An interesting deflection. Broaching the very topic for which one was accused was a business tactic he'd often employed himself to keep a prospective buyer or seller off their guard. He narrowed his eyes. "Is that so?"

"Yes, sir, most emphatically so. I discovered it was the footman Crawford who partnered with Mr. Fletcher to conduct his nefarious deeds about the house. Apparently Mr. Fletcher paid him handsomely to partake in his hijinks. When I found out, I dismissed him posthaste. Furthermore, you have no need to worry that any further tomfooleries will take place in the future, for I have banned any and all pranks."

The man was full of surprises this evening. Edmund shook his head. "What of your camaraderie building, as you call it? Are you so willing to part with that idea?"

"No, I've merely had a more civilized idea as to how to go about that. A literary circle. I shall induce household solidarity by discussing books, sir."

"Not all the staff is literate, nor do I suspect the chambermaids will relish adding one more chore to their already busy day." Edmund kneaded the back of his neck. The more he thought on it, the more absurd the idea grew. "I don't think Mrs. Buckner will be so keen on the idea either. She keeps her girls on a tight leash, and I don't imagine she'll loosen her hold for the sake of running off to spend time reading a book."

A sheepish grin curved half of the butler's mouth. "I actually first got the idea from the housekeeper, sir. We figured that if I read a few pages each evening at dinner, no time would be taken away from anyone's tasks and no shame would be incurred for not knowing how to read."

He dropped his hand, surprise mixing with a fair amount of respect. That Barnaby—and Mrs. Buckner—cared so much about the rest of the workers was commendable indeed. "I must say I am impressed. Not many other households will employ such enlightened servants. What is your first selection to be?"

"*Don Quixote*, sir."

Perfect. With his unique traits, Barnaby was as peculiar as

the man of La Mancha himself. Edmund returned his butler's grin. "Very well. Let me know how it goes."

"Absolutely, sir. Now then." Turning aside, Barnaby picked up the big tray laden with tea, a plate of scones, clotted cream, and a knife for slathering on the spread. "Would you like to join your guest in the sitting room?"

"I have a guest?"

"You do, sir, and I've kept him waiting overlong." Barnaby strode off, surprisingly fleet of foot for carrying such a large service.

Edmund caught up to his side just before the sitting room door. "Who is it?" he murmured for Barnaby alone.

"Oh, I think you will recognize him straight off, sir." A mischievous glint lit the man's eyes as he stepped aside and allowed Edmund to pass.

He strode in, then immediately grabbed the knife off the butler's tray, rattling the porcelain and startling Barnaby. Crouching, Edmund clutched the dull bit of metal and faced Gil.

"How did you get here?" Edmund growled.

Gil rose from the sofa, hands in the air, his gaze fixed on the knife. "That's quite a greeting for your business partner. Wholly understandable, though." His gaze flicked to Edmund's face. "Put away the knife and allow me to explain."

"Barnaby!" Edmund bellowed. "Summon the constable at once."

The butler merely set down the tea tray and stood placidly by the door. "Hear Mr. Fletcher out, sir, and if you still wish me to send for the law afterward, I shall do so."

Edmund could hardly believe the man's insubordination. Had his butler fallen under this devious man's spell? He eyed Gil, debating if he ought to rush him, take him down before he could spring into action. But Gil stood as calmly as Barnaby. Looking younger. Less haggard. Certainly less wild and violent. There were no bruises on his face, no fat lip, no gash on his head, as if the man hadn't been in a skirmish in a London warehouse a mere two days ago. How on earth could this be?

Edmund eased his stance but didn't let go of the knife. "What is going on?"

"I have a story to tell you, one that is best heard sitting down." Gil gestured toward the chairs near the hearth. "Please, Edmund, may we?"

He hesitated, unsure what to think, and yet oddly curious to hear what the man might say. Nodding, he waited for Gil to sit first in case this was some sort of ploy. He'd never *ever* trust this man again.

"As you'll recall," Gil began, "in my last correspondence, I said I'd travel here to Price House to discuss a recent development with you once I returned from the Continent at the end of August."

"Yes," he said, wary. "Good news, as I remember, and yet you gave me anything but the entire time you were here."

"That is because I only just arrived."

"What are you talking about?" He snorted. "I greeted you the very moment you stepped off the coach nigh on a month ago now."

"That wasn't me." Gil loosened his four-in-hand, taking a moment to inhale deeply. "Before I left London—as you know I rarely do—I first stopped off to see that my brother's needs would be met in my absence."

Brother? Edmund blinked. That was news. In all his years of dealing with Gil, the man had never once mentioned a sibling. "I didn't know you had a brother."

"Not many do. It is a dark family secret that first my father and now I have kept hidden all these years. I made a deathbed vow to my father never to reveal the disgrace that is Stuart, and yet with his recent escape, I can no longer keep that promise."

Stuart? Escape? Disgrace? So many questions pummeled him that he was glad for the support of the cushion beneath him. None of this made any sense. "I don't understand," he admitted at length.

Gil nodded. "Of course not, Edmund. It's a lot to take in at once. But as I was saying, I visited my brother to let him know

I'd be out of touch for about six weeks. He is used to my regular visits, you see. It is not an easy life at Colney Hatch, even for those kept in the rehabilitation wing, and he looks forward to seeing me for my biweekly visits."

"Colney Hatch." He shook his head, which didn't help in the least to connect all the dots. "That's an asylum. Are you telling me you have a brother who is mad?"

"One could sympathize with such a condition, but no. There is nothing mentally unfit about Stuart. It is his morals that are decayed. His . . . depravity, shall we call it, started at a young age." Gil hefted a sigh, sorrow in his eyes. "It began with small things, the pilfering of a silver spoon or one of my mother's earbobs, small but valuable household items that he blamed on others, creating a web of lies. While most lads were happy to spend time with their friends or playthings, Stuart spent his discovering compromising secrets about the household staff and using that information for manipulation. It only got worse from there. But when he ran off from reform school and fell in with the dark side of London's worst criminals, disgracing the family name by becoming an opium eater, my father had him committed to an asylum to rehabilitate his moral failings."

Edmund chewed on the information like a bite of gristle, not sure if he ought to spit it out or swallow it. He opted to remain on alert yet lessened his grip on the knife. "If this is so, then how did this Stuart end up at my home—and looking like you, no less?"

Gil shifted on the sofa, clearly uneasy. "I take responsibility for his appearance in Oxford. I'd given details of my travel plans—first to France, then to here—to the physician on staff when I went to visit Stuart. I thought I was out of his hearing range, but apparently not. When I received the telegram that my brother had escaped, I swear I had no idea he'd come to Price House. The administration assured me they'd most likely find him in one of the opium dens in the Limehouse district—if he hadn't overdosed himself, that is."

Edmund laid the knife in his lap, stunned, all his suspicions of the past weeks suddenly making sense.

Mostly.

He angled his head, once again studying Gil's unbattered face and calm demeanor. "That doesn't account for this supposed Stuart's physical appearance."

Gil shrugged. "Though he is two years my junior, we look uncannily alike. There are only minor differences that no one except my mother would notice—a mole behind my ear, a very slight height differentiation. Stuart's shoe size is one less than mine."

"And yet he looked older than you."

"Addiction to such detrimental vices will do that to a man. Believe me when I say I am sorry you got pulled into this whole sordid affair, Edmund."

Hmm. Plausible. Could be too plausible, though, yet another story to swindle him in some other way. He eyed his alleged business partner. "If what you're saying is true, then tell me something only you and I as business partners would know. Something that cannot be fabricated or guessed."

"Fair enough." Planting his elbows on the chair's arms, Gil steepled his fingers beneath his chin—a familiar pose. One Edmund hadn't witnessed this entire past month. And now that he thought on it, it was odd he'd not seen the gesture for it was a favorite of Gil's.

"Remember that negotiation with the East India Company a few years back?" Gil tapped his chin with his laced index fingers. "When we had to haggle over the shipment of rare spices for our client, Mr. Hagethorn?"

"Yes." How could he forget such an infuriating deal?

"You were so frustrated with the delays that you placed a bet on the arrival date with one of your companions in India. A Mr. Gupta, if I recall correctly. I warned you against such a rash wager, and you scolded me for being a mother hen. And you were right. You won a fair amount, and as a consolation for the delay, we gained an extra three ounces of saffron from the ship's captain—off the record, of course, as he'd smuggled it in."

Edmund sucked in a breath. True, all of it. But still, he would not be so easily deceived. Not again. "Impressive, but Gupta and the captain were both involved in that situation and so could have informed you. What about the incident in Edinburgh the winter before I sailed?"

Gil laughed, his trademark snort cutting off the end—another trait that Edmund realized had been missing with the other Gil.

"Ah yes, we were walking the horses back from a meeting with the textile merchants. Your mount got away from you, and though I tried to help, you ended up a muddied mess. Ruined your trousers and you had to borrow mine. You said you'd never trust a . . ." He thought for a minute, then grinned at Edmund. "A nip-nappety, scabby-eared horse again."

Edmund gaped. Not even he'd remembered the exact words he'd bellowed in frustration, but now that Gil reminded him, they rang true. And only Gil would have known such a detail. Plus, not once had he yet called him *old man* or regaled him with an annoying *ha-ha*.

Which meant this *was* Gil. It had to be.

Edmund leaned forward in his seat, hardly believing how duped he'd been. "It's really you, then, is it, Gil?"

"It's really me, my friend."

"I can scarce believe it."

"You likely won't believe this either." Reaching inside his coat pocket, Gil produced an envelope and handed it over. "It's the good news I wished to tell you in person."

Edmund pulled out a folded banknote, then choked when he read the staggering amount. "Where did this come from?"

"Remember that investment you gave me leave to dabble in, the steamship company? The one everyone claimed was fool's gold?"

He nodded slowly. "I do."

"Well, that shipping company is now a major force in the industry, landing a lucrative deal for exclusive cargo transport across the Atlantic. That little banknote is but the first in what I expect to be some rather hefty dividend payments."

Edmund's heart skipped a beat. With this much incoming funds not tied up in any other sort of market or investment, Sanjay would have the money he needed. Thank God! He glanced at the ceiling, nearly overcome with the unexpected blessing.

Indeed, thank You, God.

"This couldn't have come at a better time." He waved the note in the air. "I . . . I don't know what to say other than thank you and forgive me for ever doubting your identity."

"Forgiven and forgotten." Gil grinned. "Shall we celebrate the windfall with a cup of tea?" He tipped his head toward the big tray Barnaby had left unattended by the door.

"We can celebrate more than that, my friend, for I have good news of my own." Edmund rose, smiling over his shoulder as he strode to the teapot. "I am to wed—and soon."

32

Ami had read of the Mediterranean Sea. That the azure waters were unlike any colour one could imagine. How the breeze could make you forget about past sins and future troubles. Lies. All of it. For to stand at the railing of a ship and experience the enchantment firsthand far surpassed what authors penned in their travel guides. There, beneath the vast sky, she sensed God's pleasure in His creation—in her—for no other reason than His great goodness.

And nothing could begin to describe the feel of her husband's strong arms wrapped around her waist or the warmth of his solid chest at her back. Her career goals, once solitary, now had a companion in love—a profound shift that she embraced with a newly found sense of completeness.

His breath tickled her temple as he nibbled on her ear. "What are you thinking about, Mrs. Price?"

"How deliriously happy I am." She turned in his arms, the gentle purling of the water against the hull as mesmerizing as the dusky-eyed man in front of her. "And you? What occupies your thoughts, husband?"

"Potatoes." A handsome grin lit his face. "I hope they're better cooked for dinner tonight."

She arched a brow. "We are surrounded by beauty and all you can think of is your stomach?"

"Oh, I can think of plenty of other things, I assure you." An amorous gleam smoldered in his gaze. "Potatoes are merely what keep me from acting on baser impulses."

"I never knew you were such a beast, Mr. Price." Rising to her toes, she kissed him soundly. "But at least you're my beast."

"I hope you are as happy with me as you are about the dig your father has arranged for us." Bending, he whispered against the nape of her neck, "I expect a personal tutorial from you, you know."

"Mmm." She pulled away, hardly able to think straight. It'd been like this for the past two weeks now, since they married. She could only hope—and pray—this bliss would never fade. "When we arrive in Giza, meet me in the shadows of the pyramid." She winked. "I think we can work out a deal."

"Putting your shadow-brokering skills to good use, eh? I like it." He pressed his lips to the crown of her head. "I like it—and you—very much."

"Speaking of the like, there is something I've been meaning to ask you." She studied his face, seeking truth. "Are you terribly disappointed we are going to Egypt and not to India? I know how much you adored it there."

"You're right. I do love India. But I love you more. And who knows? Perhaps someday you'll fancy a dig in the Indus Valley."

"What I fancy is you, husband."

"There you two are."

They turned to see her father striding across the deck. His hair, though normally a-muss, stood out like a fluff of milkweed gone to seed. His collar hung askew, and the top buttons of his waistcoat were completely missing, not to mention a red scratch marred his cheek.

"Father!" Ami grabbed Edmund's arm for balance as the ship canted. Hopefully her father hadn't taken a tumble. With his continued joint pain, his sea legs weren't what they used to be. "What happened?"

His lips twisted as he stopped in front of them. "I'm afraid the curse of Amentuk has struck again."

"Impossible." Edmund shook his head. "Stuart Fletcher is safely tucked away at Colney Hatch asylum getting the care he needs."

"No, I meant—"

High-pitched chattering cut through the air, followed by a man's shout and a lady's screech. Ami peered past Edmund to see a monkey in a tiny green coat scurrying past a couple farther down the deck.

And headed straight their way.

"Oh bother!" The words were barely past her father's lips when he crouched low and extended his arm. "Nothing to be done for it now, though, I suppose."

The little imp raced up his sleeve, parking his rump on her father's shoulder and digging his tiny paws into the inside pocket of her father's suit coat.

Ami exchanged a glance with Edmund, then grinned at her father. "I see you've made a new friend."

"I didn't mean to. Amentuk here belongs to the captain." He pulled the monkey into his arms, the furry creature clutching a date and chewing furiously. "I merely made the mistake of offering him some leftover fruit from breakfast. Now he thinks I'm some sort of treat dispenser."

Ami laughed. "Don't tell me that monkey's name is Amentuk."

"All right. I won't. But you should know that strange happenings always abound when embarking on a journey to the land of mystery." Her father waggled his eyebrows as he patted the monkey on the head. "Come along, Tukky. Let's get you back to your master."

He strolled away, the monkey climbing to the top of his head like an oversized hat, its tiny black fingers clutching his hair.

Edmund chuckled. "I suspect your father will be occupied for the duration of this voyage."

"Between that furry friend and his obsessive cargo checking, I believe you are correct." With a light touch, she turned his face to hers, the sun bathing his skin in a golden glow. "I have no doubt he'll keep a keen eye on the griffin in particular, but are you certain you don't mind parting with it? As I recall, that statue was important to you because of your family's heritage."

"You're right." A soft smile graced his lips. "But my view of heritage has changed. I no longer feel compelled to hold on to the need to make my father proud, at least not my earthly father. Serving God is the legacy—the heritage—I wish to leave behind. I don't need a notorious little statue to accomplish that." Gently, he brushed an errant strand of hair that'd blown across her brow. "The griffin was a symbol of my past, but you, my love, are my present and future."

Love flared in her chest, warming her more thoroughly than the Mediterranean afternoon. What a treasure this man was. "Have I told you, husband, how grateful I am that you're selling not only the griffin but the rest of your artifacts to the Cairo Museum?"

"Yes, about that. I think you should know I didn't actually sell it to the Cairo Museum."

Her belly clenched. Oh dear. How had the deal gone bad? "But it's already on board the ship. Please don't tell me Mr. Harrison was so insistent that you're sending it back to England?"

"Nothing of the sort." He chuckled. "My, but your mind shoots off at odd angles."

She frowned. "It is my job to think outside of the box, or I'd not be a very good archaeologist."

"You are a stellar archaeologist. The most beautiful one I know. But what I meant to say, my love . . ." He entwined his fingers with hers, lifting her hand to kiss the back of it. "Is that I'm donating the lot to the Cairo Museum as a wedding gift to you."

She gasped. "But what about Gil's half of the proceeds?"

"I bought him out." He winked.

"Oh, Edmund!" She squeezed his hand. He was wrong. Entirely wrong. Such an act was more than a gift; it was a testament to the love that bound his heart to hers. "Thank you, a thousand times over. Thank you, thank you, thank you!"

"You sound like Sanjay." His lips twisted into a smirk. "I've lost count of his notes of appreciation for the business contract and money I wired him."

"Which will hold him over quite nicely." Reaching, she straightened his windblown collar, a frown suddenly wrinkling her brow. "But what if your lawsuit isn't successful? Others like him will crumble under that new tariff."

"Not to worry, wife." He captured her hand and pressed a kiss to her palm. "I have no doubt the crack legal team Gil and I have woven together will be victorious. The mighty men of Parliament cannot stand against an edict signed by Her Majesty the Queen even if it was over thirty years ago. No judge in his right mind will go against a royal decree. If only I'd known of it sooner, I wouldn't have bothered with Lord Bastion."

She inhaled deeply, savoring the salty tang of the warm air and the hint of curry that somehow always accompanied this man she loved. Although she'd told others God would make a way when things turned blurry, it was astounding to see how He had done so for her—and for Edmund. "How Mr. Fletcher found that old Indo-British Trade Accord still amazes me," she murmured.

"He truly is a good business partner, as I've told you time and again."

"Well, it was kind of you to remain loyal even when his brother was impersonating him. In fact, husband, I'd say you are the kindest man I know."

"And you, my love"—his tone was a caress that tingled to her toes—"are the most intelligent, beautiful, and capable woman I've ever met, so I'd say we're quite a pair, hmm?"

She grinned. "As unique as the artifacts we shall discover together."

"And after this dig, what then?" Edmund's blue eyes gleamed with a mix of curiosity and anticipation.

Guiding his arm to her waist, she turned once again toward the water and leaned against the solid beam of her husband. "There's a whole world of possibility out there, my love. A whole wide world."

EDMUND'S POEM

What soft light doth break beyond,
At dawning, in this golden morn,
In your eyes, my world's reborn
New promise, new love, forever sworn.

Eternal pledge, our hearts entwined
Forever yours, forever mine,
Light or shadow, bliss or strife
Will you, my darling, be my wife?

HISTORICAL NOTES

The House of Commons

In Victorian England—and now—getting elected to the House of Commons often requires more than just personal wealth to overcome the political and structural challenges. The sponsorship of a member of the House of Lords provides advantages such as access to networks and influential circles, political guidance and mentorship, voter appeal and endorsement, and establishment approval.

Excelsior

Bubble wrap wasn't available in the nineteenth century, so how would you pack your breakable items for transport? You could use straw, which some companies did, but others used excelsior, which is really just a fancy name for curly little wood shavings.

Bee Skep

This is a traditional form of beehive made of woven straw or wicker. Think Winnie the Pooh and you'll have the perfect image in your head. In England, the bee skep was commonly used for many centuries until late in the Victorian period. Modern hives as we know them today were first invented in America in 1851.

Lady Margaret Hall

In the late nineteenth century, women were allowed to earn a bachelor of arts degree at Lady Margaret Hall, one of the first women's colleges at the University of Oxford. This was a revolutionary landmark in women's education. However, while women could earn a BA, they were often considered unofficial students and were not granted full membership in the university. In essence, women could take the same exams and receive the same degrees as men, but they faced limitations in terms of access to facilities and participation in university life.

Cravats vs. Four-in-Hand Ties

During the latter half of the Victorian era, both ties and cravats were worn by men. A cravat is a broad piece of cloth tied around the neck that could be folded and styled in various ways. This was worn for more formal occasions. Neckties as we know them were called four-in-hands due to the specific knot that was commonly used to tie them.

Palmistry

Palmistry is the study of reading the lines of a person's hands, but it's practiced in different forms. While fortune-telling was popular during the Victorian era, so was the more innocuous pastime of interpreting palms to gain insight into a person's character or personality. The emphasis in this type of palmistry is on understanding an individual's psychology rather than predicting specific future events. Palmistry was a frequent parlour game during the 1800s, and there were books and pamphlets widely available on the subject at the time.

Mummy Mask

It was a common practice for ancient Egyptians to place masks on the mummies. These masks were made of papyrus or linen, then coated with plaster and painted bright colors. Most often they resembled the person who'd died and were designed with a serene expression and detailed facial features. The most striking—and familiar—part of a mummy mask is the large almond-shaped eyes.

Magic Lantern

This projector of sorts was a precursor to today's projectors and played an important role in Victorian society as a means of entertainment and education, though in this story, Mr. Fletcher used it for a more nefarious purpose. Basically, it's an optical device. The lantern was often made of wood. It had a chimney for the lamp's flame—usually an oil lamp—and images were created on glass slides and projected by a lens.

Congenital Word Blindness

Today we know this as dyslexia, which denotes a condition in which individuals experience difficulty with reading, spelling, or processing language. These difficulties are measured on a spectrum, so each person's symptoms can differ. Some might have trouble reading. Others writing. Many both, but not all. The term *word blindness* was used because most often dyslexia affects the recognition and ability to decode words.

Victorian Archaeology

The views of Ami and her father are unusual for the late 1800s. During this time, the era of colonialism was in full swing, with Britain actively engaging in expeditions to Egypt and other parts of the world. The prevailing mindset was one of cultural superiority. Any discovered artifacts were considered a form of conquest and viewed as prizes to be claimed by the colonial powers. Many of them were tucked away in private collections. The concept of repatriating relics wasn't widely acknowledged or respected during this period. But then again, there's nothing ordinary about Ami Dalton, her father, or their eccentric approach to preserving the past.

Victorian Asylums

Mental health wasn't the only reason one might find themselves committed to an asylum in the nineteenth century. Any behavior that was considered socially unacceptable was grounds for admission. These reasons included, but were not limited to, melancholia, hysteria, epilepsy, alcoholism or substance abuse, feeblemindedness, chronic criminal acts, and disruptive behavior.

The understanding of mental health and the criteria for asylum admission varied widely during this period—and once you were in, it was very hard to get out. Colney Hatch was such a hospital, located in Friern Barnet, London. It was designed to accommodate a large and diverse population of patients and became one of the largest asylums in Europe during the Victorian era.

DISCUSSION QUESTIONS

1. Ami struggles to be accepted as a qualified Egyptologist. Why do you think this is so important to her? Has there been a time in your life when you felt like you missed out on the recognition you should have received? How did you deal with it?

2. Edmund is ashamed of his dyslexia. Why do you think Ami didn't make a big deal about it when she found out? Have you ever grappled with dyslexia or any other learning challenges? If so, what are some ways you've learned to cope?

3. Shadow brokering is a dangerous side gig for Ami, yet she is so driven to rescue relics from the black market that she's willing to take that risk. What is the most hazardous situation you've ever put yourself into for the sake of a noble cause?

4. Phineas says, "Did ye know bees are some o' the most consistent creatures around? They've a job to do, and they do it without fail. I reckon that's a lesson fer all o' us, keepin' our commitments no matter what distractions come our way." Do you agree with his sentiment?

Has there been a time you've honored a commitment even when it would have been much easier to have quit? Is there a commitment you're hesitant to take on right now because you know it will be difficult?

5. Ami hates lemons, and for good reason. She was scarred as a child by her nursemaid, who scrubbed her face daily with the fruit, humiliating her about her freckles. We all bear emotional scars from our childhood. What is something from your past that you still deal with today?

6. Brudge's sidekick, Scupper, is always spouting words of wisdom from his dearly departed mother. What sort of sayings do you remember your senior relatives sharing with you? Are there any wise words that you share with others?

7. In Mark 11:12–25, Jesus curses a fig tree in the morning, and by evening it is dead, so in that instance, the curse was very real. The golden griffin is said to carry the curse of Amentuk, which is fictional. What are your thoughts on curses in our present world?

8. Ami feels very strongly that the Egyptian relics belong in the Cairo Museum because they are an integral part of that culture. What do you think the balance should be between cultural heritage and the placement of historical artifacts? Should antiquities be returned to their country of origin, or are there valid reasons for them to be displayed in museums around the world?

9. Who was your favorite character and why?

10. Who did you love to hate the most and why?

ACKNOWLEDGMENTS

There's only one name that gets credit on the front of the book—the author's. But the truth is, there are oh-so-many-more people that deserve a huge round of applause. So let's kick off this love fest, shall we?

To begin with, you wouldn't even be reading this page were it not for Rochelle Gloege, Kate Deppe, and the awesome team at Bethany House Publishers. This is a whole new experience for me, so thank you all for holding my sweaty little palm through the process.

Next, hoots and hollers go to my intrepid critique buddies: Tara Johnson, Julie Klassen, Shannon McNear, Ane Mulligan, Chawna Schroeder, MaryLu Tyndall, and Erica Vetsch. These women are my tribe, my peeps, my homies, the ones who slap me upside the head when I make a mistake—lovingly, of course—and wipe my nose when I'm sloppy crying.

Now it's my turn to jump up from my seat and clap my hands raw in honor of you, my awesome reader. I always like to acknowledge just a few in each and every book, so even if your name isn't mentioned here, stay tuned . . . it might be in a future novel. Thank you Mark Buzard, Susan Cornwall, Stephanie Cassandra McCall, Andi Tubbs, and Patti Wentling.

Last—but never least—a palm-stinging high five, fist bump, hip check, and a little smooch on the cheek to my husband,

Mark, who dutifully helps me out of every plot corner I paint myself into.

Cheers to one and all!

And guess what, dear reader? I love hearing from you! Be sure to visit my website, MichelleGriep.com, to sign up for my newsletter and drop me a note. I promise I'll answer because I absurdly enjoy when someone rattles my cage.

BIBLIOGRAPHY

The Boy's Own Conjuring Book: Being a Complete Handbook of Parlour Magic. New York: Dick and Fitzgerald. 1860.

Egyptomania by Bob Brier. New York: Palgrave Macmillan. 2013.

A New Look at Old Words, Street Slang from the 1600s–1800s: A Writer's Categorized Guide by Catherine Thrush. South Carolina: Urban Realms. 2023.

The Study of Palmistry for Professional Purposes by Comte de Saint-Germain. Chicago: Laird & Lee. 2010.

Victorian Alchemy: Science, Magic and Ancient Egypt by Eleanor Dobson. London: UCL Press. 2022.

The Victorian Domestic Servant by Trevor May. Oxford: Shire Publications Ltd. 2011.

The Victorians by Jeremy Paxman. BBC Books. 2009.

Direct Quotes Used in Chapter 5

"Beware the Jabberwock, my son! The jaws that bite, the claws that catch! Beware the Jubjub bird, and shun the frumious

Bandersnatch!" Taken from 'Jabberwocky' in Lewis Carroll's *Through the Looking-Glass, and What Alice Found There* (1871).

"Poetry is the record of the best and happiest moments of the happiest and best minds." Taken from Percy Bysshe Shelley's essay "A Defence of Poetry" (1840).

Read on for a *sneak peek*
at the final book in

THE
TIME'S LOST
TREASURES
DUOLOGY

AVAILABLE SUMMER 2025

The end of Eva's world started with a window she never should have left open. A small neglect, yet twelve years later, one that had culminated in a leaky roof, a ledger that refused to balance, and a blind sister. Not to mention her dead mother—for Eva wouldn't. She kept that memory locked tightly in a closet.

Hefting a great sigh, she set down her pen, trying to ignore the incessant plip-plip-plip of raindrops collecting in a nearby bucket. Inman Manor might have a long list of needs to fill, but at least she did not need to worry about their water supply.

She picked up her father's silver letter opener, taking a moment to admire the scrollwork on the handle, then slit the next missive on the pile. Thankfully this one wasn't a bill but a note from her friend Lottie, bemoaning the fact she'd not seen Eva in ages and would Eva please consider coming to the harvest ball on Saturday. A lifetime ago she would have. She'd have bought a new gown and ribbons for her hair, maybe even splurged on a pair of silk slippers. What a dream she'd lived in.

Picking up the pen, she wrote a short, yet pleasant, refusal. Lottie would understand. Hopefully. Eva sealed the note and set it in the post bin. In her haste, her elbow caught on the bottle of ink. Black liquid spilled on the desktop and crawled up the fabric of her sleeve like a disease. Bother!

She grabbed a rag and blotted up the mess on the desk, then did what she could to dab away the stain on her gown. So much ruin. A sigh leached out of her. It was the best she could do.

She sank heavily onto the chair, pressing her fingertips against her eyes, wishing she weren't the one who must hold everything together. And yet here she was, sitting in Papa's office, at Papa's desk, filling Papa's shoes.

Oh, Papa.

It had to be nigh on a year ago since the riding accident that horrid grey morn. But her father's commands hung heavy on the air as if he had just spoken them. *"Take care of your sister. Always. And the house, don't lose it."* Expected commands. Promises she easily gave and had every intention of keeping. But it was his final words that haunted her the most.

"Blackwood. Beware of Blackwoodssss . . . hissss."

A statement unfinished. A warning she had yet to decipher, for in the twelve months since, she had yet to figure out why she ought not trust the Reverend Mr. Blackwood.

"Are you unwell, miss?"

She swiveled in her seat at the steward's voice. How had she missed the thud of Sinclair's boots on the office floorboards? Yet there he stood, water dripping from the brim of his hat, adding to the cadence of the plip-plip-plipping in the corner bucket. He was a sinewy man with an incongruent softness of cheek, as if the sugar biscuits the cook slipped him now and then were never swallowed but stayed bunched up right there beneath the skin. Would that change now that she must tell the cook there were no more coins for sugar?

"I am fine." She tapped the ledger, ignoring the jagged edges of her bitten fingernails. It was a slovenly habit, one she'd picked up over the past year, but she had bigger concerns to master first. "Our budget, however, is ailing. Do you have a moment? I should like to speak with you about an idea to increase our income."

"I was just stopping by for the supply list, miss, but I have time to hear you out." He pulled off his hat, the crow's-feet at the corners of his eyes a mix of hardship and laughter. "What's on your mind?"

She pulled the list he wanted from atop a stack of papers, quickly penned an addition, then held it out. "As long as you're going into Royston, would you stop by Mavers Feed and pick up enough winter wheat for ten acres? I know it's not much, but every bit will help."

He slanted a skeptical look. "I thought the budget was strained as is."

"It is." She sighed. "But I pawned my locket for extra funds. If God wills it, no one shall purchase it, and I'll buy it back when the wheat is harvested next summer."

A frown tugged down his brow. "I hate to see you suffer such hardship, miss."

So did she, and yet there was nothing for it. Perhaps this was what came of buried secrets. "Thank you, Sinclair," she murmured.

"I can do that, miss, but . . ." He tucked away the note, rainwater collecting in a pool at his feet. "Where is this seed to go? The fields are already sown."

"Which is why I'd like you to speak with Tom. As soon as this rain lets up"—she glanced out the window, the leaden skies giving no hint of relenting—"have him begin work on the fallow plot near the northwest corner of the estate. If we can get that wheat in before a hard freeze, next season we'll increase our yield."

"Mmm." An ominous grumble rumbled deep in Sinclair's throat. "I don't think so, miss. You know it's not right."

She pulled her shawl tightly to her neck to hide her frustration. "You cannot negate the fact that eighty extra bushels—one hundred if God smiles upon us—will bring in extra money."

"I don't fault your mathematics, miss."

"Then what do you fault?"

He fiddled with his derby, inching it about in a circle, the veins on the backs of his hands sticking farther out with each twist. "It's not wise to turn earth that ought not be disturbed. You know this."

She snorted, wholly unladylike yet completely unstoppable. "Don't tell me you believe such poppycock. I should have ordered this done earlier."

"It's not called the cursed acres for no reason, miss."

"Look around you, Sinclair." She swept her hand through the air, knocking her shawl aslant. "The house is falling down about our shoulders. The Inman estate is already cursed. Besides, that tale is from centuries ago. I'm sure any truth to the legend has expired by now."

"'When the land is left alone, in peace the curse is overthrown.'"

As if on cue, a low drone of thunder added a sinister tone to the ancient words. A small shiver spidered down Eva's spine—one that annoyed more than frightened. She faced the steward with a lift to her chin. "Be that as it may, the account numbers leave me no choice. That ground must produce despite traditions—or superstitions. And even then we'll barely get by."

"I don't like it, miss." He blew out a long breath. "But I'll do as you ask."

"Thank you, Sinclair. I know it's not been easy on you since my father died. It's not been easy for any of us. I pray we will soon see better days."

"Your words to God's ear, miss." He clapped on his hat. "And may the good Lord grant us a speedy answer. Good day."

"Good day." Her words blended with the chime of the wall clock. Eleven already? Where had the morning flown? She closed the ledger cover, weary of trying to balance numbers that refused to be wrangled into any sort of common sense.

Leaving the office, she wound her way through the back corridor, passing by the open kitchen door. The mouthwatering aroma of baking bread pinched her empty stomach. Thin soup and toast for dinner again, yet she was grateful for it. Why her father had kept the abysmal state of their finances such a secret was beyond her. After managing the books this past year, she still couldn't account for how he'd kept things going, save for the odd earnings he'd labeled as sundries. She'd sure like some of those *sundries* payments now—payments that had dried up after his death. Apparently he'd had some unknown source of sporadic income to keep the manor running. Not enough, though, to provide her with a new gown for the Guy Fawkes festival. If only he had explained instead of hiding their money woes. If only she had not pushed him so hard on the matter.

For if they'd not quarreled, he wouldn't have taken out his fury on such a hard ride.

And he'd still be here today.

She sighed as she threaded her way to the front of the house. No sense fretting about monetary matters now. She simply must trust God to provide, and the devil be drawn and quartered. La! What a thought, but even so, a wry smile twitched her lips.

"There you are!"

Penelope Inman whirled from where she'd been pacing in the entry hall. Eva smirked. The girl had the ears of a dormouse.

"Aren't you eager today." Closing in on her sister, Eva straightened the girl's collar.

"You're late." Penny flinched away, waving her copy of *Little Women* in the air. "I'm dying to find out what happens now that Jo cut her hair. Do you think Marmee will cut hers? Why, I was of half a mind this morning to do away with my own."

"I'm glad you didn't, poppet. I happen to like this head of yours as it is." Bending, Eva planted a light kiss atop her sister's crown. "It is a far more respectable colour than the wildfire burning atop mine."

"Then perhaps we should clip off yours."

"Perhaps we should," she murmured, then added under her breath, "it might bring in a coin or two."

"What's that?" Penny cocked her head, a single dark wave falling over her brow.

"Nothing." She grabbed the book from her sister's grasp. "Let's find out what is happening in the March home, shall we?"

Penny spun toward the drawing room, a folk song on her lips and her skirts swishing around her legs, which didn't slow her in the least. She marched off, completely unhindered by her lack of sight, as the front bell rang.

"Be there in a moment, poppet. I'll save Dixon a few steps." Eva set the book on the entry table before pulling open the front door.

A round fellow smelling of lilies and sausage stood on the front stoop. Rain droplets dripped from his hat brim onto his moustache—which was a curled affair, the sides neatly swirled into downward circles at the sides of a stern set of lips. His direct gaze was no merrier, and she got the impression he summed her up with as much pleasure as she had this morning's ledger.

Even so, Eva managed an amiable smile. "How may I help you, sir?"

"I should like a word with the man of the house." He sniffed, his bulbous nose bobbing. One fat raindrop fell to the ground.

"There is no man. I am Eva Inman, mistress of the Inman estate, and you are?"

"Mr. Buckle, tax collector from the Royston Assessment Office. I'm paying a courtesy call to all the homes in the area, reminding owners that taxes are due by December thirteenth." He held out an envelope that might have been crisp at one time but was now damp and wilted. "Oh, and there's been a slight surcharge added. Rates have gone up. Good day."

He dipped his head as she broke the seal. Of all the inconvenient times for a tax increase!

And then her jaw dropped as she glanced down at the formal missive.

"Hold on there, Mr. Buckle." She dashed down the stairs, chasing the man to his horse in the rain. "There's nearly a fifty-pound difference here." She shoved the horrid document against his chest, blinking away the moisture collecting on her eyelashes.

He retreated, palms in the air, water dripping from his elbows. "As I said, miss, rates have gone up. If you take issue with the amount—which I can only surmise that you do—you'll have to direct your enquiries to the appeals board, not to me."

"Very well. I will." She lifted her chin, refusing to show cowardice though it cost her a face full of raindrops. "When do they next meet?"

"In January." He swung up into the saddle, leather creaking.

"But that's after the deadline!"

"So it is. Walk on." He clicked his tongue.

Leaving her standing agape. In the rain. Alone. Again.

Would God never smile upon her?

Michelle Griep has been writing since she first discovered blank wall space and Crayola. She is a Christy Award–winning author of historical romances that both intrigue and evoke a smile. Currently living the hippy homesteader life in rural Missouri, she is an Anglophile at heart, and you'll most often find her partaking of a proper cream tea while scheming up her next novel . . . but it's probably easier to find her at MichelleGriep .com or on Facebook, Instagram, and Pinterest.

Sign Up for Michelle's Newsletter

Keep up to date with Michelle's latest news on book releases and events by signing up for her email list at the link below.

MichelleGriep.com

FOLLOW MICHELLE ON SOCIAL MEDIA

Michelle Griep   @MichelleGriep   @MichelleGriep

You Are Invited!

Join like-minded fans in the **Inspirational Regency Readers** group on Facebook.

From book news from popular Regency authors like Kristi Ann Hunter, Michelle Griep, Erica Vetsch, Julie Klassen, and many others, to games and giveaways, to discussions of favorite Regency reads and adaptations new and old, to places we long to travel, you will find plenty of fun and friendship within this growing community.

Free and easy to join, simply search for "Inspirational Regency Readers" on Facebook.

We look forward to seeing you there!